Dancing
WITH A
Devil

JULIE JOHNSTONE

DAVIS &
DOUGLAS
PUBLISHING

Davis & Douglas Publishing

DANCING WITH A DEVIL
Copyright © 2014 Julie Johnstone

Cover Design by Lily Smith
Interior Formatting by Author E.M.S.

ISBN: 978-0-9910071-3-4

Published in the United States of America

Prologue

**The Duchess of Primwitty's home, London, England
In the midst of a most thrilling adventure
The Year of Our Lord 1818**

Lady Audrey Cringlewood refused to fall victim to the same fate her mother had. This was precisely why when the Marquess of Davenport crooked his long finger at her, she squared her shoulders and followed the notorious rake into the Duchess of Primwitty's guest bedchamber. He moved with such easy grace, she found it hard to look away from him, so when he stopped suddenly, she was unable to do the same. She bumped into his broad back, and her face and neck immediately heated. "I'm terribly sorry."

Lord Davenport turned. A slow smile tugged at the corners of his firm sensual lips, then spread into a wicked grin. "You never need apologize for colliding with me," he said, stepping closer and reaching around her. The door behind her shut with a soft swish, followed immediately by the click of the turning lock.

Her stomach fluttered as all her senses leaped to life. Before she could decide what she should do, Lord Davenport trailed his fingers from behind her back, across the curve of her hips and up her bare arms. Gooseflesh rose and spread across her skin. The marquess curled his fingers around her shoulders and gently pressed her against the door. Her breath hitched in her throat as her back made contact with the wood and his hooded green gaze locked on her.

Her pulse jumped and under the heat of his assessing stare, she squirmed only to meet with an immovable object. Make that two. She blinked and glanced to the left and right. He had caged her in with his arms. Powerful ones, judging by the way his navy kerseymere waistcoat strained over the swell of muscles underneath. "Is there a reason you have trapped me?"

His eyes darkened to a deep lush green that bespoke of a man who never did anything without a reason. "Would you like there to be?" A teasing note tinged his deep voice.

Audrey swallowed hard, her throat suddenly very dry. If she were sensible, she would slip out of his hold and demand he court her properly. But she suspected making demands on Lord Davenport would get her nowhere. She had to make the man realize he wanted to court her, and think the idea had been all his own. "Yes," she whispered.

A satisfied light came into his eyes. He leaned close, his golden whiskers shining in the candlelit room and his scent, a heady combination of damp earth and rain, filled her nose. She sighed with pleasure. This was the closest he had come to her in the weeks since they had met and been flirting.

His gaze softened and he raised his hand to her cheekbone to slide one finger along the edge of her jawbone. "Before this goes any further, to be absolutely clear, I do not seduce innocents."

Audrey tensed at the pronouncement. So he thought her experienced? That made sense given he had first met her when she was trying to help his cousin, Lady Whitney Rutherford, infiltrate the secret hellfire club, The Sainted Order. Audrey was not a fool. She had considered that his playful banter and looks of the past several weeks might simply be foreplay to his trying to seduce her, but they had been alone several times and he had not made one improper overture toward her.

What to do now? If she confessed her innocence, he would undoubtedly walk away from her without a backward glance. If she chose her words carefully, though, she would not be lying and would hopefully receive the kiss she was sure would change her life. The moment his lips left hers, she would be forthright about her position.

She tossed her hair over her shoulder and pursed her lips. "It's good to know you are a man of such high honor."

A chuckle rumbled from his chest. He cupped her chin, his strong fingers making her feel safe as they cradled her face. His dark thick lashes veiled his eyes for a moment before they swept up to reveal his intense shimmering gaze. "You surprise me."

"Do I?" Her heart skipped a precarious beat. Since she had run away from her father's home and only narrowly escaped being dragged back there by deceiving him, Audrey had begun to surprise herself with the lengths she would go to in order to avoid being forced to marry for anything other than love.

The devilish grin on Lord Davenport's lips twisted into a humorous smirk. "You do." He shifted slightly, the heat of his body enveloping her and his massive shoulders blocking out the bedchamber behind him. "Surprise me again."

"I beg your pardon?" The breathless question made her wince, but at least she had managed to get coherent words out.

"Tell me exactly what you want from me."

What she wanted was to know if the attraction between them was as real as she thought. The kind of desire that would lend itself to a marriage of love and not one of inconvenient convenience. She never wanted to find herself in the same position her mother had, preferring to end her life with a lethal dose of laudanum rather than live with her cold husband another day. She was not lying to Lord Davenport in the strictest sense, given what she was about to say was true. "I want you to kiss me."

Light reflected from the overhead candelabra. It glimmered over his fair skin and the elegant ridge of his perfectly sloped cheekbones. She studied him, not believing she had admitted her heart's desire to this man.

Scandalous as it may be, she would do it again. Everything about him lured her in—including the small white three-inch scar that ran down the length of his right cheekbone. Maybe one day she would learn how he had received it. With shaking fingers, she reached up and touched the jagged line. He barely twitched in response, but his jaw flexed.

"Well, Lord Davenport—"

"Ah-ah," he interrupted, a glint of humor flashing across his face. "If you tell a man you want him to kiss you, you should address him by his Christian name. I insist you call me Trent."

A devilish streak rose up in her. "Maybe I should call you Sin, as your cousin does."

"I'm tempted to let you, but alas, you have to have saved my life in order to call me that."

Audrey blinked in surprise. "And your cousin saved your life?"

"Yes, when I was younger."

"How?"

His lips twitched with amusement, but his gaze had grown guarded. "I do not divulge the secrets of my past."

She opened her mouth to question him more but then thought better of it. From all she could tell, he was a very private man, and if things went as she hoped, she would learn all his secrets eventually. Fighting her curious urge, she said, "Are you going to kiss me or not? I do not believe it will take your cousin long to figure out we have both disappeared from the courtyard, and since I met you, she has become more like a pesky chaperone than a companion in adventure."

Teasing laughter filled his eyes. "I'd say she was never a willing comrade in your escapades, given you blackmailed her into accepting your help with her absurd schemes." He smirked at her. "Let us not forget your demand that she assist you in duping your father."

Guilt pricked Audrey and made her shift from foot to foot. She had not wanted to blackmail Whitney, but when Father had come to retrieve her from Whitney's home, and Whitney had been only too eager to send her with him, desperation had made Audrey resort to drastic measures.

To save herself she had threatened to use the secret she had learned about Whitney. She never would have actually told anyone, but Whitney had not known that.

Fresh shame made her stomach roll. With a sigh she said, "I daresay that was not my finest moment, but the fear of having to go back to my father's home robbed me of my normal, logical thinking." And her morals. She gulped. "I needed a quick plan to attain more time away from Father."

Trent narrowed his eyes. "Why must women be so deceptive?"

Audrey dug her nails into her palms. She hardly wanted to get into a quarrel with him. She wanted him to kiss her, but she could not let him stand here so pompous and superior and speak such fustian nonsense. "Women have much fewer options than you men. Sometimes, we are forced into deception to protect ourselves."

His brow furrowed. "Come now. Do you not think that is a lie you tell yourself to justify what you are doing?"

"I most certainly do not!" she snapped. "Women are expected to bend to the will of our fathers, whether they love us or not. Whether they give a fig whether we are happy or not, just as long as they can get us out of the house and no longer be responsible for us."

The line of his mouth tightened a fraction and the tic from moments before returned at the side of his jaw. She glanced toward her slippers. Heavens! Why had she admitted such a personal thing? She rubbed at the sudden ache in her temples. She had gone and ruined everything, once again, with her too verbal opinions. Perhaps her father was right about her after all. "I'm sorry," she mumbled. "I seem to say all manner of unsuitable things around you. Perhaps we ought to return to the courtyard now."

Cupping her chin, he turned her face up to meet his. Her heart turned over at the gentle, contemplative look in his eyes. He released her, only to slide one hand to the back of her neck. The other came around her waist and pulled her firmly against the unforgiving hard plane of his abdomen and chest. Anticipation for what was to come filled her to an almost excruciating point. She held her breath as he leaned close. "You do not say the wrong things," he whispered in her ear. "You surprised me yet again with your refreshing honesty."

Overwhelming guilt blanketed her. Blast everything! She could not stand here a minute longer and allow him to believe her utterly truthful when in reality she was holding back the entire truth. With a resolute sigh, she opened her mouth to ruin her hopes and dreams.

He pressed a finger to her lips. "If you think I'm going to let you leave this room without obtaining the first of many kisses to come, you are mistaken."

She tried to throttle the dizzying current racing through her and focus on what she needed to say, but when his hot breath caressed her neck, it was all she could do to stifle her cry of pleasure. He brushed his lips against her ear, once, twice—dear heaven, she was going to explode from longing. She ran her hands up his coat, marveling at the corded muscles contained just below the surface of the fine material.

Whatever small thread of sense she had left fled the moment his lips descended on hers. The gentle press of his lips against hers sent spirals of pleasure through her body. She sought something to hold on to, to try to keep herself grounded in reality, but when her hands touched his thick hair and he growled, she abandoned herself to his kiss. And my, did he know how to kiss.

His lips whispered against hers, then covered her mouth with an urgency that filled her veins and made her match his hunger. She rose on her tiptoes to press her mouth firmer against his. He broke away to trail hot fiery kisses down her neck to the pulsing hollow of her throat. She threw her head back and clung to his neck as he kissed his way across her collarbone, then lower, lower.

All she could think was that she never wanted this kiss to end. Her toes curled. Her heart thumped and her happiness swirled in her belly. When he pulled her gown down to reveal her right shoulder and pressed his warm lips to her skin, her eager response to his touch shocked her. She tried to order her thoughts, but his tongue flicked over her shoulder and her mind reeled once more.

She moaned, but when his warm finger slipped inside the top of her gown to caress dangerously near her breast, she gasped and jerked away. Dear havens, this was what she deserved for not admitting her innocence.

He kissed her neck and whispered, "The door is locked."

With a pounding heart, she pressed her palm against his chest until he gazed at her. "What's wrong? Are you worried that we will be discovered?" He grinned, making him look every inch the rake. "I was not planning on taking you here and now, my dear. This is a prelude of what is to come."

Audrey cringed, her mother's words ringing in her head. *A million tears will not change a lady's life, but a well-thought-out plan can alter her future.* Clearly, she had failed to consider thoroughly all consequences of her plan. She cleared her throat. "Please do not be mad."

His grin vanished, replaced by a frown. "Experience has taught me that when a woman says that it's because they know they have done something they should not have."

The knots inside her stomach grew tighter. The only thing to do now was to be truthful and hope her kiss had affected him as much as his kiss had her. "I might have misled you just a bit about how experienced I am."

He shifted away from her and gazed at her without blinking. "Exactly how experienced are you?"

Heat singed her cheeks. "I've been kissed several times."

His eyes blazed with sudden anger. "What game are you playing? I told you I do not seduce innocents."

She flinched at the harsh tone of his words. A terrible tenseness swept through her as she struggled to find the right words to say. "I had"—she cleared her throat— "what I mean to say is I suspected there might be something special between us, and the only way I knew to discern for certain was to get you to kiss me."

"What?" Astonishment colored the one word, though his face betrayed not a hint of what he was feeling.

Tense silence enveloped the room, broken only when she inhaled a shaky breath. The desire to flee was strong, but she refused to bend to embarrassment. Never with any other gentleman had she experienced anywhere close to the thrill as she did when simply bantering with Trent. And their kiss... Well, his kiss had filled her heart with hope that she had found the man for her. She squared her shoulders and notched her chin up. "I was hoping your kiss would astound me."

His right eyebrow arched high. "For what purpose? Obviously a dalliance was never your intention, yet I overheard you tell my cousin you had no intentions whatsoever of ever marrying. I assumed you wanted—"

Audrey quickly shook her head before he said anything too embarrassing, her mind racing back to the conversation with Whitney. What had she said? Heavens! She *had* told Whitney she never wanted to marry—for anything but love. Trent must have quit eavesdropping before she had carefully made clear her position to his cousin. This certainly explained a great deal. "I believe there has been a terrible misunderstanding."

"I'm inclined to agree. I would have never brought you in here had I realized your lack of experience. You may not want to marry, but I am not the man you can seduce into taking your innocence so you can thwart your father, or whatever it is you are trying to accomplish."

Shame swept over her. "I am not trying to thwart my father!" At least not in the way Trent now thought.

His lips pressed together in a hard line. "What exactly are you trying to do? This time, please do be honest."

Audrey twisted her hands together. She had done this to herself by lying. He deserved the utter truth, no matter how embarrassing. The knots in her stomach screamed for release. "I was rather hoping you might want to court me."

His slips parted, and a bit of the anger in his eyes dulled. "Though I applaud and appreciate your honesty now, it was rather scheming of you to mislead me. I cannot court you. I do not wish to marry."

"I see," she choked out, glancing down at the floor and wishing fervently that Whitney would bang on the door right now and save her from her utter embarrassment. *Nothing* would save her from her misery.

"Ah, Audrey."

Trent's silken voice washed over her while he took her hand. She whipped her head up. Was that confusion on his face? Before she could decide, the look was gone. He pressed her hand to his lips. "I am sorry."

How horribly humiliating. She had wanted his affection and eventually his love, and instead she had his pity. She shrugged. "I'm perfectly fine. We should return to the others." She tugged her hand away and went to turn toward the door, but Trent caught her arm.

"Can we still be friends?"

His suggestion startled her and left her unable to immediately reply. Her aunt and uncle had been friends before they married. And her mother had believed men and women could be friends. Audrey frowned. She had always thought it rather preposterous that most people considered it impossible, yet she had never suspected Trent might think so as well. This was not exactly what she had hoped for, but maybe—"I suppose," she forced out, her voice wobbling even though she tried to make it steady.

"Good."

What sounded like regret filled his voice. Her heart skipped a beat. Heavens, no doubt she was hearing what she wished. "We should leave," she said, determined not to make a further fool of herself.

"Yes," he agreed but did not release her arm.

She glanced pointedly at his hand. When she looked up, her stomach flipped at the intensity of his stare. "Trent?"

He refocused on her. "Do you not think some ideas people hold to be antiquated?"

This had to be about being friends! Her jaw parted. She clamped it shut and prayed he would say more.

He increased his hold on her arm with gentle pressure before speaking. "We'll show them all men and women can be friends."

He released her arm and she swiveled quickly toward the door to hide her grin. He may have vowed he wanted only to be friends, but the hunger in his eyes told another story. As friends for now, she would continue to see him socially. Now all she had to do was be so irresistible that he would not be able to help falling in love with her and forgetting his ridiculous objection to getting married.

One

**One week later
London, England
Inside the gaming halls of Wolverton's Den**

Trent stared at the cards in his hands, but they blurred, refusing to fight for his attention. In all his years of playing *Vingt-et-un* he had never lost a game, unless purposely in order to obtain information, but he was about five seconds away from losing.

From across the table, his cousin Whitney's betrothed, Drake Sutherland, glanced up from his cards and smirked, causing fine lines of amusement to appear around his keen brown eyes.

"I seem to be winning," he drawled, his American accent making the words sound slower than they ought to.

Trent narrowed his eyes, refusing to bandy words, though given this last week it was unlikely a simple look would stop Sutherland from prying. The previous seven rude warnings had not deterred the man. Irritating as it was, Trent had to forgive him. Sutherland was only following the well-intended, though misguided, directives of Whitney. Since she was his favorite cousin, by nature of their similar personalities, Trent forgave her too, but when he saw her next, he was going to have to set her straight on meddling in his life. He refocused on his cards, hoping Sutherland's attempt was over.

"Say, Dinnisfree, do you not think Davenport has been rather preoccupied this last week?" Sutherland boomed. Trent snapped his head up and shot Justin Holleman, the Duke of Dinnisfree, a warning look.

The duke flicked his red hair out of his eyes and acknowledged Trent's look by tapping his right index finger on the table, a signal no one but one of the prince regent's spies—or retired spies in Trent's case—would understand. Sometimes using one of the old secret signals would twist his gut with regret and make him question whether giving his resignation to the prince had been the right decision. Then he would remember the little matter of his revealed identity thanks to his deceitful, double-crossing deceased French wife. May her black soul rest in peace.

Dinnisfree picked up a card. "I've noticed nothing unusual in Davenport's mannerisms. The man is aloof, as always." Dinnisfree's bored tone offered no friendly avenue to continue the conversation. Trent relaxed, until Sutherland grinned.

Sutherland laid his cards faceup. "I've won again, gentlemen."

"So you have," Trent agreed, working to keep his tone carefully neutral.

Sutherland drew his winnings toward him, the coins scraping the wood as he did so. Once he had a neat gleaming pile, he spoke. "This is exactly what I mean, Dinnisfree. You cannot deny Davenport's preoccupation." Sutherland glanced at Trent. "Someone has your attention to the exclusion of everything else. Very unlike you."

A trace of humor underlay the words, but the remark still set Trent on edge. He gripped his whiskey glass and downed the contents with a single gulp. Fire blossomed in his belly. As he set the glass down with a *clank*, one of the many demireps Nash Wolverton, the club's owner, employed to keep the men in his hellfire club happy and present, strolled past, only to stop in front of the elaborately painted Chinese wall where she turned slowly to face Trent.

She ran one hand down her sheer jade costume. The

woman's long dark hair reminded him of Audrey's. It was almost the same shade, but not nearly as shiny, nor did it have the soft waves Audrey's hair possessed. Trent's fingers flexed in remembrance of the way her locks slid like silk through his hands the one time he had touched the strands.

Damnation. This preoccupation with her was getting worse with each passing day—not better. As the demirep sauntered toward him with an open invitation of sin on her parted moist lips and her eyes slumberous with desire, he shook his head subtly. Her eyes opened wide, but she took his hint and twisted away. This was the seventh open invitation to sleeping with a woman he had turned down this week.

What the devil was wrong with him? The only thing he could pinpoint was Audrey. Had asking her to be his friend been foolhardy? Should he have handled things differently with her when the truth of her innocence and what she wanted had surfaced? Even if he should have, he was not sure he could have. A picture of her standing in the Duchess of Primwitty's guest chamber flashed in his mind—disheveled hair, swollen kissable crimson lips. Her face tinged a lovely shade of pink with the heat of her embarrassment. When her confession of her innocence and desire tumbled out of her mouth in a rush of words, he had not been able to retain his anger for her misleading him. Not only that, he had been incapable of ending their acquaintance.

The idea of being friends had come to him and seemed a fine plan. Learning she was innocent and wanted him to court her, he had assumed the nightly fantasies of her would cease. But she still appeared in his dreams every night naked and writhing on his bed with his cream silk sheets tangled about her slender body, her dark hair fanned out around her in sable waves and her bodice undone to expose the swell of creamy flesh her elaborate gowns always pushed up enticingly. He groaned at the mental picture.

Laughter erupted across the table, almost drowned by the dull roar of conversation from the lords gambling and talking nearby. His former training as a spy to hear everything and nothing at once allowed him to pick out a trace of a slow American guffaw. He narrowed his gaze on Sutherland. Before he could warn the man not to pester him further, Sutherland spoke. "You can deny it all you want, but ever since you got the preposterous notion in your head that you and Lady Audrey can be friends, you've been preoccupied by thoughts of her."

Trent ground his teeth. "I'm not preoccupied by any woman." Dreams of his dead wife Gwyneth's betrayal surely did not count. When he slept, he could not block the memories of being deposited by her and her Napoleon-crazed brother in a French prison to be tortured and killed. As for Audrey...England would go a year without rain before he ever admitted to fantasizing about her. Besides, it was temporary. He was sure of it. Once he bedded another woman, his lust would slack.

Sutherland shrugged. "As I said, refuting it is useless. I see it in your eyes. You may as well abandon your stance against marriage and give in. Now that Lady Audrey is under your skin, you will fall. I predict sooner rather than later." Sutherland whipped out a cigarillo and lit it. He took a long draw before continuing. "Mark my words."

Trent did not consider himself a violent man, but he had the urge to mark something—as Sutherland had put it—like the man's smirking face. A nice sound facer would likely make Sutherland quit looking at him as if he knew his inner thoughts better than he did, but that would ruin their friendship, and since Sutherland was to marry his cousin next week, thereby becoming a relative, fisticuffs did not seem the best solution.

He drummed his fingers against his thigh. It got so tiresome fending off his friends and family's well-meaning efforts to understand—and because they never could quite comprehend—then try to change the fact that he did not presently have nor ever want a wife. He would love to give up the sham of the perpetually carefree rake, but he could not.

Trent yanked on his cravat. His own questioning of his ability to stick to what he said was one thing, but he despised another man doubting him, especially when the man did not know all the facts.

Hell, he had ended up becoming a spy because of a situation similar to this one. His father's long-ago revelation that he had formerly been a spy, followed by his laughing comment that Trent did not have the bollocks for such a commitment, had sent Trent straight to Prinny to offer his services. In less than a week, he had given up gambling, drinking and chasing women to go into training to serve his country. It had transformed his life. Thank God, his father had still been alive to see the change.

That old training now echoed through his head. *Every movement you make gives your enemy a clue*, his father had once told him. He moved his hand and Sutherland's gaze followed. Sutherland was not an enemy, but he was attempting to meddle. Trent forced himself to hold perfectly still. "As usual, Sutherland, you have no idea what you're speaking about."

Marriage required trust and faith, and after his disastrous marriage to Gwyneth, no trust and faith remained in him to give to another woman. Of course, Sutherland did not know that. No one, except Dinnisfree, knew he had not so long ago been a spy for Prinny. And the only living individuals who knew he was the widower of a clever French spy who had duped him and betrayed him were Dinnisfree and Gwyneth's brother. Frustration coiled through his body.

As usual, he could not explain himself. There was no explaining his dead wife without lying about who she was and who he had been, and he'd had enough lies to last a lifetime. Besides, he would never put his family in danger by relenting to his wish to make them understand why he did not want to marry. No words could aptly describe how being duped into marrying the very enemy he was working for England to guard against still twisted his gut into pulsing hard knots.

"This conversation is boring me," Dinnisfree said, shoving his chair away from the table. He clamped a hand on Trent's shoulder. "If you aren't going to accept that bit o' muslin's invitation to bed her, I will."

Trent flicked his gaze toward the woman in question lingering by the grand piano in the corner of the room.

She had one hand placed cleverly above her head to best display her ample charms. It rested, as if naturally, on the large white column that reached to the vaulted ceiling. Her other hand lingered on the curve of her tiny waist. Trent waited for a surge of lust. Interest. Anything. By damn, there was not a hint of desire, same as all week.

He pushed the bothersome thought away and focused on the two men talking to her. She stepped toward the shorter of the two gentlemen and slid her arms around his neck. "Looks like she has already found another patron for the night."

"Probably best," Dinnisfree said. "If she is willing to sleep with a drunken dandy like Richard Cringlewood, then I'm certain I would not be impressed by her."

Trent chuckled as he stared across the smoky room. Audrey's brother, Cringlewood, reached behind his neck and untwined the woman's hands. "It appears that Cringlewood is declining her invitation as well. Perhaps he is not as cork-brained as you think him to be."

Dinnisfree slapped a palm on the table, making the glasses rattle. "Do not let your lust over the man's sister cloud your senses. You know as well as I do Cringlewood has a gambling problem and is overly fond of liquor."

Damned the duke for his loose tongue. Typical of his unapologetic friend, he shrugged when Trent glared at him. "I'd wager Cringlewood only declined the demirep's offer because he lacks the funds she would expect from any gentlemen as payment for services well rendered."

Ignoring the stares of the few men who had dared to look their way, Trent sought Cringlewood out once more. "I've heard rumors that his debt at many of the clubs is mounting."

"I've heard the same," Dinnisfree said with a nod. "I've also seen him and his partner in misadventure, Thortonberry, at every club I've been to this week."

"As have I," Trent said. "I don't care for Thortonberry. The man acts as if he is hiding something. Not only that, I have seen him with a different demirep for seven straight evenings."

"That part does not bother me," Dinnisfree quipped.

"But I agree he has the shifty-eyed look of a man concealing a secret."

"I think he is simply reserved," Sutherland said. "I had a chance to become better acquainted with him this week, as Whitney has dragged me to a different ball every night, and last evening I spoke with him after he danced with Lady Audrey."

Trent narrowed his focus on Thortonberry's black evening-attire-clad figure in the distance. The man was dressed for an evening at a ball. Was he planning to seek Audrey out again? Trent studied him, not liking what he saw. Thortonberry grasped the demirep by the elbow and led her under the warm glowing light of six gleaming chandeliers and out of the gaming hall toward the direction of the pleasure rooms. Trent considered Sutherland's revelation. The desire to ask which dance Audrey had granted Thortonberry and if they had danced more than once gnawed at his belly, but he refused to give in to the emotions. Instead, he focused on learning more about the man's character. "Did the marquess seem a forthright man to you?"

"He did, though I will say he acted rather bumbling around Lady Audrey, as if she made him nervous. I thought that rather odd for a man who has no problem bedding a different woman every night, unless of course Lady Audrey makes him self-conscious because he cares for her."

Dinnisfree snorted. "Or that is his ploy to seduce her. Rather a smart one if you ask me, though I'd never resort to such measures."

Trent squeezed the ledge of the table until a jagged splinter pierced the flesh of his index finger. Without a sound, he jerked his hand away and plucked out the splinter.

"Is something a matter?" Sutherland asked, his mouth turned up in a sly smile, his gaze locked on Trent's hand.

"Not a thing." Jealousy may be pounding through him, but he would be damned if he would give in to it or reveal it in his tone.

When Cringlewood glanced in their direction, Trent waved the man over.

Sutherland grinned. "Are you quite sure your cousin is not right and that you do actually care for Lady Audrey?"

Trent gave Sutherland a long hard look. "I'm concerned for her welfare as I would be for any friend."

"Yet she is not your friend," Dinnisfree said, his reddish-blond brows pulling together. "She is a woman."

"I'm aware of that fact," Trent drawled. "I'm of the opinion"—albeit a new one—"that men and women can be friends. As her friend, I'd be utterly remiss if I did not alert her brother to the potential threat to her innocence."

Sutherland gawked. "Are you saying Thortonberry is threatening her innocence? This is rather ironic considering you were a threat to her virtue, don't you think?"

Trent clenched his jaw. "Unwitting threat," he muttered.

"I find that hard to believe," Sutherland countered, amusement lacing his tone.

Trent ground his teeth until pain shot up the right side of his face. He was not about to defend himself by besmirching Audrey's reputation. No one need ever know they had shared a kiss and then she had informed him of her innocence. "I suppose you are correct. I learned first hand how chaste the woman is when I tried to kiss her. I can tell you, she has quite a smart slap." He rubbed his right cheek as if remembering.

"I'll be damned," Dinnisfree blurted, showing surprise, which was not like him at all. "I never thought I would live to see the day a woman turned you down."

Trent shrugged. "Now you have."

Sutherland frowned. "Your confession is noble, Davenport, but what does it have to do with you thinking Thortonberry is trying to seduce Lady Audrey?"

"I'm telling you from personal experience a man who sleeps with a different demirep every night has no intentions of properly courting any woman anytime soon. If he did he would refrain."

Sutherland nodded. "I'm inclined to agree."

Trent raked a hand through his hair. Since he had met Audrey, he had not slept with a single other woman,

let alone seven like Thortonberry. For that matter, he had
not even felt a sliver of desire for any other than her. Not
good. Not good at all. He did not want to be infatuated
with Audrey or any other woman ever again. When a man
relented to those sorts of emotions it gave a woman
power over him, and a woman who could bend a man
with her smile could unhinge him body and soul.

Again, he had the prickling notion that asking her to
be his friend may not have been wise, but it was done.
He prided himself on his ability to control his emotions
and he never turned his back on a friend. As her friend,
it was his duty to make sure her brother was keeping a
sharp eye on her. And if he learned she was not being
properly chaperoned now that she was home, he would
warn her away from Thortonberry himself, as any good
friend would do. "I have to keep Thortonberry away from
her," he muttered.

Sutherland leaned forward. "I'm not so sure.
Thortonberry may not have decided if he wants to court
her yet or not. Perhaps when he makes the decision he
will give up the demireps, as he should. Besides, how do
you plan to tell her brother you think he is doing a poor
job of supervising his sister? How well do you know
Cringlewood?"

"Not well, but I plan to be extremely tactful."

Dinnisfree leaned forward. "I suggest you start now,"
he whispered.

"Good evening, Davenport," Cringlewood slurred as he
pulled out a chair and plopped into it. "I assume you
need a fourth for a card game." Cringlewood swayed in
his chair before steadying himself. "I can only play one
more hand. Shouldn't play that, but I need my luck to
turn."

Trent shuffled the cards, assuming the banker
responsibilities. "Well, hopefully this is your lucky hand.
Do you have chips?"

"He does not," a deep voice grumbled behind Trent.

Nash Wolverton stared down at Cringlewood. A fierce
frown marked the club owner's rugged face, and his dark
hair hung over his eyes. He shoved it back as if only now
remembering it. "Need I remind you, Cringlewood, that

your account here is frozen until you pay down your debt?"

"Come now, Wolfie, if you'll advance me a bit more blunt I vow I'll take these gentlemen and pay you back." Cringlewood's words ran together, making Trent want to grab the man by his lapels and shake him for his foxed state. How the devil was this fool to keep his sister safe?

"Do not call me Wolfie." Wolverton's clenched jaw and his steely tone left no room for doubt that the man was close to throttling Cringlewood. And if one still doubted, Wolverton's hands clenched by his side were an excellent indicator of his irritation. Trent could not blame him for wanting to throw Cringlewood out, but he needed Audrey's brother to remain here long enough to reveal where Audrey was tonight. Cringlewood's chair squeaked loudly as it teetered backward. Sliding his booted foot behind the chair leg, Trent slowly tilted the man back toward the ground.

"Give him a rouleau," Trent said. "I'll be responsible for paying you back."

Wolverton nodded. He raised his hand and within seconds, his moneyman appeared, suit and glasses askew and silver hair sleeked back. He looked past his hawk nose and over the rim of his spectacles at Wolverton. "Sir?"

"Give him twenty guineas," Wolverton said and motioned to Cringlewood. "Lord Davenport has taken on responsibility for Cringlewood's losses."

"For this roleau only," Trent clarified.

Wolverton flashed him a grin. The man's gleaming teeth reminded Trent of a wolf. *Fitting.*

"Of course, Davenport." Wolverton leaned down, a long a haul considering his great height, and clasped Cringlewood by the shoulder. "After this hand, call it a night."

Cringlewood shoved Wolverton's hand away. "I intend to. I'm simply killing time waiting on Thortonberry. I've better places to be than this."

"Good. You should go there." Wolverton departed without a backward glance. His assistant gave a perfunctory bow and scampered after him.

Trent dealt the cards before asking, "What event are you attending tonight, Cringlewood? Anything exciting?"

Audrey's brother picked up his cards, glanced at them and then looked up. "Nothing you'd be interested in. I don't wish to go, but my father insists I help keep a watchful eye on my sister." Cringlewood opened and closed his eyes, as if he was having trouble focusing. "Did you know I had a sister?"

Trent did not look at his friends. Dinnisfree coughed and Sutherland shifted in his chair. What should he say? Audrey's family had no idea she had never been betrothed to a private investigator named Roger Wentworth. Audrey and Whitney had concocted the tale so Audrey would not have to leave London and go back to the country with her father. Whitney had posed as the investigator and duped Audrey's father. Trent cleared his throat. "I met her when she was betrothed to Mr. Wentworth, as he is a personal friend of the Duke of Primwitty's, an old school chum of mine."

Cringlewood nodded. "Makes sense. I suppose you know she mucked that up, as she does everything."

Trent pressed his lips together. He did not care for the man's negative view of Audrey. As her brother, he should be one of her most stalwart supporters. "It's my understanding that Lady Audrey caught Mr. Wentworth with another woman."

Whitney and Audrey had contrived the explanation so Audrey's father would not blame her for what he thought was a genuine broken engagement. Pity her father and brother seemed only to care about the fact that she had not ended up married, whether the man respected her or not.

Cringlewood took a card and frowned. "All men have mistresses. My sister has a false notion of what marriage should be about, which is precisely why my father is forcing me to attend the Allreds' ball tonight. He is determined to see her married and out of the house before this season ends."

A very odd feeling tightened Trent's insides into hard knots. He did not need to hear anymore to know her father was uncaring and her brother was an addle pate.

Convenience and arranged marriages were the norm, but usually the father arranging such things loved his daughter and did his best to ensure she would be in a good marriage. Trent laid his cards down in front of him faceup. "*Vingt-et-un*, gentlemen."

"Damnation!" Cringlewood cried and threw his cards on the table. "Would you be willing to let me pay you back next month?"

"Let this be a gift between friends," Trent replied. "I'm sure your mind was occupied with concern for your sister, as well it should be. Does she have any particular suitors currently that bother you?"

"No. No," Cringlewood replied, standing. "In fact, she is not aware of it yet, but Father has lined up several interested gentlemen for her to meet tonight." Cringlewood looked away from Trent and across the room. "There's Thortonberry now, gentlemen. I better take my leave before I'm too tardy for the ball and join my sister in Father's bad graces."

Trent raised an eyebrow at Cringlewood, though he wanted to stand, forcibly detain the man and demand answers. With a casualness he did not feel, he asked, "Is Thortonberry one of your sister's suitors?"

Cringlewood chuckled. "Hell no. Thortonberry thinks of Audrey as a sister. He is our neighbor and they have known each other since we were all in leading strings. If I thought I could hoist Audrey off on Thortonberry I would, but as you can see"—Cringlewood waved toward the marquess who stood some twenty brown-lacquered wood tables away, locked in the embrace of the demirep he had been speaking with—"he has no interest in marriage. But he did generously offer to do me the favor of helping to keep an eye on my sister, so we really must go."

Trent did not like the sound of that at all. He did not trust Thortonberry to keep nothing but his gaze on Audrey, even if her doltish brother did. His gut told him Thortonberry was not as he seemed, and intuition had saved him more times that he could remember when he was on assignment for Prinny in France. The only time it had ever failed him was with Gwyneth. He had never suspected she was anything other than the simple

Frenchwoman she had pretended to be, working in a bookstore with her brother.

His thoughts were interrupted by Thortonberry's appearance. The marquess regarded everyone at the table with assessing green eyes before his gaze locked with Trent's. "I seem to be running into you at all the hellfire clubs this week, Davenport. Have an itch you cannot get scratched properly?"

"I could ask you the same," Trent replied, making sure his sarcasm laced his tone, instead of the irritation strumming through him. Thortonberry's caustic remark had touched a nerve.

Thortonberry's gaze sharpened. "I'm perfectly satisfied, just voracious. And late." He glanced at his pocket watch, then turned to Cringlewood. "I took the liberty of requesting the supper dance with your sister. I thought that way you would be free to do as you please at supper, and I can keep a watchful eye on her."

"That's grand of you," Cringlewood boomed. "Gentlemen, many thanks for tonight."

As Cringlewood and Thortonberry disappeared into the crowd, Trent stood. "I'm going."

"Going where?" Dinnisfree asked.

"To the Allred ball."

"Devil take it. I knew you were going to say that."

Sutherland stood, a grin stretching his face. "I'm going there as well. Whitney is expecting me. Are you coming, Dinnisfree?"

Dinnisfree shrugged into his overcoat and shook his head. "Even if I did not have somewhere else pressing to be, I would not willingly go to a ball crammed full of supposedly perfectly proper lords and ladies. I cannot think of anything phonier or less enjoyable."

Sutherland shrugged. "Suit yourself."

"You know I will."

"I'll see you there, Davenport," Sutherland said before taking his leave.

Trent shrugged into his own coat before speaking. "Why do you always do that?"

"Do what?" Dinnisfree asked.

"Keep everyone at arm's length."

"Because I have to, just as you once did. I cannot afford to trust anyone, but tell me, lately I find myself curious if that feeling has ended for you since retiring."

The question made Trent uncomfortable. "Are you considering retiring?"

"Never. And do not try to avoid what I asked. Do you trust as you once did?"

Trent knew what Dinnisfree meant. His life would never be the same as before he was a spy. He rubbed his chin for a moment, the already burgeoning whiskers prickling his fingers. He had been trained extensively— just like Dinnisfree—to trust no one but his fellow spies, yet he had slipped with Gwyneth. She had broken down his walls one by one and gained his confidence. He'd been too in love to recognize what was happening and too late he had realized that Gwyneth was a French spy on a mission to secure the secret correspondence it was his job to transport between Prinny and the men who guarded Napoleon.

"No. I don't trust as I once did." And he never would, but that had more to do with what Gwyneth had done to him than anything else. She had shown him just how wrong he could be about a woman, and it was a lesson he would never forget.

Dinnisfree nodded. "I did not think so. You have that same haunted look in your eyes as you did the day I rescued you from Bagne de Toulon. Which begs the question of why you are going to the Allred ball to help Lady Audrey if she will never be anything to you."

"She is something to me," he said, surprising himself with the verbal admission. "She is a friend, and I don't bloody well know why, but I'm compelled to watch over her. Speaking of which, I need to be departing." They strolled through the crowded room side by side, retrieved their hats from the coatroom and walked down the brick steps of the club and into the dark night made glowing thanks to the lit street lamps. "Will I see you at Gritton's tomorrow?" Trent asked as his coachman slowly pulled his carriage up to the curb.

Dinnisfree shook his head. "No boxing for me tomorrow. I'll be headed to France."

Trent stilled and checked the streets for anyone who might overhear them, a habit that would likely never fade. "Is this a job or are you running away to wrestle your demons?" Not an unusual occurrence for Dinnisfree. Sometimes Trent envied the man's lack of family ties that enabled him simply to go as he pleased, but then he would see his mother, brother or cousins and his envy for Dinnisfree would be replaced by pity.

Dinnisfree compressed his lips into a thin line. "I keep my demons in a steel box and I threw the key away long ago, my friend. They can't get out and I can't get in."

Trent grunted. It was typical of Dinnisfree to refuse to talk about his past, or even acknowledge he had one. With a wave, the duke disappeared into his carriage and Trent stood on the cobblestone streets without moving until it pulled away. He closed his eyes and breathed in the crisp scent of soil and grass that accompanied the aftermath of a sunny day ending.

An ache he recognized as loneliness seeped into his bones as a pleasant breeze blew around him. Slowly, he opened his eyes and stared up at the sky. The moon and stars overhead reminded him of many long summer nights when he had been a lad. He would sneak out of his room to go and fetch his cousin Whitney when she was visiting, and they would swim in the creek at night, oblivious to the dangers or the pain of life. He yanked his greatcoat tighter and climbed into his own carriage before tapping on the side and telling his driver where to go.

As the carriage prattled down the street and past St. James Square, he reconsidered if he could ever trust a woman enough again to open his heart and soul. His carriage rounded the corner and the canal became visible in the distance. With the stone wall rising to one side of the canal and the trees lining the banks, it reminded him of the small sliver of the Oise he had just been able to make out from a crack in his cell wall in Bagne de Toulon.

He curled his hands into fists, then spread his fingers out and examined his nails. It had taken over a year, but the ridges and constant blue tinge underneath the nail had faded finally. No one would look at them now and wonder what had happened. If he allowed himself to remember too long his time in the dark, dingy rat-infested cell, the intense sharp pain of each nail being yanked out one by one would shoot through his fingers and up his arms like it was happening again. He had been starved, beaten and mentally sliced to shreds, all because he had trusted a woman.

Yet every woman was not Gwyneth. His gut twisted with the knowledge. It did not matter. His head knew this, but it did not matter. No. Much better to be lonely for the rest of his life than to risk getting close to anyone ever again.

Two

Most debutantes would have been thrilled if the Duke of Clarington had singled them out for conversation at a ball. Not Audrey. Long ago, she had realized she was not like most other debutantes. If she had wanted to marry simply for money, then she would be thrilled to be trapped conversing with Lord Clarington and his friend Lord Spencer, but she wished to marry for love. She peeked at Lord Clarington's hard-set face and shuddered. She could never love him. He appeared colder than a frozen pond. She stole a look at Lord Clarington's friend, Lord Spencer. He had a smile on his face, but it was a practiced smile. The vain peacock probably sat in front of a looking glass for hours to get the effect he desired.

How long had it taken him to pick out the blue-and-white striped jacket he wore tonight? Hopefully not long since it obliterated the boundaries of good taste for evening attire, not to mention the elaborate peeks jabbing his cheeks appeared quite painful. As for Lord Clarington, it did not matter what he wore, because his pinched face and cold eyes told her everything she needed to know.

As the men stood directly in front of her and argued over which one of them was the best huntsman, she raised her fan and flicked her gaze across the guests at the Allreds' ball. She searched the grand ballroom to see whether her father still watched her, while simultaneously she hoped to catch a glimpse of Trent and discover that by some happy fate he had decided to attend the ball tonight.

She started her examination at the right side of the room, which shimmered with warm light provided by hundreds of candelabra and dozens of enormous crystal chandeliers. Near one of the large white columns that circled the perimeter of the marble dance floor she caught site of broad shoulders and light hair. Could it be Trent? Gripping her fan, she discreetly rose on her tiptoes to see the man's face.

As she got a good look, disappointment filled her. How could she have mistaken his almost white hair for Trent's beautiful golden hair? Wishful gazing she supposed.

Where was Trent? Perhaps the more pressing question at this moment was where was her father? If he was preoccupied in conversation and no longer watching her like a hawk maybe she could slip away and hide in the powder room until the supper dance. Then Lord Thortonberry would come to claim her for their dance, and at least she did not have to worry about pretending with him or being concerned her father would try to get a marriage offer from him since Lord Thortonberry was a longtime family friend and most definitely not interested in her.

As the notes of the cotillion drifted over the balmy orchid-scented air to her, the dance floor drew her gaze once more. Since Lord Clarington and Lord Spencer still stood arguing with each other, she allowed herself a moment more to pay them no mind. In the center of the ballroom, lords in exquisite black evening attire and gleaming shoes twirled ladies in delicate silk gowns of jonquil, cerulean blue and Pomona green.

Whitney's sister Gillian and her husband, Lord Lionhurst, spun by Audrey. Longing flittered in her stomach. She wanted to look at a man and have him stare back at her as those two did, as if no one else was in the room. Perhaps it was because they had just returned from their extended wedding trip abroad that their faces held a certain enraptured glow. Audrey swallowed hard. That was silly. They were in love. Very much so. She peered at Gillian. Her friend looked magnificent in a rose gown of satin covered in pearl rosettes.

Self-consciously, Audrey ran a smoothing hand over her favorite gown from last season, a silk indigo creation with a layer of white spider gauze over it. She had felt like a princess in this last year, but now it was a tad faded and not quite as fine. Well, it would have to do since father had denied her request for new gowns, no doubt to punish her for what he called her most recent colossal failure to catch a proper husband.

She trailed her tongue over the sore she had developed on her inner cheek. Every time her father lectured her this week since she had returned home, she bit her cheek to keep herself from speaking out and defending herself. She could not very well tell him the truth that she had not mucked up her betrothal to Mr. Wentworth, because Mr. Wentworth did not exist and there had never been a betrothal. Admitting to her father that she had fabricated the whole story to avoid having to return home to him because she feared whom next he would try to force her to marry would not help his anger at her at all.

Distinctive throat clearing snapped her attention back to the gentlemen, who both stood staring at her expectantly. Heat singed her cheeks. She hated nothing more than being caught unaware. Lord Clarington held out his arm to her. "I do believe we have come to the dance I requested from you."

She nodded. She wanted to be dancing with Trent, not Lord Clarington, but it was hard to dance with a man who had made himself scarce for an entire week. It no longer seemed quite so lucky that he had told her he wanted to be friends as it had when she thought that meant she would see him often and still have the chance to make him fall in love with her.

She slipped her hand into the crook of Lord Clarington's elbow, and as she did, she saw her father, not five feet away, drink in hand and a fierce frown on his face. He stood just behind a large suit of gleaming armor. Had he been watching her this entire time? Given the way he now glared at her, he must have noted her preoccupation as Lord Clarington and Lord Spencer had talked.

Forcing a smile to her lips, she searched her mind for what she could do that might please him and make him think she was really giving Lord Clarington a chance. Ah! "Lord Clarington, tell me, have you read any good books lately?"

"Nothing that would interest you."

She gritted her teeth, then forced her smile bigger. "I daresay I'm interested in quite a great deal. What is it you are reading?"

He moved them into place for the quadrille. "I'm reading *Rob Roy*. You would not understand it."

If her father were not watching her, she would tell Lord Clarington what an offensive bore he was and leave him standing alone. Instead, she tilted her head. "Ah, *Rob Roy*. Quite a good novel. I already read it, of course."

Lord Clarington's mouth fell open as he moved with the dancers. "You could not have."

She barely resisted the urge to pinch the man. "I assure you I could and did."

His mouth puckered as if he had sucked on something tart. "What is it about?"

Once she moved back toward him she said, "Do you wish for me to give you a synopsis of the entire book? The main narrator is Frank Osbaldistone. He falls in love with Diana Vernon, whose father is in hiding because of his Jacobite sympathies." She took a deep breath, rather enjoying the increasing pinched look on his face. "Then—"

"Enough," he snapped and jerked away. When once again he faced her, his nostril flared so wide he looked comical. "Women should not tire their minds by reading such heavy tomes. You should read magazines or some such thing."

"If you say so," she murmured. Arguing with this foolish man was a waste of her time. Instead, as she kept up with the dance she recommenced her search for Trent. The conspicuous line of wallflowers in various hues of light pinks, blues and yellows standing without dance partners by the large potted plants made her angry at the stupidity of men and envious that the wallflowers did not have to endure Lord Clarington. She prayed he did not offer for her. Her father would surely demand she marry him and that would be a lifetime of misery.

At the end of the quadrille, Lord Clarington led her off the dance floor, opposite of where her father had been. She simply had to have a moment alone. As Lord Spencer approached them once more, she released Lord Clarington's elbow. "Thank you for the lovely dance and conversation. If you will excuse me, I think I will go freshen up."

"There is no need," Lord Spencer said. "You look exquisite."

"Careful with this one," Lord Clarington said, eyeing her. "She reads *Rob Roy*."

"*Rob Roy*?" Lord Spencer exclaimed. "Really? How fascinating. My sisters read nothing but *Lady's Monthly Museum*. They love the gossip and fashion."

Lord Clarington locked his hands behind his back and looked down his nose at her. "That is what ladies should read."

She should not comment. Her lips trembled with need. She could hold it in. All she need do was excuse herself without offending the man, so he would not report her behavior to her father.

"I see you are finally mute on the subject, as is proper."

"If I became mute, it is because your arrogance astonished me."

"I beg your pardon?" His tony was icy.

"As well you should," came a patronizing voice from behind her.

She swiveled around and could not stop the genuine smile that lit her face. He had come. Trent was actually here and looking gorgeous, dressed head to toe in black evening attire save the snowy white cravat that contrasted with his sun-kissed skin. Her heart fluttered at his nearness and the fact that his gaze, narrowed on Lord Clarington, glowed with anger.

He shifted closer to her, and his vitality captured her as always and made her pulse skitter. "I do believe Lady Audrey meant you are a fool when it comes to women, because women are rather smart creatures and have just as much right and ability to read *Rob Roy* as you." He glanced at her. "Am I correct?"

"You are." At this moment, staring into Trent's burning gaze, she did not give a fig if Lord Clarington bemoaned her name for hours to her father.

Trent's mouth pulled into a slow knee-quaking smile. "Is your next dance taken?"

She was quite certain her father would rather her try to ensnare a duke like Lord Clarington than a marquess like Trent, but she could not make herself care. Tonight she would dance with a devil and tomorrow she would gladly pay the price. "No. The next dance, the supper dance, is spoken for, but this one is free."

A slight frown appeared on Trent's face, before it vanished and he proffered his arm. "Come, then. Let us not waste another minute."

The second her gloved fingertips pressed against the curve of his bicep, she knew what she felt when near him had nothing to do with reason and everything to do with attraction. Emotion. The invisible pull from one person to another. A physical ache to be with him blossomed inside her.

Without a parting word, he led her away from Lord Clarington and Lord Percy and to the dance floor. As he turned her to face him, he rested one hand gently on the curve of her back and with his other hand clasped hers and raised their joined hands into position. With a thudding heart, she placed her other trembling hand on his upper arm near his shoulder.

She took a shaky breath and traces of whiskey and smoke underlying the scent fresh soap that clung to his skin tonight filled her senses. He pulled her slightly closer, so that the heat radiating off his body nearly overwhelmed her, but she noted he did not bring her closer than was proper.

"You're shaking."

His deep, sensual voice made the blood rush through her veins. She wet her lips. "Yes. I'm sorry."

He quirked his right eyebrow, a gesture she now recognized could either mean he was jesting with her or he was surprised by something she had said. She cleared her throat and tried desperately to give a good reason, besides the truth, why she would be trembling. Telling him that simply being near him made her shiver uncontrollably would not do. Not yet. She did not want to scare him off now that he had shown himself once more.

"I do that sometimes when I'm angry."

"Don't let what Lord Clarington said upset you. The man is an idiot who incorrectly assumes women are not bright." A devilish look brightened his eyes. "Enough about Lord Clarington. I want to talk about you."

"Me? What about me?"

His fingers curled tighter around her gloved hand as his gaze bore into hers. "To begin with, I can honestly say I've never seen a woman who looks more beautiful than you do at this moment."

She could have been dancing in the clouds for as light as his words made her feel. "Thank you. I did not have a new gown to wear, so I was rather self-conscious..." Her words trailed off at the abrupt change of expression on his face. His playful smile disappeared and his mouth opened slightly. Perhaps she should not have spoken so freely. She missed a step as nerves set upon her. "Normally, I would have had new gowns. We are not poor. Father is angry with me, so he is punishing me. I'm sure in his eyes I deserve it. I do try to be as he wishes, but I simply cannot marry a man I cannot countenance." She clamped her jaw shut when his right eyebrow shot high. Now she had gone and done it with her nonsensical babbling.

He threw his head back and laughed as he twirled them around and pulled her closer to him, so that their bodies nearly touched. When his eyes met hers, his open, intense gaze made her knees weak. He pressed his mouth close to her ear. "You never fail to astonish me. I've never met a woman quite like you, or at least how I think you are. I know firsthand you can be cunning and lie like an expert when the need suits you, yet I've yet to see your lies be any that would harm another. And take just now—"

She was not sure if he was complimenting her or not,

but she was thrilled he had clearly given her enough thought to consider this much about her. "My gown?"

"Yes. I do not know a woman who would admit that their gown was old, or they felt self-conscious or that their father was angry with them because they were willfully disobeying his commands. Yet you admitted all that, as if it was the natural course of conversation."

Her face flushed with pleasure and just a bit of embarrassment. "I did not say exactly that I was willfully disobedient."

Trent grinned, then frowned. "You are confounding me and making me question things I have no wish to question."

Her heart lurched. "And that is bad?"

A deep crease appeared between his eyebrows. "I like to stick to what I have planned."

"Did you plan to come here, seek me out and dance with me?"

"No," he said, his tone slow and careful. "I had not planned it at all. Then I became worried about you, so I decided to seek you out and warn you. When I arrived and saw you, standing by the balcony"—his gaze traveled down the length of her gown and ever so slowly climbed back up to her face—"well, let me say your beauty has a way of making me forget myself. I could not pass up the chance to dance with you. And when I overheard Clarington being so rude, I wanted to rescue you, though thinking back upon it and the way you matched him comment for comment, you did not need my help." As the waltz ended, he brushed a finger against her hair before dropping his hand away and offering her his elbow.

Her heart thundered painfully. She slipped her hand into the crook of his arm, wishing the dance, his admissions and this night would never end. Yet not ten feet away, her brother stood with Lord Thortonberry, poised to snatch the moment away from her. Richard waved at her to join him. She bit her lip and slowed her steps.

Trent caught her gaze, then stopping, turned to face her. The deep crease between his eyebrows appeared once more and a tic pulsed at the left side of his jaw. "How well do you know Lord Thortonberry?"

Of all the things she had been expecting him to say, that was not one of them. "I've known him all my life. Why?"

"Do you trust him?"

Whatever was this about? "Of course. He is my brother's closest friend and our neighbor."

"That may be, but sometimes those we think we know the most are the ones we know the least."

She had no idea what he was trying to tell her, but she did not like the glassy look in his eyes. On top of that, the music for the supper dance had started and Lord Thortonberry was striding toward them with an angry frown. She squeezed Trent's arm. "Who is it you are telling me I should not trust?"

"Lord Thortonberry. He consorts with questionable characters, men as well as light skirts. He's not appropriate company for you to keep, especially in light of the fact that you are searching for a husband and marriage of mutual affection."

Mutual affection? Audrey gritted her teeth, thinking. Could Trent not even say the word "love"? Whitney had told her previously that he had been madly in love with some Frenchwoman who had killed herself, but she did not seem to know much more than that. Maybe the woman had broken his heart. As much as she hated to think he had loved another woman with such devotion she could see the good in the knowledge. If he had loved fully, then that would make him capable of the deep love she wanted. Another less pleasant thought occurred to her. "How do you know what sort of characters Lord Thortonberry consorts with, including light skirts?" Right as the words left her mouth, she realized in her burgeoning anger, she had forgotten to whisper.

Lord Thortonberry stepped next to Trent with a smile at her and a hostile gaze for Trent. "Yes, Davenport, do tell us how you know what sort of characters you think I consort with."

If Trent had been surprised at Lord Thortonberry's sudden appearance, he did not show it in the least. His face looked made of stone. "I've heard rumors." His tone, just like his face, revealed nothing.

Whatever was occurring here? Was Trent jealous? If so, that was marvelous, because it meant he liked her more than as a friend. Audrey tsked. "You shouldn't listen to rumors."

"No, indeed," Thortonberry concurred, with humor underling his words. "Besides, even if the rumors were true, Lady Audrey would never be in any danger from me. She is safe in my care, and this dance is mine, so you can go along and enjoy the rest of your night."

When Trent's gaze became cold and hard, a part of her reveled in his anger, though it was positively wrong of her. He was jealous! She was so incredibly happy, she could not keep the smile from her face as Lord Thortonberry led her to the dance floor.

She glanced over her shoulder as Lord Thortonberry positioned them for the cotillion and inhaled sharply. Trent had not moved and his face— There was no mistaking the hard pressed line of his lips or the angry slant of his eyes. This was turning out to be a glorious night! She forced herself to move her attention to Lord Thortonberry, only to find him frowning at her.

"How do you know Davenport?"

Lord Thortonberry's sharp question angered her. She already had to answer to her father and brother. She was not about to submit to questions from another, apparently disapproving, man. She raised her eyebrows at him. "I know a great many lords. I could not really say with certainty how I first met him."

"Cannot or will not?"

She was glad that the dance forced her to switch partners. She moved away and ended up facing Mr. Sutherland. She smiled at Whitney's betrothed. "Good evening, Mr. Sutherland."

"Indeed it is, Lady Audrey. Are you having a pleasant time?"

She stepped back in time with the other dancers and came back toward him, then nodded. "I am now."

"Now that Davenport has arrived?"

Heat flushed her chest. "I suppose Whitney told you that I rather like her cousin?"

He nodded. "She did. And we both agree the feeling

appears mutual, but I worry you will have a hard time getting Davenport to admit it. Try to be patient."

She really wished she knew the details about the woman from France, but she certainly could not ask Mr. Sutherland. She suspected he did not know much anyway. Whitney was closer to Trent than anyone, so she would be privy to the most information. Audrey sighed. She could be as patient as a saint if she thought Trent truly cared for her but just had not admitted it to himself yet. Her father was another story, of course, but she could probably hold him off for a bit longer.

The tempo of the music rose and signaled a partner change that put her back with Lord Thortonberry. She cringed at the ridged set of his mouth. Before she could think of a different topic to discuss, other than Trent, Lord Thortonberry spoke. "Davenport is not the sort of man to marry. I do not wish to see you hurt by him."

"Your warning sounds more like opinion than fact. How can you know if he is the sort to marry? Is this the same way he knows you consort with unsavory characters and light skirts? Have you been listening to gossipmongers as well? If not, that leads me to the conclusion that the two of you were at a questionable club and saw each other there. If that is the case—" A hard knot formed in her throat. She did not want to think about the possibility that Trent might be bedding other women.

Lord Thortonberry jerked a hand through his hair and then let out a grunt. "No, no. I would never go to a hellfire club. You know me better than that. I suppose I am as guilty of listening to rumors as Davenport, but I only mentioned it because I care for you."

The anger that had knotted in her throat released. She patted Lord Thortonberry on the arm. "I care for you too." He was like a brother to her, after all. A strange look flashed in his eyes but was gone before she could read it. Left standing in uncomfortable silence, she cleared her throat. "The dance has ended."

He blinked and glanced around them. "So it has." As the dining bell chimed, he took her by the elbow and led her off the dance floor and toward the supper room. She wanted to look back to see if Trent was still watching her, but she did not. Perhaps it was better to kindle his jealousy just a bit and not seem too desperate. With that in mind, she gave Lord Thortonberry all her outward attention, though Trent had her thoughts and her heart.

Three

As Trent followed Audrey and Thortonberry into dinner, he made sure to keep enough distance that if either one of them happened to glance behind them, they would not catch him observing them. Not that there was much concern in that. They appeared to have eyes only for each other. He expected one of them to collide with a piece of furniture or another guest any moment now. If fate were at all kind, Thortonberry would be the one to trip and go sprawling face-first to the floor. Maybe he would twist an ankle and need to keep it elevated for the next several weeks, giving Audrey time to meet a more suitable prospect for a husband.

The scenario made Trent smile, until he imagined her married and the man caressing her hair or skin or bandying wits with her late at night under the bedcovers in the privacy of their bedchamber. He scrubbed a hand over his face. He was turning into someone he did not recognize.

What the devil was wrong with him? He would never offer for her, so he could not allow himself to imagine such things. He had become a sorry excuse for an honorable man.

They abruptly stopped ahead, and he made a quick scan around the crowded supper room for the perfect place to watch Audrey without anyone noticing or bothering him. Most of the guests lingered near the refreshment table, around the high tables set up on the periphery of the room or near the warming table where footmen served the food. After a moment, Thortonberry, the bounder, slid his hand to the small of Audrey's back and guided her toward the refreshment table.

Tension vibrated through Trent as he forced himself not to stride over there but to find a place to stand that would place him where he could observe Audrey best, in case she appeared to have need of him. Directly across from her was the terrace. Excellent. The doors to the garden stood ajar. His pulse quickened. To the right of the double doors a row of large windows with long, heavy cream curtains lined the wall from the terrace to the dining room entrance.

Trent smiled. Gold-corded ties held all the curtains back, except the ones on the last window. They hung loose in a billowing fashion. Perfect to conceal oneself. Even better was the large oil painting displayed on a wooden stand positioned partially to the side of those loose curtains. If anyone glanced at him, they could easily assume he was looking at the painting. The host, Lord Allred, was known for his love of art, after all.

Midway across the room, he spotted his cousin Gillian by the table that held the food, but luckily in deep conversation with her husband, Lionhurst. To avoid walking where they could see him, he switched directions, doubled back and made his way to the outer edge of the crowd to use the people as cover. Once at the curtains, he positioned himself directly behind the edge of them but far enough out that it was not obvious he was attempting to hide.

He sought Audrey out and immediately found her. He loved that she had worn her hair down, though it was uncommon. She was not common. And he liked that more than he cared to admit. Thortonberry handed Audrey a plate, and when she took it, the man's hands lingered too long on hers and he tilted his head slightly down as if he were staring at her breasts.

The muscles along the backs of Trent's shoulders throbbed. Thortonberry needed to understand Trent was watching him. As he was about to stride across the room,

Audrey's brother stumbled into his view, took her by the elbow and whispered something in her ear.

Her brows came together in a pucker and she handed Thortonberry her plate before following her brother out of the supper room. This would be the perfect time to warn Thortonberry to behave or else. Trent stepped out from the space between the curtains and the painting and started to weave through the crowd toward the marquess. Halfway across the room, his cousin Whitney moved into his line of sight with a smirk on her face and her gaze trained on him.

He did not bother trying to avoid her. One of many reasons Whitney was one of his favorite people was her tenaciousness. She never gave up on what she wanted. He hoped to hell what she wanted at this moment had nothing to do with him. He had enough to think about right now.

Within a moment, Whitney stood in front of him, a mischievous twinkle in her eyes. "I have been watching you."

"Have you?" He made sure to infuse his tone with amusement, though wariness surged through him.

"I have," she chirped. "You would not have noticed, because you were busy watching Lady Audrey."

The best way to confuse a suspicious person was to give them what they wanted. Trent shrugged. "Of course I was."

Whitney's eyes widened. "I must say this is easier than I expected. I did not think you would admit it."

"Why would I not? She is my friend, and I am concerned about her and the current company she is keeping with Thortonberry."

"She is your *what?*"

He chuckled at the way his cousin's mouth was hanging open. "My friend. It's a new view I've developed."

Whitney set her hands on her hips. "It is an excuse, that is what it is. A rather ingenious one, but no matter how you cloak it, it is still an excuse for not wanting to admit how you really feel about her. I have not wanted to push you, because honestly ever since you returned from your trip to France you have not been the same."

"Whitney—"

She held up her palm. "Let me finish, please. I know you feel guilty over that Frenchwoman." Whitney stopped speaking, glanced around the room and gripped his elbow. "Follow me."

Within moments, they stood back by the window with the billowing curtains. Whitney leaned close. "You cannot punish yourself forever because that woman—what was her name?"

"Gwyneth," he choked out. *Damnation.* He tugged a hand through his hair. Fabricating a story that Gwyneth had killed herself because he had pushed her away had been foolish. At the time, it had seemed a good way to accomplish his goal of getting Whitney to admit the truth to Sutherland of why she had left him, so she would not lose him. And it had worked. When she heard how not telling the truth about himself had cost him the woman he loved, Whitney had immediately opened up to Sutherland.

Whitney nodded. "Yes, of course. Gwyneth. I know you loved her and her killing herself wounded you desperately, but Audrey is not Gwyneth. Audrey is strong and truthful. I have seen the way you have looked at her these last two months, and it is not a look of friendship."

Knots pulsed in his shoulders and neck. Reaching around, he rubbed the back of his neck and considered what to say. Whitney trying to match him with Audrey had to end now and the only way he knew to ensure that happened was to be shockingly, bluntly honest. "You are working under a disillusion about me, Whitney, and I adore you for it. You think I'm better than I am, but I'm not. I am a man with baser needs who has no desire ever to marry but still wishes to fulfill those needs. I did start to pursue Lady Audrey, but only because I mistakenly thought she never wanted to marry either and that—"

Damn, this talk was deuced uncomfortable. "Well, to be perfectly honest, I thought she wished for an affair and had the experience with men to know what she wanted."

Whitney clamped her jaw shut with a snap. She stared at him in silence for a second, then raised her hand and toyed with the plume in her hair before finally speaking. "I see. Well, clearly you were wrong about her and yourself."

"Myself?"

"You do not wish for an affair with her, Sin. That is another lie you tell yourself because, well, I think you are afraid to fall in love. It is too late, though. She is under your cravat. You just have not accepted it yet. Friends, you say?" Whitney shook her head. "I think not. You could have spoken with her about this nonsense regarding Thortonberry and then been off to a din of ill repute to fulfill those *baser* needs you mentioned. Instead, you lurked behind a curtain and watched her every move with an intensity that left me breathless."

Was that true? Was Audrey somehow becoming more to him? His mind flatly rejected the notion. He desired her, plain and simple. Well, not so simple. He liked her as well. In fact, he liked many things about her, except the fact that she was an innocent seeking a husband. "I never said I did not desire her still, but I will not act on it. Whether you believe me or not, all I wanted to do tonight was watch out for her, since it seems her brother is too drunk to fulfill his duties and I have yet to see her father here."

Whitney pursed her lips. "If you say so. I'm afraid I have to end this conversation now. I see Drake heading this way and I'm sure you want to depart and go fulfill your baser needs." She quirked a haughty eyebrow at him and turned on her heel, so quick her gown smacked his leg as it swung around.

Damn his cousin. She had him questioning himself, and that was the last thing he cared to do. He would go to the Sainted Order and this time, by damned, he would bed a wench and quit fantasizing about Lady Audrey immediately.

TWO HOURS LATER IN THE underground candlelit pleasure room of the Sainted Order, Trent downed his glass of whiskey, smacked it against the bar and motioned for the barkeep to pour him another. While he waited for his drink, another beautiful demirep sashayed up behind him. She leaned over him, her perfumed fiery hair swinging down the left side of her face into a long shimmering cascade that almost touched his crotch and trailed her hands over the back of his shoulders, then over them and down the front of his chest. He should have been aroused to a painful state. Yet he felt nothing.

"Do you want to come with me?" the woman whispered in his ear. She took the tip of his lobe between her teeth and gave it a playful tug.

Before Audrey, that naughty little gesture would have brought him to arousal. Now his blood might as well have been ice in his veins. *Hell and damnation.* He wished he wanted to bed this woman. The sad fact was he did not, and despite thinking earlier he could make himself, imagining himself lying with this woman left a sour taste in his mouth.

He shook his head. "Not now. I have somewhere to be." Like home. If he could not bring himself to bed another woman tonight and forget the green-eyed Siren consuming his thoughts, then he might as well go back to the comfort of his own home. He much preferred his cozy study to a damp room that reeked of too much perfume and smoke.

Plus, he needed to consider the very real fact that he might need to avoid Audrey until he had himself firmly in hand.

"Maybe tomorrow night?" the demirep purred in his ear.

"Yes, perhaps." He took the last swig of his drink, put on his coat and made his way out of the room and down the dark, damp winding corridor toward the door that led up to the stone stairs that would take him to the main entrance of the club.

He paused when a shriek came from the corridor to his left. He eyed the shadows dancing on the stone walls. The oil lamps flickered because of the constant breeze. Another shriek rang out, but was it trouble or pleasure? The corridor did lead to the bedchambers and some women did shriek when they were enjoying themselves.

Undecided as to whether he needed to go investigate to make sure one of the hellfire members was not being too rough with a demirep, he stood there. A bursts of female laughter erupted from the same direction the shriek had come from, followed by a woman's voice. "You are a very naughty boy, Lord Thortonberry."

Trent froze. Thortonberry was here.

"Come back to the bedroom with me," Thortonberry coaxed.

"This is your third night in a row here," the woman replied. "Are you not tired of me?"

"No."

"What would your wife say if she discovered you were coming to see me?"

Thortonberry chuckled. "I'm not married, but even if I was, I would still be here with you, whether my wife liked it or not. Not that I would tell my wife about this, at any rate."

"Probably wise." The woman's voice grew suddenly softer as if they were walking away or she was whispering.

Trent itched to move toward them but in this empty corridor, every sound echoed. A door creaked and light from a bedchamber spilled into the dark hall. Trent pressed himself against the wall and held his breath.

"Some ladies are prickly about their husbands going to hellfire clubs," the woman said, right before wood scraped brick and the door smacked shut.

Trent exhaled his breath in a whoosh, then slowly inhaled as he counted to twenty to cool his temper. Thortonberry was exactly the sort of man Trent had thought. There was no bloody way he would quit watching over Audrey now. She was in danger from the marquess whether he intended to seduce her or marry her. He was no good for a woman like her. She deserved—" He scrubbed a hand over his face. What did she deserve? Certainly more than having her reputation ruined or being duped into marrying a man who presented himself to her one way, then played her false and spent all his nights in the arms of other women.

He had to make sure Thortonberry did not ensnare her. For now, he would work from a distance until he developed an indifference to her laughter, wit and beauty.

Trent grunted. This should not present a problem. He would not let it. He could be around her and not flirt with her. He was a former spy trained to deflect, defeat and defend. Of course, that training had utterly failed him when he met Gwyneth, but he had learned from his colossal mistake with his former wife.

Four

The next night Audrey's nerves tingled as she took her seat beside Whitney in Mr. Sutherland's theater box at Drury Lane. From below them, the pit hummed with the excited conversation between men and women who came to the theater to socialize. Audrey leaned over and grasped Whitney's hand. "Thank you for inviting me."

"It is my pleasure. I'm glad, between the two of us, we were able to convince your father I would be an acceptable chaperone for tonight's outing."

Audrey snorted quietly. "I think the fact that you told him Trent was going to be attending the theater as well, and in the same box as us, is what convinced him. Now that Father has concluded Lord Clarington will not offer for me, I do believe he has pinned his hopes of getting rid of me on Trent." Which suited her perfectly.

"I've pinned my hopes on him too, which is why I orchestrated tonight," Whitney said in a mysterious tone.

Audrey quirked an eyebrow. "What do you mean *orchestrated*? What mischief are you creating?"

"You'll see," Whitney sang as she dug her quizzing glasses out of her reticule, put them up to her eye and peered into the crowd below. After a moment, a slow smile came to her lips. "Ah. The first of my pawns has entered onto my board. Look over there by the stairs." Whitney pointed to her right.

Audrey peered over the balcony to where Whitney indicated. The thick crowd in the pit and the dim theater lighting made it difficult to see whom Whitney spoke of. Audrey moved to the edge of her seat and squinted. "Who are you looking at?"

Without a word, Whitney handed Audrey her quizzing glasses. "Hurry. Before he delves too deep into the crowd and is no longer visible."

With a tremor of excitement, Audrey stared through the glasses and her breath caught. Below her but towering above most men and women around him, like the golden god he appeared to be, Trent strode with the Duke of Primwitty through the crowd toward the stairs that led to the second level of the theater. Audrey's pulse skittered as her gaze traveled up Trent's long legs to his wide powerful shoulders. He turned for a second and she smiled. He had worn crimson, which she distinctly remembered telling him was her favorite color. He had commented that it was a wicked color and did not at all suit her, but it was perfect for him.

Wild excitement coursed through her veins. Soon he would be parting the curtains of this box and sitting next to her. Maybe tonight, he would start to see her as irresistible, a woman he could not live without. A woman he loved. Her brow furrowed as Whitney's words came back to her. Slowly, Audrey lowered the quizzing glasses and glanced at her friend. "What do you mean your pawns have entered your board?"

A low chuckle came from Whitney. "When I asked Sin to come to the theater with us tonight, he declined."

Audrey's stomach dropped to her slippered feet. "But that is awful. Why are you only telling me this now?" Her head instantly pounded. "I would not have agreed to come."

"What nonsense you speak," Whitney said in a chiding tone. "He claimed he had already agreed to accompany the Duke of Primwitty tonight. After leaving Sin's home this morning, I took it upon myself to call on Sally to see if Sin was telling me the truth. Normally I would not question him, but he acted rather uncomfortable when talking to me. He paced the room and avoided my gaze.

Sally told me the duke had no theater plans with Sin tonight."

"Is this story supposed to make me feel better?" Audrey asked with a trembling voice.

Whitney's grin faded. "Well, yes, but I see I'm mucking up the telling. Sally came to see me this afternoon. Sin called at their home not long after I departed, and Sally overheard Sin begging a favor of the duke to accompany him to the theater tonight to keep a watchful eye on *you*."

"*Me*?" Confusion made her thoughts dance around in her head. "I'm not sure I understand."

"It makes perfect sense to me. He wants to make sure you do not fall into the hands of a rake, but he wants to do it from afar. He is avoiding you." A wide smile lit Whitney's face.

Audrey frowned and pressed her fingers to her temples. "Your explanation is still not making me feel better."

"Honestly." Whitney shook her head. "Sometimes I think I'm the only one who can clearly see when people are trying to hide something."

"And what is Trent trying to hide?"

"He likes you, but too much for his comfort. He has spent the last year involved with women who demanded nothing from him but payment for services rendered."

Audrey gaped at Whitney, not shocked but amazed that her friend spoke so bluntly on such an intimate matter.

Whitney shrugged. "Sorry, dearest, but I must speak the plain truth and since we are alone..."

"Yes, of course. Go on." It was not as if she had not known that Trent was a rake.

"My theory is that you present a problem to him because his heart was broken, and he is afraid to love again. He is afraid of you, because *you* are the first woman who has awakened the desire for something more in him. Do you agree with this theory?"

"I do think he must have been hurt," Audrey said with hesitation. "I daresay I want to agree with the rest of what you have hypothesized, but I fear it is because I long to believe he cares for me and not because it is actually true. I'm certain that along with my heart my pride is involved."

"That is quite understandable. The important thing is that I am correct. And because I'm so sure of what I have said, I set a plan into motion that I'm positive will have Sin springing from his seat and striding over to our box to sit near you. After that, the rest is really up to you." Whitney paused and patted her hair.

Audrey stirred uneasily in her chair. Whitney's plans had been known to cause quite a bit of trouble before. "What exactly have you done?"

"I asked Drake to invite Lord Thortonberry to join us in our box tonight." Whitney frowned and then spoke again. "Asked may not be the exact right word. I had to cajole Drake, and it took rather a lot of effort. He does not want to promote a tender between you and Lord Thortonberry, but I explained to him that was not a concern. It isn't, is it?"

Audrey laughed at Whitney's probing gaze. "Certainly not. Lord Thortonberry thinks of me as a sister, and as I said I think of him as a brother."

"I knew I was correct," Whitney exclaimed. "I usually am," she added with an air of supreme confidence. "Then my plan is perfect. Last night at the Allred ball, I watched Sin watching you and glaring at Lord Thortonberry. I decided he is jealous of the man, which is probably why he is convinced the marquess is no good. I guarantee you when Sin sees Lord Thortonberry sitting beside you tonight he will come straight to our box. All you need do is get Lord Thortonberry to flirt with you. Can you do that?"

Audrey bit her lip. "I suppose, but I'm not sure I'm comfortable using Lord Thortonberry for my gain."

"Posh!" Whitney waved her hand. "How can it harm him for you to flirt with him? You just told me he thinks of you as a sister, so his heart is not in danger."

"Well, that's true. Still, I feel inclined to tell him what I'm doing."

As the curtains rustled behind them, Whitney's forehead creased. She glanced over her shoulder and a smile shone on her face. When she turned back to

Audrey, she whispered, "He is here. Do what you must, but be quiet and quick about it. Drake would not like my plan and would most definitely inform Sin."

Audrey nodded and ran a smoothing hand over her gown and hair as Mr. Sutherland and Lord Thortonberry entered the box. Whitney rose, which at first surprised Audrey, until her friend directed Lord Thortonberry to take the seat she had vacated.

"Might I sit by you?" Lord Thortonberry gestured to the empty chair beside her.

"Of course. I was pleased to hear you were joining us."

His bright green gaze assessed her. "I'm glad," he said, taking the seat beside her. "You look lovely tonight."

She glanced down at the cerulean gown she had worn. She had chosen it specifically because Trent had told her blue was his favorite color. "Thank you." She regarded his dark navy evening attire. "You look quite dashing." She blinked, realizing it was true. He was a handsome man with his long lean figure, strong jaw and compelling eyes. For the first time, she wondered why he had not taken a wife yet. Whitney clearing her throat behind Audrey caused her to dismiss the errant thought and focus on Whitney.

"Drake and I are stepping just outside of the box for a moment."

Audrey supposed that was her cue to ask Lord Thortonberry for his help. The minute the box curtains swung back into place and she was alone with Lord Thortonberry, she turned to him. "Would you mind helping me tonight?"

"It would be my pleasure. What sort of help do you need?"

Her face heated. This was rather embarrassing, even though she had known Lord Thortonberry all her life. "I need you to flirt with me."

His mouth curved into a smile. "I think I can do that."

She was about to thank him, but his gaze stopped her and caused her to draw a sharp breath. Was that a flame of desire in his eyes? Surely not. She wet her lips and swallowed. "I need you to flirt with me, because I am trying to make Lord Davenport jealous."

Lord Thortonberry's warm gaze turned cold. "Why would you want to do that?"

She stiffened, momentarily abashed. This was no time to let embarrassment deter her, though. She may not get another chance like this. "Because his jealousy will make him realize he does not want to lose me to you or any other."

Lord Thortonberry's eyes widened. "Really? Is that truly the way it works?"

It had worked that way for Whitney with Mr. Sutherland. When he had thought Whitney was in love with another man, Mr. Sutherland had realized he could not live without her. Audrey nodded her head. "Of course."

"And does it work that way for women to? If I wanted to make a certain woman realize she cared for me, would trying to make her jealous be the way to do it?"

Audrey considered the question. The mere thought of Trent liking another lady made Audrey's stomach ache. Of course, she already knew she cared for him, but if she did not, jealousy would probably help her to realize it. She gave a decisive nod. "Yes. That would most definitely work for me."

Lord Thortonberry leaned back in his chair. "All right. Then I will help you, but only if you help me."

Audrey blinked. "With what?"

"I wish to make a lady jealous."

"You do?"

He smiled slowly. "Yes. I do."

"Well, that is grand," she exclaimed. It was much better if she could repay his help by helping him in kind. "Who do you wish to make envious? Is she here?"

Lord Thortonberry's gaze darted across the way to the boxes facing them. Audrey glanced in the same direction and tried to decide which lady he might be looking at.

"She is here," he said abruptly, his gaze still trained in the same area. "Do you know Lady Caroline Rosewood?"

Audrey found the petite blonde in the sixth box to the left of them. Lady Caroline was considered an incomparable this Season, but Audrey did not really know her. "Only by name and face. We have not been formally introduced. I'm sorry." She assumed he had hoped she might be one of Lady Caroline's confidants.

A thoughtful smiled curved his lips. "That is probably better. I would not want to ruin a friendship between the two of you."

Audrey nodded. "What of you and Lord Davenport? Are you concerned helping me will cause a strain between the two of you?" Further strain would be more apt, but she could not say that.

"We are not friends, so there is no concern there."

His cold tone bothered her. She wanted to ask more, but the curtains parted and Whitney and Mr. Sutherland strolled in. As they took their seats, the lights dimmed to signal the beginning of the play. Below them, in the pit, the noise quieted to a dull roar. She raised the quizzing glasses and sought out the Duke of Primwitty's box. It was still empty. Blast Trent! Where were they? Had they stopped for him to speak to some other ladies? She dug her nails into her palms.

The lights on the stage illuminated and the actors and actresses strolled out to begin the play. Audrey's heart pounded in her chest. Maybe Trent would not take his seat at all. Then what? Suddenly the curtains to the duke's box parted and Lord Primwitty strolled into his box followed by Trent. Both men sat down. Lord Primwitty looked immediately toward the stage, but Trent appeared to be looking their way.

Trembling, she lowered the glasses and turned to Lord Thortonberry. "He is looking at us. What of Lady Caroline?"

"I believe she is watching as well. Shall we give them a show to rival the play?"

She giggled. "Yes. What should we do?"

Lord Thortonberry ran his fingers down the side of her hair and tucked a strand behind her ear before leaning over and pressing his mouth near her ear. "We are already doing it."

She cut her gaze to Trent. Was he sitting forward in his seat? "It's rather hard to tell how Lord Davenport's face appears from this distance."

"I'm sure he is livid," Lord Thortonberry replied,

sounding rather pleased. "Do you have a fan with you?"

"Yes." Her fingers went automatically to the strings of her reticule. Behind her, Whitney whispered fiercely to Mr. Sutherland. She prayed he was watching the play and not taking notice of her and Lord Thortonberry.

"Get it out, open it and raise it above your face, as if you are telling me a secret," he instructed in low tones.

She quickly obeyed and raised her fan. When Lord Thortonberry reached up and moved it over his face for a moment, she gasped and tried to pull it away, but he held firm. She dropped her tone low. "What are you doing? Someone may think we are kissing behind the fan."

"Davenport will likely think it, and that is what you want, is it not?"

Angry, she yanked the fan away. "I do not wish to ruin my reputation in the process of making him jealous," she hissed.

Lord Thortonberry spread his hands apologetically. "I'm sorry. But it is dark in here, and no one else is watching us but him, I feel sure."

"And Lady Caroline," Audrey inserted in a cool tone.

"Yes, of course," he agreed. "And Lady Caroline. Please don't be angry. I did not mean to overstep any boundaries. I only wished to help you. Please." He grabbed her gloved hand and raised it to his lips. "Say you forgive me."

Audrey frowned at him and slowly pulled her hand away. "You are acting rather odd tonight."

"I do believe your prey is coming to find you," Lord Thortonberry said in a dull voice.

A tremor of excitement ran through Audrey. She sat up straighter, pressed her shoulders back and said a silent prayer of thanks for Whitney's ingeniousness.

TRENT PAUSED OUTSIDE DRAKE'S BOX and took a moment to compose himself. His heart pumped at an unmerciful beat. Could worry kill a man? If so, Audrey was going to put him in his grave early with her apparent interest in Thortonberry. It had taken a moment to figure out who it was in Drake's box sitting by Audrey, but the minute recognition struck it was like a knife plunged into his gut and deftly twisted when Thortonberry had whispered in Audrey's ear.

Trent drew open the curtains and strode in to the box, making an effort to show no reaction when everyone turned to look at him.

He forced a casual smile to his lips and walked slowly toward the seats. Pausing near Whitney's side, he inclined his head to his cousin, then gave Sutherland a cold stare. The man better have an excellent reason why he had invited Thortonberry to the theater.

Forcing a casual tone, he said, "Imagine my surprise when I looked over from Primwitty's box and realized you had a little party in yours. I did not realize there would be four of you here tonight. If you had told me, I would have made arrangements to join you."

Whitney giggled, capturing Trent's attention. No doubt, his irrepressible cousin had something to do with Thortonberry being here. She patted the seat beside her, a definite pleased look in her shining eyes. "Come sit by me and enjoy the play."

"I'll sit up front," he said and strolled to the seat on the other side of Audrey. He dropped down beside her and faced her. Taking her hand as he had seen Thortonberry dare to do, he kissed it. Her smell of honeysuckle lingered on the silk of her white gloves. He inhaled deeply before releasing her and peering into her eyes. Audrey on an ordinary day stole his breath. Tonight, Audrey's appearance rendered him speechless. He let his gaze soak up every aspect of her appearance. The way the lights lent a soft glow to her porcelain skin. The gentle slope of her high cheekbones. Her long thick lashes that could alternately veil her eyes like a seductress or make her look the picture of utter innocence.

He moved his gaze lower to the inviting slopes of her breasts displayed by her low-plunging iridescent blue gown. His blood thickened as he counted each beat of his heart. Shadows lay between her curves, taunting him, heating him and promising many nights of sinful pleasure in her arms.

A physical ache for her that rivaled the raw desire to escape that had plagued him the many months he had been imprisoned gripped him now. He stared, unable to look away and unable to speak yet. The jolt of his heart and surging of his blood was far from what he felt for any friend he had ever known. He did not know what to do. How to proceed with her. Yet he knew he would not get up and walk away. That was out of the question.

He cleared his throat. "Your beauty left me speechless. Forgive me."

She grinned, but to the other side of her Thortonberry grunted.

The marquess leaned over and met Trent's gaze. "I imagine you've said that before."

"Never," Trent replied, supremely glad it was the truth. Gwyneth had been beautiful but in a calculated way. He had never been rendered speechless by her. Lust crazed? Certainly.

Audrey tsked at Thortonberry. "It's not well done of you to accuse Lord Davenport of giving the same compliment to another woman that he just gave to me."

"I do apologize," Thortonberry said, his tone bitter and leaving no room for doubt that he was anything but sorry.

"I expect no less from a man of your caliber," Trent replied.

"Gentlemen, if you cannot behave nicely to each other, I am going to make one of you leave," Audrey threatened.

Wanting to say more but believing Audrey might just do what she had said, Trent sat back. What he really wanted to do was reveal Thortonberry's proclivity for sleeping with a different demirep every night, but then he would also need to explain why he had been at the hellfire clubs all those nights. He had a sinking suspicion once he did that it would make what he had to say about Thortonberry seem less credible or possibly false. Women could be unpredictable in their temperaments.

As Audrey relaxed back into her seat and trained her gaze on the play, Trent studied her and tried to plan the best course of action. He could not let her be seduced, or worse, end up married to Thortonberry. When she suddenly bursts out laughing at a scene in the play, his heart jerked and an odd warm feeling infused him. What the hell was that? Lust? No, not lust. He felt...happy. Damnation. Her laughter made him happy. When had that become possible?

She leaned forward in her seat and peered intently at the stage. Her face, filled with delighted rapture, made his blood warm further. Her emotions showed in a delightful display of half smiles, dimples and grins.

Gwyneth had rarely laughed and her face had exposed little of what she felt. Whitney had been partially right last night—Audrey seemed nothing like Gwyneth, yet that still did not mean he would ever want to allow himself to be vulnerable to her. One could never be certain what secrets a woman concealed behind her smile. What he did know was those secrets could be sharper than any blade he had ever felt when they cut into you.

Thortonberry drew close to Audrey and whispered something in her ear. She tilted her head back, a smile gracing her lips and her chest shaking with her laughter.

Trent tensed. He did not like seeing another man make her laugh. He frowned, crossed his arms and waited for Thortonberry to try to speak with her again. It took less than a minute.

Thortonberry leaned near her and Trent spoke up. "Do you like the play so far, Lady Audrey?"

She turned to him. "Yes, very much."

He eyed Thortonberry, gratified to see the man's lips twitching. Ten minutes later, when Thortonberry shifted his body as if he was going to attempt to speak with Audrey again, Trent launched a countermove. He tapped her on the arm. When she looked his way, he said, "I particularly like this actress. I think she commands comedy very well. Tell me, who are your favorite actresses and why?"

"Oh, that's easy. I adore Sarah Harlowe. She has wonderful comedic timing. I also love Miss Maria Foote. She is wonderful. Do you care for either of them?"

He did actually. He nodded slowly. "I like them both a great deal. I think they are excellent at what they do and true ladies."

Thortonberry snorted. "No true lady is an actress."

Trent frowned. "I disagree. I find it small-minded to say a woman is not a lady merely because she is an actress."

He stiffened when Audrey gaped at him. Belatedly he realized he had freely spoken an opinion he had never voiced. "I realize I'm in the minority."

"The minority," Thortonberry exclaimed. "I'd say you are the only one in the entire *ton* that holds that opinion."

"No, he is not. I too do not think an actress can not be considered a lady in the sense that being an actress means she is worth less than me. To me, she is the superior woman. She has a talent, whereas I have none."

Shock rendered Trent unable to speak for a moment, but then a deep admiration filled him. "You are a constant surprise." He meant it in the best way possible.

She blushed.

"For once we agree, Davenport. Lady Audrey, I am shocked to hear you voice an opinion so contrary to what I know your father and brother believe."

Trent watched Audrey. The smile on her face vanished and her lips turned down in a frown, then pulled into a tight line. He had the urge to throw Thortonberry out of the box for making Audrey lose her smile. He was contemplating actually doing it, when she spoke.

"I fear you do not know me very well, Lord Thortonberry, but I cannot blame you for that. I do not voice my opinions on the matter of women overly much, because to do so would be to risk my father's anger. I beg you not to mention this conversation to Richard."

To Thortonberry's credit, he nodded immediately. "I swear I will not. Perhaps I need to expand my views."

Trent narrowed his gaze. Thortonberry said one thing with words, but his flared nostrils and tight jaw told Trent the man was lying. This was the perfect opportunity to cut Thortonberry out of the conversation for the rest of the night. "What do you think about the new acting techniques being displayed on stage?"

Audrey turned her body toward him and gave Thortonberry her back as she started telling him her views. He relaxed into his seat and listened to her melodic voice. He could sit and listen to her for hours. He had a sudden picture of them strolling in his garden arm in arm and talking for hours on subjects that interested them both such as the theater. His self-control was slipping.

When the theater lights rose, he blinked, surprised to realize that the play was over. Time had passed quickly while he talked with Audrey. He stood, wanting to see the night finished so he could put needed distance between himself and Audrey. "I assume you came here with Whitney?"

Audrey nodded and rose. On the other side of her, Thortonberry stood there like the nuisance he was. Trent pressed his teeth together, intent on removing Thortonberry's ability to touch Audrey again or even walk beside her, for that matter

"May I walk you to Sutherland's carriage?"

She spared a glance at Thortonberry, which made Trent's head pound. Biting her lip, she said, "Yes, that would be lovely. We can all walk together."

Trent barely contained his growl. He moved swiftly and offered his left elbow to Audrey to maneuver her to his other side and away from Thortonberry. Damned if the marquess did not move right along with her. Thortonberry had bollocks. Trent would give the marquess that much, but not any more.

An awkward silence, made more pronounced by the excited chatter around them, descended as they made their way out of the theater and onto Catherine Street. Whitney strolled up to Lord Thortonberry, but Trent could not hear what they were saying over the sounds of clopping horse hooves, whistling wind and calls of farewells.

Whitney pulled Sutherland toward her and away from their group. "Darling, I'm freezing. Audrey, dear, make quick goodbyes and hurry to join us."

Audrey nodded as Whitney and Sutherland walked a few feet up the row of carriages and disappeared into his.

The night was unusually cool, so when Audrey shivered Trent pulled her closer. The bright moonlight and blazing oil lanterns made spotting his carriage and Thortonberry's easy enough. They stood one behind the other in the long row of carriages. He did not see Primwitty anywhere, but the duke understood Trent was on a mission and had likely headed home to Sally. Trent turned to dismiss Thortonberry since the man had not made a move to bid farewell. Thortonberry's gaze lingered on the valley between Audrey's breasts, exactly where Trent had stared earlier.

A fierce wave of possessiveness nearly choked him. He drew Audrey more firmly against his side. Her small frame pressed against his, and satisfaction coursed through him when she leaned into him and not away. When she swayed, he slid his hand to her back to steady her. The heat radiating off her skin singed his fingers and beckoned to areas of his body that needed to be oblivious to the soft feminine creature so near him.

With a ruthless determination born of hours of solitude in his small cell with nothing but darkness and a desire to live as his company, Trent turned his focus back to Thortonberry. "I've something I wish to say to Lady Audrey, Thortonberry. Alone. So good night." Trent specifically eyed the man's coachman, who stood waiting for the marquess.

Lord Thortonberry glowered at Trent before asking Audrey, "Do you need me to stay?"

Who the devil did Thortonberry think he was? Trent itched to smash his fist into the man's smug face.

"That is quite all right," Audrey replied. "I'm perfectly safe standing here on the street with Lord Davenport."

A flash of the one time they had kissed filled his mind. Her creamy skin. The swell of her firm, warm flesh in his hands. Honeysuckle filling his lungs and her taste of honey and lemon filling his mouth with each velvet slide of her tongue against his. Hell and damnation, he wanted it again. He wanted her.

He blinked and focused on her face. The air nearly left his lungs. Her eyes shone with such utter trust the weight of it burrowed into his bones. Clearing his throat he said, "You can be assured the lady is safe in my company." He would make it so, no matter how difficult it was.

Thortonberry nodded curtly. "Then I'll see you tomorrow, Lady Audrey."

"Tomorrow?" Trent demanded.

"Yes. Your cousin invited me to her picnic. It seems you could not attend, and she had games planned that require an even number, so she can match people in pairs. I volunteered to pair with you, Lady Audrey."

"That's kind of you, Lord Thortonberry."

"Actually, I'm able to attend now," Trent said, a tic in his jaw beating a furious tempo. "I suppose that means you can stay home."

"Lord Davenport," Audrey chided. "There is no need for you to stay home, Lord Thortonberry. I'm sure Whitney can invite one more person to even the numbers again."

"It's settled, then," Thortonberry crooned, his eyes shining with glee. "I'd hate to miss a picnic with games."

Trent balled his hands at his side. Bloody Thortonberry was a liar. The man shifted from foot to foot with a darting gaze. Typical of a liar. Thortonberry no more wanted to play games than Trent wanted to contract the plague.

With a nod, Thortonberry walked away. Trent stared at Audrey while trying to decide what to say. Her thick dark hair was swept up to expose the long, slender column of her neck. He wanted to press his lips to her silken skin. Instead, he swallowed hard and pushed the desire away. "I don't want you to allow yourself to be alone with men like Thortonberry."

"What sort of men should I allow myself to be alone with? Men like you?"

"Certainly not." He tugged his cravat. It was too damned tight and the night was not near as cool as he had previously thought.

She took a deep breath, her breasts swelling upward invitingly. "Yet here we are, you and I—alone."

Her husky voice slid over him like cool water on a humid summer day. Irresistibly tempting. He scowled at the way her luminescent eyes made him forget his purpose. "Do try to listen to me."

She nodded.

He captured her gaze and held it, trying not to think how

lovely her eyes were and how he could actually see little specks of gold in them. *Blast and damn. Concentrate, man.* "Thortonberry is a fox disguised as a puppy."

Her eyes twinkled. "I think he is rather more like a puppy, cute and cuddly at that."

He shifted uncomfortably. She was baiting him. What he needed was to watch her from a distance, yet she was forcing him to stick close to her. "Will you promise to partner with me tomorrow, and only me?"

Her mouth tugged into a grin. "That sounds perfect."

He grunted. She had not promised nor rejected the idea. He had just been outmaneuvered by a slip of a woman. The other spies he had once worked with would have laughed their bloody heads off if they had been privy to this exchange. Wary he regarded Audrey, the large smile still firmly on her face made her dimples show. "Why are you grinning at me?"

"Because tonight I got the answer to my question."

"What question was that?" God only knew, considering her complex mind.

"Oh, I'll never tell," she said breezily and brushed past him to walk toward Sutherland's carriage.

A secret smile replaced her grin and that made him nervous. What answer could he have unknowingly placed in her mind? And was it correct? He caught her by the elbow just as she neared the carriage. "Audrey, I don't want you to think—" Hell, this was hard. He couldn't simply blurt out he didn't want her to mistake that his intentions toward her had changed. "That is, just now, when I seemed to act possessive, I, I mean to say—"

"You were jealous?"

He nodded before he realized his idiotic confirmation would give her the complete wrong idea.

She squeezed his arm discreetly. "I know, and I'm so glad." She scrambled into the carriage before he could stop her.

He watched the carriage disappear down the street. He had to get Thortonberry out of the picture quickly. Once that was accomplished, he would keep his distance from her even if it meant going abroad for a short time until she was married. The thought made his heart jerk peculiarly.

Five

The next morning Audrey rose and chose her best walking dress made of French twill silk with cap sleeves that happened to be in Trent's favorite shade of blue. The snug bodice with small crimson roses showed off her figure rather well, she hoped. She left her hair unbound but well brushed, grabbed her bonnet and raced out of her room and down the stairs to where her coachman was waiting to drive her to the picnic.

She loathed a confrontation with her father, but she needed to remind him she had an outing, lest he accuse her of being sneaky again. She made her way to his study and knocked on the closed door. "May I come in?"

"Yes, and shut the door behind you." Her father's tone was sharp, as usual. "No need for the gossiping servants to hear what I have to say."

Audrey stepped into the room and forced a smile. "I'd say you've no worry of that since you've gotten rid of half the staff in the last month. I daresay the remaining servants have too much work to stand around eavesdropping."

Her father's mercurial black eyes sharpened. "Are you complaining?" he asked with deceptive calm. The red splotches on his cheeks gave his burgeoning temper away.

"No," she said, sighing inwardly. She sat in one of the two green velvet chairs across from his desk. "I'm sorry to interrupt you. I am about to depart and wanted to remind you I am going to Lady Whitney's picnic. Ms. Frompington will serve as chaperone." Ms. Frompington was nearly deaf and had terrible vision, which to Audrey made her the perfect chaperone.

Her father leaned back in his chair, crossed his arms over his chest and nodded. "Fine. I've something to discuss with you first."

She bit the inside of her cheek. She did not want to be late for the picnic but there was no hope for it. "Yes, Father?" Making her voice meek was always a battle. Her will wanted to be bold but her head knew better.

"Mr. Shelton has asked for your hand in marriage, and I've told him you'll accept at the Lionhursts' fete."

She stiffened in her chair; her father's cold announcement unleashing a burning fury within her. The fete was less than two weeks away. "Father, please, if you hold any love for me, don't ask me to marry Mr. Shelton. He's twice my age and only wants to parade me as another prize he's collected to his friends. He doesn't love me. Good heavens, the man doesn't even know me. We've not exchanged more than twenty words in the last year."

Her father's expression hardened. "I'm not asking you." The words resounded around the room like a clap. "I'm telling you. And here is something else you need to understand. You've been nothing but trouble for years. You're entering your fourth Season." Disgust filled his tone. "You're two and twenty and on the verge of being on the shelf. I won't have it." He slapped his palm against the desk. "I'll not be burdened with you anymore."

His words were like a smack across the face. With effort, she forced herself to shrug in mock resignation, though her hurt was so acute she wanted to run out of the room. Too many times, she'd attempted to gain his love. She was done trying. Clearing her throat, she prayed her voice would not tremble. "I'm sorry you feel that way."

His face turned crimson, and a vein pulsed at his right temple. "How else could I feel? You have turned down every decent offer of marriage that ever came your way."

It was on the tip of her tongue to say it was because

she had never loved any of those men, but he wouldn't care. Instead, she sat in stony silence and waited for him to speak.

"If it had not been for your mother, I would have forced you to marry long ago, but she begged me to let you chose your husband." He raked a hand through his hair and stared at her with eyes glittering with anger.

"I had not realized you loved Mother enough to do anything she wished." The accusation had flown from her lips without thought, but she didn't care. A sense of recklessness gnawed at her as hot tears stung the backs of her eyes.

"Don't disrespect me, girl." His voice was as hard as granite. "For the last three years I've stood by and said little as you ruined your chances with suitor after suitor and even botched up the betrothal to that private investigator, Wentworth. How you managed to drive away a man so obviously desperate for a woman, I'll never know—but you did."

"We all have our special talents," she said flippantly, falling back into her old habit of pretending his hurtful words did not bother her. What she really wanted to do was scream at him that she had never truly been engaged to Roger Wentworth because he did not exist. The contrived scheme had bought her temporary immunity from her father. Tense, she maintained her silence.

Tapping his fingers against the desk, her father continued to glare. "No doubt your tart tongue is the reason you've never married. Take Davenport for instance. You have now danced with him and Richard told me you sat by Davenport at the theater last night, but has the man called this morning to ask to properly court you?"

Audrey's head pounded. "No," she whispered hoarsely. "It is early though to make calls." How ridiculous her defense sounded.

Her father thumped the desk. "He won't. Mark my words. I had stupidly hoped last night, but I realized this morning when I received the offer from Mr. Shelton that his was likely the best offer you will get."

She lifted her chin. "I am going to see Lord Davenport at the picnic today."

"Did he specifically ask you to meet him?"

"Well, no, but—"

"Foolish, stupid girl. Of course he did not. You live in a fantasy. Wake up."

Audrey flinched at the cruel words that pierced too close to her secret doubts. Leave it to her father to know exactly how to hurt her most.

"Do you not wonder why he will not ask to court you?" His low, mocking tone battered her, yet somehow she managed to remain perfectly still. Her father laid his palms against his desk. "I'll tell you why." His voice had lost any pretense of niceness and came out as a snarl.

She refused to show fear. Staring him straight in the face she said, "Somehow I knew you would." Her voice now trembled. Damn her father for succeeding in hurting her once again.

He pointed a finger at her. "A man like Davenport can have any woman he wants. He'll never offer for you because he knows as a wife you'll bring him misery with your tart tongue and willful ways. You are but a diversion to pass his time but never to chain himself to."

A wave of hurt crashed over her, but she would never show her pain to her father. After a moment, she flicked an imaginary speck of dirt off her dress, then forced a smile. "If that's truly what you think of me, it seems to me you should be a better friend to Mr. Shelton and not do him a disservice by agreeing to let me marry him. I better say no. Perhaps I shouldn't marry at all but just live here and spare men my tart tongue."

Her father rose and stormed around his desk to stand in front of her or rather loom over her. "You may have reached your majority but you'll either obey me with reverence or leave my house. You'll accept Mr. Shelton's offer or else pack your bags and make your own way in the world."

Frustration threatened to overwhelm her and make her say something that would really cause her problems. Instead, she clutched at her dress and stared down at her hands. What she wouldn't give to shout at him that she would leave this instant and set out on her own. But she wasn't stupid. If she was going to be forced to leave, she would buy as much time as possible. She was no simpering lady to sit idly by while her father shoved a life on her that she didn't want. The fact that she was seriously contemplating leaving gave her a sense of self-control she had never felt. Resolve welled within her chest and rushed like blood through her veins.

Unfortunately, fear of the unknown future beat a fast path behind resolve and left her feeling as if she wanted to slump in the chair. She gripped the cushion of her seat and sat straighter. Unless a miracle happened or she left, misery would be a permanent part of her life.

Tilting her head back, she studied her father's face. Lines of anger carved mercilessly into his forehead, around his eyes and at his mouth. There would be no changing his mind. Stubborn determination settled in her shoulders, leaving them tense as if she held a heavy weapon. "Can I go now? I am late for the picnic."

"Go." He looked down at his papers and waved a hand at her. "But resign yourself to the fact that you are to be married to Mr. Shelton."

She marched out of her father's door without a word. She would resign herself to no such thing, except the very real fact that she had little time left to make Trent realize he loved her or she would have to flee the only life she had ever known.

UNDER THE BRIGHT SUN AND cloudless sky, Trent leaned against an enormous oak tree at Richmond Park and stared in Audrey and Thortonberry's general direction. Something was amiss with her. She had arrived late and her eyes had appeared red and swollen, as if she had been crying. Then, before he could even approach her, Whitney had paired Audrey with Thortonberry for the ridiculous games. And now they were sharing a blanket for lunch.

Damnation. His plan to keep her away from Thortonberry was unraveling before his eyes. That was unacceptable. He would put himself between them. He pushed off the rough tree trunk and as he did, Whitney rounded a hedge of high bushes, her green skirts swishing with her rapid pace and a few tendrils of her blond hair coming loose as she strode toward him. She motioned for him to stay. "I want to talk to you," she called.

A few of her picnic guests swiveled around from their blankets to look at them, but they all turned away just as quickly, too busy enjoying their scones. Or maybe it was the scowl he could feel tightening his forehead that made them look away. He struggled to smooth his face and even smile at Lady Caroline and Sally, who had once again glanced his way. Lady Caroline smiled back, but Sally arched her eyebrows at him.

Whitney strolled up to him and gave him a sidelong glance before a smug smile fleetingly touched her lips. "You were staring at Audrey again."

Some former spy he had become. He was making all kinds of mistakes and Audrey was the reason. "I wish you would not have invited Thortonberry," he said, maneuvering the conversation away from what he had been doing.

"Then you should not have declined my original invitation to come to the picnic today," she replied tartly. "As it is, you deciding to come caused me a great deal of trouble." She averted her face, and Trent knew why. She did not want him to see her amused smile, but even with her head turned toward the pink, purple and yellow azaleas in bloom, the upturned corner of her mouth was impossible to miss.

"I had to scramble around early this morning to find another guest to invite, so that everyone could pair off for the scavenger hunt I have planned," Whitney said, once again facing him.

Her face may not have shown a hint of the lies she was trying to feed him, but her fingers busily twirled a thin white ribbon hanging from her sleeve. Round and round she twined the ribbon until the tip of her index finger turned pink. He barely contained his laughter. Unbeknownst to her, she told him her story was false without ever uttering a confession. The busier a person's hands became, the more they were attempting to hide.

He had once watched a French spy who lost a message he was supposed to deliver to Trent from a guard at Saint Helena unravel the end of his overcoat while he attempted to offer false excuses for what had happened.

Trent kept his gaze on Whitney's hands. "I'm terribly sorry if I inconvenienced you."

She stilled immediately. "Apologies are not like you at all." She had the funniest lopsided frown on her face. "What are you trying to get me to admit?"

Trent struggled not to smile. "Nothing really. Though it did occur to me, you might be trying to manipulate me into courting Audrey. I specifically told you I did not think Thortonberry was good company for her and yet you invited them both to the theater last night and today to this picnic. You knew if you did that, I would come to both, though I had declined your invitation to get me in close proximity to her."

Whitney tugged on her dress, then pressed a hand over her hair. "Good gracious, the grand scenarios you conjure with you mind! As if I could predict you would come scrambling to be by Audrey's side when you realized Lord Thortonberry was with her."

Trent grunted. "You lie so prettily, cousin dear. If I did not adore you I might be irritated that you seem to be disregarding my expresses wishes for you to understand I never want to marry, therefore Audrey is better off without me, and certainly without Thortonberry."

Whitney bit her lower lip and then huffed out a long breath. "Fine. Fine." She stood before shrugging. "I ignored you. I admit it. I cannot say I'm sorry for it either." She set her hands to her hips. You are my favorite cousin and Audrey is one of my dearest friends. Things seemed so promising when the two of you first met. All sparks and smoldering looks, and despite your explanation that it was only because you thought her a woman of loose morals, I refuse to believe that."

Trent snorted. "That is not the first time you have chosen not to accept reality."

She pressed her lips together. "No need to dredge up the past. It may have taken me almost a year to realize I needed to tell Drake the truth about why I had fled him and our betrothal, but at least I realized I had to do it, so I would not lose him. I was not blind to what was before me. You need spectacles."

"My sight is splendid," Trent said. "Perfect, in fact."

She frowned. "Then you should see you are about to lose Audrey to another man, unless you act to court her and get over whatever ridiculous fear is holding you back."

He crossed his arms over his chest and leaned back against the tree. He refused to be forced into anything by anyone. "I fear nothing." The lie rang hollow in his ears.

Whitney arched her eyebrows. "Nothing? That is probably for the best, if it's true, because it seems my plan has backfired. Look at Audrey." She waved a hand in Audrey's direction. "I believe she likes Lord Thortonberry, and to think all this time I thought she truly cared for you."

Jealousy pricked him, which exploded when Thortonberry reached over to the dense azalea bush beside his blanket, plucked a bright pink flower and tucked it in Audrey's hair. Trent stood, his head spinning with his thoughts. He could not stand by and let Thortonberry swoop her into his web of deception. Simply trying to watch over her was not working. He had to act. But what to do? The first thing was to make sure Thortonberry had no other opportunity to be alone with her today. Once that goal was accomplished, Trent would contrive another plan.

"I'd like you to partner me with Audrey in the scavenger hunt."

Beside him, Whitney chuckled low. "I think I can manage that since I am the one pairing everyone off. Luckily, I invited Lady Caroline, and I know she will be thrilled to be paired with Lord Thortonberry."

He winked at Whitney. "You are a minx through and through. I hope Sutherland knows what he is getting into by marrying you."

She winked back. "It's because I am a minx through and through *that* he wants to marry me. Watch me work and save your compliments for later."

In a swirl of green skirts, Whitney rushed to the center

of the picnickers who sat in a semicircle on the grassy knoll. As his cousin clapped her hands and called out eagerly for everyone's attention, the conversation slowly died and left a shocking quiet in its place, punctuated by the whistle of a low breeze and the chirping parakeets that lived in the trees of the park.

Within moments, Whitney had explained the rules for the scavenger hunt and called, "Get with your partners, everyone."

Trent closed the distance between himself and Audrey and, leaning close to her, said, "Hello, partner."

The happy smiled that stretched her lips and lit her eyes turning them from a deep lush green that matched the leaves on the azalea bushes to a color more reminiscent of the crisp grass caused a tightening in Trent's chest.

"I want to win," she exclaimed with a twinkle in her eyes, "so be prepared to keep up with me."

"You shall have to endeavor to match my pace," he teased, enjoying the moment of levity. He could not remember the last time he had relished simple bantering so much. When Thortonberry cleared his throat, Trent flicked the man an annoyed look. Why was the marquess still standing here? "You should make your way to Lady Caroline, Thortonberry. The hunt is about to begin."

With a pinched face, Thortonberry turned on his heel and strode over to the rocks where Lady Caroline stood.

Audrey shook her head. "He is acting so odd. I do not understand it. He told me he has a tender for Lady Caroline, but he has ignored her so far and he did not seem very eager to pair with her, did he?"

Trent shook his head. "He did not. I'd say—"

The chiming of the bell to start the scavenger hunt cut off his intended warning about Thortonberry to Audrey. Laughing, she grasped his hand and tugged. "Come on," she called over the laughter from the participants taking off. "I know just where we should look for our item."

His warning died away, replaced by a surge of warmth and desire for the innocent beauty so eagerly tugging on his hand. He allowed her to pull him in the direction of a hill covered with purple wildflowers and away from the scattering pairs. The flowers brushed against his breeches as they trudged up the slope.

Audrey moved slightly ahead of him, but he did not hurry to rush to her side. Instead, he enjoyed the gentle swaying of her hips as she walked. Once at the top, he followed her lead to the far side of the hill and glanced down at the city displayed below.

"Breathtaking," she murmured.

"Yes," he agreed, not sparing another look at the city when such a beautiful woman stood by his side with her hand still firmly curled around his. He drank in every detail about her. The long slender slope of her neck. Her silky tresses cascading around her shoulders. Her high cheekbones and those generous lips. He curled his fingers tighter around hers. Desire pounded through him. He wanted to feel her lips once again. A sudden errant thought assailed him. If she were his, he could kiss her quite often. Yet she was not his, and never would be, but it did not matter. He wanted to kiss her one more time. Just once. Never again.

"Where is your chaperone?" He winced at the hoarseness of his voice.

She swiveled away from him, crossed back to where they had ascended the hill and peered over. "She's coming. Rather slowly but surely." Turning back, she tilted her head to the side. "Whatever is the matter, Trent? Are you afraid to be alone with me?"

A bark of laughter escaped him. She was teasing him. Tempting him. And he would crumble. He was only human, after all. "Come here," he commanded, curling his index finger at her.

She moved toward him without hesitation. He gently grasped her shoulders and drew her near. "I want to kiss you."

"Then why do you not?" Her cheeks colored to a bright pink.

"Because I can promise you nothing. I am taking without giving." *What the hell am I doing?* He was not sure what he might be considering, but he was certain there was no time to think on it now, not with her chaperone pressing down on them.

Unblinking, she gazed at him. "Take. Later you can give. I believe in you."

Good God, he didn't even believe in himself anymore, but her words battered his control to nothing. He cupped her delicate face in his hands, and as his lips descended on hers she exhaled with a sigh and her sweet breath filled his mouth. Knowing it was dangerous to let go completely, he started the kiss slow, but when Audrey delved her hands into his hair and tugged him closer, he could not hold back. The tether that held him snapped.

He ravaged her mouth, wanting to consume and possess her. Questions ceased, replaced by wonder. Her soft lips molded to his and she met each stroke of his tongue with a velvet one of her own. Behind him, the snap of a twig and the huff of an exhausted breath alerted him to the approach of her chaperone. With a growl, he ended the kiss.

Bemusement flittered across her face and as much as he did not want to turn away, he did in time to greet her chaperone and offer a helping hand up the last step of the hill.

"Now you help me," the silver-haired woman muttered and pushed past him to waddle by. She plucked her hands on her hips as she faced them. "You two must slow your pace. I cannot keep up and I will not be lapse in my duties."

"Of course, Ms. Frompington," Audrey replied, her voice raised.

Trent arched a questioning eyebrow at her.

Audrey inclined her head to her chaperone. "Ms. Frompington has a little trouble hearing, don't you?" Audrey said in a loud voice.

"You say you saw a deerling?" the woman demanded. "Is that some sort of special breed of deer?"

"Yes, indeed," Trent inserted with a smile.

Audrey rolled her eyes and pointed toward the ground. "I actually came up here for a purpose."

"Me too," Trent said, unable to resist baiting her.

She gave him a sidelong glance and a lovely smirk that caused his chest to tighten.

"According to Whitney, you and I are to find a pair of

quizzing glasses. And I thought what better place to hide a pair of quizzing glasses than at the spot in the park with the best view."

Admiration filled his chest. "By Jove, you are brilliant."

"I like to think so," she said, humor underlying her tone.

"Shall we?" he asked, kneeling to his haunches and patting the grass around him.

"I'm far too old to kneel," Ms. Frompington declared.

Trent caught Audrey covering the smile on her face. When she moved her hand, she had impressively schooled her features. "Why don't you sit on that bench over there?" Audrey pointed to a wooden bench a few feet away that faced out toward the city below. With a nod, Ms. Frompington walked toward the seat and plopped down with her back to them.

Audrey knelt beside him, their heads almost touching. The afternoon sun shone down on her head and made the black strands of her hair gleam like a stone polished to perfection. His breath caught in his chest. The picture was perfect, except for the offending flower Thortonberry had put in her hair. Trent plucked the bud from behind her left ear.

She raised her hand to her hair and tucked the dangling strand behind her ear. "Why did you do that?"

He threw the flower to the ground. "I don't want you taking anything from Thortonberry. What were you doing earlier with your head pressed so close to his?"

She stopped her search of the grass and gave him a sidelong glance. "Trying to see if I could make you jealous two days in a row."

"You say the most surprising things," he grumbled. The devil of it was he loved that about her. She was utterly capable of artifice when needed yet somehow still seemed honest to a fault at her core. She was a contradiction, and part of him wanted to believe such honesty existed in a woman, but another part of him was attached to his vow to never allow a woman to unhinge him body and soul again.

Audrey stared at him without blinking. "I'll take the fact I can surprise you as a compliment, though my father has assured me time and again, I should endeavor to be silent lest I drive whatever man has interest in me away with my audacious opinions."

"Your father is an addle pate. I love your intelligence."

"Do you?" A sly grin pulled at her lips.

Damned if he didn't. "I do," he admitted with some hesitation, wanting to make her feel good but not wanting her to think his admiration changed his stance on marriage.

"That's nice to hear," she murmured with a tremor in her voice.

He flicked his gaze to Ms. Frompington, who still had her back to them. Satisfied he was not putting Audrey's reputation in any danger, he ran a finger down her smooth cheek. "Do not let your father quash your spirit."

Her eyes widened and she nodded.

With a will born out of silently enduring countless nights of torture in Bagne de Toulon, Trent forced himself to pull away from her. His heart squeezed in his chest as a frown flittered across her face. He needed distance. Strange thoughts invaded his head, such as not wanting to see her marry anyone else. "We better find those quizzing glasses if we are going to beat the others back to the brook and claim the prize."

Before she responded, a sharp cry came from the park bench. Trent scrambled to his feet, helped Audrey up, and they rushed over to her chaperone, who was struggling to stand while holding a pair of crushed quizzing glasses. The woman's face twisted in a scowl. "I shifted in my seat and sat on these!" She shook the glasses in the air. Tiny shards sprinkled down. "What sort of beetle head brings quizzing glasses to the park?"

Trent glanced at Audrey and they burst out laughing. He held his hand out to a now glaring Ms. Frompington. "I'll take those. I do believe you inadvertently located the item Lady Audrey and I were to find for the scavenger hunt."

Ms. Frompington nodded and set the glasses into Trent's palm. "Excellent," she crooned. "Now we can join the rest of the group and bid our farewells."

"Farewells?" Audrey asked.

Ms. Frompington nodded. "I'm injured." The chaperone pointed to the rip in her dress close to her backside. "I believe I've been cut in a most delicate place. I'm afraid I need to go home, my lady, and tend to my injuries."

"Of course," Audrey said with a sigh.

Trent frowned. He should be glad his goal was about to be accomplished. Audrey was going home and would be out of Thortonberry's reach, at least for the rest of the afternoon. Yet he didn't feel glad. Disappointment was more apt. She would be out of his reach as well and he would miss her company, which irked him immensely. He did not want to miss her presence. What he needed was a better plan of how to protect her from Thortonberry, but devil take it if he knew what that was at the moment.

NOT LONG LATER AUDREY STROLLED toward her carriage arm and arm with Whitney. Her friend pressed close. "You're sure you have to leave?"

Audrey nodded. "Yes. Ms. Frompington is not the resilient kind. If I insist we stay, she'll spend the rest of the day complaining about her wounded backside and making me and all of you miserable."

Whitney frowned. "You should tell your father you need another chaperone."

"No. no. I truly like Ms. Frompington. Besides that, she is half-deaf which suits nicely when I'm trying to have a conversation with Trent."

Whitney paused near Audrey's carriage where Ms. Frompington waited. "And did you have a good conversation?"

They'd had a great deal more than good conversation, but Audrey wanted to relish her kiss with Trent a bit more before she shared it with her friend. "I think so, and I hope he thought so too."

Whitney touched Audrey's arm. "You do not appear overly pleased."

Audrey nibbled on her lip, thinking on the conversation with her father. "I am pleased with the time

I spent with Trent. I was hoping to have more. My time is running out to make your cousin realize he loves me. Father told me this morning that I am to accept an offer of marriage from Mr. Shelton at the Lionhursts' ball."

"No!" Whitney exclaimed, gripping her arm. "Mr. Shelton is awful."

"I know. So you see my predicament has become dire."

"Lady Audrey." Ms. Frompington popped her head out of the carriage. "I do not mean to rush you, dear, but I'm developing a terrible megrim to go with my aching wound."

Audrey locked gazes with Whitney. "I better go."

"Do not worry," Whitney whispered. "I shall think of some way to help you expedite Trent's realization."

Audrey nodded, though really she was not sure exactly what else they could do.

Six

Early the next day, Audrey's stomach fluttered as she followed Sally and the duke down the center aisle of Saint James chapel for Whitney and Mr. Sutherland's wedding. The Primwittys' stopped at the second row to the front to speak with Whitney's sister Gillian and her husband Lord Lionhurst. Audrey hung back, feeling rather awkward as the two couples took turns reminiscing over how they each had met the other and their own weddings. Everyone was married or getting married.

A pang of jealousy tightened Audrey's stomach, but she forced it away. She was thrilled Whitney was marrying the man she loved, and she refused to let envy have any part of this special day. "I'm making progress," she muttered under her breath.

"Making progress with what?" a deep velvet-tinged voice demanded directly behind her.

She grinned and faced Trent, her breath catching in her throat and her heartbeat tripping then speeding ahead. He looked marvelous. The dark blue frock coat did nothing to conceal the fact that he was a well-built man and she rather liked that. What she liked even better was the way his light trousers clung to the muscles of his thighs.

He flashed a rather wolfish smile at her. "Have you forgotten what it is you were making progress with?"

She blinked, whipped up her fan and tried to ward off the blush that crept up her neck. She certainly could not tell him she believed she was making progress with him. That would likely make him run in the other direction. "Progress with taking my seat," she whispered. "I did not want to be rude and ask anyone to move."

Trent's eyes danced with amusement. "Allow me." He offered her his elbow and then tapped the Duke of Primwitty on the shoulder. "Excuse us, Primwitty. We're going to sit down."

"Yes, of course," the duke replied. "I'm terribly sorry, Lady Audrey, for making you stand there."

"That is quite all right." It was better than all right, she thought as Trent led her around the chatting couples and into a pew. If she had not been standing there she may not have gotten to sit by Trent. Yesterday, she had been sure she had seen something different in his eyes when he looked at her. Something akin to tenderness mixed with longing. She was certain she was breaking down some barriers. Hopefully they would crash in time to save her from her father's plans for her.

She settled into her seat beside Trent, a thrill running through her when his hard thigh momentarily brushed hers. She could have sworn his muscles tensed upon contact, but he moved his leg so quickly it was impossible to know for certain. Did he desire her as much as she desired him? If so, she wished he would stop fighting it.

She focused her attention on the front of the church where Whitney and Mr. Sutherland would stand and tried to stop the racing of her heart. She had to get herself in hand. The vaulted ceiling let in a flood of sunlight that shone down on the hundreds of roses decorating the marble stairs leading to the altar. She inhaled deeply of the rose-petal scented air and her pulse slowed just a bit until Trent leaned so close to her his crisp scent of soap and lemon filled her nose and his heat enveloped her. "You look so serious," he murmured. "What are you thinking about?"

She turned her head to look at him. A frown creased his brow. She wanted to be truthful and give up the game of trying to make him realize he loved her, but she was afraid. She swallowed. A little truth was better than none at all. "I was just thinking that I want to get married here as well. And I would like hundreds of roses just like this. They look so lovely and have such a wonderful scent. Don't you think?"

His frown increased. "I had not given it any thought. Do you have a candidate in mind for your wedding?"

Sally's sudden appearance by Audrey saved her from having to either boldly lie or confess. The duchess looked at her with sparkling humor-filled eyes. "Darling, may Peter and I squeeze onto this row?"

Audrey glanced over her shoulder to the empty row behind her and her mouth fell open. Lord Thortonberry sat directly behind her, but other than that, the bench was empty. He smiled and waved and she returned his greeting as she scooted over to make room for Sally and the duke. Whitney had to have contrived inviting Lord Thortonberry to her wedding to try to continue to make Trent jealous. Audrey faced the front again and spared a glance for Trent. She barely contained her delighted laughter. He was glaring between her and Lord Thortonberry.

"Is that your candidate?" he demanded in a harsh whisper.

"Do be quiet!" Sally shushed. "Do you not hear the music signaling the bride's march is starting?"

Audrey craned her head around and exclaimed with delight, quickly scampering to her feet along with all the other wedding guests. Whitney, with a wreath of white and orange roses in her hair and in a gown made of the finest Brussels lace, slowly moved down the aisle.

Before long, she stood before the altar and she and Mr. Sutherland pledged themselves to each other. As the ceremony came to an end, Whitney turned arm and arm with Mr. Sutherland and beamed at the crowd. Audrey beamed back. She was so happy for her friend. When Whitney and Mr. Sutherland strolled down the aisle, Audrey followed their departure, then stood with the crowd.

Trent was unusually silent beside her and a dark

scowl had set on his face. She stepped into the aisle and was about to ask him what was wrong, though she suspected, rather gladly, that it was Lord Thortonberry's presence, when Lord Thortonberry spoke. "Would you care to ride to the wedding breakfast with me? I'm taking Lady Caroline and her aunt as well."

"She would love to," Sally replied before Audrey could decline the offer. Behind Audrey, a disgusted huff came from Trent. His reaction brought a smile to her lips. Perhaps riding with Lord Thortonberry and Lady Caroline would be the proverbial last feather that broke the horse's back.

NOT LONG LATER, TRENT PROWLED through the wedding guests gathered at his uncle's home for Whitney and Sutherland's wedding breakfast. Where the devil was Audrey? They should be here by now. As he rounded the dozen tables set up in the ballroom, he darted around his uncle and dodged his mother, who shot him a withering glance.

He strolled the perimeter of the room, then stopped, relief and tension flooding him at once. Exhaling at the same time the muscles between his shoulder blades bunched together, he stared across the room at Audrey. She stood to the left of the table that held the wedding cake and directly in front of the coffee and tea table. Beside her, under shadows cast from the large trees outside the window that blocked the filtering sunlight, was the fiend Thortonberry. This had to stop.

Trent pushed away from the column he'd leaned against, intent on striding across the room and sweeping Audrey away. Before he had taken two steps, Sutherland moved into his path. "I would not do that if I were you."

"Do what?" Trent snapped, giving half his attention to Sutherland while keeping the rest on Thortonberry.

"I would not charge over to Lady Audrey and interfere while she is talking to Thortonberry, unless of course you have decided you want to court her. Then by all means, charge."

Trent ground his teeth until his jaw throbbed. "I thought you did not like Thortonberry."

"I don't. But Whitney believes he has every intention of courting Lady Audrey and—"

"Maybe he does," Trent interrupted. "But he has no intentions of ever giving up his mistresses, even when he is married. Lady Audrey deserves a man who will be devoted to her."

Sutherland nodded. "I agree. But sometimes we cannot get what we deserve. Whitney told me on the carriage ride over here from the church that Audrey confessed yesterday at the picnic that her father intends to try to force her to marry some old lecher he has picked out for her. A man Lady Audrey cannot stand. Better she should marry Thortonberry than a man she detests."

Trent shook his head, his body shuddering. "She would grow to hate Thortonberry as well when he left her alone in her cold bed night after night to go lie in the arms of some lesser lady."

Sutherland eyed Trent with a critical squint. "Perhaps, but perhaps not. It is not your place to interfere. Do not be so selfish."

"Selfish?" Trent growled.

"Yes." Sutherland's face hardened. "If you are not willing to court her, let her go."

Trent opened his mouth to consent but snapped it shut. Sutherland was right. It was better she choose who she married than to have the choice forced on her. Yet the words of acknowledgement that Sutherland was correct would not come. Trent glanced at Audrey. She had her face turned up as Thortonberry spoke and a smile tugged at her lips.

Jealousy coursed through his veins and twisted his heart into a painful knot. "I could marry her." *Hellfire.* Had he said that? He turned the idea over in his head. *I could marry her.* He would give her fidelity. Friendship. Passion. What he could never give her was his heart. Why had this idea not occurred to him sooner? He was obsessed with her, unable to quit thinking about her, because he desired her so much. Once he bedded her, the longing would ebb to a manageable level and what would remain would be perfect. A marriage of convenience with a woman he found beautiful and brilliant.

"Excuse me," he said, not looking at Sutherland or waiting for him to reply.

He started toward her, intent on talking to her about them, but before he could reach her side, the bell for breakfast chimed and his mother appeared, demanding he see her to her table. Once he had his mother situated, he looked around for Audrey and found her at a table with Lord Thortonberry, Lady Caroline, Sally and Primwitty. There was not an empty seat at the table.

Briefly, he considered going over, but to what purpose? He would look like a jackanapes if he demanded she come sit with him. All through breakfast and the toasts to Whitney and Sutherland, Trent kept an eye on her. When she caught his gaze, he smiled and was gratified by the smile that lit her face and eyes in return. As he was considering the best way to go about asking her father if he could court her, his mother appeared at his table. "Dearest, I've a megrim. I wanted to stay until the happy couple set out on their wedding journey, but—"

"They are not taking a trip, Mother. Sutherland cannot presently leave his shipping company. It's been several rough months for the business and he and Whitney decided to postpone a trip until things were settled."

"I hadn't realized," his mother murmured. "Do you think they will notice if I depart early?"

Trent shook his head. He had already seen a few of his other family members slip away.

His mother smiled. "Will you fetch your brother? I believe he is in the billiards room. He promised to see me home."

The conversation seemed to be flowing at Audrey's table, but he was reluctant to leave and take his gaze off her. Blast his brother Marcus. It was just like him to thumb his nose at propriety and, instead of remaining in the ballroom, wandering off to see to his own pleasure. "All right," he said when his mother began wringing her hands. By the time he located Marcus, who was in the garden flirting with a maid and not in the billiards room where he was supposed to be, Trent informed him that Mother was ready to depart and hurried back to the ballroom, only to run into his cousin Gillian, who was on her way out.

"Oh, Trent, I'm glad I saw you. Lady Audrey told me to bid you good day. Peter was not feeling well, so Lady Audrey hurriedly departed with the duke and Sally."

Damnation. He had wanted to talk with her and tell her he was going to speak with her father about a courtship, but it would have to wait until tomorrow. He needed to relax. Tomorrow wasn't so long, and it was not as if anything would change between now and then.

Seven

Early in the evening, Trent barged through his front door, swinging it open with such force his normally poker-faced butler, Pickering, gaped. Recovering quickly, Pickering drew to his full five-foot-six height and said in a dry tone, "A letter arrived for you, my lord."

Trent shrugged out of his coat, handed it to Pickering and faced the graying man. The letter could wait. One thought consumed him. He had to send a note to Audrey's father requesting an audience in the morning. "Fetch Harris to me." Trent would jot down a missive and send his footman over to Audrey's home tonight.

"Certainly, my lord." Pickering turned on his heel and then paused and looked back. "Will you be going out tonight?"

Trent nodded. "Have Shaw set out my clothes for dinner at my cousin Gillian's home. I'll leave in an hour."

"Excellent, my lord."

Trent strode toward his study with thoughts of Audrey in his head. He had never intended to offer for her, but now that he had made the decision he was glad he had. This was the best course of action for both of them. He wanted her, and once they were married and he had her, this gnawing need to be around her would diminish and they could enjoy each other as friends. No. More than friends. He cared for her, but it would be in a reserved, careful way.

He opened the door to his study, went to his sideboard and poured himself a glass of whiskey. The liquid filled his mouth with bursts of smoky flavors and warmed his belly. Satisfied, he strode to his desk, propped his boots on the ledge and turned his chair so he could stare out into the darkening sky. He was going to be married. Sweat dampened his palms. He rubbed them against his trousers and peered out the window at the blooming rosebushes, but he no longer saw the bushes.

He saw Audrey in the pale lilac dress she had been wearing the day he met her. The image was one he'd recalled countless times. Once they were married, he could seduce her all the ways he'd fantasized about since that initial encounter. Most marriages were matches of convenience that benefited two people, and there was no reason he and Audrey couldn't have exactly that sort of marriage. He had made things too complicated. Now they would be simplified.

Feeling lighter than he'd felt in ages, he smiled. Soon he'd ask her to marry him. She'd say yes. She was a sensible, astute woman. Immediately, he recalled her and Whitney's schemes. Perhaps sensible didn't exactly fit her.

He grinned. She was shrewd anyway. He had no doubt she'd see the value of a mutually beneficial marriage. If she didn't, now that he was determined to marry her, he could easily show her the worth of their match one sweet caress at a time. His blood hummed through his veins with the thought.

A hard rap resounded on his door, followed by Pickering calling, "May we enter, my lord?"

"Of course," Trent replied, wincing at the gravelly sound of his voice. He had to quit daydreaming about Audrey.

Pickering entered with Harris, the young footman, directly on his heels. The butler eyed Trent's cluttered desk and his lips pressed together in a thin line. "Did you see the letter that arrived, my lord?"

Trent glanced down absently, prepared to hold it up to satisfy Pickering's need to make sure he had done his duty in delivering it. Absently, he read who it was from and stilled his hand suspended in midair. Dinnisfree never wrote letters, let alone when he was on assignment. Trent turned the heavy cream paper over in his hands, broke the wax seal and opened the correspondence.

This letter will reach you before I do, but I had to tell you right away I believe Gwyneth is alive.

Shock slammed him in the chest and set his blood to rushing in his ears. He blinked and read the line again, yet it remained the same. Bloody, bloody hell. She couldn't be alive. He'd seen her body himself. The image of her form burned beyond recognition became clear in his mind. He squeezed his eyes shut, his held breath filling in his chest until he felt he would explode. His cynical inner voice cut through the roaring noise that was the cacophony of swirling thoughts. *I never saw her face.*

Somewhere in the room, the loud crackling of paper made him cringe. Something hard jabbed his right palm. He dismissed the mild irritation, pushing every distraction away but the night he'd escaped Bagne de Toulon and gone to find her to confront her for what she'd done to him.

Her body lay in her bedroom burned black and reeking of charred flesh. The only way he'd known it was her was his signet ring he'd given her when they'd married. His thumb went automatically to his finger to caress the ring he'd retrieved from whom he'd thought to be Gwyneth. He inhaled sharply and the acrid, sickly sweet smell he would never forget filled his nose. Confusion clouded his thoughts. Instantly, he started to gag as he'd done that night.

"My lord?"

The words were like a shot in his ear, the warm hand on his shoulder intrusive and threatening. Trent jerked up and out of his chair. The years of ingrained combat training resurfaced in a flash. Blindly, he grabbed the unseen hand and twisted. *Strike first for best protection.* A loud yelp filled the room. Behind him, hands grasped and tugged. *I won't go back to prison. Can't.*

"Lord Davenport, you're hurting him!"

The voice was urgent, desperate and *familiar*. Trent blinked and his study came back into view. He stared in horror at Pickering hunched before him, his face twisted in a grimace of pain. Trent released his butler and helped the man to stand. "Jesus, I'm sorry."

Sweat dripped down Pickering's face as he straightened his coat and carefully pushed back the lock of silver hair that had become dislodged from its neat side-swept position. Once he was perfectly presentable again, the butler met Trent's gaze. "Are you quite ready for Harris to run your errand for you?"

Trent looked between his gaping footman and his unflappable butler. *The errand.* His intended letter to Audrey's father to speak with him about courting her. Trent shook his head. "Leave me." He choked out the words.

With a swift nod, Pickering elbowed an unmoving Harris into submission. When the door closed, Trent collapsed into his chair and gripped his head. He stared at the dark wood of his desk. It was so dark it was almost black. Blackness threatened to consume him. Damn Gwyneth. Only she could manage to destroy a man's life twice. Shame swept through him. To wish for his wife to be dead was deplorable and dishonorable. He was both. Had to be, because he did not want her to be alive. Yet she might live.

His gut twisted as hollowness filled his chest. He could not write that letter to Audrey's father now. Hell, he really should not even go near Audrey. He wasn't sure he could control himself around her. He couldn't offer her marriage. He laughed bitterly. The muscles in his neck knotted, the tension moving down his shoulders in spiraling waves to his back. The scar on his right cheek throbbed. Another gift from Gwyneth delivered personally the one night she came to see him in prison.

His chest ached as if something were crushing him. Was that loneliness? He turned the feeling over and stilled. Shock reverberated through him. Not loneliness. Loss. Growing deeper and curling around his heart. Squeezing. Squeezing. He had not allowed himself to truly want a real connection with a woman in so long and now that he had— He roared in anger, picked up the glass on his desk and threw it across the room.

It smacked against the wall, glass shattering everywhere and showering the room with shiny slivers. It wasn't enough. Tension throbbed in his veins. His muscles. His bones. Gwyneth had taken everything from him. His ability to trust. To love. And now she had marched back from her grave and taken Audrey. He shoved back from his chair, hooking his hands under his great wooden desk and heaving it up and over. It crashed against the floor with a thundering boom that reverberated throughout the room. Papers, pens, books and ink spilled across the floor a cream, white and black mess. A disaster. Just like his life.

Kicking out at the still-twirling clock that had been on his desk, he caught his foot on his chair, lost his balance and went down hard on his back. His head smacked the wood floor, making his teeth rattle together in his head. He lay there, staring up at the ceiling, and all the rage and bitterness pent inside flowed out in peals of laughter.

His study door swung open with a bang, but he could not seem to make himself care or move. Footsteps tapped slowly across the floor and Pickering loomed above him, his bushy silver eyebrows raised. "I take it you fell, my lord, and tried to use the desk to catch yourself?"

Pickering's offered theory was utterly implausible, but Trent nodded, knowing they would both cling to the charade to keep a semblance of normalcy.

"Indeed." He pushed to a sitting position, his boots sliding against paper and his palm landing in a wet ink spot. Without a word, Pickering produced a cloth, which Trent gratefully took and wiped the dark ink off his palm as best he could.

The first thing he needed to do was protect Audrey from himself. Stretching to his right he grabbed several sheets of parchment paper scattered on the rug. Before he could search or ask for his quill, Pickering reached behind the overturned desk, and when he stood again, had Trent's quill in his hand and the inkpot. Pickering eyed the pot. "I believe there is enough ink in here to write a few correspondences."

Despite everything, Trent chuckled and took the inkpot and quill Pickering handed him. "Where is the stack of invitations I was going to have Jones respond to?"

Pickering glanced around the floor, his mouth turning down in a frown. Then he moved toward Trent's chair, knelt and reached under it. "Here, my lord. But the steward can do this. Why don't you—"

He waved his hand at Pickering. "I want to do it. Give them to me, please."

Without a word, Pickering handed him the invitations. Trent glanced at them briefly before fanning them against the crimson and green carpet. Dinners. The theater. A trip to the museum. All social events where Audrey would likely be present. He reached beside him, grabbed one of the tomes that had been on his desk and a sheet of foolscap and responded no to the first invitation he had been intending before to respond in the affirmative to.

Once finished, he reached for another invitation when Pickering cleared his throat. Trent glanced up at his butler. "Go to bed, Pickering."

"My lord, I can straighten your study and allow you to answer these correspondence in a dignified manner."

"No," Trent said more sharply than he had intended to. "The business that has brought me low is not dignified. It's messy and occurred because of a single mistake I made." Giving his trust to Gwyneth would never quit costing him.

"As you wish, my lord," Pickering responded with a steady, no-nonsense voice. He bowed out of the room and shut the door. Trent did not move. He stayed on the floor, legs thrown out in front of him, and summarily responded no to each invitation that would put him in contact with Audrey in the next week. He knew he would see her in public eventually, but he needed a bit of time to reestablish his guard.

The thought that she might be betrothed to another man the next time he saw her filled his mouth with a bitter taste, but the knowledge that his abruptly ending their friendship would likely make her despise him twisted his insides into knots. And knowing there was no way to explain his actions made it all the worse.

So Gwyneth might be alive. If he were still a praying man, he would pray it was not so. Looking around him, he spotted Dinnisfree's letter, and leaning on his side, stretched his right arm out and picked the letter up with his fingertips.

Once resettled, he unfolded it and read.

> *I should be home within a week.*
> *Your loyal friend,*
> *Lord Justin Holleman, the Duke of Dinnisfree.*

A wry smile pulled at Trent's lips. *Leave it to Dinnisfree to leave me in the dark. A week?* He glanced to the top of the letter for the date. If this letter had gone out the day Dinnisfree had written it, that meant the duke would be home in roughly seven days, if travel went well.

He set the letter down, stood and picked his way around the mess on his floor toward the bar. Three glasses of whiskey later, the iciness inside his chest hadn't thawed in the least and the same acute sense of loss gnawed at him. Audrey had never been his, and now she never would.

Eight

With a week passing since Audrey had last seen Trent
and the deadline for her accepting Mr. Shelton's proposal
arriving tomorrow night at the Lionhursts' fete, Audrey's
nerves made it fairly impossible to stand still, let alone
think clearly and rationally. Luckily, she, Whitney and
Mr. Sutherland stood close to the balcony, which put
them out of the line of direct sight and most people
mulling around the Marlow's ballroom were either
dancing or trading the latest on dits and paying her no
heed. Gripping Whitney's arm she whispered, "Are you
sure Trent said he was coming here tonight?"

Whitney gave her a sympathetic look and nodded. "He
said he was recovered from whatever ailed him all week
and would be here. I feel certain he will. Aunt Millie
specifically requested he attend, and I've yet to ever see
him deny his mother a thing." Whitney quirked her
mouth. "Except, of course, getting married, but I'm
certain that will change with you!"

Audrey wished she felt as certain, but after a week of
not seeing him, the warm feeling that had infused her at
Whitney's wedding breakfast when she had caught him
gazing at her from across the room had now all but
disappeared.

Once more, she glanced around the ornate ballroom
for him and groaned. Mr. Shelton was striding toward
her. "This night has taken a decided turn for the worse,"

she muttered. For a moment, she contemplated giving Mr. Shelton the cut direct, but there was no reason to start a war with her father before absolutely necessary. She forced a half smile as Mr. Shelton strode up to the little group she was standing in.

He bowed slightly, which made the excess skin under his chin jiggle. Audrey struggled not to wince as she acknowledged him. "Mr. Shelton."

"Lady Audrey," he said in a stiff, formal tone. "I believe this is our dance."

Only because she glanced up and caught sight of her father staring down at her from the overhead balcony did she relent. "Yes, indeed, my lord. I hope you have light feet," she said in way of joking. "I've been known to crush some toes."

Mr. Shelton raised his eyebrows but didn't crack a smile. "I assure you, you'll not step on my feet."

Was that a command or a reference to his superior dancing abilities? She didn't know, but she didn't care for the haughty way he spoke to her. Yet if she could just keep her father happy long enough so that she could see Trent tonight, perhaps he would indicate his feelings and she could offer her father a very real and promising reason not to try to make her marry Mr. Shelton. With an inward sigh, she took his preferred elbow and allowed him to lead her to the dance floor.

Once the dance began, and Mr. Shelton started moving her about with jerky motions. She forced herself to smile, so her father would think they were getting along nicely. "Tell me, Mr. Shelton, what hobbies do you enjoy?"

"Hobbies are frivolous. I'm a busy man."

She nibbled on her lip. She could ignore his superior attitude, if only she were the meek kind of woman. "I suppose I'm rather frivolous," she said gaily. "I love horseback riding, gardening and painting. Oh, and I like to pound away on the pianoforte, though I must confess I'm dreadful."

He regarded her for a long, silent moment with an odd expression before a faint smirk twisted his lips. "Women are frivolous by nature and need a good husband to show them better ways to occupy their time. Speaking of a good husband, has your father talked to you about anything special?"

"No," she immediately lied, feeling no qualms about it. Father had not talked. He had demanded.

Mr. Shelton's eyebrows bunched together. "Hmm. I'm surprised, but I'll say no more."

"That's probably best," she said, struggling against the instinct to clench her hands. "Father really likes to do things on his own terms."

"Understandable," Mr. Shelton agreed. "I like to do things my own way as well."

She did not care for his suggestive tone, but she cared even less for the slow slide of his beefy hands down her back. He came to a stop just above her derriere. Glaring at him, she arched her back away and stepped back a pace. "I believe you have lost control of your hands," she snapped, turning her face purposely away from him. Not even to keep the peace with her father would she allow this man to maul her. She swept her gaze around the outer edge of the ballroom, past the refreshment table, the line of wallflowers, the chairs of six staring matrons and toward a shadowy alcove near the hall that she knew led to the portrait gallery.

Either it was her imagination, the flickering candlelight or something had truly moved. She held her breath, a strange feeling consuming her and her heart beginning to race. The notes of the waltz picked up pace and Mr. Shelton danced them closer to the alcove. She squinted, unsure, and then her breath caught. Her gaze locked with Trent's. He leaned casually against the wall, but his rigid stance and fisted hands at his side bespoke of anything but calmness coursing through him at this moment. A happy thrill shot through her body. She grinned and gripped Mr. Shelton's hand tighter. When he squeezed her hand back, she immediately lessened her hold.

The rest of the dance passed in silence and when the song ended, Mr. Shelton led her back to Whitney, her husband, Sally and the duke. Squeezing her hand with entirely too much familiarity, he said, "I'll see you tomorrow night."

"Perhaps," she said, so as not to seem too unsociable.

Whether things went her way or not, she would never dance with this man again. When he departed she turned to Whitney and Sally. "Trent is here!"

"Where?" Sally demanded, gazing out toward the dance floor.

"Not there." Audrey cocked her head toward the alcove. "Over there, but do not look at—"

Before she could get the rest of her warning out for Whitney and Sally not to look at once so they would not indicate they noticed him, both women had turned to stare at the alcove and then began to wave Trent over.

Audrey huffed out a breath. "I had hoped he would come to me on his own accord."

Sally patted her hand as she exchanged a smile with her husband. "I'm sure he would have, darling, but this way we have just hurried things up a bit. No need to waste perfectly good time waiting for a man to be sensible when they so rarely are."

Sally's and Whitney's husbands both grunted in unison.

He approached slowly. Too slowly, as if reluctant, but aware that to ignore his own cousin would be a terrible faux pas. Something was not right. Audrey's stomach flipped. Perhaps it was her imagination. The closer he came, his facial expression grew clearer. His eyebrows slanted into a frown, but in four more steps he had smoothed them. Audrey clenched at her dress, then forced herself to release it as he came upon them. She tilted her head and forced a trembling smile to her lips. "Lord Davenport, I'm so glad to see you well once again."

"Thank you," he mumbled.

She frowned. Trent didn't mumble. He'd never mumbled once in all the time she'd known him.

"Oh, the quadrille," Whitney exclaimed. "How lovely. Audrey was just saying this is her favorite dance and she luckily still has it free."

Audrey gaped at Whitney, not sure whether to be thankful or angry. If Trent was trying to avoid her, she did not want Whitney forcing his hand, no matter how much she longed for his strong hands to belong to her. Forever.

When Trent scrubbed a hand over his face, Audrey's stomach flipped again. It was not her imagination. He did not want to be with her.

Heat singed her cheeks and she peered down at her slippers for momentary respite. She'd say she needed to freshen up. That was what she would do. Then she would go home and bury herself under her covers. She glanced up to make her excuse, and his gaze was on her.

An uncomfortable silence stretched as he stared and she cursed the burning shame no doubt made evident by her flaming skin.

His expression darkened before softening. "One last dance can hurt no one."

Last dance? Was he upset with her? Was that this sudden change? Had she gone too far in flirting with Lord Thortonberry? As all the couples headed to the dance floor, she determined to ask him. Once they took their places in the dance line, she hurriedly tried to speak with him before the quadrille began. "Trent, are you upset with me?"

"No."

That was it? No. One word, nothing further! The man was infuriating. The tempo of the music started to rise, signaling that soon she'd have to move. "Are you jealous? Is that why you're acting so different than last time I saw you?"

His brittle smile softened slightly. "I'll always be jealous when another man touches you."

Everyone around them started moving. Blast, blast, blast. She went through the motions while counting the seconds she'd be with Trent long enough to continue their conversation. After a few beats they came together and she hissed, "There's no need to be jealous. You must believe me."

The dancers moved again, forcing Trent to step away from her. She watched him for a moment and when he appeared to think she was no longer looking she caught him staring at her with the special look he'd given her before—the one that pierced her to her soul and branded her his. Gooseflesh rose on her arms as her hope was renewed. Absently, she finished the dance and curtsied to him at the end. Now they could talk. "Trent—"

"Lady Audrey," a low voice said behind her. "This next dance is mine."

She sighed and turned to greet Lord Tilly. She would throttle her father if she could for requiring she accept any lord who asked her to dance tonight. "Yes, of course, Lord Tilly. Let me just say goodbye to Lord Davenport."

Lord Tilly smiled kindly at her. "He's left, Lady Audrey."

Denial closed her throat as she swiveled around to empty air. Trent had slipped away without so much as a goodbye. There was no denying something was dreadfully wrong. The teasing, laughing man who had kissed her at the picnic and the one who had stared longingly at her a week ago at Whitney's wedding breakfast was gone. Along with her hope for a marriage filled with love between the two of them. Tomorrow, her time was up with her father and once she disobeyed him she'd be kicked out of his home and become an outcast in Society.

THE POUNDING ON HER BEDCHAMBER door early the next morning did not wake Audrey up, because she had never actually fallen asleep. She had spent the night worrying. "One moment," she called as she dragged herself out of bed, threw on her dressing robe and went to the door. She gasped in surprise to see her Aunt Hillie, her mother's sister, standing there. She threw her arms around her aunt and hugged her. "When did you arrive? I did not know you were coming for a visit."

Her aunt gave her a firm hug back. "I just arrived and I did not know I was coming for a visit either, until my financial circumstances became so dire that they took my home yesterday."

"Oh, Hillie," Audrey murmured, pulling away enough to look at her aunt in the face. "I'm so sorry."

"Don't be, dear," Hillie said with a cheerful note. "I get to visit with you and I'm certain I'll be all right. I somehow always am."

Audrey nodded and took in her aunt's appearance. A bit of dust clung to the outrageous ensemble her aunt wore. Audrey bit her lip. Clearly, her aunt's unusual way of dressing had not changed, even if her financial circumstances had. Seven feathers of various hues of green adorned Hillie's hair, and her gown was two sizes too big, in an altogether outdated fashion and made of Hillie's signature color of carrot—according to her. In truth, the color clashed horribly, as it always had done, with Hillie's red hair, but Audrey happened to know orange had been Uncle Fred's favorite color.

Audrey took her aunt's hand at patted it. "How long have you been here?"

"Not even twenty minutes," Hillie said while reaching up to straighten one of her feathers. "I went straightaway to speak with your father, but after assuring me I could stay, he refused to hear the rest of what I wanted to say. He told me to come fetch you, because he needed to speak with you and then he said he would endure listening to the mess I had made of my life later."

Audrey squeezed her aunt's hand. "I'm sorry, Aunt." Her father had never liked Hillie. He said she was dicked-in-the-nob, but Audrey knew that wasn't true. Hillie was different, with her insistence on every gown she owned being orange, never wearing less than seven feathers in her hair and adding a proverb to almost every conversation she had, but being different didn't bother Audrey. She knew firsthand Father's lack of tolerance for anyone who didn't fit the mold Society expected. Audrey tugged her aunt inside of her room. "I'm glad you have finally come for a visit, despite the circumstances."

"As am I," Hillie said, warmth infusing her tone. "I would love to visit with you now, but your father demanded you come right away and I'm to get my chance to plead my beggarly case afterwards."

Audrey nodded as she plodded over to her wardrobe, chose a gown and went behind her dressing curtain. "You are never a beggar with family," she called from behind the screen.

"Hmph," Hillie replied. "That's not what your father thinks. But enough about me for a moment. Do you know what your father wants to speak with you about?"

Audrey came out from behind the dressing screen and turned her back to Hillie. "Would you fasten me?"

"Of course, dear. Where are the servants?"

"Gone," Audrey replied as Hillie tugged on her gown. "Father has gotten rid of them. I believe we may be on hard times."

"Oh, my," Hillie murmured. "Is that what your father wishes to speak with you about?"

She faced her aunt and shook her head before retrieving her brush and pulling it through her hair. "Heavens, no. He does not deem me sensible enough to discuss such things with. Believe me, I have tried several times to find out what is happening only to be met with derision. No, Father is trying to force me to marry a man I do not love. Actually"—she set the brush down and slipped her feet into her shoes—"I rather detest the man." She quirked her finger at her aunt. "Come, let us walk before my tardiness makes matters worse for me."

Her aunt fell into step beside her. "We can chat as we walk. It is not fit that whilst good luck is knocking at our door, we should shut it."

"Who said that?"

"Thomas Shelton," Hillie answered with a sly smile.

Audrey nodded. No one who was simpleminded could recall proverbs word for word and tell you who said them. "I think you're rather smart, Aunt Hillie."

Her aunt smiled. "I've always thought so too, dear, but it's nice of you to say so."

As they descended the marble stairs and entered the portrait gallery, they paused in unison in front of her mother's portrait. Staring at her mother, she noticed what she always did, that even though there was a well-placed smile on her rosy lips sadness filled her green eyes and made them tilt unnaturally downward. Of course, the painter had not known her mother did not always look that way. Audrey sighed. "It was not well done of Mother to die before she could tell me whatever a lady is to do when her well-thought-out plan goes awry."

Her aunt clicked her tongue. "Taking her life was not well done either, but we cannot complain to her now. Bless her. I hope she's happier now."

Tears stung the backs of Audrey's eyes as she whispered, "I hope so too."

"Dearest." Her aunt turned to her. "What was your plan for your life? Does it involve a gentleman other than the one your father wants you to marry?"

Audrey swallowed the hard lump in her throat. "It did. I wanted to marry for love like you and Uncle Albert did, and not have an arranged marriage of loveless quiet desperation like Mother and Father's." A shudder passed through her at the idea of such a marriage. "I'd rather be dead than stuck in a loveless marriage."

"Tsk. It's a good thing death is not your only option. What happened to your plan and your gentleman who I assume you love?"

"I tried to make him jealous and I think it may have backfired. Aunt, considering the desperate position you now find yourself in, would you change the fact that you went against your parent's wishes and married for love?"

Aunt Hillie shook her head. "Never. From what I've observed of those I know, marriages of convenience hardly ever turn out to be convenient."

"Do you—" Audrey hesitated, thinking of her own predicament. "Do you regret anything about running away from home to marry the man you loved?"

Her aunt cupped Audrey's face much like her mother used to. Audrey gulped back emotion. Aunt Hillie smiled sadly and ran her fingers across Audrey's cheek before letting her hand drop away. "I regret that ten years went by that I did not get to see your mother, because of Father forbidding it. When she grew old enough, married and left Father, I hurried to see her again."

Audrey nodded. "Mother talked several times of how sad those years without you were. She also hated that you did not live nearer to us."

Aunt Hillie dabbed at her moist eyes. "Tell me of this gentleman you tried to make jealous."

"His name is Lord Davenport. He is kind. Smart. Handsome. Mysterious."

"Ah!" Aunt Hillie quirked an eyebrow. "Did your father not approve of him?"

Audrey laughed, despite the tension rolling through her stomach. "Oh, no. Father would wholeheartedly approve of Lord Davenport, *if* Lord Davenport had ever asked to court me. But he hasn't, and that's the problem. Father is not inclined to wait, as I am. Or was. Or rather—" Audrey furrowed her brow. "I would be inclined to wait if I thought Lord Davenport wanted me to. But last night he was rather cold, which makes me think he may not wish to court me at all. And now I'm sure father is calling me to his study to demand I accept Mr. Shelton's proposal tonight. Father wants me to marry immediately. He's quite tired of having me here." Saying the truth out loud hurt more than she thought it would.

"Ah, I see," Aunt Hillie said slowly. "So are you going to submit to your father's wishes?"

"Never."

"Excellent, my dear. I think you must make certain Lord Davenport does not care for you and them we can decide what must be done from there."

Audrey fingered the locket her mother had left her. "Sage advice, but how do I go about finding out how he feels?"

Her aunt smiled. "Why, ask him, of course. Make a time you can speak with him privately, and until then you must pretend you are submitting to your father's wishes. We shall worry about what happens next, when next it happens."

She kissed her Aunt Hillie's cheek. "Do you want to walk the rest of the way with me?"

"No, dear. I think I'll stay here and visit with your mother."

With emotion clogging her throat, Audrey nodded. She squared her shoulders and marched toward her father's study. It wouldn't do to face Father with fear. Once at his door, she rapped on the dark wood. "Father, may I come in?"

"Yes."

She slipped inside and took her usual chair across from him. "You wanted to see me?"

"Tonight is the Lionhursts' ball."

She stared at the top of her father's balding head, since he had not deemed her worthy enough to look up and stop what he was doing. "Yes, I remember." Her steady voice pleased her."

"You will accept Mr. Shelton tonight."

She sent a silent thanks above. Father had not stated exactly what she was to accept, so she was not exactly lying by agreeing. He could mean she would accept a dance. Her conscience niggled, but she ignored it. "Certainly, Father."

Finally he looked up, his eyes cold as ever. "It's good to see you've come to your senses." He waved at the door. "You may go. I've work to do."

For once, his utter lack of real interest in her was a blessing. Not bothering with a goodbye, she dashed out of the door and almost crashed into her brother, Richard.

Audrey eyed him with a frown. He appeared to have the same clothes on he'd worn last night, yet his gray eyes looked blurry, as if he'd just awoken or perhaps never slept. His brown hair was a tousled mess. She'd give him the benefit of the doubt, though he did smell like a bottle of Father's whiskey he was so fond of partaking in nightly. And overly much. "Richard, whatever are you doing up so early and why are you lurking in the hallway?"

He leaned close to her and her nose wrinkled involuntarily. The acrid smell of smoke joined the lingering scent of liquor. "Have you been smoking and drinking?"

He gave her a lopsided grin that tugged her heart with the memory of how sweet Richard had been before Mother died. Mother seemed to have taken the best of Richard with her to the afterlife. Richard tousled her hair. "I just got in." He pressed a finger to his lips, then removed it and pressed it to hers. "Don't tell Father."

Swatting his hand away, she started to nod and then stopped, narrowing her eyes. "What have you been doing out all night?"

He winked. "This and that." A sudden frown puckered his brow. "I only wish I had done it better."

"You are making no sense, Richard."

He reached up and pulled a lock of her hair, as he used to do when they were children. "I know. Say, did Father tell you the plan?"

She felt her brows come together. "No." Unless of

course Richard meant Father's plan to force her to marry Mr. Shelton. Surely, Richard was not supporting Father's idea. Her stomach dropped. That would be the ultimate betrayal. "Richard—"

"Richard!" her father roared from within his study, cutting off Audrey's question to her brother. "Get in here now."

Richard patted her on the arm. "Go draw or some such ladylike thing," he said with a wink. "It's my turn to be lectured."

Richard disappeared into the study, leaving her staring at the now closed door for a moment. Had Richard been talking about Mr. Shelton when he referred to a plan? She toyed with the idea of eavesdropping, but she didn't want to chance being caught. As she walked toward the portrait gallery she thought about what her aunt had said and made a decision. If she was going to ask Trent how he felt about her it would have to be tonight and it would have to be at the ball.

To ensure he would come and meet her somewhere they could talk privately, she had to act quickly to get a note to him. Once at the portrait gallery she did not see her aunt. Pressed for time, Audrey made her way to her room instead of searching out her aunt. She hurried to her escritoire, sat and retrieved a sheet of foolscap. She toyed with her quill pen for a moment before writing,

> *Dear Trent, will you please meet me at seven sharp at your sister's party tonight? Meet me in the terrace on the far side near the garden path. I need your help with an urgent problem.*

That should do the trick. Trent was a man of honor. He would not fail to show if he thought she needed his help. She sealed the note and rushed downstairs to have the coachman take it for her. With any luck when she asked Trent how he felt about her tonight he would profess his devotion. If not, her life would be changing dramatically, but she would endure somehow.

Nine

When Trent wanted to avoid thinking about his past, or his future, he came to Gritton's Boxing Arena on Drury Lane. At Gritton's, a man didn't don the gloves one wore at Gentleman Jackson's to protect oneself from being pummeled to a bloody mess. If a man stepped foot into Gritton's ring it was bare-knuckled and he better concentrate on nothing but the fight at hand, move fast and strike first.

The strain of being with Audrey last night and treating her as a mere acquaintance had left him feeling as if a lead ball sat in the pit of his stomach. All he wanted to do at this moment was forget himself. He stepped into the arena to warm up for his match and wait for his partner, whoever Gritton might have paired him with. It did not really matter, as long as the man hit hard. He started dancing around the ring and jabbing his fist in the air. Within minutes, blood surged through his veins and left a dull roar in his ears. Perfect.

"Davenport!"

Dinnisfree's familiar voice cut through the daze Trent was attempting to reach. He whipped around and stopped jabbing. A smile, though his friend could very well be bringing the worst news of Trent's life, tugged at his face. It was not Dinnisfree's fault Gwyneth might be alive, and he was glad to see Dinnisfree, no matter the circumstances. "Home exactly when I suspected you would be," he said, eyeing the duke's morning suit. Unusual for him, he looked every inch a gentleman of the *ton* with his face freshly shaven and his red hair neatly combed. Curiosity struck him to know what Dinnisfree's latest mission had been.

The duke strode up to the ring favoring his right side and stuck his hand through the ropes to grasp Trent's extended hand. "I can tell by that fierce scowl on your face that you are trying to forget something. It would not be Lady Audrey, would it?"

Trent shot Dinnisfree a warning look, and ignoring the duke's question, asked his own. "How did you hurt your leg?"

Dinnisfree shot a wary glance around the ring. "Dodging."

Trent nodded, knowing his friend had left the bullet part unsaid.

"I assume my message sent you into a tailspin, judging by your pleasant nature this morning."

Trent gritted his teeth. "Your message changed some plans I'd made, but it's nothing I cannot live with." Because he would have to.

Dinnisfree shrugged. "If you say so. I'm not one to question what another man can live with."

Trent leaned over the ropes closer to the duke to ensure privacy, though realistically no one was near enough to hear them. Old habits died hard.

"I gather you were on business in France." They both knew business was code word for a mission for Prinny.

"Not the sort of business you would think. This was more of a personal trip for Hawkins."

Trent mulled over what sort of personal situation Prinny, known as Hawkins in code, would have that would require Dinnisfree to go to France. "A woman?"

Dinnisfree nodded, his face blank.

Trent grunted. "Care to explain how your personal business for Hawkins led you to an area where you thought you might have seen Gwyneth?"

"Hawkins was inquiring after an interest whom he believed now resides in Paris."

Trent raised an eyebrow. "And does she?"

"She does, but she wishes to have nothing more to do with Hawkins. Anyway, whilst I was there, I found myself in a theater near where Gwyneth once lived. Imagine my shock when I thought I saw her at the theater. The woman had her height, build, coloring and by God, she had her face. I could not simply ignore it. I thought you would want to know."

Trent swallowed, feeling like he'd been handed a death sentence, and associating the possibility of his wife's possibly being alive to a death sentence for himself made his gut twist with shame.

Dinnisfree cleared his throat. "I can see by the vein pulsing at your temple and the way you are twisting your mouth that you are mentally damning yourself for wishing she were still dead. Or maybe you were hoping I'm possibly wrong and it's not her because you have developed an attachment to Lady Audrey."

Trent tensed.

"Listen, man, if you have developed a tender for Lady Audrey—"

"Are you ready to box?" Trent interrupted. He didn't want to talk about Audrey or Gwyneth or anything at the moment. He wanted to hit and be hit. Forget himself and his life.

Dinnisfree pressed his lips together and nodded. "Give me a minute to change."

Trent occupied himself with warming up until his friend returned and they commenced sparring. At first, the fight was exactly what he needed, and he was able to narrow his thoughts to nothing but the task before him. It was such a relief that he managed to let his guard down. He must have, because one minute he was considering his following move and the next he was remembering Audrey in her blue gown. He blinked and a fist was flying at him. Trent dodged the punch coming toward his face a second too slow.

Dinnisfree flashed a triumphant smile as his fist connected with Trent's jaw. The blow sent him flying onto his back with a thud that made his teeth rattle. His head hit the hard floor, and for a moment, his ears rang in time with the flashing specks of silvery light dancing across his vision. He blinked several times and then lay there panting with his eyes closed.

After one solid hour of boxing and being knocked down four times in a row, his jaw bloody well ached and his lower lip pulsed with every crimson drop that dripped from the previously received cut. Trent rolled onto his side, spit out a mouthful of blood and slowly opened his eyes. How had things grown tangled so fast? A shadow loomed beside him. He didn't move. He knew well enough his friend stood above him, likely smirking. Trent had spent enough days and nights in France holed up on assignment for Prinny with Dinnisfree that not even blindness would stop him from recognizing his friend's rattling inhalation of breath. It had a certain short, short, long pattern and occurred whenever his friend was bone weary.

With a grunt, Trent pushed himself to an upright position and grasped the outstretched hand in his face. "Come on." Amusement laced Dinnisfree's tone before his face pinched up to display his discomfort. "If you care to talk now, I'll endeavor to listen." The duke's voice sounded strained, like the mere act of what he'd just offered made him ill.

Trent staggered to his feet, and without saying a word he brushed past his friend and lumbered under the rope of the ring. As he was passing the entrance into Gritton's, the door opened and his footman strode inside.

Trent came to halt in front of Harris. "What the devil are you doing here? Is something amiss?"

Harris held out a cream missive. "I'm not sure, my lord. Mr. Pickering ordered me to bring this here to you at once. He said to tell you specifically the lady's coachman told Mr. Pickering the matter was urgent and you needed to get this right away."

Frowning, Trent took the letter. Dinnisfree drew near and peered over his shoulder. "Is it from your mother or cousins?"

Trent turned the letter over to rip it open and froze. At the top in perfect curvy writing was Audrey's name. *Jesus.* Something had to be wrong. He ripped it open and gaped. Flicking his glance to Harris, he said, "You may leave."

His footman nodded and went out the way he had come in. Dinnisfree raised a questioning eyebrow at Trent. "Who is it from?"

Trent motioned to the wooden bench in the far corner of the room. The two of them walked silently over and sat down, well away from the other men at Gritton's. "It's from Lady Audrey. She says there is an urgent matter and she must see me tonight at my cousin's ball."

Dinnisfree cocked his head. "And will you?"

Will I? He gripped the paper in his hand and thought. The smack of fist against flesh rang out like a drum accompanied by a rough underlying tune of butchered English and interesting curse words. He should not meet her, but he would. The compulsion to ride directly to her house, learn what urgent matter her note referred to, and fix everything for her was almost irresistible. Except he couldn't ride there and he knew it. Bitterness filled his mouth with a sour taste.

"I should not meet her in light of the new turn of events in my life, but I will. This one last time to ensure she is okay and to explain to her somehow that our relationship must be more distant."

"What words will you use to explain that?" Light humor laced Dinnisfree's tone.

Trent shook his head and glanced down at his battered red hands. "I don't know. But I will have to find the right words. I cannot pursue her when my wife may very well still be alive."

Dinnisfree grunted. "If you want her so badly, have her. From what I observed the lady seemed to want you as much as you desire her."

Trent's fingers automatically curled into fists. "She is not the type of woman to simply be taken."

"Do not get your hackles up. All I'm saying is that if I were in your shoes, I'd just seduce her and be done with it. What matter is it that your duplicitous wife may or may not be still alive? It is not as if you intended to marry Lady Audrey anyway, so I do not see the difference."

Trent's whole body tensed. "I do not want to talk about it anymore."

"My God." Dinnisfree's eyes narrowed. "You were planning on marrying her. Do you love her?"

"No," Trent snapped. "I am incredibly fond of her, think she is brilliant, actually, and since I desire her I thought a marriage between us could actually be quite convenient."

"Yes, I see. Marriages of convenience are excellent ideas. She gets a protector, and you get a serviceable, delectable woman who would never have expected any sort of soft emotions from you."

Trent glared in his friend's direction. "I don't like your sarcastic tone."

"Sorry. In my defense, a mocking tone is better than actually telling your friend they are a bloody fool, is it not?"

"Yes, I suppose it is," Trent said, filling his own response with a sharp edge. "I knew what I was doing."

"So you say. Do you know what you're going to do now?"

Trent hadn't allowed himself to really consider his future, because he knew what honor bound him to do and there was no part of him that wanted to find Gwyneth alive. Reluctantly, he met Dinnisfree's gaze. "I'll go to France and see if I can locate Gwyneth."

"And if you do?"

The question reverberated in his head. "I'll ensure she's safe, give her enough money to live her miserable life out on and then come back here and live out the rest of my miserable life." Trent jerked the towel off his lap and swiped at the sweat trickling down his forehead as Dinnisfree stared at him with that annoying assessing gaze he liked to use when he was trying to make a point.

"Sounds rather cheery and promising."

"Do you have a better suggestion?" Trent snapped.

"You could tell Lady Audrey the truth."

"You know I can't," he growled. "It's not as if I can explain how it is I married a woman who turned out to be a double-crossing spy whose real name I did not even know when I married her. She'd want to know how I know such things."

"Good point," Dinnisfree said. "Tell her a version of the truth."

Trent shook his head. "No. No matter how much I want her, I would not make myself an adulterer nor would I put her in such a tenuous situation as not to actually be my legal wife. What if we had children? They could be bastards."

"I'm sorry. I did not think it all the way through. I tend to do as I wish and damned the consequences or moral implications."

Trent clasped Dinnisfree's arm. "You do not give yourself enough credit."

"What if I'm wrong and just saw a woman who looked almost exactly like Gwyneth? Would you marry Lady Audrey then? Do you want me to scare away any possible suitors while you're gone?"

A strangled laugh escaped Trent. "I'd like to say yes, but God only knows how long it might take me to be certain whether Gwyneth is dead or alive. I'd be a selfish cad to prevent Lady Audrey a happy marriage if the right gentleman comes along, knowing I may very well still be married. No. I have to let her go. Do me two favors, though."

"Name it."

"Her father is going to try and force her to marry a man she does not want, according to Sutherland."

A wicked smile pulled at the corners of Dinnisfree's mouth. "You want me to persuade the man not to ask her."

Trent nodded. "I do, indeed. I'll get the man's name to you before I leave."

"Consider it done."

"Nothing nefarious," Trent amended, seeing the gleam in Dinnisfree's eyes.

"I'm offended," Dinnisfree said cheekily. "I can be persuasive without being nefarious.

Satisfied, Trent nodded. "Favor number two has to do with Thortonberry."

Dinnisfree smirked. "I thought it might."

"Keep him away from her."

"Have you considered you might particularly dislike Thortonberry and not been giving him a chance to prove himself worthy of her, because it is her he is after?"

"No." Trent left no room for argument with his hard tone. "I have not. I overheard the man say he would never be loyal to a wife. She does not deserve that."

"There are worse things, my friend. She could end up married to a man who beats her or verbally abuses her or treats her as if she is less than nothing. I frankly do not see Thortonberry as that sort of man."

Trent jerked to his feet and glared down at his friend. "I don't care what sort of man you see him as. Just do as I have asked."

Before Dinnisfree could reply, Trent stormed to the locker room. He could not explain to his friend that the thought of Audrey being in a marriage that made her unhappy twisted his insides. Then again, the thought of her happy in another man's arms twisted his insides as well. "Hell and damnation," he muttered.

LATER THAT NIGHT AFTER MAKING the necessary polite greetings at his cousin Gillian's fete, Trent made his way to the terrace to meet Audrey. Tension vibrated through him with every step he took. He needed the exact right words to say to her, so she would not walk away from here tonight doubting herself. Damned if he had any idea what he was going to say. If only he could simply tell her the truth, but the truth was something he couldn't give her. Tonight would have been so different if Dinnisfree hadn't gone to France and seen the woman he thought might be Gwyneth. Trent pushed the useless thought away. If Gwyneth was alive, he couldn't offer Audrey marriage, so there was no point in lingering on what might have been.

He would never hold Audrey in his arms and caress her bare silken skin. Nor would he ever plunge himself inside her or feel her laughter tickling his neck or listen to her witty rejoinders that always made him laugh. He would never fill her belly with his child.

He tensed. Where the hell had that thought come from? Not once after he had concocted his plan to marry her had he considered the children they might have, so why now? Angry with himself, he focused outward as he stood near the terrace door for a moment and studied the chattering, milling crowd. Somewhere in this room was a decent man who had the ability and desire to marry and offer Audrey the world and maybe even his trust. He was not that man. Had never been that man. Perhaps things had turned out for the best, yet still, the idea of her marrying another man, even a good one, made Trent's heart constrict oddly.

Opening the door, he stepped into the cool moonlit night then took a deep breath, filling his lungs until they ached. Something felt wrong. He paced the silent terrace, examining his thoughts and releasing his breath bit by bit. It was the same deep breathing ritual he'd come to rely on in the past when he was on assignment in France.

As the last bit of air expelled from his lungs, he frowned. The problem was he was bloody selfish. He longed to feel Audrey's soft body underneath his and he knew he never could. The sooner tonight was over, the better.

He moved to the outer edge of the terrace near the garden and away from the windows or door. No one could see them in this alcove and if anyone chanced onto the terrace he would hear the door open and move them farther into cover onto the garden path. The terrace door creaked open as if connected with his thoughts, and Audrey emerged into the moonlight and blazing torches, a tormenting vision of beauty in green velvet that contrasted alluringly with her creamy skin. As she neared him, the heart-stopping picture she presented made a physical ache burn within him. He took a ragged breath and tried not to stare, but it was hard. Her emerald eyes sparkled and her low-cut gown displayed her ample, creamy breasts to perfection. A bolt of lust shot through him as it always did when he was near her, but this time the strangest sense of pride accompanied the lust. Ridiculous. She was not his.

If he were smart, he would keep distance between them, hear what her problem was, tell her they could no longer carry on as they had and depart the terrace before the dance that had just begun in the ballroom came to completion. Dread cut him to the bone, but was also the thing that made him open his mouth to be done with it. "Audrey—"

She stepped close to him and into the shadows. "You have no idea how glad I am to see you."

He scrambled to find some kind words to say to put the needed distance between them, but her flowery perfume filled his nose and made it difficult to remember to control himself, let alone think how to terminate their relationship. All he wanted to do was circle his arms protectively around her; instead, he forced himself to step back. There was just enough moonlight that he could see the hurt expression that crossed her face and it felt as if a knife had been driven into his heart.

"Are you not glad to see me?" she asked.

The uncertainty in her voice tightened his chest further. He had never been afraid to do something difficult in his life, but he couldn't seem to make himself say what needed to be said.

"Trent, whatever is the matter? Is it the same thing that was wrong at the Marlows' ball?"

Frustrated, he tugged a hand through his hair. When the devil had he become a coward? He needed a few more minutes with her. Stolen moments. "Nothing's the matter. Your beauty astonishes me, as always, that's all." Her eyes widened, and he couldn't resist moving close enough to touch a dangling curl of her silky hair. "I've never seen hair with glistening waves like yours. My fingers twitch to plunge my hands into your hair." This was foolish. He had to stop. In one moment.

"I always thought I looked rather like a witch." She spoke in a breathless whisper.

He felt winded himself but from the need pounding through him. The desire between them swirled in the air with the breeze. "Not a witch." He brushed his fingers against a particularly enticing curl that lay against her bare skin. "The word conjures the wrong image."

Her lashes swept down, veiling her eyes. "What word would you use to describe me?" The tremble in her voice betrayed her anxiety and made him want to soothe her.

No matter what, he never wanted her to be uncertain of her worth. He cupped her chin and raised her face until her shining green gaze met his. "I'd label you an enchantress. The word brings to mind a woman who is irresistibly charming, fascinating and beautiful."

Her perfectly kissable mouth parted slightly. He had to have one last kiss and then he would tell her. His hand moved up her arm of its own volition. Underneath his touch, she trembled and gooseflesh covered where his fingers trailed. Her response caused a rush of possessiveness to grip him and he curled his hand around her shoulder and squeezed gently before moving to trace the long slope of her neck while his blood roared in his ears. "Of all the women I've known and encountered not one has had a complexion to match yours. I've never seen skin so smooth in my life."

"Never?" Amusement vibrated her tone. She darted out her pink tongue and licked her lips.

He groaned. Jesus, this was too hard. "One kiss," he mumbled more for his benefit than hers. She nodded.

Walk away after this, bloody fool. It was hard to concentrate on anything other than the fact that the soft shadows he wanted to explore filled the hollow of her neck.

Attraction was a fiendish thing. Why did he have to want her so much? Why couldn't he have desired a courtesan, or a widow, or any other woman who he could have simply bedded? Audrey's tongue darted out to lick her lips, and his pulse took off in a race against his good senses as he fisted his hands into her hair and tilted her head back. "I've something I must tell you."

She took his hand and pressed it against her chest. Underneath his fingers, her heart pounded wildly. "And I've something I must ask you. But not yet. *After our kiss.*"

When he groaned, a knowing smile came to her lips.

"Enchantress," he taunted as he ran a thumb across her lips. She was so soft, so very kissable and so very likely to make him forget himself.

"Sorcerer," she whispered back as his lips descended over hers.

Ten

Now, this was a kiss a lady could rationally think meant the man loved her, or desired her in the very least. Trent's lips were heaven on hers. She couldn't fathom why he'd only kissed her twice. Blast the man. He needed to unleash the passion he kept under such tight control more often. Heavens, she was glad he was finally letting loose. His warm, sweet lips tantalized her, even as her brain registered surprise when he pulled away.

Please, God, don't let the kiss be over. A wicked grin tugged at his lips as he tilted her head back and kissed her forehead, the tip of her nose and then her eyelids. "Every time I see you, when I lie down to sleep at night I dream of kissing you." His voice was a strained growl.

She delved her hands into his hair and pulled his lips close to hers so with each breath he exhaled the fire within him washed over her. An uncontrollable shiver took hold. "I hope that is not all you dream of."

The hunger and tenderness in his eyes made her knees weak. A softer smile graced his lips. "No."

The admission sent a jolt of satisfaction through her and took all her inhibitions away. Standing on tiptoes, she twined her arms around his neck and kissed him with all the longing, love and need in her heart. Her mouth burned with each stroke of his tongue against hers. She could not stop the moan that escaped her, nor could she prevent her smile when he tugged her closer.

He stroked his fingers down her neck and followed the path he created with feather-light kisses that made her dizzy.

When he flicked his tongue across the hollow of her neck, an ache blossomed in the pit of her stomach and nearly stole her breath away. He circled his hands around her back, kneading her burning flesh as he went. She clung to him, digging her fingers into his arms while savoring the waves of pleasure his kisses sent through her body.

Her father was wrong about Trent. Satisfaction filled her chest. He wanted her just as much as she wanted him, and he'd never kiss her like this if he didn't intend to marry her. Her future would not be miserable but filled with love. With her pulse leaping, she reached back and grasped Trent's hand to place it over her thundering heart. She wanted him to understand exactly how he made her feel before she asked him how he felt about her.

At first, his hand stiffened and then he growled before curling his fingers around her breast. Blinding need pounded her and she arched farther toward him. When he traced his finger back and forth over the material covering her nipple, her body responded instantly. Her nipples grew taut beneath the fabric of her dress as his mouth became more demanding and his fingers rubbed harder and with frenzied urgency.

In her haze of pleasure, a melody filled her head followed by a strange sound. Almost like boots against the cobblestone of the terrace. The thought froze her for a second before her mind screamed a warning.

"Good God." Her father's harsh voice echoed around her. Before she could react, Trent released her and swept her behind him with a firm hand. He stood erect before he spoke.

"Lord Bridgeport, let me explain."

Notes of music and the chatter of the crowd gushed in from the now open terrace door. Audrey trembled uncontrollably where she stood. What had she done? Staring at the broad expanse of Trent's muscular back, she shook as she hurriedly tugged her dress to try to make herself presentable to her father. Things would be fine once Trent asked for her hand.

"Explain?" a harsh voice she didn't recognize demanded. "I hardly think Lord Bridgeport or myself are in need of an explanation. It's plain enough by what we just happened upon what is going on," the man snarled.

Audrey's belly cramped so fierce she had to dig her fingers into her sides and breathe deeply. A sickening suspicion increased the pains coursing through her. She could not see around Trent, but she didn't need to. Mr. Shelton was the only man other than her father who would be angered, rather than scandalized, by finding her on the balcony in Trent's arms.

"Look, Shelton, I don't know what has your bristles up, or frankly why you're even out here, but I'd suggest you take your leave. This is a private matter between Bridgeport and myself," Trent snapped.

Shame swept over Audrey as she cowered, hidden from her father and Mr. Shelton, behind Trent's back.

"No, you look, Davenport." Her father's violent tone made her jerk. "Shelton has every right to be out here. It's you who has no right. Shelton is going to marry Audrey."

"What?" Disbelief filled Trent's voice.

"Not anymore," Mr. Shelton shouted. "I'll not have a wife that has been soiled by another man."

"Wait a bloody minute, Shelton," Audrey's father said. "I'm sure we can work this out."

Hurt flooded her at her father's pleading words. He cared nothing about her or her feelings. It was the match that was important to him. He'd not stood up for her or her reputation. If he had any love for her, he would have. Tears burned the back of her throat.

In front of her, Trent shifted his stance, widening his legs and rounding his shoulders. He looked very much as if he was preparing to fight. Was he? Heavens, this was going too far. She had to do something. She opened her mouth to speak but Trent's deep voice drowned her out. "I demand you take back your insult against Lady Audrey. No one has been defiled, as you so nastily suggested."

Audrey pressed a shaking hand to her forehead. She most definitely had wanted to escape marrying Mr.

Shelton, but not this way. She'd never intended to shame or anger the man. And Trent—*heavens*. She squeezed her eyes shut for a second. She prayed he wouldn't think she had intended to trap him into marriage. She was going to be sick. No. She refused to allow herself to be ill. Swallowing hard, she squared her shoulders and stepped to Trent's side.

She met her father's contemptuous gaze first and instantly wished she hadn't. Her mouth watered as her nerves jumbled into tighter knots inside her belly. Pressing her nails into the soft flesh of her palms, she forced herself to look at Mr. Shelton and speak. "I'm terribly sorry, Mr. Shelton. I—"

"You should be," he spat. "I would have given you wealth beyond anything you've ever known, you silly fool. I'll not have you now."

She struggled not to breathe a sigh of relief. "I understand. And since I never formally accepted your marriage proposal"—she added that for Trent's benefit—"there are, of course, no ill feelings. Despite what you saw, I vow to be guilty of a kiss but innocent of anything else."

Mr. Shelton glared. "You'll understand, I'm sure, that I'm disinclined to believe you. But, ever the gentleman, I won't repeat what I saw."

Now, Audrey did breathe out a sigh of relief while thanking God for small reprieves. At least Father couldn't hold a ruined reputation over her head. "You're too kind for being so discreet."

"It's not for you." Mr. Shelton laughed, but the sound was abrasive and cutting. "I don't give a fig about your reputation. I don't want people knowing I was almost made a fool of by marrying a woman like you."

Trent stiffened beside her. Discreetly, she shifted toward him to try to calm him. Mr. Shelton gave her one last contemptuous look before stomping off the terrace and back into the ballroom. She stood for a moment, caught between an overwhelming sense of relief and a foreboding of what was to come. Intent on heading off her father's oncoming tirade, she spun toward him and stilled. His face was an unnatural shade of purple. "Father, I—"

"Shut your mouth, you disgraceful, ungrateful lightskirt."

Sadness squeezed her chest like an unrelenting fist. "Father, let me explain."

His face twisted with rage as he advanced on them. Trent pushed Audrey back behind him and stood between her and her father. "It's not what it seems."

"Were you or were you not taking liberties only a married man should take?" her father bellowed and shoved Trent in the chest. Trent's body swayed, brushing against hers, but he did not lose his footing nor, thank God, did he try to retaliate. Audrey tried to move out from behind him, but he raised his arm and blocked her.

"Stay put," he commanded in such a lethal tone, she was afraid to move. She'd never heard Trent's voice raised in anger in all the time she'd known him.

"You've not answered my question," her father roared while shoving Trent yet again. His body remained unmoving as stone. Good thing. Her father sounded mad enough to charge through the thickest of walls.

"I did take liberties I should not have and for that I'm ashamed, regretful and incredibly sorry." Trent spoke in a stiff, apologetic tone.

His words, though perfectly proper and likely exactly what her father wanted to hear, made her shudder with humiliation. Confusion swiftly followed and left her feeling as if she was drowning under the thoughts and doubts bombarding her mind. Did Trent regret kissing her or just regret they'd been caught? Did he love her or not? Would he marry her or was she the biggest fool to ever live? *Please, God, not the last.*

"I'm glad you're gentleman enough to agree you crossed a line." Her father's voice was cool and impersonal, all traces of anger seemingly gone. The foreboding she'd felt moments before raced across her skin, leaving gooseflesh in its wake.

"For what has just occurred, I'm sure you'll agree the only recourse is to marry," her father said. "You may call on me tomorrow morning and we will work out the terms of the betrothal contract."

Audrey darted out from behind Trent. He stared at her

father with a hard cold-eyed smile. As if he sensed her looking he turned and met her gaze. Bitterness—or was it remorse?—swept over his face, making him appear less a man chiseled of stone and more one molded of regrets. Her heart gave a tremendous jerk.

Slowly, he turned fully toward her. His eyebrows were drawn together in a deep frown. Her breath caught and a lump formed in her chest. *No. no. no.* She wanted to run and hide. Or cover her ears. He'd said nothing, yet she knew what was about to come. Her heart cracked within her chest.

"Audrey, I'm sorry, but I cannot marry you. I started to tell you. Or, that is, I meant to tell you." There was a bitter, strange edge to his voice, yet the despair roaring in her ears like a funeral bell made it hard to care what could have made him so rancorous, unless he truly believed she'd tried to trap him.

She grasped the notion in desperation. If only she could make him see. Clasping his arm she said, "I vow I did not plan this."

He carefully withdrew his arm from her hold. "I don't think that." His voice was low and shaking.

Behind Trent, her father sneered at her. The idea that her father was correct, and she was no more than a diversion Trent never intended to marry made her stomach turn. She inhaled a shaky breath.

Trent's face twisted, as if he was in pain. "Your fear is groundless and not the reason I can't marry you."

His voice chilled her like a cold wind. Tears blurred her vision. Gathering her frayed pride, she blinked the tears away and forced a laugh, albeit a bitter one. "Well, it was amusing while it lasted."

"Amusing," her father growled. He swung toward her. "You may accept that, but I'll not." Before she realized what was happening he barreled into Trent with a roar. Both men flew back into the balustrade. Trent jumped sideways, sending her father crashing alone into the railing, his weight and height working against him to fling him almost sideways in the air. For a horrified moment, she held her breath. He was going to topple over the barrier to his death three stories below.

"Father!" she screamed, hoping Trent could save him. She blinked at the blur before her. Trent grasped her father by the arm and jerked him backward toward the terrace floor.

With her heart pounding in her ears, she rushed to her father and grasped his other arm to help steady him. "Let me help you."

"You've helped enough." He snatched his arm out of her hold and shoved her away with his free hand.

Her slipper caught on the edge of a chair and caused her to stumble backward toward the ground while reaching out blindly for something to grasp. Air rushed from her lungs with a harrumph as Trent gripped her under the arms and hauled her to her feet. For a moment he held her pressed against his chest. "I've got you." His warm breath whispered across the back of her neck before he gently pushed her down. She landed with a thud in a chair. Her gaze locked behind Trent on her father advancing like a madman, his face twisted and his fists raised to fight. Anther scream ripped from her throat, but this one was to warn Trent. He jerked around in time to duck the punch her father threw.

Audrey jumped up, caught the hem of her dress under her slipper and careened forward to land on her hands and knees with a jarring impact that cracked her teeth together and caused an instant headache. Pain shot through her knees and hands, but she scrambled to her feet, determined to stop her father. As she stood straight, he swung at Trent again, then his face screwed into an expression of pain. Groaning, he grabbed his chest and collapsed to the ground.

For a moment, she froze as wave after wave of shock slapped at her. When Trent dropped to his knees by her father, it was as if whatever invisible string had held her still was cut. She raced to his writhing form and knelt down. He tugged frantically at his evening coat as he struggled to breathe. "My chest," he wheezed as drool ran down the side of his cheek and his eyes rolled back in his head.

"Dear God, what is happening?" she cried.

"I think it's his heart," Trent snapped.

Trent grasped her father's hands and pulled them out of the way. She tugged at his shirt as he mumbled a jumble of words she couldn't understand. "Father, what is it?" Trent shoved her hands away and with a violent yank, ripped her father's shirt in half. His face turned a deep shade of red as his hands fluttered to his chest, then fell away. "Father, Father!"

"Audrey," Richard's sharp voice called behind her. She did not bother to turn. She scooted closer to her father, her heart thudding so loudly in her ears they rang in time with each beat. The silence seemed too long. "Why is he not talking?" Desperation made her shake. "Why are his eyes not opening?" She spoke to Trent's back as he huddled over her father. Why wasn't he answering her? Grasping Trent's arm, she tugged on him. "Move over. Let me see him."

Trent gazed back at her, his eyes glazed with the same emotion she'd recognized earlier—regret. "No, no, no." She moaned and tried to shove him out of the way to get at her father.

Trent sat up and crushed her to him. "He is gone, Audrey, I'm sorry. I'm so very sorry."

Before she could make sense of what Trent was trying to tell her Richard knelt beside her on his knees. Audrey flung herself at her brother and buried her head against his silky coat.

"He's dead. I've killed him. I've killed him with my disobedience. He came upon me kissing Trent on the terrace and it killed him." Tears slid unchecked down her face. Her father hadn't loved her, but that didn't mean she hadn't spent night after night wishing he had and years trying to make him see her and not through her.

Richard's brow crinkled with obvious confusion. God, she was tired. So very tired. With a sigh, she pushed a lock of fallen hair out of her eyes. "Richard, do you understand me?"

He shook his head. How could she find the strength to explain? She swallowed and suddenly Trent was there, his hand firm and reassuring on her shoulder, his voice explaining in low tones what had happened. Then his hand was gone and Richard stood. Their voices seemed louder, but hardly compared to the noise in her ears that made it hard to think. Audrey was aware that something did not seem right with them. *Concentrate.* She had to focus. It was so hard. Her thoughts fluttered around her like rings of white smoke rising from a fire. They disappeared before she could grasp what she thought they might be saying.

Their deep voices grew louder. Angry. Snarling.

She opened her eyes and gasped. Her brother and Trent stood toe to toe, her brother's face mottled and red, Trent's mouth pressed tight and grim. She pressed her hands to her ears, desperate to stop the deafening ringing so she could hear what they were saying. All fell quiet then noise erupted through the silence like a blast from a pistol.

"You leave me no choice but to challenge you to a duel if you refuse to marry my sister."

Mortification weighed upon her almost heavier at this moment than her grief. How utterly selfish of her. Appalled with herself, she struggled to her feet and squared her shoulders while staring at Trent. She wanted to sound as if she were perfectly fine, so he would never know how he had hurt her. "You're free to go. I don't expect you to marry me."

"By God he will," Richard roared. "He told me what Mr. Shelton said. He has ruined your chance for marriage."

She winced as Trent blanched, which made her feel a thousand times worse, smaller than the smallest, most insignificant bug she'd ever quashed under her slippers. She was the bug. Insignificant to Trent. He'd stomped on her heart and crushed her hopes. "Please, Richard, let him leave before someone comes out here and then gossip starts. As it is we can say Father simply had a heart problem."

"I'll stay and help you see to your father," Trent said to her.

"That will not be necessary." It was so hard to keep the bitterness out of her voice, but she had managed, she believed. Now to deal with Richard. "Richard, please."

"Cease talking," he snapped.

She bit her lip, unsure how to proceed. From where

she stood, she could see a couple strolling toward the terrace. Any minute they would come out here and hear the ugly truth. But if she pressed Richard he'd likely grow angrier. Whatever transpired, she would fix it tomorrow.

He rose to his full height. "I demand satisfaction."

Trent nodded. "You deserve it and more. But duels are foolish. There must be another way—"

"No," Richard interrupted with a vicious slice of his hand through the air. "My second will contact you with the details of the duel."

Trent nodded just as the terrace door opened and the couple stepped onto the balcony. "All right," he agreed under his breath, turned, moved without a sound toward the garden path and slipped into the dark night.

Audrey bit down hard on her lip to stop the scream that was lodged in her throat from escaping. Her brother was a worse shot than she was. She couldn't lose him on top of Father all because she was an utter fool. It was too late now to talk sense into Richard, but tomorrow, she would beg Richard to call off the duel.

SEVERAL HOURS LATER, AUDREY'S HEAD pounded and her stomach threatened to empty its contents as she climbed the steps to their home on Mayfair with her coachman's help. Scenes from the ball played relentlessly through her head and no matter how she tried, she could not stop them. Her father's mottled face. His wheezing and grasping at his chest. His hateful words. Trent in the glow of the moonlight refusing to marry her. Huddling by her father's still form as the doctor came and pronounced him officially dead. The stricken look on the faces of the guests at the Lionhursts' ball as her father was carried out.

Ringing commenced once more in her ears. Moaning, she released Mr. Barrett's arm and pressed her hands to either side of her head. She swayed and as she did, he gripped her elbow. "My lady, shall I try once more to get your brother to come into the house."

Weary, Audrey turned to the carriage. In the darkness, she could not see inside the window to glimpse Richard's face, but she suspected he wore the same scowl as he had since they had alighted into the carriage from the ball and she had tried to talk to him. He had refused to look at her or acknowledge anything she way saying. Her shoulders sagged and when she caught the look of pity on Mr. Barrett's face, she released him and straightened her spine. She may want to crumble to the ground, but she refused to do it in public. "Go back to Richard. Watch over him if you can and see that he makes it back home eventually."

"Certainly, my lady." Mr. Barrett tipped his hat, strode down the steps and clambered onto the coachman seat. With a word from him, the horses let out a neigh, the carriage wheels turned on the cobblestone street and Mr. Barrett and her brother disappeared around the corner.

As she touched her hand to the brass knob of the door it opened and her aunt flew out the door, her face creased with lines of worry. "Oh, my dear! The Lionhursts' sent their footman round with a note to tell me what has happened. Come in, come in!"

Audrey folded into her aunt's warm, flowery embrace and wilted against her. She clutched at her arm as her aunt brought her into the house and closed the door. "I can't believe he is dead," Aunt Hillie murmured while shaking her head and leading them into the parlor. "Sit, here, dearest. Your face is pasty and"—her aunt pressed a hand to Audrey's forehead—"your forehead is damp. Let me get you some tea. You look as if you may faint."

Audrey collapsed against the settee. "I feel as if I might faint," she whispered, swallowing against the nausea threatening to rise. Her mouth began to water profusely and the pounding of her head grew tenfold. Suddenly she jerked upright. "I'm going to be sick." She pressed a hand over her mouth and watched as her aunt raced to the tea tray and ran back with tea splashing over the side of the cup and falling on the faded Audubon carpet.

"Drink this." Aunt Hillie moved Audrey's hand out of the way and pressed the china cup to her lips.

Audrey inhaled deeply of the honey-scented steaming tea as she took a tentative sip. The warmth slid down her throat and pooled in her belly. Aunt Hillie peered at her with a worried frown. Audrey sat still for a moment, waiting to see if the tea would settle her stomach or be the thing that made her lose the contents of it. The rolling of her stomach continued, but did seem to subside a bit. She gave a tentative nod and then took another sip. After a few minutes, the tea cup was empty and her stomach was still, though her head still pounded dreadfully.

"A bit better?" her aunt asked in a hushed voice.

Audrey nodded and closed her eyes, lowering the teacup to her lap. She slit one eyelid open when her aunt's warm fingers grazed her hand and took the teacup. "Thank you," Audrey murmured.

"Of course, dear."

The soft clank of the teacup being set on the side table resounded throughout the parlor along with the swishing of Hillie's skirts and the soft pat of her slippers across the carpet and back. The settee sank a bit to the left as Hillie once again sat by Audrey, took up her hands and grasped them in hers.

Audrey did not open her eyes, but the much-needed comfort of having someone she loved who actually seemed to care about her take her hands and hold them made the tenuous control she held over herself break. Warm tears seeped out of her closed lids and trickled down her face and off her chin.

"There now," her aunt soothed and wiped at Audrey's face with a soft cloth. Every moment of the terrible night played repeatedly as she cried softly. After a bit, the front of her dress was soaked, her nose stuffy, and her body felt as if it weighed a hundred stone. She could not make herself move, all she could muster was to open her eyes into mere slits.

She turned her head on the cushion of the settee and glanced at her aunt, who peered intently at her, her brow puckered and her bottom lip between her teeth. Her aunt released her lip and squeezed Audrey's hands. "Are you able to tell me what happened? The note from Lady Gillian said your father died suddenly on the balcony and there seemed to be something wrong with his heart as he was clutching his chest."

Audrey let out a shuddering sigh. "He and Mr. Shelton happened upon Lord Davenport and me while we were kissing."

"Oh, dear." Aunt Hillie pressed a hand to her chest.

"Yes, oh dear is correct. It was not pretty. He screamed and yelled. Mr. Shelton, of course, declared he no longer wished to marry me, and once he departed Father demanded Lord Davenport marry me."

Aunt Hillie's eyes opened wide in surprise. "And Lord Davenport agreed?"

Heat singed Audrey's cheeks and she darted her glance to her lap. "No," she choked out in a hoarse whisper. "He told Father he would not." Anguish threatened to close her throat. She gulped hard, desperately wanting to finish the explanation, race to her room and be alone. She turned to meet her aunt's sorrow-filled gaze. "They fought. Father fell in the midst of it, clutched his chest and...and he...he died." Her voice cracked on the last word and consumed by guilt she tugged her hands free of her aunt's and covered her face.

"Dearest. Dearest." Her aunt pressed a soothing hand to Audrey's forehead but Audrey moved away and lowered her hands.

She did not deserve to be soothed. "Please do not," she said, feeling as if she wanted to crawl out of her skin.

Aunt Hillie narrowed her eyes. "His death is not your fault," she said in a stern tone.

Audrey bunched her hands into fists. She refused to fight with another member of her family, so she simply stared silently at her aunt.

After a moment, her aunt heaved a sigh and shook her head. "We'll talk more on it tomorrow."

"Yes, thank you," Audrey murmured and pressed a hand against her aunt's arm before dropping it away and rising on legs that felt like pudding. She locked her knees and glanced down at her aunt. "I'm going to bed now."

"Yes, of course." Aunt Hillie rose as well. "Dearest, where is Richard?"

"I'm not sure. He would not talk to me after it happened. He came onto the terrace as Father was dying. I think he must have been looking for us."

"Yes, of course. I'm sure Richard does not blame you, dearest."

Audrey was sure he did, but she kept her silence on that matter. "There is more, Aunt Hillie." Audrey wrapped her arms around her mid-section, feeling as if she was coming undone. "I was so upset about Father that I blurted to Richard what had happened with Lord Davenport and Richard demanded Lord Davenport marry me. He denied Richard's request as well." Hysterical laughter threatened to spill out. She bit her lip, breathed deeply and continued. "Richard demanded restitution for me by a duel with Lord Davenport. It's all so senseless! No one knows of my folly and the damage to my pride and heart is mine alone to be concerned with."

"My gracious, yes, it's senseless, but I'm afraid Richard is correct in that the man should marry you. He took liberties no gentleman should without the intention of marrying the woman. I can hardly believe I'm saying this, but I agree with Richard's inclination to protect your honor, but I daresay there is a better way to settle this. Perhaps Lord Davenport felt it was somehow a trap gone wrong?"

Audrey shrugged, though she had considered that too. Trent was not the sort of man to allow himself to be forced into anything, but if he loved her what did it matter how they ended up betrothed? She ground her teeth, considering the notion, but wariness blanketed her mind in fuzziness and made it hard to think properly. "I don't know. I'm very tired."

"Of course you are, dearest. Go to bed. I'll wait up for Richard and we will somehow set everything straight tomorrow."

Audrey nodded, though she did not possibly see how this could ever be set straight.

Eleven

The next morning, after a humiliating hour of trying unsuccessfully to talk Richard into calling off the duel, Audrey retreated into her drape-drawn darkened room and huddled under her covers. Richard's merciless berating continued to ring in her ears. She needed to think and plan but it was desperately hard to quiet the noise in her head. She longed for her mother and realized with sickening awareness that she didn't long for her father. If she had an ounce of decency and true compassion, she would.

It didn't matter he'd only been dead since last night. She should have desperately wanted to see him again. The fact that she didn't sent her scrambling out of her bed and to her chamber pot, where she retched up whatever was left in her stomach from lunch yesterday.

After she was certain her sickness had passed, she collapsed against the hardwood floor and welcomed the early-winter chill from the bare wood that seeped into her cheek. The tiredness she'd felt on the balcony last night and then in the parlor was nothing compared to the bone-deep weariness that gripped her now.

She squeezed her eyes shut as the door to her bedroom creaked.

"Audrey, dear, are you in here?" her aunt called.

Oh, thank heavens it wasn't Richard. "Down here," Audrey replied, too tired to move just yet.

Her aunt's footsteps padded across the floor and stopped just above Audrey. Skirts swished and her aunt's knees cracked and popped as she knelt. She pressed a warm hand to Audrey's forehead. "Oh, dearest," her aunt murmured. "I was afraid your brother's ghastly behavior would send you back into your bedchamber."

Audrey cracked her eyes open, her vision blurry from crying and lack of sleep. Slowly, she turned her head to take in her aunt's concerned face. "Richard is right in saying I make him ill. I make myself ill."

"No, dearest. Richard is wrong and angry. You did not kill your father."

Audrey swallowed. "My actions did." When her aunt inhaled sharply as if she would argue, Audrey shook her head. "Please do not try to convince me otherwise. My actions killed him, and what is worse, I don't miss him," she whispered. "I'm wicked."

Her aunt leaned over her and hugged her. "You are not wicked."

Audrey's body sagged with relief and she blinked in surprise, not realizing how afraid she had been that her aunt might agree with her. "I don't wish him dead," Audrey rushed out, wanting to confess all, "but I can't say there isn't the smallest part of me that isn't relieved he won't be throwing me from the house today because of last night." Warm tears trickled out of her eyes and down the sides of her face to trail along her neck and pool at the back of her hair.

"Oh, my, you poor dear," her aunt soothed and gathered Audrey into a tighter hug. Audrey grasped Aunt Hillie's back and allowed herself to be pulled into a sitting position. Shame heated her face and clenched her belly. She buried her head in her aunt's fragrant hair. "He was right," she blurted. "There's something wrong with me."

"No, shush. He was wrong. He just had a hard time appreciating you. You are kind and intelligent and independent. The independence scared him, I do believe." Aunt Hillie rocked her while patting her hair.

Audrey hiccupped with tears. "Maybe if I hadn't been so opinionated and headstrong?"

"I do not think so, dear. Your mother was neither of those things and he never could relate to her either. We must not be harsh. Who knows why he was the way he was."

Audrey's heart constricted. She untangled herself from her aunt's warm embrace, pulled her knees to her chest and rested her chin there. "I never understood him and he never understood me. And now it's too late." Her eyes suddenly stung once again. She would not cry anymore. There was no time. *Blast it all.* Tears began to leak, despite her furious blinking and willing herself to be strong.

The look of pity on her Aunt Hillie's face made matters worse. Audrey struggled to breathe deeply but her efforts turned to racking sobs that went on so long her head pounded in time with her heart, and her nose became so stuffed she had to breathe through her mouth. All the while, Aunt Hillie ran her hand up and down Audrey's arm and made soothing sounds. Once the tears stopped and her breathing returned to normal she forced herself to focus, as well as she could in her state. "The time for crying is over."

Aunt Hillie nodded, the seven feathers secured in her hair bobbing as she patted at her own moist eyes.

Audrey sat up straight. "I need a plan to repair the damage I've created."

"A stich in time saves nine," Aunt Hillie said.

Audrey smiled. "Who said that?"

"Thomas Fueller. I do believe he meant if you act immediately when a problem occurs the problem will require fewer actions to fix."

"Yes." Audrey nodded as her belly clenched. "I need to stop the duel between Richard and Lord Davenport."

"And get Lord Davenport to offer for you."

"Aunt Hillie,"Audrey said in a dark warning voice.

Her aunt frowned. "All right. Let us work on what we agree on, which is stopping the duel. I think you should go to Lord Davenport and ask him to try to reason with your brother and get him to call off the duel."

"Yes." Audrey nodded. "I was thinking the same thing, though I doubt he will have any effect. He already tried to reason with Richard. If that does not work, then perhaps Lord Davenport can simply not show for the duel. I would rather Richard feel I am dishonored by Lord Davenport than Richard be dead. He is a terrible shot and I happen to know from Lord Davenport's cousin that he is a renowned shot with a pistol."

She met her aunt's gaze. "I wish Richard would come to his senses. I truly do not wish to see Lord Davenport."

"Quite understandable, dear. The man has wounded your pride by not offering marriage."

He'd done more than that, but Audrey remained quiet. Her broken heart paled in comparison to her father's death and Richard's impending duel. "How will I escape the house? Richard will never let me visit Lord Davenport. For one thing, we're in mourning. Beyond that is the obvious reason that an unmarried woman has no business calling on a bachelor like Lord Davenport."

Her aunt looked contemplative for one moment. "If your brother's drunkenness last night is any indication of how he plans to handle your father's death, then slipping away unnoticed tonight shouldn't be that difficult."

Audrey sighed. "You're right. Richard will likely be in his cups not long after dinner."

"I'll be ready to depart," her aunt said.

Gratefulness washed over Audrey, followed by a realization. "No." She shook her head. "I need you here on the chance Richard comes looking for me. You stay in my room and tell him I'm sick."

"You're sure? I don't like the idea of your going alone."

"I will not be alone. Mr. Barrett has always had a fondness for me. I'm sure he will agree to take me to Lord Davenport's and keep my secret as long as I explain the situation."

"Excellent. It's all settled. What shall we do now?"

"I'll go talk to Mr. Barrett. You go about your normal routine. We don't want Richard to become suspicious."

"All right," her aunt agreed.

Audrey moved to stand, but her aunt caught her hand. "Dear, when you go to talk to Lord Davenport do try not to look so forlorn. He may realize just how much you love him."

Audrey's breath caught in her chest. "Loved him," she corrected, though it was a lie. If he told her today he loved her and was sorry she knew she would fly into his arms.

Aunt Hillie smiled up at her. "Have I ever told you my take on the proverb that says you can lead a horse to water but you can't make it drink?"

"No, Aunt." Audrey hoped she didn't look as irritable as she felt. What in the name of all that was holy did a proverb about a horse have to do with her?

"I think any horse can be made to drink if a person simply makes the horse realize he's thirsty."

Audrey frowned. "Aunt Hillie, I don't understand what this—" Heat flushed her neck and face instantly as realization dawned. Audrey gaped at her aunt. "Is Lord Davenport the horse in this instance?"

"Of course."

"Am I to take it that the water is equivalent to marriage for the sake of this conversation?"

"Clever, clever girl." Her aunt clapped her hands. "Just make him realize he's thirsty for marriage. It's plain by your face that you love him. Do not forsake happiness for pride."

There was no point repudiating what her aunt knew. Audrey squared her shoulders. To try to deny it would only make how she felt more obvious. "Lord Davenport made it clear he couldn't marry me."

"Did he say he didn't want to marry you?"

Audrey started to beg her aunt to drop the matter, but she stilled. Her heart skipped a bit and her chest foolishly filled with hope. He'd never said he didn't want to marry her. "Well, no. He said he couldn't."

"Then you'd be a fool not to want to find out why. Maybe it's something silly you can help him solve. Like a ridiculous fear. Men are bursting with foolish fears they feel the need to stoically hide like ninny hammers. My own dearly departed Frank didn't want to marry me at first, because he was sure he'd be destroying my life by taking me away from my family's wealth."

Audrey's heart pounded in her chest. What if her aunt was right? What if Trent really loved her but feared something from his past? She knew, according to Whitney, that he had regrets about a woman he'd known in France. "How did you convince Uncle Frank otherwise?"

"Simple, dear." Her aunt grinned wickedly. "I merely showed my horse that he was parched and would perish from thirst without me by his side."

"I do not think I can do that, Aunt Hillie. I think I may be too hurt and as much as I hate to admit it, I am scared he will simply tell me he does not love me."

Her aunt hugged her close. "Those are valid fears, yet I beg you to think on what I've said."

"I will," Audrey promised before leaving her aunt to find Mr. Barrett.

TRENT HAD PASSED THE DAY in a bloody foul mood, pretending not to be home when Whitney, Gillian and then Sutherland called on him. He knew what they wanted. They wanted him to go to Audrey, but he could not do that. To see her would make matters worse for both of them. His mood worsened throughout the day as the reality of what his loss of control with her had set into motion. By the time evening fell and the darkness of the sky deepened to the black of gaining night, he headed to White's and was shocked to see that Audrey's brother was there with some other addlepated dandies.

Trent took a seat on the far side of the room in a dark corner and contemplated what this could mean. If he could get Cringlewood—ah hell, correction, the man was now Bridgeport—if he could get Bridgeport alone, maybe the man would be more willing to be reasonable tonight than he had been last night.

Three hours later Trent gritted his teeth as Bridgeport raised his hand to order another drink. Damnation. The man had been here for hours consuming one whiskey after another. It took every ounce of self-control Trent possessed not to simply stalk over to him, grab the man by his coattails and force him outside where they could speak privately. That wouldn't serve his purpose, though. Personally, Trent thought a well-placed bullet might be just the thing to snap Bridgeport out of his drunken, self-indulgent behavior, but then Audrey would be hurt and protecting Audrey was the sole reason Trent was still here.

When Bridgeport suddenly stood, Trent let out a hefty sigh of relief and allowed the man a few seconds to stumble toward the door and collect his coat. When none of the marquess's addlepated mates followed, Trent ambled out of the room toward the exit as if he hadn't a concern in the world.

He stepped into the dark night and smiled. Finally, he was getting a bit of good luck. Audrey's brother was leaned against the side of the building, retching up the contents of his stomach. Trent waited for a moment, until it seemed the deed was done, and then strode to Bridgeport. He didn't turn or acknowledge that he heard Trent approaching, though Trent made sure to walk loud enough his presence would not be a surprise.

"Bridgeport, might I have a minute?"

Audrey's brother swung around, swayed dangerously to the right, then steadied himself by throwing his arms out. A comical smile came to the man's face. "Thought I was going to fall on my bloody arse, didn't you?"

Hoped was more like it. "No," Trent replied, examining the marquess's trembling hands still splayed haphazardly in the air. Hell, the man had the shakes that came with drinking far too much. The situation was worse than Trent had thought. Bridgeport would be no match in a duel. The man would be lucky if he could shoot an immobile object right in front of his face. "I'd like you to call off the duel tomorrow."

"You're scared!" Bridgeport bellowed.

Trent almost nodded. He was scared. Scared he'd kill Audrey's brother right here and now, devil take the idiot. "Lower your voice, man. Would you have everyone knowing you think your sister's honor has been impugned?"

"It has," Bridgeport raged.

A noisy crowd of men had gathered at the front door of White's. Trent eyed the group and prayed they'd quickly go inside, or else his hope of talking sense into Bridgeport was going to have to be abandoned. He couldn't risk him making the situation worse for Audrey by alerting half the *ton* to the duel. "Listen carefully to me, Bridgeport." Trent purposely lowered his voice, hoping the fool would do the same. "I admit I took liberties I ought not have, but your sister's innocence is well intact. I'm in no position to marry her, as you demanded, but I vow to stay far away from her and do everything in my power to see she makes a respectable match.

"Your power!" Bridgeport roared. "We'll see how powerful you are come tomorrow."

Disgust ripped through Trent's body, leaving a trail of singeing heat behind. The group of men at White's door had grown quiet and a few had taken a few steps in their direction. "Think of your sister, man. This duel could ruin her, no matter how it turns out. If word somehow got out, or worse, you died."

"I'm thinking of my sister," Bridgeport yelled.

Trent furiously shook his head and yanked Bridgeport to him by the lapels of the man's coat. Once they were face-to-face, Trent spoke. "I'll meet you tomorrow, because you've left me no choice. But if you've any real love for your sister, you'll shut your bloody mouth and keep our meeting to yourself. There are people watching us." Disgusted, he shoved Bridgeport away and strode toward his waiting coachman.

Once inside the carriage and headed for his home, he squeezed his eyes shut with a groan. What the hell was he going to do now? He was an excellent shot. It was not bragging, but a fact. One had to be a superb shot to make sure one stayed alive when on assignment. Trent examined his options but found only one reasonable enough to contemplate. Tomorrow, he could notch his gun ever so slightly to the right to ensure Bridgeport suffered nothing short of a surface wound on his arm, but would the irrational fool feel vindicated if he was shot? Trent's gut twisted. He didn't want to wound Audrey's brother. The man was the biggest imbecile, but he was defending Audrey's honor.

"Damn it all," he growled. His own idiocy and lack of control had caused this whole sordid situation. If he'd simply learned why she had called him there, tried to help her if he could and kept his bloody distance between them.

He brooded the rest of the way home and by the time he reached his house, his mood had gone from foul to lethal. He stocked past his butler Pickering and into his study.

Trent growled as he entered the room and flopped into his chair. He yanked his cravat off, threw it on the settee and pulled open the collar of his shirt. It might be cool outside, but his study was suffocating. Or maybe it was his conscience weighing so heavily that the air around him felt smothering. How the devil he'd ended up in such a shocking position in a public place with Audrey tonight confused him. Not only had he compromised her, but he might have been disloyal to Gwyneth. It didn't matter there was not a speck of love inside of him for his wife. He had loved her when he married her, and he'd treat her honorably regardless of how she treated him. "Hell and damn."

He kicked his boots off, thumped his feet on a stool and laid his head back to squeeze his eyes shut. He needed to think. Clearly, calmly and methodically. Audrey deserved nothing short of a marriage proposal, but he couldn't give it to her. If it were possible, he would do it. He wiped at his brow, seeing not his cozy study but the rat-infested French prison Gwyneth had left him in. That was what marriage had brought him before. Not trust and fidelity, but lies and betrayal. And he had been about to willingly marry again. But this time would have been different. He would have protected himself better.

"Pickering," he bellowed, needing a drink now more than ever.

His butler appeared within seconds.

"I need a drink," Trent said before Pickering was fully through the study door.

"Yes, my lord, but—"

"No buts. Just my drink."

Pickering opened his mouth to speak and Trent held up a forestalling hand. "Listen, Pickering, I hear myself. I know I'm being an ill-mannered, unmitigated tyrannical bore, and I beg a thousand pardons. But tonight has been tedious. I'm beginning to think it will never end and I'm stuck in some earthly dimension of my own personally created hell."

Pickering cleared his throat. "My lord, you have a visitor."

"A what? I just got home."

Pickering smirked. "Yes. And your visitor just arrived. I take it you didn't hear the door."

"I've things on my mind," Trent grumbled, squeezing his eyes shut and mentally ticking off the possibilities of who would dare to come here this late. "Is it Dinnisfree?" The duke had been the only one close to him who had not already stopped by today.

"No, my lord. It's—"

"My mother? My cousin? My brother? Tell whoever it is I'm indisposed. I'd likely offend whoever has come to see me."

"Don't worry," came Audrey's throaty voice, heavy with sarcasm instead of its usual warmth, "I doubt there's anything further you can say that will offend me more than you already have."

Trent surged to his feet and nearly shoved Pickering out of the way to get to Audrey. He had her in his arms and crushed against his chest before he realized what he'd done. Hell. He stiffened. He was doing it again. Putting them both in a terrible situation.

Before he set her away, he took one long inhalation of her fragrant honeysuckle hair. He nearly groaned aloud at the lust and yearning her smell ignited. Disentangling himself, he stepped back. Her cold eyes and withdrawn expression chilled him to the bone. Gone was her smiling radiance. He had done that.

For one indomitably long moment, she stared at him, and then her lips parted, her nostrils flared and her green eyes glistened like polished emeralds. She whirled away so he could not see her face. Her skirts swished around her ankles in her haste. He could not blame her. "I've come to speak with you about the duel."

Of course. She wanted to protect her brother, even at the risk of ruining herself. His admiration for her grew.

Damn the duel for a moment. "Audrey, I'm sorry."

"You should be." Unmistakable hurt vibrated her tone. Her back arched slightly and her hands clenched at her sides. His gut twisted into painful knots. For once in his life, he was completely at a loss for what to say to a woman. "I assume I've upset you."

She whirled to face him. Blistering color stained her cheeks and made her freckles turn red.

"Of course you did," she snapped. "But I am not here to talk about my feelings. I am here to beg you not to fight my brother. Will you grant me this one wish or will you deny me that as well?" Her foot tapped rapidly in front of her, but her trembling lip gave away the riotous emotions inside her.

That he was causing her pain made him feel as if someone had plunged their fist into his chest and was slowly squeezing his heart without mercy. Self-loathing filled him. He couldn't rectify any of this. If he died right now, it would be a well-deserved fate.

For a breath, he half expected his heart to seize yet the damnable thing beat on. The only reparation he could offer was the smallest sliver of the truth. "Audrey." He stepped closer to her, but she scuttled out of his reach, looking very much like a wounded deer. His heart tugged in the strangest way. "I want you to know I would marry you if I could."

Her shoulders sagged and the quivering of her lip increased until she bit down on it. She notched her chin up and squared her shoulders. By God, she was brave and beautiful.

"*If you could?*" Her tone was a harsh accusation. "Are you trying to tell me you are incapable of marriage or just not desirous of a marriage with *me*?"

Pain spiraled through him at the sudden whiteness of her complexion and the way she crossed her arms as if to protect herself. He had to tell her more. She deserved more of the truth. Damn everything else. He would pay all the consequences later. "I'm trying to tell you I'm already married." Saying the words aloud made him wince. He teetered between the feelings of relief and failure.

"Married?" Her brows came together, causing a deep crease between her eyes. "Surely you jest?"

"I wish I did, but it's true. I'm married or at least I think I still am. I can't say for certain."

"You can't say for certain?" Her hushed broken tone made his chest tighten.

When she swayed, as if she might faint, he grasped her by the elbow and curled his fingers around her slender arm. "Do you need to sit down?"

DO I NEED TO SIT down? Trent's question echoed through Audrey's mind. Considering her world seemed to be tilting at a precariously odd angle, Audrey decided that yes, she did indeed need to take a seat. Her legs gave way beneath her the second she let go of her pride. She fully expected to crash to the floor, but Trent circled his strong arm around her waist and crushed her to his side. At the force of the impact against his solid thigh and chest, her breath released from her body with a shuddering whoosh.

For a moment, she was too dazed to speak. He was married? A fiery ball of anger formed in her chest. No, he'd not said he was married. What he'd said was he thought he was married, but he couldn't say for certain. The ball in her chest burst and sent sparks of humiliation to every corner of her body. Her scalp burned with the heat of disgrace; her toes tingled with regret.

There was no way to deny it now. Her father had been one hundred percent correct. Or had he? She had to know for sure. Did Trent love her, but the fact he was married held him back? She wanted to throttle him, but she desperately needed to hear the whole story. The heat radiating off his body and his breath hitting her neck in puffs of deliciously warm air invaded her senses. If she didn't ascertain how he really felt she would always regret it. Of course, once she knew, she may regret that more, but not to ask was unacceptable. She wriggled in his arms. "Let me go. I'm fine to stand on my own now."

"Audrey."

The pleading note in his voice almost undid her. Part of her wanted to stay in his arms and part of her wanted to slap him. What she needed most was distance. She shoved hard against his chest and ducked under his arms when his hold loosened. Scampering backward, she put several paces between them. "It's interesting you aren't sure whether you're married or not. I don't suppose you care to explain how one comes to be in that state or why you didn't mention it sooner?"

"I came to be married as all people do. I met a woman I loved and asked her to marry me."

His nonchalant reply twisted her gut. So he had loved his wife. Or he still loved her. Did it really matter? Audrey felt wretched. On the way over, she'd been quite certain she could never feel worse, but she'd been wrong. "Then why the secrecy?"

"There's no secrecy. I thought my wife was dead, and now I've learned I might have been mistaken."

"So that's why you didn't tell me?" That at least was half-honorable.

"Among other reasons."

Any charity she felt fled out the door. "Such as?" She hated that she couldn't control the angry tone of her voice.

Trent rolled his shoulders, a habit she knew he reverted to when he was uncomfortable. Good, the devil deserved to be more than uncomfortable.

He cleared his throat. "No one but two other people know I was married and I prefer to keep it that way."

Didn't that just take some bollocks to ask her to keep his dirty little secret? The anger inside her threatened to consume her. She advanced on him with a pounding heart. "Whatever were you doing with me?" she demanded. "Or is that quite naïve of me to ask?" She poked him in the chest and forced back the scream lodged in her throat. "Were you simply seducing me?"

"God, no," Trent thundered.

"What then?" Her blood roared in her ears. She was going too far. She knew it, but she couldn't rein herself in. "Tell me what I was to you." The wounded tone of her voice made her cringe but she forced herself to continue. She had to know. *Had to.* "If you weren't possibly married would you have asked me to marry you? Do you—" She could barely force the question out, but now was not the time to be meek. "Do you love me?" The whispered question was so low she barely heard it herself. How appalling to have asked such a thing, yet she wouldn't take back what she had asked. To never know would be torture. All her loneliness welled within her in one large knot of yearning. She wanted his love. Even if she could never have him, knowing she had his love would be enough.

He stared at her, his complete shock evident in the widening of his eyes and the color leeching from his face. "Audrey, I would have offered for you last night if I knew I was free to do so."

That was no answer. She gritted her teeth before speaking. "Last night? *Only just last night?* Not before we were caught? Your hand seemingly forced." She was helpless to stop the rage mingled with humiliation that made her shiver.

He yanked his hands through his hair, a loud sigh coming from him. "I had made up my mind to offer for you at the wedding breakfast. I even went home to send your father a note so I could ask him to court you, and then I got notice that my wife might be alive." His gaze raked over her face. "I thought we could have a very beneficial marriage."

"Beneficial marriage?" She would have sworn she'd heard him wrong except his nod confirmed she'd heard him correctly.

He reached for her and she reacted without thought by whipping her hand through the air and slapping him. The contact of her open palm against his cheek echoed in the silent room. "That's what I think of your beneficial marriage idea."

Her hand stung but no more than her pride. With as much dignity as she could muster, she clasped her hand to her chest and glared at him. "I would call you a fool, but I daresay you're too thick skulled to realize the truth." The mocking tone of her voice masked her bleeding heart. She had to get out of here before she dissolved into tears or worse threw herself at his feet and begged him to love her. Raising her chin, she said, "Now that matters are settled between us, I demand as repayment for you toying with me that you not show up to duel my brother."

"For God's sake, woman," Trent growled, "I did not toy with you."

She cocked a disbelieving eyebrow at him. It was either that or scream, and screaming would hardly make her look unaffected by him. "You may say whatever you like, but we both know the truth. I do not want you shooting and killing my brother. You've done quite enough already."

The tic at Trent's temple beat so furiously she worried for one second she'd gone too far. His mouth compressed into a thin, hard line before he seemed to calm enough to speak. "I'm sorry for my part in your father's death, and I'm sorry for kissing you on the balcony last night."

His words obliterated whatever shred of dignity she had. "I feel so much better now," she replied, each word punctuated with icy loathing, of herself as well as him.

"Damnation, Audrey." Like a flash of light, he grabbed her and yanked her to him, her chest crashing against his. "You misunderstand me." He pressed his face close to her head, his lips brushing against her ear. "I care for you very much."

That was not love.

"I intended last night to never touch you, but you undo me."

Audrey struggled out of his grip and clutched the material of her dress. She wanted to press her hands to her ears to block out what he was saying, but she never wanted him to know how much his words hurt her. The aching sincerity of his voice told her he was truly trying to explain himself and that he'd never meant to hurt her, but his words made everything worse. What was between them had nothing to do with love, on Trent's part, and everything to do with lust and convenience. If she'd wanted to marry for mere passion or suitability she could have done it five times over by now. She wanted love. His love.

She clenched her teeth and forced her thoughts to order. "Before I leave, I'll need your promise that you won't go to the duel."

"Did you hear a word I just said to you?" Exasperation

was evident in his tone and rigid stance.

Had she heard him? It was hard to keep the disbelieving laugh inside, but she did. "Your promise, please," she said levelly, choosing to ignore his question. It was the only way she'd escape this room without tears.

His features hardened. "I cannot give you that promise."

"You blackguard," she spat, unable to hold back her anger. How dare he refuse her request?

The small scar on the right side of his face reddened. She'd seen it do that several times before when he was irritated about something. What nerve he had to be irritated with her. She inhaled a sharp breath, gathering air to blast him with stinging words of anger. As if he could read her mind, he held up a silencing hand, the look on his face one of fierce warning.

"My failing to show up at the duel will not appease your brother. I believe it will anger him further. He will take it as a further slight, though it is the furthest intention from my mind. I fear he may take out his anger on you if he cannot get to me."

She blanched, knowing he was undoubtedly correct. For a moment, she was tongue-tied. The fact that he seemed genuinely concerned for her welfare touched her and confused her. "Then what's to be done? I can shoot a pistol better than my brother, and that's not saying much."

The smallest smile graced Trent's lips and the strangest look skittered across his face, gone before she could truly read it. *Scorn?* No. The smile had been real, not mocking. It had appeared more like... Her breath caught in her throat. *Admiration.* But for who? Surely not her. *Focus, silly nitwit.* Nothing else but her brother mattered. "Do you have a plan?" For the oddest reason, she felt sure he would.

Trent shrugged. "I'll simply delope. Our seconds will call the duel. The wrong to your honor will be answered and your brother's pride will remain intact."

A reluctant surge of gratitude filled her. She offered a sharp nod. "I thank you. And now I must be off, before I'm discovered gone."

Trent snorted at that. "If you're worried about your brother discovering you missing, I left him not more than an hour ago on the street in front of White's. He'd had quite a lot to drink and didn't appear near in the mood to be heading home."

Audrey frowned at Trent's news. "Did you run into Richard or seek him out?"

"I sought him out in hopes of avoiding the duel for his sake, as well as yours."

"Oh." The large lump now lodged in her throat prevented her from saying more. The fact that Trent had gone out of his way to try to end this mess affected her, and she didn't want to be touched by him. Or rather she did, and that was the problem. Irritation at herself and Richard made her clench her teeth. *Blast Richard.* It was unseemly for him to be cavorting around Town with Father not even buried in his grave. She understood better than anyone the differing tugs of sorrow and strange nothingness he likely felt in relation to Father's death, yet Richard owed Father's memory respect. Tomorrow, after the mess of the duel was behind them, she would speak to him and take him to task on straightening out his life now that he was the new marquess. His drinking simply had to stop.

"Audrey?"

Trent's gentle question snapped her out of her musings over Richard. Trent now stood so close to her the flecks of gold in his green eyes were visible. The fluttering of her heart frightened her. Even now, after everything she knew he still affected her—blast him. She turned sharply toward the door, not wanting him to see the longing probably written all over her face. Before he could stop her, she flung open the door and called over her shoulder loud enough for him to hear, "I must be going now that our business is concluded."

She raced into the hallway and nearly barreled into the butler. "Please see me out now." Her rushed words got no visible reaction from the man other than his inclining his head and striding at a brisk pace down the hall. Audrey's heart thundered in her chest. She strained to hear footsteps behind her as she hurried down the hall. Perhaps Trent would call out and demand she stop? When she got to the front door and the butler opened it for her, she was trembling all over.

Trent hadn't come after her. He hadn't halted her departure, begged her to stay or even bothered to bid her farewell. It was for the best. She was so hurt and angry she thought she very well might slap him again, and that wouldn't do. She didn't want him to know how much he'd wounded her. At least she'd never told him she loved him. He would never know for certain what a fool she'd been for him.

She repeated the thought to herself as she settled herself in her carriage and waited for the door to be closed. The minute it clicked shut and the carriage dipped down with the weight of Mr. Barrett taking the driver's seat, she buried her face in her hands and cried all the way to her home. Once there, she wiped her tears and took a deep, steadying breath. It was time to harden her heart and forget Trent. The devil wasn't worth her tears.

Twelve

Early the next morning, Trent stared across Hamstead Heath Park and tried to force his thoughts to the impending duel. The green grass of the park blurred and Audrey's anguished face appeared in his mind. The sleepless night had done nothing to fill the hollowness that had taken up residency in his chest since the moment he'd forced himself to let her leave yesterday.

A man who didn't know for certain whether his wife was dead or not didn't bloody well deserve to contemplate a future with anyone else, especially when it seemed the woman he'd been considering a future with wanted more than a marriage of convenience. She wanted his love and that was the one damned thing, married or not, he could never give her. Love was for blind fools.

A sharp jab in his side snapped him out of his meanderings. He shot a glare at Dinnisfree. "Why did you elbow me?"

His friend returned his glare. "It's my job as your second to keep you focused until the duel begins, and you're hardly focused. Snap out of whatever, or rather whoever, has your thoughts, though I'm sure I know who."

Heat crept up Trent's neck. He jerked his head in agreement. "There'll be plenty of years to question whether I've made the right choices."

Dinnisfree paused in inspecting the pistol that

Thortonberry had given them. Trent clenched his teeth. Considering the way Audrey was suffering because of him, it served him right that he had to suffer Thortonberry as Bridgeport's second. Dinnisfree raised the pistol to his chin and slid the metal back and forth over his beard, an ironic smile coming to his lips. "You need years to figure out if you made the right decisions, you say?"

He hated the way Dinnisfree liked to make his point by leading with questions. Trent was about one second away from smashing his fist into his friend's too-perfect nose. Instead, he held out his hand for the pistol, which Dinnisfree slapped handle-down into Trent's palm. He curled his fingers around the weapon, weighing it and calculating the distance from himself to Bridgeport and what would be the opportune time to delope. Calculations completed, he flicked his gaze across the dewy grass where Bridgeport stood, pistol in hand and feet spread to shoot. A rush of anticipation surged through Trent. Despite the fact he fully intended to delope once Bridgeport took a shot, Trent couldn't control his body's natural defensive reaction. He rolled his shoulders to try to relax.

Dinnisfree clasped him on the arm "Are you sure about this?"

Trent nodded, keeping his gaze on Bridgeport. "The man doesn't have a chance in hell of hitting me. I'll delope and it will be over and for the best."

"If you say so, but I don't like the looks of Bridgeport."

Trent focused in on Audrey's brother. His features were tight, his eyes narrowed and his nostrils flared.

The duke shook his head. "There's more on that man's mind than his sister's reputation."

"Likely you're right," Trent agreed. "But whatever is weighing on Bridgeport's conscience isn't going to make him a better shot."

"Take your marks, gentlemen," Thortonberry called out.

Dinnisfree cleared away from Trent as he raised his pistol for show. There was no need to announce his plans to delope. He wanted Bridgeport to feel as vindicated as possible. Hopefully the man would think Trent considered him a superior shot and was acknowledging it with his actions.

Time to concentrate. He shoved all thoughts aside as Thortonberry called the firing signal. Bridgeport's pistol recoiled with a harsh bang across the clearing and Trent jerked in reaction. The shot, just as he'd known it would be, was no danger. Trent raised his pistol straight to the sky and fired.

His plan completed, he found Dinnisfree to his left to assure himself the duel was over. Dinnisfree nodded his head in acknowledgement while walking toward Thortonberry to formally agree the duel was completed.

The rushing of blood in Trent's ears blocked out all sound around him but that of his own heart's effort to send blood throughout his body. Considering and discarding the best thing to say to Bridgeport, he turned his gaze back to Audrey's brother.

Odd. He was hunched over, fussing with his ankle like he'd twisted it. When Bridgeport straightened, the hairs on the back of Trent's neck stood on end. What the hell was the man doing? Bridgeport held a second pistol and strode toward him.

The call for action shot through Trent's body. *Hell and damn.* His fingers curled around an empty pistol.

Bridgeport's mouth twisted into a sneer.

"Bridgeport," Trent barked.

Audrey's brother stopped five feet away. *Close enough for the bloodthirsty idiot to hit him.*

He pointed the pistol at Trent.

Trent tensed. *Too late to run and nowhere to hide. Hell of a way to die.*

"Bridgeport," Dinnisfree roared. "I'll kill you if you take that shot."

A spark flashed in the distance.

Powder. Fire.

Trent dived to the right, the pistol shot filling his ears. The ground came hard and fast, forcing air from his lungs in a powerful explosion. He greedily sucked air back in. Rolling into a crouch, he scanned the park. Bridgeport lay prone under a raging Dinnisfree.

Footsteps thundered to a halt by his side. Thortonberry, huffing out air, loomed over Trent. "Lay back, Davenport, you've been hit." Thortonberry said dully.

"No." Trent shook his head. "He missed me."

"I beg to differ." Thortonberry pointed, his lips pursing.

Trent could not tell if the man was fighting a smile or trying not to grimace.

"He got you in the arm."

Trent glanced down, surprised to see blood dripping on the grass and his shirtsleeve stained dark crimson. Delayed pain exploded, searing a fiery path of agony up his arm. "Bloody fool," Trent snarled, trying to stand even as the ground tilted in front of him. Above him the physician appeared. Trent frowned. Was he on the ground? Unsure, he set his good palm down. Cool, wet grass caressed his skin. Hell, he'd fallen on his back. Numbness crawled up his injured arm at an alarmingly rapid rate. "Thortonberry," he growled as the doctor pushed him all the way down and ripped his shirtsleeve to get at the wound.

Thortonberry knelt and quirked his eyebrow. "Do you have some dying words you want me to convey to Lady Audrey?" Unmistakable amusement laced his tone.

Fierce anger surged through Trent. He used all his strength to reach up and grab the man's coat lapels to jerk him near. The effort caused bright spots of light to pepper his vision before little dots of black appeared. "Keep quiet about this and stay the hell away from Lady Audrey."

Thortonberry smirked. "I hardly think you are in a position to demand anything, not that you ever were. However, you can rest or die assured, be that as it may, that I would never mention a word of this duel. My every thought is for Lady Audrey and how to protect her."

Even though most of the man's words angered Trent, he was satisfied that Thortonberry meant what he said and would never utter a word of the duel. Trent released his hold and thudded back against the grass. He tried to fight the darkness shutting out all the light, but it was hopeless. As blackness started to consume everything but a picture of a brilliantly shining Audrey smiling at him, Trent realized Thortonberry had failed to promise to stay away from her. He struggled to form a proper threat, but his numb lips refused to cooperate.

THE MOMENT AUDREY HEARD THE carriage wheels rolling across the gravel drive she abandoned her pretense of embroidering and turned to her aunt. "Aunt Hillie, please let me speak with Richard first. He is likely to say more if it is just the two of us."

Her aunt nodded. "I'll be right here if you need me."

Audrey pressed a kiss to her aunt's cheek and raced out of the house to meet the carriage. Lord Thortonberry, his eyebrows drawn together in a fierce frown, descended the carriage first, followed swiftly by her brother. She scanned Richard, saw no signs of a wound and let out a breath she hadn't realized she'd been holding. Trent had been true to his word. Clearly, he'd deloped, because otherwise her brother would be injured or dead. Despite the deep hurt Trent had inflicted on her, gratitude swelled within her chest.

She waited for a moment to speak, assuming Lord Thortonberry would excuse himself and take the path that led from their house to his, but when it became clear he intended to stay, she slipped her arm through her brother's. She chose her words with care, so as not to alert him that she knew Trent had deloped. "Tell me what happened. I hope Lord Davenport is not too wounded."

Richard met her question with silence. Uneasy, she shifted and studied her brother. His wild gaze, nothing like a man who had put part of his troubles behind him, caused icy tendrils of fear to race across her skin and made her shiver. "What have you done, Richard?" The question was a shaky whisper.

Richard wrenched away from her, ignoring her completely. He wheeled toward Lord Thortonberry. "See how accusing her tone sounds," he bellowed. He waved a hand at Thortonberry. "Tell her how Davenport mocked me."

She met Lord Thortonberry's gaze. When he lifted his head upward, it appeared as if he might be agreeing, but then he gave the slightest shake of his head, his lips pursing in the strangest way, as if he had been reluctant to tell her. Probably he did not want her to know her brother had done something dishonorable. Her stomach twisted. "Richard," she said in a low, patient tone, though desperation nearly choked her. "You must tell me what happened."

"You cannot command me." Richard bit out each word.

Audrey barely stopped herself from screaming. She took a ragged breath and swung her gaze to Lord Thortonberry. "I am begging you to tell me. All of it. Honestly."

Lord Thortonberry narrowed his gaze, then dipped his head to her. "He shot Davenport *after* the duel was over and had been called."

Stunned and sickened, she repeated the information, certain she must have heard incorrectly "Richard shot Lord Davenport?"

"Yes. In the arm. Davenport deloped." Lord Thortonberry's words displayed nary a hint of emotion.

"Get off my property," Richard shouted, charging at his oldest and dearest friend.

"Stop it," Audrey shrieked, instinctually lunging for and wrapping both her hands around her brother's arm. Richard dragged her across the grass for a moment before he seemed to realize what he was doing.

He stopped, panting where he stood, and glanced down at her, his eyes glazed and blazing. Slowly, he pried her fingers away from his arm. "I'm quite collected now. You've no need to worry."

She nodded, though uncertainty filled her.

Her brother breathed deeply before speaking. "Davenport mocked me, I tell you, and therefore showed me your honor meant nothing to him."

She shook her head, tears sliding down her face. "No, Richard, he wasn't mocking you." Lord Thortonberry raised a questioning eyebrow at her, as if he agreed with Richard. She pressed her hands to her cheeks. "I asked Lord Davenport to delope." No need to go into the exact details of how she'd asked him. Let Richard think she'd sent a note. "I was worried for your safety. I—" Richard scowled at her. She stepped back, putting more than an arm's length between them. She didn't want to further wound Richard's pride, but he had to know he was wrong about Trent. The hatred burning in his eyes worried her. Swallowing, she forced herself to continue. "I was concerned if the duel went forward as planned. I—" She gulped. "Everyone says what an excellent shot Lord Davenport is."

"And you think me incapable?" Richard bellowed.

"No." But that was partially a lie. Probably, Richard could be a rather good shot *if* he would quit drinking and practice but that was likely never going to happen.

Richard advanced toward her, but Lord Thortonberry stepped in front of her and blocked him. "Bridgeport, you need to calm down."

Richard's face mottled red. "You think to tell me what to do, standing on my property? Why did you move in front of my sister? She needs no protection from me." Richard's voice was so loud Audrey had the urge to press her hands against her ears.

"Are you certain?" Lord Thortonberry's hard, doubt-filled tone made Audrey cringe. Though she appreciated his concern, his tactics were sure to further anger Richard.

Richard pointed to the stone path that they had taken a thousand times over the years to go from their home to Lord Thortonberry's. "Leave. You are no longer welcome here."

"Richard!" Horror filled Audrey. "You do not mean that."

"I do. Now go, Thortonberry."

Lord Thortonberry glanced at her with raised brows. She nodded. Presently, the best thing to do was comply, until Richard calmed himself. Tomorrow, surely, his temper would abate and he could apologize to Lord Thortonberry. Without a word, Lord Thortonberry turned on his heel, his boots clicking against the stones they struck as he walked. She watched as he disappeared around down the brushy, bush-lined path. He seemed to be swallowed into the overhanging vines from the looming trees. Once she no longer heard his footsteps, she turned to Richard.

Pain twisted his features. He eyed her. "You have ruined your chances of marriage with Mr. Shelton and everyone else who ever asked you. Now, you seem not to care that Lord Davenport refuses to marry you. You're selfish," he hissed. "We need money. Clearly more desperately than you comprehend. What shall we do now?" Richard threw his hands up in the air. "You are in mourning now! How will we go about quickly finding you a husband?"

Stunned at his tirade, it took her a moment to think what to say or ask. "How desperate is our financial situation? I tried asking Father several times, but he turned me away every time I asked."

"We're penniless," Richard said tonelessly. "At first Father was trying to marry you off, so he'd have one less mouth to feed, but then he concocted the idea to sell you to the highest bidder, or the first."

She wrapped her arms around her waist, shoved away the pain and invited numbness. It started in her toes, spread like an uncontrolled fire up her legs, across her belly, climbed toward her chest and settled in her mind. There. That was much better. She felt as if she stood apart from herself and looked at a woman she did not know. She was an observer, for the moment, in her own life. "Was Mr. Shelton the first bidder, or the highest?"

"The first. All you had to do was cooperate and we could have been saved but you ruined everything with your lusting after Davenport."

She supposed in a way that was true. Another question formed in her mind. "What happened to Father's money?"

Richard shrugged. "What didn't happen? Bad investments. Gambling. Drinking."

She couldn't help but glare at Richard, suspecting he had a part in their demise.

He narrowed his eyes. "It was not only me. Father gambled and drank long before me. Where do you think I learned my behavior from?"

"I don't know," she whispered. Reality crashed back

over her and made the numbness fade away. Her head pounded so harshly it was making thinking hard. "Is that everything?"

"Is not that enough?" His words dripped sarcasm. "The rest can wait for another day."

"The rest?" Good, gracious. There was more? She clutched at her roiling stomach.

Richard snorted. "I'm tired and I'm done talking." With that pronouncement, he stomped down the drive, up the steps and into the house with a bang.

She stood on the drive, unmoving. A soft breeze blew the scent of roses around her and the sun beamed down over her head. Normally, she would have considered this a glorious day, simply because of the weather. She pressed her hands to her face and tried to think what to do first. How could she help her brother and herself?

"Audrey."

Lord Thortonberry's soft tone directly behind her made her entire body tense. She whirled to face him. "I thought you had left," she murmured. Something about the way his eyes appeared hooded bothered her. He blinked, as if reading her thoughts, and smiled. Perhaps she was being too touchy because of her strained nerves.

"I waited at the end of the path until I saw your brother go in. I wanted to make sure you were all right."

"Yes, yes. I'm fine."

"How can I help?"

"Tell me how Lord Davenport is," she blurted, wishing, as she saw the widening and then narrowing of Lord Thortonberry's eyes, that she had found a more subtle way of asking the question.

"The doctor said it's too early to tell. The biggest concern is infection. If that doesn't kill Davenport in the next few days, then he has a good chance of living. The bullet lodged itself in his upper arm, but the doctor felt certain he could get it all out." He sounded detached and hurt as he spoke, but that was surely wrong. What did Lord Thortonberry have to be hurt about?

"I see," she managed to choke out before turning swiftly away. She'd rather he did not see the stark fear surely displayed on her face. Panic rioted within her and threatened to steal her self-control. No matter how Trent had hurt her, she had to see him, but now, more so than before, Richard would not allow it. Even if there wasn't her brother to consider, it wasn't as if she could appear unannounced as she'd done last night. No doubt Trent's family was there tending to him. Maybe she could get a note to Whitney and find out what was happening? Perhaps Whitney could help her? They'd always been there for each other in the past.

Behind her, Lord Thortonberry cleared his throat.

"Are you very distraught for Lord Davenport?"

She made herself turn to face him and forced a scoff between her cold lips. "I'm no more distraught for him than I'd be for anyone possibly on death's door. Do not mistake my feelings. I decided after the theater that we would not suit."

It occurred to her that Richard might have told Lord Thortonberry about Father finding her on the terrace kissing Trent. She held her breath and waited for what he would say.

"That's good." He smiled. "I didn't believe for one minute you'd fall under the spell of a man like Lord Davenport."

She pressed her fingertips to her aching head. "A man like Lord Davenport?"

"Well, yes." He shrugged. "I do not care for gossip, but perhaps you should know some people say he is a rather frequent visitor of the more notorious hellfire clubs."

Her heart flipped in her chest. From her time spent scheming with Whitney, she had inadvertently learned many secrets about Trent, so she had known he had been a visitor of the clubs, but she had assumed he had stopped frequenting them. She bit her lip hard. More truthfully, she had assumed he had stopped visiting them, because he was enamored of her. A new well of hurt trickled within her.

"I see. Well, it's a good thing I no longer desire his attention, then." Had her voice wobbled? She thought it had, but she had done the best she could. She shoved her hurt aside. No matter what Trent had or had not done, if he was dying, she had to see him. The fact was even though he had wounded her so that she felt the ache of the pain with every breath she took, she couldn't instantly make the love she had for him go away. Pressing her lips together as she'd often seen the matrons at the balls do, she sighed and then said, "I really have to go in and start preparing the house and myself for the mourning period." That was the nicest way she could think to tell him, without actually saying it aloud, to go home.

He nodded. "I'll be looking forward to seeing you out and about once your mourning period is over."

"Yes, of course," she mumbled, her mind on how she was going to see Trent and not on Lord Thortonberry at all.

Thirteen

Trent awoke with a start to candles flickering in the darkness. He attempted to sit up and intense pain shot through his right arm. Groaning, he squeezed his eyes shut and fell back to the bed. The creaking of an opening door filled the room, followed by shoes tapping against the wood.

"Pickering, I need a drink."

Two sighs floated in the silence, trailed by a definite feminine tsk. The maid perhaps? His damp sheets did need changing. Still, he was in no mood to oblige anyone right now. "Go away and come back when I call for you," he growled.

"We'll not," came his cousin Whitney's reply.

Damnation. He opened his eyes and his two nosy, albeit well-meaning, cousins were walking toward him.

He gave Gillian a wink to let her know in no uncertain terms that she could quit worrying he was going to die, which clearly she had been doing since her face was drawn tight. Then he cocked an eyebrow at Whitney, who looked amused rather than concerned. He tugged the dangerously low sheets up over his naked torso. He'd rather not shock his cousins any more than he'd likely already done. They could only be pushed so far before they'd go running to his mother and then there'd be the devil to pay. "Either I'm dead or in hell."

Whitney smirked. "Why hell?"

"Simple," he said. "I've always said I'm a firm believer that hell is where your worst nightmares come true."

Gillian's hands came to her hips. "And having two people that love you at your bedside when you awake from participating in a colossally stupid duel is one of your worst nightmares?"

A bark of masculine laughter erupted from the doorway. Trent squinted toward the entranceway at Sutherland. "What the devil are you wearing?"

Sutherland tipped the odd rounded hat on his head. "It's American fashion."

"You'd do well to remember you live in England now," Trent jokingly reminded his friend while shoving all the way into a sitting position. He clenched his teeth against the pain of his wounded arm. If he was going to be bombarded with relatives telling him what he should have and should not have done and what he should now do, he wanted to be sitting up.

Whitney moved silently behind him, placed a quilt around his shoulders and patted his back. "Lean forward."

He did so without question. She was the one person in the room he'd allow to order him about somewhat, but only because she was likely the only one here who wouldn't presume to tell him what a fool he'd been or demand answers to questions about his past. Whitney pulled the bunched blanket down his back and arranged a mound of pillows behind him before gently pushing him against them. "All better?"

"Yes." He gave her a wink and then said sternly, "You can all go home now."

She frowned but didn't budge. Trent slanted his gaze at Gillian. She shook her head at him as she settled herself at the foot of his bed. "You're being rude," Gillian said, smoothing a hand over his wrinkled bedcovers.

"Oh, pardon me," he said grumpily. "I'd like to see how you'd act if you'd been shot. So come, tell me, how did you know? Did Dinnisfree tell you?"

Whitney tsked at him as she reached back and grasped her husband Drake's hand. Drake shook his head at Trent. "Dinnisfree didn't alert us to your duel or the fact that you were shot."

Trent's three uninvited guests exchanged a glance, no one offering up the unknown informant. Someone on his staff perhaps? They wouldn't dare defy his direct order not to contact his family in the event he came back wounded from the duel. Well, that is, none of them but Pickering. Pickering just might have had the bollocks to do it if the man had been worried Trent was going to die. But he'd only been shot this morning. Hadn't he? "How long have I been unconscious?"

"Two days," Whitney immediately provided.

"Pickering," Trent muttered while reeling from the news that he'd been out for two days. He must have had a bloody awful fever. A quick glance around the room confirmed the fact. Washbasins and rags littered his bedchambers. The window was cracked to allow fresh air, even though the air was chilled. Still... "When did Pickering contact you?" For Pickering's sake, the man better not have gotten in touch with them before today. Trent could forgive Pickering if his butler had truly thought Trent might die, but not if the man simply didn't want to be bothered to care for him.

"It wasn't Pickering," Whitney said and ran a hand over Trent's forehead. "Your fever is gone." She twisted toward her husband. "Drake, darling, will you close the window? I don't want Sin to catch a chill."

"A chill might do him good," Sutherland said. "He seems in a rather hot mood to me."

Trent glared at Sutherland while pushing Whitney's hand off his forehead. "Enough avoiding my question. If not Dinnisfree and not Pickering, who the hell told you about the duel and the fact that I'd been shot?"

"I did."

Trent's chest tightened with recognition. Audrey strolled into the room, dressed head to toe in foreboding black with her hair swept off her delicate face. His chest squeezed further and an undeniable surge of happiness swept through him, followed by a spasm of tension.

"What are you doing here?" he snapped, wincing at the way he sounded. It wasn't that he didn't want to see her. He did, which was part of the problem. "Jesus Christ," he roared, both his cousins jerking at once from their perch on the bed to their feet. He didn't care that he sounded harsh. There was much more at stake than the women's sensibilities. "Am I the only one with sense enough to know she shouldn't be here? Her reputation must be preserved at all cost."

Whitney stared at him with eyes shrewder than any spy he'd ever faced. He got the uncomfortable feeling she was trying to understand him. He didn't want to be understood by her or anyone else. Hell, he didn't even comprehend himself. Seeing Audrey here, knowing she willingly risked her reputation to see him, made that strange tugging on his heart occur again. As he looked at her he wished he had never learned Gwyneth might be alive. He loathed the longing for Audrey. It made him weak. It made him wish for things that would never be. "Get out." He didn't like the faint tremor in his voice, as if some emotion had touched him. He couldn't afford sentiments.

The room grew uncomfortably quiet. Why wasn't anyone leaving? He glanced around at his cousins and Drake and realized they were all staring at Audrey. "I didn't mean Audrey," he said, their honest misinterpretation of his harsh command belatedly dawning on him. "You, you and you"—he pointed in turn to everyone but Audrey—"out. I need a moment to speak in private with Lady Audrey."

Gillian opened her mouth as if to protest, but Whitney—God love his unconventional-to-the-core cousin—linked her arm with her sister's and tugged. "Gillian and I were just about to retire for the evening." When it appeared as if Gillian might protest, Whitney leveled her with an intense glare that made Trent smile. She'd learned that look from him.

"Well, I suppose if my wife is retiring for the night," Sutherland said, nodding toward Whitney, "I should retire as well, unless of course, you need me, Rutherford, to help you get to the chamber pot or wherever else your weakened body won't take you on your own accord."

"My body is not so weak I can't get out of bed and use my good arm to plant my fist in your face," Trent replied, reminding Sutherland of the last time they had crossed each other and the black eye Sutherland had received in the process.

Sutherland grinned. "That's the spirit, Davenport. Good to know you're back from the dead."

He was back all right. Now what to do about his less than cheery future? He waited in silence and tried to keep his gaze off Audrey, so he wouldn't give her the wrong impression. It wouldn't do either of them any good for her to think there could be anything between them. Once the door closed, he caught Audrey staring at him.

Whatever happened, he would not touch her. Her tongue darted out to wet her lips and his loins tightened. "Come closer so we can talk without shouting." Had he just said that?

She shook her head. "I'm perfectly fine over here."

He'd never liked being foiled, whether it was for his own good or not. "Talking too loud might strain me." Was that really a concern? By damn, he had to be stronger than this when it came to her.

She walked near his bed and hesitated by the side. He motioned toward the bed. "Sit, please." And as if that wasn't stupid enough of him, he touched her invitingly curvaceous hip as she sat. Only to position her, so she'd be comfortable, of course. Bloody hell. Of course not. His fingers burned with the contact to her flesh. When Audrey shivered, he snatched his hand away.

The desire to bed her was so strong his blood surged in his veins. He would not touch her again, yet he felt a pull to her that was incredibly hard to resist. It was as if his need for her was a separate part of him with a mind and a plan of its own. He had to master his weakness. Clearing his throat, he affected a neutral tone. "Why are you here further risking your reputation to see me?"

"I—" She dropped her gaze to the floor. "I felt responsible for your being shot since I asked you not to shoot my brother. I had to know you would be okay," she said, her voice tight with emotion. When she looked up · her face was smooth, her eyes neutral, yet her arms were crossed protectively over her chest. The only person for her to guard herself against in this room was him.

Pain that had nothing to do with his injury ripped

through his chest. This was the perfect opportunity effectively to cut all ties between them. He could thank her for her concern and send her on her way back home where she belonged. He hadn't intended to open up another discussion about them, but a deep curiosity to know exactly how she did feel about him gnawed relentlessly in his head. It changed nothing, of course, but he had to know. If she had wanted his love, did she love him? "There's no other reason you came here? Say, for instance, because you care for me and whether I live or die, despite whatever guilt my death might have caused you?"

The heavy lashes that shadowed her cheeks flew up. "Of course I—" She halted her words with a jerk, but she failed to disguise her emotions. Her green eyes burned bright. Trent's breath snagged in his throat as he glimpsed longing, love, desire and desperation flitting across her gaze. She blinked and the emotions were gone.

Had he imagined feelings that weren't truly there? Was he such a cad that he wanted this woman to yearn for him, even though they couldn't be together? An enigmatic smile graced her lips. "I care for you, as past good friends will always care for each other."

Well, that certainly answered his question. Still, something niggled. "How did you slip away from your brother again? It seems he's doing an incredibly poor job watching over you."

She bit her lip and, standing, cast her gaze toward the door. "Father's death has been incredibly hard for Richard, not to mention the guilt he now feels for shooting you dishonorably."

"So he's in his cups?" The addlepated man deserved to be lynched for shooting him after he'd deloped, but for Audrey's sake Trent hoped her brother pulled himself together, and quickly.

She fiddled with her dress. "I believe so."

Trent frowned. Something wasn't right. It wasn't like Audrey to give cryptic answers or not look at him or anyone else in the face when she was speaking. She wasn't a wallflower. Quite the opposite. He grabbed her arm and pulled her back down to his side, forgetting his decision not to touch her. "What's afoot, Audrey?"

When she stubbornly held her silence, he increased his grip. His heart beat with worry for her. "I won't let you leave here until you tell me exactly what's happening with your brother."

"Then we will be here all night," she snapped and pressed her hands against his chest. "Let me go."

It hurt his arm like hell but he held her tight, not letting her budge an inch away from him. He drew her nearer to his side, every beautiful streak of gold in her green eyes shining back at him defiantly. He studied her. The way her black lashes curled up against her creamy eyelids and the perfect slope of her pert nose made her appear delicate yet she was anything but. He wanted her with an intensity that pounded him to the core. Struggling to bring his thoughts away from his lust and to her precarious position, he said, "What is your brother doing?"

"I really couldn't say." She wiggled and grunted with no effect except that he thought her incredibly beautiful. Likely, that would not please her to hear.

"Where is he at this moment?" Her honeysuckle scent tickled his nose and did nothing to help cool his desire.

"Here. There. As I already told you, I really can't say," she answered flippantly.

"Can't or won't say?"

"Does it matter?" She moved restlessly in his arms and glared at him when he increased his hold.

"It matters to me." An awful suspicion filled his mind. "Which is it?"

A deep shuddering sigh came from her and her body went from still to slack as her soft chest pressed against his. "I don't wish to say that I can't say."

God, she was confusing. She'd have made a wonderful spy. She could have talked a thousand circles around Gwyneth, who'd been the smartest woman he'd ever encountered before he met Audrey. "Do you or do you not know where your brother is?"

"*Not.* At this moment."

"When was the last time you did know where your brother was?"

She took a long, deep breath. "Late last night when I came home from seeing you—"

"You were here last night?"

She nodded.

Jesus. She'd not risked her reputation only tonight, but last night as well. It was mindboggling how little care she took for herself and her future. The truth slammed him in the chest like a log. He grunted and released her at once, so that she almost fell off the bed. Immediately, she shoved to her feet. From the day he'd tried to seduce her in the Duchess of Primwitty's bedroom, to the stolen kisses at the picnic and on the terrace, all the way to this moment where he'd hauled her on the bed beside him, he'd taken no more care for her future than she. One of them had to be levelheaded. "You were saying." It took all the will he possessed to sound calm.

"I hired a hackney to bring me here last night, because my brother had taken the coach. When the hackney dropped me at my home I had him leave me at the end of the drive so as not to be discovered in case Richard had returned home." She said this as if it were an everyday occurrence that a lady go gallivanting around at night in hired hackneys to visit a possibly still-married man.

"Of course," he said through clenched teeth. "What else could you do but sneak?"

"Exactly." She gave a perfunctory nod. "I came upon my brother outside of the house arguing with a man."

Alarm shot through Trent. "Who was the man?"

She shrugged. "I didn't recognize him."

"What about his coach?"

Audrey's nose wrinkled and she gazed thoughtfully for a second. "It had no emblem I knew on it."

He swallowed, his throat suddenly dry. "What did the emblem on the coach look like?"

Her brow furrowed together and then she took a quick breath. "I don't recall."

He pressed forward, recognizing her lie the moment it left her lips. "Perchance a snake swirled around some coins?"

Her face drew closed like a shudder. "How utterly ridiculous. No one has an emblem like that."

Nash Wolverton did and he prided himself on always personally collecting the money men deep in debt owed him. Wolverton always did it in his carriage embossed with a snake and coins. The club owner thought it rather funny to poke fun of the way those in the *ton* had their emblems on their carriages. Trent's simmering anger became a scalding fury. "Did you question your brother?"

"Not last night."

The mild unease of earlier exploded. Trent grasped her by the hand. "When, then? This morning? This afternoon? Tonight before you came here?"

She shook her head, mutiny shining from her eyes like sharp daggers. "When I awoke this morning he was gone along with all of his personal belongings."

"God damn your coward brother to hell."

"How dare you!" She wrenched free of him and glared. "He'll come back. I know him. He's scared and embarrassed by what he's done to you."

Trent scrubbed a hand over his face. Fighting wouldn't help her. What would? He scanned through ideas and seized on one. "You need a husband—a protector. Even if your brother does come back he isn't fit to watch over you."

The look of disdain she gave him skewered him. She tossed her hair over her shoulders, her back straightening and her chin rising. "Did you have someone in mind?"

"Me." Where the hell had that come from? Hadn't he put that possibility to rest?

Audrey's eyes widened, then narrowed. "*You.*"

If words could slap, that one was a zinger. He flinched. "I'm partially responsible for the position you find yourself in, so yes, me—if I'm available." He wiped a hand across his damp brow. "I'll go to France and find out one way or the other if my wife is really alive, and if she's not, we'll marry as I told you I'd been planning to suggest before. That is, if you are not already betrothed." He forced himself to say the last sentence. He did not want to take the possibility away from her, as much as it rankled him to leave the chance there.

Obvious contempt contorted her face before she poked him in the chest. "I don't care if you're married or not. I wouldn't have you if...if"—she slapped her palm against his chest with a huff—"if you were the last man on earth and I was being threatened with death."

Trent forced a wry smile to his face, though coldness had set in to every inch of his body. "Careful, my dear, your flattery may go to my head."

"Flattery!" She grunted. "I could say the same to you for your sweet proposal. I will marry for love and then to *only* a man who loves me. There will be scores of them tripping over themselves to adore me the rest of my life. Do you hear me?"

"How can I not? You're screaming." Self-preservation had taken over his tongue. He should soothe her, but his pride demanded he defend himself. Obviously, he'd hurt her, but he hadn't meant to. He'd meant to make things right, if he could, but she was being unreasonable, demanding more than he could give, and damn it all, he wouldn't lie to appease her.

A warning cloud settled on her angry features.

"Audrey," he cautioned. "Don't even think of slapping me again."

She eyed his cheek for a moment, and he could practically see her mind turning and judging. She stiffened and drew her shoulders back. "You." The word was accusatory. "You bring out the worst in me. I've never slapped a soul in my life before you. You make me forget myself."

He knew the feeling. She did the same to him. "What do you want me to say?"

"You're quite incapable of saying what I wanted to hear," she snapped. She turned away, her skirts swishing in the room as her footsteps hurried across the wooden floor and out the door.

"Audrey!" He stumbled out of bed, started toward the door and stopped when the draft hit his bare skin. "Damnation!" he yelled and scanned the room for his clothes. "Pickering, stop her," he shouted as he stumbled toward his wardrobe, not caring if he woke the whole household. Bloody likely his imposing guests had probably all scattered to hide the minute Audrey flung open the door. He grabbed a shirt and pair of breeches out of his wardrobe and struggled into the trousers first. As he gritted his teeth and forced his arm into the shirt, his door swung in with a bang.

Fourteen

Trent gaped at Whitney as she stood in the doorway, hands on her hips and eyes narrowed. "What's this nonsense about you being married?"

He ignored her question and tugged his shirt into place. "Move. I need to speak to Audrey before she leaves."

Whitney blocked his way, unless he chose to bodily move her.

He was considering it when she said, "Audrey's gone. She ran out the door and scrambled into her carriage like the devil himself was after her. I do believe her parting words for you were never to contact her again and that you could read about her in the Society paper when her wedding was announced. Sin," Whitney huffed, "what have you done?"

"What haven't I done?" He moved to his bed and sat.

Within seconds, Whitney was beside him and took his hand. "Tell me."

He wanted to. He suspected he could use a feminine perspective. Trent considered for a moment before speaking. He trusted Whitney. "I can't tell you everything."

She nodded, wise and aware as always. "I assumed you could only say so much based on your rather cryptic answers when questioned previously about your time spent in France. Say—" Her lips pressed together for a moment, then she quirked her mouth. "Does this mean that story you told me so long ago about the woman you loved killing herself because you tried to protect her by leaving her was untrue?"

He stared at her, unsure how much he could admit without giving away too many clues of who he'd been and what he'd done to help Prinny get his messages safely to and from the men guarding Napoleon.

Whitney's eyes searched his. "You do remember, don't you? The one you told me to convince me to confront Drake and tell him I loved him instead of continuing to try and push him away?"

Trent tugged a self-conscious hand through his hair and held his cousin's earnest gaze. "It wasn't true. I was trying to show you how lying could destroy love, so I made the story up. I'm sorry."

"How would you know how lying can destroy love if you've never been in love?"

"I didn't say I'd never been in love."

"Ah, so we are finally at the heart of the problem."

"We are?" He hadn't realized they were trying to get to the heart of his problems. His cousin was for too astute for her good or his.

"Indeed." She nodded. "You loved your secret wife, but she didn't love you."

"Good God, you're blunt." *And correct.* Damn if the truth didn't still smart after all the time that had passed. "I loved my wife and she used me."

"How?"

"I can't say." Damnation. He sounded like Audrey moments ago when he had questioned her.

"Cannot or won't?"

This was ridiculous. It was as if Whitney had taken his role and he was playing at Audrey's evasive one. "Does it matter?" He balled his hands into fists. He wanted his cousin to understand. Someone needed to understand. He didn't want all the women he knew thinking the worst of him. "My wife needed something I had, and to get it, she knew she had to gain my love." He laughed bitterly. "Do you know, thinking back, I do believe she didn't foresee my asking her to marry me. It was never part of her plan."

"No?" Whitney whispered and squeezed his arm comfortingly. "Was she cruel to you?"

His chest tightened unmercifully. Would Whitney consider it cruel that his wife delivered him to the French, knowing they had no qualms about torturing him to the death to get him to decode the message from Prinny to his men guarding Napoleon? Yes, his cousin would. Despite her previous adventure with running away, she'd mostly lived a sheltered life. He clasped her hand. "She has a black heart, but it's been charred by the circumstances she was brought up in, I do believe."

Whitney placed her other hand over their clasped ones. "Listening to you, I wouldn't think you would ever have wanted to marry again, yet I couldn't help but overhear you tell Audrey you would come back and marry her if your wife is not alive. Why do you think you would offer such a thing?"

Because he cared for her. Admired her. Wanted her and if she had to accept a marriage that was not for love as she desired, then by damn he wanted it to be him to marry her if it could be. No longer wishing to discuss his life or feelings, he said, "My, but you have good hearing. Was your ear pressed firmly to the door?"

Her cheeks pinked instantly. "Don't try to circumvent the inquiry."

His cousin's hawk like attention to getting answers would have impressed him at any other time but this one. Now he was annoyed. "I'd like you to stay out of my business," he said pointedly, deciding he definitely no longer wanted another feminine perspective. One angry perspective from Audrey was quite enough.

Whitney smiled. "Like you stayed out of mine?"

He clenched his jaw. "You were mucking things up with Sutherland. I had to intervene."

"Yes, I know you did. But if you'll remember, I specifically told you not to, yet you plotted, lied and pushed Drake and me into each other's company."

"It's not the same," Trent snapped. "You loved Sutherland. You admitted it."

"True." She smirked at him. "I'm a woman; therefore I'm smart enough not to try to deny my true feelings."

This was more than uncomfortable. His cousin was poking where he did not even wish to look himself. "Audrey hates me," Trent said, simply wanting Whitney to quit asking him questions about himself.

"She hates the things you've said to her. Don't men hear *anything* properly?"

Trent started to respond, then stopped. "What does any of this matter? If you were really listening, then you know I may very well be married to someone else."

"Yes, yes. I heard. Will get to that situation in a moment. You still have failed to explain to me why you offered for Audrey just now."

"Honor. Plain and simple." Now maybe his cousin would leave him alone.

Whitney quirked an eyebrow. "Do you really believe that nonsense?"

His cousin's superior attitude was really grating on his nerves. "It's true."

"You love Audrey," Whitney said matter-of-factly.

"No. Certainly, I care for her, amongst other feelings, which is why I was going to offer for her in the first place." He rolled his neck to loosen his tightening muscles, then looked at his cousin. "I think Audrey's smart, witty and beautiful."

Whitney regarded him for a moment while nibbling on her lip. "I could not hear as well as I wanted at the door." Whitney blushed a bit at her confession. "Did you tell her all of that?"

"No. I told her I was partially responsible for the position she now finds herself in and—"

Whitney's snort stretched Trent's patience to the snapping point. "I've had enough of answering your questions. I never liked when I was a schoolboy and someone brought me to task and I like it even less now."

Whitney rolled her eyes, then craned her body toward the door. "Gillian," she called.

Trent expected it to take a minute for his cousin to appear, but she stepped through the entrance seconds after being summoned. Could no one mind their own damn business? He took quick inventory of Gillian. She still wore the gown she'd had on before she'd claimed she was off to bed. Eavesdroppers and meddlers, the lot of them. She'd probably been huddled outside the door this entire time. Behind Gillian a sheepish-looking Sutherland strolled into the room. At least one person in this household had the wherewithal to look as if they were embarrassed for how they were acting.

Sutherland shrugged. "Sorry, Davenport. I told them we ought to stay out of your affairs."

Gillian nudged past Whitney's husband and came to stand by Whitney. "I told you," she said, looking directly at her sister.

"Told you what?" Trent demanded, not liking the fact that his cousins were discussing him and his life as if he weren't here. Their plotting and scheming would invariably wreak havoc for him.

Whitney sighed. "She told me you were just like all other men, but I defended you. I argued that certainly you were not a blooming idiot as most men are when it comes to matters of the heart."

"Now see here," Sutherland protested.

"Sorry, darling." Whitney blew Sutherland a kiss. "You're an exception now. Not before we were married, though."

"Enough," Trent snapped. "I need sleep."

Whitney shook her head. "What you need is a smack on your wounded arm to get your attention. How is it you failed to mention to us in all the time you've been home that you were, or rather possibly still are, married?"

Gillian sat close to his other side. Trent felt caged. Two females who cared for your welfare could be infinitely more dangerous than a hundred who didn't.

Gillian touched his arm. "Can you tell us why it is you don't know for certain if you're married still? Was this the reason you didn't say anything about the marriage in the first place?"

"Yes and no." He refused to say more. The sharing had become ridiculous and relentless.

Gillian's brows puckered together. "Which is which?"

Damn it all. He needed peace. And time to think. Or maybe not, as the only thought in his head was for Audrey. That couldn't be good. He focused on his cousins. "I didn't mention my marriage because I bloody well didn't want to. And I thought my wife was dead. Now it seems she's miraculously resurrected."

"How can that be?" Whitney demanded.

How, indeed. Hadn't he asked himself that same question, but for different reasons. How come he'd been blind and stupid? He took a breath. "I cannot tell you much. Suffice to say I had very good reason to think she was dead. I'm ashamed to admit her loss didn't sadden me."

"Trent," Whitney whispered.

"I know. I feel the weight of my words even as I sit here, but the guilt doesn't make them less true."

"What an unexpected and odd situation," Whitney said, her voice raising a hitch.

"Exactly," he replied. It was like old times. Say something but nothing at all. Sometimes he thought he missed being a spy, but now he was positive he didn't. The life had been exhausting. Never making connections or contacts. Never growing close. Never allowing anyone to truly know you. Maybe that had been the problem? He and Gwyneth had never really known each other. He discerned more about Audrey than he ever had about Gwyneth, and despite the fact that Audrey didn't realize he had been a spy, she comprehended more about him, his likes and dislikes, than Gwyneth ever had. The realization sent an ache through his chest.

Gillian nudged him. "What else will you say?"

"Not much." It was as if he were back in prison, but without the beatings. He frowned, trying to recall if since becoming a spy he'd had a conversation with his family where he uttered more than two nondescript words about his past. No, he didn't think he had.

She gave him a faint smile. "Will you say for example what your wife did to make you hate her so?"

"No," he replied as he caught Whitney's gaze.

Gillian glowered. "Will you explain at another time?"

"Certainly not."

Whitney leaned closer. "Will you tell us anything?"

"Yes." He jostled them both so that they almost fell off their perch on the bed. Across the room, Sutherland chuckled and Trent shot him a grateful smile. "I'm tired and I wish to go to bed.

"How can you sleep at a time like this?" both women cried as one.

"A time like what?" he demanded, his irritation getting the better of his self-control.

"Trent Loxley Rutherford," Whitney huffed, reminding him exactly of how his mother spoke to him when she was angry with him. Even now at four and thirty. It was ridiculous. Truly.

"Yes?" He struggled to regain his cool and manage an even and calm tone.

"How can you retire knowing you've ruined Audrey's life?"

Every muscle in his body tensed at Whitney's accusation. "She told me in no uncertain terms she would have scores of suitors lined up to marry her who worshipped and loved her." The moment the words left his mouth, his jaw dropped open. She had hurt him with that comment, and he hadn't even known it until this second. That she already had the ability to wound him bothered him. If they did marry, he would have to be vigilant in guarding against weakness.

Whitney's eyes rounded with sympathy and her hand came to rest gently on his arm. "What do you plan to do now?"

The tension in his shoulders unknotted at the easier question. "As soon as I recover I plan to go to France and learn the truth of my wife."

Whitney nodded. "That's exactly what I'd do."

"I'm so glad you approve." What if Gwyneth wasn't alive? What if Audrey was still not betrothed when he came home and he could convince her a marriage of convenience would truly be best for her? Even now, surrounded by his cousins, he could feel Audrey's soft skin under his fingertips, smell the honeysuckle scent that lingered on her and hear her tinkling laughter that warmed his heart.

He blinked and realized Whitney was staring steadily at him, her annoyance obvious in the way she tried unsuccessfully not to frown. "It's awful to say this, but I too hope you no longer have a wife."

Shame washed over him. He couldn't chastise Whitney when he'd just had a thought similar in nature. He firmly shut his eyes, praying to God everyone would leave. Silence filled the room, followed by his cousins each leaning in and pecking him on the cheek.

"Good night," Whitney whispered.

"Sweet dreams," Gillian followed in his other ear.

Of late, his dreams had been of nothing but Audrey and it was sweet—torturously so. As the door creaked, he whipped his eyes open and called out, "Whitney, wait."

She turned and hurried back into the room. "Do you have something you want to share?"

He chuckled at the eager anticipation on her face. "No. I have a request."

"Yes?"

"Can you have your modiste make an entire new wardrobe for Audrey and make sure Audrey does not know it came from me?"

Whitney nodded. "I can, but it would be remiss of me if I didn't point out men who simply care for women don't commission secret wardrobes."

"Let it never be said you're remiss."

Whitney heaved a loud sigh. "All right. I'll see it accomplished for you. Does this mean you think you won't be back from France by the time Audrey emerges from mourning?"

"I don't know." He did not want to reveal all of Audrey's problems to Whitney. That was Audrey's choice what to tell and when. As much as he did not want her to find a husband, he wanted her to have the best chance possible and he was the first to admit it was often the pretty picture that caught a man's eye before he was smart enough to look deeper. Ridiculous but true. People of the *ton* would talk if she appeared in shabby gowns when she emerged from mourning, and it was going to be hard enough for her with her father dead and her brother possibly gone for good. He wanted to help her, even if it meant destroying his chance to marry her. As much as he wanted to deny the reality, it could take a long time to discover the truth about Gwyneth and then the truth might be that he was indeed still married.

Aware of his long silent pause, he said, "Sorry. Woolgathering."

Whitney nodded, but her eyes held a gleam of disbelief.

"I simply want to do what I can to help ease Audrey's transition back into Society."

"Are you sure you should? If you help her look too lovely, she may find a husband that much quicker." A frown pulled at Whitney's mouth.

He nudged her chin as he used to do when they were young children. "My wife may still be alive, and it could very well take a long time to discover the truth. Should I ask Audrey to wait? I hardly think she will agree since she is determined to marry for love."

"Oh, Trent." Whitney sniffed and leaned down to give him a tight hug.

He gently pushed her away. "One last favor?"

"Of course." She dabbed at her eyes.

"Watch over her."

Whitney tsked. "As if you need to ask me such a thing."

"That's excellent." Trent felt somewhat better about leaving Audrey to go to France, knowing she would have people looking out for her. "It's all settled, then. Off to bed with you."

Whitney stood. "Will you write me and tell me what you have learned?"

He would not write until he was coming home and only then if he was sure it was safe to do so. "I will," he agreed, hating to add the necessary lie to the hundreds that already weighed him down.

Fifteen

Six Months Later
Kent, London

Audrey sat slumped in her brother's study staring at the mounds of notes from creditors that had piled up since Richard's disappearance. She nibbled on her lip as hopelessness threatened to overwhelm her. However was she going to manage to pay off all the debt they owed? They had only survived this long because she had found a bag of blunt stashed in her father's bureau. It had not been a great deal, but between Ms. Frompington's unexpected but rather well-timed decision to retire and Audrey rationing the remaining food and going to market to only by what was on sell or already cheap, they had managed to get by. But the money was almost gone.

She pursed her lips. She now despised potatoes. And darkness. Going from room to room at night with one lone candle was frustrating but necessary. Bah, she had to quit wallowing in self-pity. Things could be worse. And soon. She had no practical job experience, and even if she had, no trade she could work at would make enough money to pay the current debt, keep the estate running at a bare minimum and feed and clothe herself and her aunt. She laid her head on her forearm and squeezed her eyes shut. If she didn't do something soon they'd starve to death. She wished Richard would come back, so at least the burden of worrying about him would be lifted and they could work to fix things together, but she had not heard a word from him and had no extra money to hire someone to try to find him.

She might have lain there all day, but a knock at her study door forced her to rouse herself. "Come in," she said, trying to force a note of cheerfulness into her voice. To her ears, she sounded strained and anything but cheerful but at least she was making an effort.

Aunt Hillie strolled into the room in such a shocking shade of orange Audrey felt her lower jaw drop open. Even for her aunt, the color was outrageous. Audrey swallowed and chose her words carefully as not to hurt her aunt's feelings. "I see you've wasted no time disposing of your black silk mourning attire."

"Your father's been dead six months and a day. The mourning period is over, and I say we've done his passing more than justice. You've not stepped foot outside of this house in all that time except to bicker at market nor have you let anyone besides that shifty-eyed fox Lord Thortonberry in here."

Audrey frowned. "I don't understand why you dislike Lord Thortonberry so much. He's been nothing but kind to us. What has he done that's gotten under your bonnet? Was it the sweet treats he brought? Or perhaps it was the freshly baked bread from his cook? Yes, that must be it. It wasn't as warm as it should have been, was it?"

Her aunt snickered. "I admit he's done several kind deeds. Of course," her aunt said slowly. "Others—take for instance your three friends that tried to call on you numerous times—would have done kind things for us too, if you'd let them. Yet Lord Thortonberry was the only one you allowed past the front door. You turned everyone else away with paltry excuses that I've no doubt they all knew to be made up."

Audrey stiffened. "You know I had to turn Whitney, Gillian and Sally away."

"I know no such thing." Her aunt plopped in the chair on the other side of the desk and set something down with a clank.

Whitney eyed the tarnished silver tray her aunt's fingers still lingered on. Letters peeped out from underneath Hillie's hold. Undoubtedly, more bills. Audrey looked away from the tray and caught Aunt Hillie's gaze. "Are you playing butler today?"

Her aunt nodded. "You can play cook. I think potatoes are on the menu."

They groaned in unison.

"About your friends," her aunt said, never one to give up on something she wanted to know.

"My friends are too kindhearted and good to end our friendship. What sort of person would I be if I allowed them to remain my friends and become tarnished by the rumors that will swirl about our family when people start to question where Richard is or worse our financial predicament becomes public knowledge?"

Her words were partially true. She did want to protect her friends, but she was also afraid. She'd refused to see them when they tried to visit, because, well, what if they decided once they knew about her family's problems to end their friendship with her? After the betrayals she'd suffered at her father, brother and Trent's hands, she didn't think she could withstand one more person letting her down. It had seemed wise to take the initiative and put distance between herself and the ladies rather than have them do it to her.

Her aunt sighed. "You chose the coward's way. It's not like you, my dear. It's not your nature. You need to be brave now. It's time to live again, my girl." Her aunt speared her with a knowing look. "No more hiding from life behind the excuse of your father's death."

Audrey swallowed hard. One of the things she'd learned in the past six months of keeping company with only her aunt was that her father had grossly underestimated Aunt Hillie more than Audrey had previously considered. The woman was as shrewd as they came. Audrey pretended to straighten the stacks of bills on her desk. "I'm not hiding," she lied.

"Excellent," her aunt replied. "Then you and I can open these letters you received and reply yes, if they happen to be invitations." Her aunt slid the tray she'd brought in across the desk until it was directly in front of Audrey's nose.

The envelopes were small, thick and sealed, much like an invitation would be. She picked them up and a large lump formed in her throat. Tears burned the backs of her eyes when she read whom the correspondences were from. One by one, she opened the notes and gratitude flowed through her. Each of her friends had invited her to various entertainments occurring in Town as the Season was in full swing, and all three women had included a separate note imploring her to come and to let them call on her.

Audrey blinked away the moisture pooling in her eyes. "These are from my friends."

"Oh, really?" Her aunt smiled gently at her.

Audrey walked around the desk, sat in the chair facing her aunt, took her aunt's hands and squeezed them. "Whatever shall I do? I ought not to go."

"Pish posh," her aunt said. "They're grown women. Give them a chance to hear the truth and decide for themselves what they shall do."

"Yes, I suppose," Audrey mumbled, but her hidden fear blossomed in her chest as she thought of going back out into Society and possibly running into Trent. "What if I see *him*?"

Her aunt patted Audrey's knee. "It's bound to happen someday. But if you're truly too desperately afraid to venture back out into Society, then stay here. I won't try to force you, but soon we need to find some sort of employment or we shall starve to death. I can sell my wedding ring." Her aunt held up her hand and her gold wedding band gleamed. For the first time Audrey noticed her aunt's hands shook badly and were oddly misshapen. Audrey clasped her aunt's hand back in hers, and when she did, Aunt Hillie hissed ever so slightly.

"Did I hurt you?" Audrey asked, lessening her grip on her aunt.

"Just a bit. My hands have been bothering me of late."

Her aunt was in no condition to work. She was gaining age and needed to be cared for. It was up to Audrey to provide for them since Richard had fled. The best way she knew to secure their future was to marry, and marry well. The thought left a bitter taste in her mouth and made her stomach turn.

She didn't like the idea of hunting for a husband because she had to. That went against the very grain of the dream she'd always held in her heart and in her hopes to marry for love. Quickly, she cataloged in her mind the jewels of her mother's she'd found in her father's dresser after his death. There wasn't much left but there were four pieces that were worth enough money to get them by for the next several months. She had recently written to Lord Thornberry in London and inquired if he knew of someone who could sell them for her. He was the only one who knew of their circumstances since he had practically forced his way into her home to help her after he had suspected Richard had fled. But she was glad Lord Thortonberry had done what he had. She had come to rely on him in a way.

"I can practically hear you thinking about your plan," Aunt Hillie said.

Audrey nodded. "I was just wondering when I might receive a response from Lord Thortonberry. I do hope he knows someone who can assist us. Those jewels could sustain us for next several months until I can secure a proper husband to save us both from ruin."

"I suppose Lord Byron did say *carpe diem*, but it saddens me to think you would settle for anything less than love."

"It saddens me too, but nevertheless, if I can find a way to sell Mother's jewels, I could buy us a good three months I'd wager."

Her aunt's forehead creased with lines Audrey suspected were caused by worry.

Audrey took a fortifying breath. "You never know what can transpire in three months." She forced a smile. She was determined to sound positive so her aunt wouldn't worry any more than she already was. "Maybe Prince Charming will fall at my feet and declare his love for me." An image of Trent filled her head, and she nearly gasped. For these past six months, she'd not allowed herself to think of how she'd loved the rake, and she wasn't about to permit herself to remember those feelings now.

"I hope so dear."

A knock at the front door echoed down the hall, and Aunt Hillie stood. "You stay here and plan how you're going to find your Prince Charming. Mayhap we'll be able to hire the butler back once we sell the jewelry."

Audrey nodded absently, only briefly wondering who it could be. She knew Lord Thortonberry was in London on business and wouldn't be back to the country for at least three weeks, which was precisely why she had written him when the idea to sell Mother's jewels had struck. She did not have three weeks to wait for Lord Thortonberry to return. Secretly, she suspected he was going to pursue Lady Caroline, who was undoubtedly in London for the Season. Selfishly, Audrey would miss his company, but she would never voice that to him. She wanted him to win the heart of the woman he loved. Someone should have the happiness Audrey had always dreamed of.

Immediately her thoughts turned to Trent. The man was no longer part of her life. Had he gone to France to search for his wife as he had said he was going to? Was he back in London? Was he a widower or not? Gracious alive, she had to stop this. Trent had only offered for her out of a sense of obligation or at best desire. He didn't love her, and he never would. If she couldn't marry the man she had loved, and she didn't fall in love again, maybe she would find a man who had the potential inside him to grow to love her. She didn't want to enter a marriage where she was in love but it wasn't returned. She never wanted to be that vulnerable to a man. Her mother's plight had proven that to her.

Calling on the same will she'd invoked when her mother had died, Audrey shoved the lingering feelings for Trent away. She was a strong woman. She would create a happy life out of the ashes of havoc that swirled around her now. What she needed to figure out immediately was exactly how to go about building that happy life.

Dread filled her chest when she contemplated going to London for the Season once again, but she had little choice. She ran a hand down her mourning dress. If she was going to face possible scorn and cuts direct from people in the *ton,* it would be preferable to confront them in style, but she had no spare blunt to purchase new gowns.

She nibbled on her lip and dismissed her silly wish. There was no place for pride in battle. Any man she wanted to marry would not desire to wed her for her taste in clothing. They should want her for the woman she was on the inside, not how she looked on the outside. Still, she would pull out all her dresses from last season and do her best to make them as presentable as possible since experience had shown her men rarely bothered to try to discover the secrets of a woman's heart if they didn't care for the flesh that encased it.

She drummed her fingers against her thigh. Money was the immediate problem. She may be able to go without new dresses, but they simply had to have a butler in Town. There was no getting by without one there, as she could here in the country. And they needed blunt for food and to keep the house warm and lit.

The tapping of footsteps brought her to her feet and tuning toward the door. Her aunt came through first with a frown on her face. Immediately after her, Lord Thortonberry strode into the room with a huge smile and offered her a leg.

"Lord Thortonberry!" Audrey brushed past her aunt, discreetly giving her a pleading look as she did, and made her way to stand in front of her guest. "Whatever are you doing here? I thought you said you'd be gone several weeks."

"I received your letter and I came right away to assist you."

Audrey was about to ask him why he would do such a thing, when Aunt Hillie harrumphed and then spoke. "Fools rush in where angels fear to tread."

"Aunt Hillie!" Audrey chided.

Her aunt gave her a look of wide-eyed innocence, then leveled Lord Thortonberry with a stare that could only be described as hostile. "Lord Thortonberry, do you know who wrote that?"

He shook his head. "I don't believe I do. I'm terribly sorry."

Aunt Hillie cocked her head. "No matter. I wouldn't

have thought you would, but I'm not above recognizing there's the slightest chance I misjudged someone's character."

Audrey's face heated as she hurried to her aunt and gripped her by the arm. "Aunt Hillie, I think it's time for your nap."

"I don't take a nap."

"Yes, I know," Audrey whispered in her aunt's ear as Lord Thortonberry coughed, Audrey suspected, to cover the sound of Audrey and her aunt's frantic exchange of words. Even now, when her aunt had purposely insulted him, the man was kind. Audrey practically dragged her aunt to the door and gave her a gentle push out of the study. She stepped into the hall for a moment, and making sure to keep her voice low so she wasn't overheard, she said, "I don't know why you dislike him so, but he's my friend and I'm begging you to be kind."

Aunt Hillie pursed her lips. After a moment, she heaved a sigh. "On his own, I don't dislike him particularly, though I feel he is being less than honest, and I'm positive he's not the man for you."

"Heaven above, Aunt Hillie. He doesn't even like me. We're simply friends." With a glance over her shoulder, she confirmed that Lord Thortonberry was sitting and not paying their conversation any mind. She stepped closer to her aunt. "What makes you say he's not the man for me?" Gracious, what possessed her to ask that?

"Your eyes."

"My eyes?" Audrey blinked. "Whatever do my eyes have to do with love?"

"A great deal, my dear. When you look at him, there is no flame in your eyes. Whenever you spoke of Lord Davenport your eyes burned with your feelings."

Audrey clenched her jaw. "My eyes may have burned for him," she whispered low, "but I'll bet if you'd seen his gaze it barely flickered for me."

"Well, it's true I never met the man," Aunt Hillie reluctantly admitted.

Audrey sighed. "Enough. Lord Davenport is no longer of any matter to me, and Lord Thortonberry shouldn't concern you. He isn't here to court me."

"Just remember, *Marry in haste, repent at leisure.*"

Audrey huffed out a breath. "The man is not here to ask me to marry him."

"Perhaps not today," her aunt replied breezily and swirled away to stroll down the hall.

Audrey turned back toward the study and paused before reentering. Lord Thortonberry possessed hair the color of mahogany, dark brown with tints of red. His back was to her and she noted the way he wore his hair longer than fashionable, the edges of his tresses hugging the nape of his neck. His broad shoulders led to a trim waist and well-built form. If memory served correctly, his complexion was kissed by the sun and flawless. He didn't have a single scar, like Trent had on his right cheek. Her belly tightened and a soft sigh escaped her. She'd rather liked Trent's scar. It had made him real and attainable, less like the perfect specimen he was.

Audrey squeezed her eyes shut and struggled to force Trent out of her mind once again. When she reopened them, she focused her gaze on Lord Thortonberry. In truth, the man was very handsome and many debutantes had often giggled when he strolled by. Was her aunt right? Did he want to be more than friends? What of Lady Caroline?

She waited for her breath to catch in her throat or her heart to pound, or her pulse to skitter as it had always done with just one glance in Trent's direction, but she continued to breathe normally, her heart beat steadily, if not dully, and her pulse kept an even, uninterrupted rhythm. Perhaps her feelings would change in time? Egads. This was ridiculous to stand here and ponder her emotions for a man who wanted nothing more than her friendship.

Hurrying back into the study, she decided to take the seat on the same side of the desk as him. "Now," she said while sitting and arranging her skirts, "you must explain why you would rush back home to aid me when you could have simply written and told me who to see about selling my mother's jewels."

A smile tugged at Lord Thortonberry's lips. "The matter is too delicate for you see to it. A man needs to do it, and I assumed you would rather not tell anyone else of your predicament. Also, it occurred to me you might like to go to London for the remainder of the Season now that your mourning period is over, and since you no longer employ anyone but your coachman, I would be remiss not to come back and offer to accompany you for safety reasons."

Truly, she barely employed her coachman. Mr. Barrett was working for her for free and doing odd jobs around Kent to make money. She was too embarrassed to admit that on top of everything else. So she said simply, "Ah, I see." Audrey leaned back in her chair. Her aunt had been dead wrong. Not that it mattered ever so much. "That's very kind of you. I'm sure returning here to so generously offer your services took you away from courting Lady Caroline."

"Lady Caroline?"

Lord Thortonberry's puzzled look baffled Audrey. How could the man forget the name of the woman he was supposedly in love with? A niggling suspicion tried to take root. Blast her aunt. Her words were filling Audrey's head with silly notions. "Surely you've not forgotten Lady Caroline Rosewood, the woman you confessed to caring for. I assumed you'd gone to London to court her."

Lord Thortonberry shifted in his chair. "Did you? No. I went to London on business as I told you. I have to confess I didn't give a thought to Lady Caroline while I was there. Perhaps I'll run into her when I return to London with you."

Audrey narrowed her gaze. "That's not a very good plan. If you like her, you must put yourself in her path. Not rely on fate to help you. Take it from me, fortune doesn't seem to be very accommodating." Lord Thortonberry frowned. Perhaps he was less confident than she'd given him credit for. "Are you shy to approach her? I can help you, you know. Not like last time, but we could think of something."

He cleared his throat. "I couldn't ask you to do that."

"Don't be silly," Audrey said, staring at his twitching lip. She had definitely hit a nerve. "You'd be helping me."

He blinked. "I'd be helping you?"

He sounded so astounded that she laughed. "Yes, indeed. With the estate destitute and Richard gone I have decided I need to go to London and try to find a husband, and assisting you will help to take my mind off the dreaded husband hunt."

His gaze locked on her with the most peculiar expression that for one moment, she considered perhaps her aunt was right and he did care for her. She swallowed, suddenly afraid he might offer for her. He didn't make her tremble just being near her, as Trent once had.

How silly she was. Hadn't she just had the thought that marrying someone who had the potential to love her was better than nothing at all? Why was he still staring so peculiarly? "Is something the matter?"

Lord Thortonberry crossed one leg over the other and studied her for a moment. "Lady Audrey, I wish to—"

"Audrey," Aunt Hillie shrilled, making Audrey startle. She glanced toward the door as her aunt strode into the room.

"I thought you were napping, Aunt," Audrey said pointedly.

"Pish posh." Her aunt waved a hand toward the door. "There are three very determined visitors here to see you."

"Visitors?" Now who could it be?

Her aunt nodded. "They told me to tell you Ladies Sally, Gillian and Whitney are here to visit and they won't take no for an answer."

Despite her misgiving about allowing her friends back into her life, happiness bursts within her chest. She glanced at Lord Thortonberry. "I really must take these callers." Audrey scrambled to her feet and retrieved the jewels from her locked desk drawer. Striding back to Lord Thortonberry she handed them to him. "Take these. We can discuss it further tomorrow, if need be."

He surprised her by clasping her hand and kissing it. "Until tomorrow, my lady." With a quick bow, he turned and headed out the door.

Audrey stood for a moment, gaping, until her aunt's chuckle snapped her out of her stupor. "So," her aunt said, linking arms with Audrey. "Do you believe me now, that Lord Thortonberry doesn't wish to be merely friends with you?"

"Perhaps." Audrey strolled toward the drawing room with her aunt but pulled them to a stop before they drew too near. "Aunt, I've determined that I'll give myself a month to hopefully meet someone I believe I can fall in love with."

"So I take it you don't trust you could fall in love with Lord Thortonberry."

"I'm not sure." Audrey wrung her hands. "I don't feel that strange fluttering I wish I did, but if he declares for me and I've not met another, I may very well consider him. At least if Lord Thortonberry loved me or thought he could, then one of us would be entering the marriage as I always dreamed it would be. Don't you agree?"

"I don't believe I do. I think you should only marry if *you* fall in love. Otherwise, I feel certain you'll be unhappy."

Audrey stiffened her spine. "Aunt Hillie, marrying a man I love may not be practical for me or within my reach." Unspoken was the fact that she had loved Trent. She'd never give her heart to a man who would not return her love. At least she knew if she married someone who loved her, she'd always treat them kindly and surely grow to love them in some sort of way.

"Yes, I suppose that much is true, though I've never cared much for practicality myself, and I've survived thus far."

Audrey clenched her jaw on her response. Her aunt was surviving because she was living here. If things didn't work out for love, then Audrey had to eventually be practical enough for herself and her aunt. Their existence depended on it.

A moment later, Audrey opened the drawing room doors to a hum of chatter that stopped immediately when she entered the room, and then erupted into exclamations of delight. As she was embraced in her friends' arms one by one, her eyes grew teary and a lump of happiness lodged in her throat. Once the welcoming hugs were over, she pulled back and looked at each of them. "If you came all the way from London to insist I attend your parties, there was no need. I already decided I'm coming."

"That's wonderful to hear, dear," Whitney replied, stepping away from her sister and Sally to link her arm through Audrey's left one. "We did come here for that purpose, but we also came to strategize with you."

"Strategize with me?"

"Yes, silly goose," Sally said, moving forward and taking her other arm. "We know your brother has fled."

Audrey tensed and tried to pull away, but both women tugged her toward them at once. "How could you know that?" she demanded.

Whitney quirked her mouth. "Sin told me before he left for France that your brother had disappeared and he bade me to look out for you."

For a moment, Audrey considered asking Whitney to loan her the money to hire someone to find Richard, but since she saw no hope of repaying it, she reluctantly pushed the thought aside and focused on what Whitney had revealed. "Trent asked you to watch over me?" The way his name rolled off her tongue set her heart to racing and made her toes curl in her slippers. Ruthlessly, she mentally quashed her feelings. "How is your illustrious cousin?" The scratchy tightness of her voice was appalling. She didn't want anyone to know how desperately he'd hurt her.

"I'm not sure," Whitney said, her gaze level on Audrey.

Audrey looked down, afraid her face would betray her pounding heart. She ran a smoothing hand over her dress. "Has he not returned from France, then?"

"No, not yet."

Whitney spoke in gentle tones as if Audrey was delicate. Drat it all. It didn't matter if Whitney could see Audrey's face or not. Her friend clearly could tell Trent still had the ability to affect her. That simply wouldn't do. She raised her chin and squared her shoulders. "Well, I hope he's well, but I no longer wish to discuss him."

"We had no intentions of discussing Trent with you. Why would we? You both pointedly told me there is no future between you as things stand," Whitney said with a matter-of-fact tone.

Audrey swallowed to hold the emotions back that suddenly seemed all too raw again. "Well, I'm glad he comprehends where I stood on the matter of us." Her voice hitched, betraying the swirling tempest inside her. Whitney, Sally and Gillian exchanged a swift look that Audrey caught, which included Sally and Gillian inclining their heads toward Whitney as if agreeing on something. Audrey clenched her fists at her sides. Why did her belly clench and her chest feel hollow? If she was so relieved Trent would never bother her again, she should feel nothing but pleased.

"Let's sit for a moment," Whitney murmured and tugged on Audrey's arm to guide her to the settee with Gillian and Sally trailing behind. All three women settled around Audrey, and then Whitney spoke. "I didn't plan on telling you this, but I—"

"Ahem." Gillian and Sally cleared their throats at the same time. Audrey suppressed a smile at the pointed matching looks both women directed at Whitney.

"I beg your pardon," Whitney said. "*We* think you should know that before Sin left he confessed to me that he did not think you would wait for him if he asked you to because you wanted to marry for love. Is this true?"

"Of course it is," Audrey retorted, her anger at Trent slipping out to singe her innocent friend. To Audrey's immense irritation, she found that her hands were shaking. "He so generously offered me a marriage of convenience," she exclaimed with a false note of gratitude. "Of course his very princely proposition was contingent upon his returning without a wife in tow." She laughed in an attempt to cover her pulsing annoyance, but it was useless. She'd never been good at controlling her temper once it got away from her. "I'm afraid I had to decline his proposal, and yes, I said I wanted to marry a man who loves me." She bit down hard on her lip, aware how utterly bitter and angry she sounded. "I'm sorry," she whispered. Losing control of her emotions and unleashing her simmering rage with Trent on her friends was disgusting. He'd reduced her to a deplorable human being. The fiend.

"Darling, don't be sorry," Sally crooned as only a

duchess could do. "If I'd been in your shoes I might have found a pistol and shot the man in the other arm."

Audrey laughed again, but this time it was genuine.

"Truly, you've no need to apologize," Gillian added. "Trent is..." Her face took on a thoughtful look.

"Enigmatic," Sally said.

"Emotionally scarred," Gillian added.

"Unpredictable." Whitney cocked her head and eyed Audrey.

Audrey took a deep breath. "Unforgettable," she blurted, then slapped her hand over her mouth. Her cheeks blazed with embarrassment. After a long awkward silence, she slid her hand away. "I meant to say unforgivable."

"Of course you did. The words are so very similar." Whitney gave her a sage look. "Well, enough talk of him since it won't help you now. We need to discuss your return to Society."

Audrey nodded. "Are there any rumors swirling about me?"

"Not at all." Whitney smiled cheerfully. "No one knows about the duel or whatever else occurred that night. We don't even know all the details. Do you care to share?"

"No," she said with a smile, feeling lighter now that she knew her secrets were safe. "Not being the talk of the *ton* should make finding a husband much easier."

"I never said your family wasn't the latest on dit."

"You just did," Audrey exclaimed.

"No." Whitney shook her head. "I said your ruination wasn't all the gossip. Unfortunately your family's debt was leaked by someone and your, um, lack of funds, for a nicer way of putting it, *is* all the chatter."

"Heavens." Audrey pressed a hand to her aching head. Disturbing quakes disrupted the brief serenity she'd experienced for a moment. "That won't make finding a husband easy, especially in the short amount of time I have."

"Just to be clear so we all know the terms we are working under." Sally leaned forward, her brows rising high over her eyes. "You require that you love your husband."

Audrey bit her lip. "I do, but I concede that I may have to be willing to settle for man who thinks he loves me or can grow to love me." A vivid memory of her mother's constant unhappy face filled Audrey's mind. She shuddered. If only she would meet a man who made her feel as Trent did. Or had. She feared that would never happen, but she had to try.

$\mathcal{Sixteen}$

Paris, France

After six months in France of trying to discover if Gwyneth was dead or alive Trent was on the verge of securing his answer, he hoped. He peered out the window directly to his left and stared at the blue waters of the Seine. He counted the many boats navigating down the river, but the ritual did not calm him as it had many times before. Needing an anchor of peace, he wandered his gaze across the stone Pont Neuf bridge. The beautiful construction of the bridge filled him with wonder as always. He tried to imagine how long it must have taken the workers to build the five arches that joined the left bank to Île de la Cité and the seven arches that joined the bridge to the right bank of the city. And how they must have agonized to create the perfectly jutting bastions.

Clanking glasses broke his concentration and stole his peace like a swift pickpocket. Tension once again coiled through him. The sun faded fast in the bright orange sky and cast lengthening shadows through the windows and into the pub. Shadows were good, though. The corner table he had chosen at L'abreuvoir now sat in near darkness. A pub girl came around to light a taper, but he shook his head and with a smile she moved away. Smoke lay heavy in the pub's air, which suited him perfectly.

The haze of grayish white made seeing difficult and helped to disguise him, though he'd taken pains since the moment he set foot in Paris to mask himself. He had taken even longer with his disguise today, since Gwyneth's brother, Pierre, would soon be here and he didn't want Pierre to recognize him.

At this moment, he would have given a week of his life to rid himself of the lengths he'd gone to in an effort to mask his appearance. The full beard covering his face bothered him like an itch he couldn't get to, even after three months of it being completely grown in. He smelled of fish, which he'd never cared for and liked even less now that he'd rubbed the slimy things on his body to attain the stench of a seaman. The wool coat, its collar high and pressed against his cheek, irritated him, but that could have been his damn surly mood.

Paris stunk and he was sick of French accents. He longed for London and the clipped tones of his family and friends. Audrey's image swirled in his head as it did every day since he'd been gone, but he forced it away. Now was not the time to allow his focus to waver. He took a large swig of ale to keep up his pretense of a sailor on a mission to get deep in his cups. His hair ended up in his mouth as he drank.

Damnation. He gripped the large mug of ale in an effort to quell his instinct to put the long hair that hung around his face to order. After years of wearing his hair much shorter, having it touch his neck rankled him but served the purpose of further shielding his face and most importantly his scar. He covered it every day with the makeup Claudia, a theater girl he had met when he arrived here, had given him when offered the right amount of money to do so without questions. Unease danced over his skin. Under the clump of cream, he could detect the raised line that was uneven with the rest of his skin. If he could distinguish it, then so could Pierre, and Gwyneth's brother discovering he was still alive would be tedious and potentially dangerous, considering the man wanted him dead possibly bad enough to follow him to London and put his family in danger. It was much simpler for Pierre to continue to think Trent had died trying to escape France.

"Did you hear me, Monsieur Bernard?"

Trent jerked with the belated realization that he was being spoken to. God, how he'd grown soft. He would have never failed to respond immediately to his cover name before. He set his mug down and flicked his eyes toward the table directly to his right and within easy hearing distance. "Non. Pardon me. What did you say?"

From the creaky wooden chair she sat in, Bridgette Morel gave him an irritated glance that made her so startlingly resemble Gwyneth, Trent was robbed of the ability to speak for a moment. His mind turned like a slow crank, foggily reminding him Bridgette was not Gwyneth, but the younger sister he'd never known existed.

Bridgette shook her head and muttered something about Englishmen Trent couldn't quite make out. She cleared her throat and cocked her head. "I said it shouldn't be long now." Even when she spoke English, her heavy French accent made her hard to understand.

Trent nodded. Five months of research had uncovered the very well hidden, seemingly harmless Bridgette, who was a poor seamstress struggling to make ends meet. It hadn't been hard to convince her he was a former discarded lover of Gwyneth's who was still desperately in love with her and wanted to find her. It had been even less difficult to convince Bridgette to help him after she'd seen the full bag of coin he offered to pay her to contact her brother and find out for certain where Gwyneth was.

"Il est ici," Bridgette murmured.

Trent took in her flared nostrils and tightened features.

His entire body tensed as he pushed his chair farther into the shadows. Without moving a muscle, he scanned the room. "Where. Where do you see your brother?" he asked low enough only she could hear.

"At the bar," she said out of the side of her mouth.

Trent searched the row of men at the bar but did not see Pierre. He slowly retraced the men once more. Too short. Too tall. Bald. Pierre had a thick head of hair. The bald man lifted his hand and waived at Bridgette.

"Mon dieu," Bridgette murmured, raising her hand and waving back. "Pierre looks terrible."

Trent squinted through the haze of smoke at the bald man weaving his way toward Bridgette. Once the man was near enough to see his face, a cold knot formed in Trent's stomach. He'd recognize Pierre's slanted cat like eyes anywhere. Automatically, Trent hunched over his table, affecting the look of a man deep in his cups and pulled the hat on his head down farther to make it impossible for Pierre to see his eyes.

If Trent didn't hate Pierre so much he'd pity the man. He'd been robust and healthy last time Trent had seen him. Now he was a hollow-eyed skeletal figure with a sallow complexion. Pierre was sick. Fate had found Pierre and dealt him the cards he so richly deserved.

As Pierre walked slowly past Trent's table, a sneer twisted the man's thin lips while he briefly took in Trent and dismissed him in the same instant. Trent held in a snort. Pierre clearly still considered himself better than most men. Blithering fool. Trent's fingers twitched with the need to grasp the pistol hidden under his coat. He remained still, not breathing until Pierre stopped in front of Bridgette.

For a long moment, there was an awkward silence, and then Pierre leaned forward, appearing as if he would embrace his sister, but right before touching her, he awkwardly stopped himself. Trent frowned. It was as if Pierre had remembered something. He spoke with a scratchy, strained voice in rapid French. It took several seconds for Trent to start to translate fast enough to understand their conversation.

After saying hello, Pierre eased himself into the seat across from Bridgette. Bridgette was smiling, but her nostrils were still flared, her shoulders held rigid and her hands clasped tightly in front of her. Damnation. *Don't come apart, Bridgette.*

Keeping up his charade, he took a sip of the bitter ale in front of him and swiped his filth-covered hand over his mouth. The scent of fish nearly gagged him. If he could stand this, then surely Bridgette could remember to pretend she was here to reunite with Pierre and

Gwyneth. Trent knew she would have never agreed to meet her siblings and get the information he sought if she didn't so desperately need the money. After tonight, he'd supply Bridgette with enough coin to move far away to a much cleaner, nicer place where Pierre and Gwyneth, if she was alive, wouldn't find her, if she wished it.

Where was Gwyneth? He scanned the room and as he did, Gwyneth's name being spoken in conversation caught his attention. He abandoned searching for her and concentrated on the conversation going on at the table beside him. As if Bridgette had read his thoughts, she voiced the same question to Pierre. Gwyneth's brother shook his head, his face falling. "Morte."

Dead. Trent leaned forward, his pulse quickening. There was no reason for Pierre to lie to Bridgette. Still, Trent wanted to hear the details, watch Pierre's expression and discern his voice to judge the truth of the matter. Then once he thought he had heard the truth, he would meticulously check what he had heard. Bridgette knew this. She unclasped her hands and swiped at the moisture pulling in her eyes. "Comment est-elle morte?"

Trent listened intently as between bouts of coughing Pierre's voice hitched and wobbled while he described Gwyneth's death from consumption and Pierre standing with Nicolaus Comier, the priest who had blessed Gwyneth, read the last rites to her and stood with Pierre as they burned her body for fear of the consumption lingering and spreading. Trent's gut twisted tighter with each gritty detail revealed. She had wasted away day by day, coughing up blood and shrinking to nothing. Icy pinpricks danced across his skin. Pierre took a shuddering breath, grew quiet and then coughed violently into a handkerchief. He was young, but a stranger would never know it by glance. His sallow skin clung to his bones. When his coughing bout was over, Pierre laid the wadded linen square on the table, the crimson clots of blood against the cream easily discernible.

Trent's stomach clenched with a strange mixture of emotions. Bitter sadness, disbelief and pity squeezed his chest. No matter what Gwyneth had done, he wouldn't have wished such a slow, torturous death on her. Pierre coughed again.

Bridgette swiped at the tears coursing down her face. "Et vous?"

Pierre nodded. He too had consumption.

An hour later with Pierre freshly departed, Trent stood alone in the bitter cold and dark with Bridgette. She took his hand and squeezed. "I'm sorry you never got to see her again, but I fear it was for the best. She had an unkind heart."

Trent nodded. He didn't want his voice to betray to Bridgette how much he agreed with her. There was no point causing her unnecessary pain.

Bridgette sniffed as she took the blunt and coin and then her eyes widened considerably as she counted the money. "Monsieur, this is not what we agreed on." She held some of the money out to him.

He shook his head. "Take it. Move away if you wish. Buy a new life. You seem a nice woman. Give yourself the chance your sister never got."

Bridgette sniffed again. "Thank you," she whispered and then looked up at him with tears shimmering in her eyes. "What will you do now? Go home to England?"

First he would double-check what Pierre had told Bridgette and speak to the priest who had delivered Gwyneth her last rites, but he would not tell Bridgette any of this. Trent nodded. "Yes, home to England. Shall I fetch you a carriage?"

"No. I'll walk to clear my head. Part of me wants to flee this place immediately but part of me feels obligated to care for my brother since he's dying."

Trent wanted to encourage her to flee Pierre, but he kept his silence. It was her decision to make and Pierre was so sick now, Trent didn't think he could gather enough energy to harm anyone. Besides, why would the man harm the sister he seemed to love? "I need to be going."

She gave him a tremulous smile. "Au revoir. I hope you meet a nice Englishwoman to fall in love with." She pulled her coat closed and walked in the opposite direction he would be going.

Trent fought memories of Gwyneth and Audrey as he waited for a hackney to pass by that he could wave to him. All he needed to concentrate on now was the task at hand. After a few moments, a hackney rattled down the cobblestone street and pulled up to him. He directed the driver to the small church that had been near where he and Gwyneth lived for the short time he thought they were happily married. If that was not Nicolaus Comier's parish, perhaps someone there would know of him and could point Trent in the right direction.

As the hackney rattled across the bridge he studied Notre Dame Cathedral, determined not to think on his future but simply the architecture, yet all he could think was he would love to bring Audrey here and roam the streets of Paris, filling her inquisitive mind with the rich history of the city. He balled his hands into fists. If he received the needed confirmation of Gwyneth's death from the priest, he intended to head home and see if he could convince Audrey to marry him, if she still hadn't met anyone else.

His desire for her burned no less than the day he last saw her. In fact, it was like a disease consuming him. If he could have her in his bed, the ache for her, the need to be near her, see her, touch her, hear her, would go away. Or lessen to a dull roar he could live with. It had to.

The hackney jerked to a halt and Trent descended, gave the man some coins and strode into the tiny white chapel not three streets from where he and Gwyneth had lived. His footsteps echoed on the wooden floor as he strolled toward the front of the chapel where a priest, dressed in his robes, stood lighting candles. Trent quelled the anticipation building within him. Likely, this would be the first of many chapels he had to visit.

The priest looked up as Trent neared the front of the church. He blew out the candle he held and walked down the steps to Trent. The man was young with kind blue eyes and a bulbous nose. He smiled, showing rather brown teeth. "Puis-je vous aider?"

Trent certainly hoped the priest could help him. And in English preferably. "Parlais-vous anglais?"

The priest broke out into a grin. "Yes, but of course. What can I do for you?"

"I'm looking for a priest named Nicolaus Comier."

"But that is me!" he exclaimed, his deep voice echoing in the empty room.

Trent felt his lips pull into a smile. "Excellent. Finding you is the least uncomplicated thing I've done in a long time."

The priest tipped his head. "I'm glad to be of service, monsieur."

Trent dug into his coat pocket and pulled out the only picture he had ever had of Gwyneth. It was the size of the ends of two of his fingers and encased in a silver locket. He ran his hand over the smooth outer surface before opening the locket. He handed it to the priest. "Do you know this woman?"

The priest held the locket close to his face and squinted. A memory of when he had accidentally found her locket flashed in his head. She has asked him to hand her some unmentionables. The rough wood of the drawer scraped his fingers as he pushed the skirts aside to look for the unmentionable. Something cool was at the bottom. He took the locket out and grinned. He would have her picture fitted into a nicer one and surprise her.

Forcing his attention back to the church, he found the priest staring at him. "I knew her. She's dead. Of consumption. I helped her brother burn her body. I'm so sorry. Was she a friend of yours?"

No. "Yes. I had heard she was dead, but I wanted to be certain."

The priest clasped a hand on Trent's shoulder. "I'm sorry. Would you like a minute alone? Or I could stay and pray with you?"

"Alone would be good," Trent replied. He would feel an utter phony praying with the priest over Gwyneth. Once he was alone he sat in the first pew and stared at the tiny picture of her face. He had dropped the locket when Gwyneth knocked him over the head with the end of a pistol. When he had gone back to the house after escaping prison and seen her burned body, he had picked up the locket, which was lying by the door on his way out. He did not know why. Maybe to remind himself never to be a damned fool again for love.

She was dead. He did not feel happy, thank God. He felt sad for her. For himself. Placing the locket on the dark pew, he stood and walked out the door.

England

AUDREY STOOD IN THE MIDDLE of her entrance hall while directing which trunks to load onto the carriage first and which should be settled last. Somewhere above stairs, the sound of her aunt's humming, as she undoubtedly dressed for their trip to London, drifted down to Audrey. Her stomach tightened with nerves. Soon she would be in London and attempting to reenter Society and find a husband. It was imperative nothing went wrong.

A knock at the door made her smile. Lord Thortonberry was punctual as always. She wasn't sure how she could ever repay him for all his kindnesses. These past few days, he had been an invaluable help getting the house ready to depart for the Season. The man didn't have a pretentious bone in his body, and she'd grown to value his friendship, even as she'd come to suspect he might possibly want to be more than friends.

She still wasn't sure how she felt in that regard, since her heart had yet to flutter when he entered the room. Then again, considering the devil who'd last made her heart flutter then broke it, a calm heart was probably a good thing.

"Shall I get the door, my lady?"

Audrey glanced at Mr. Barrett, who precariously balanced an enormous trunk on his shoulder. "Goodness, no. I'll get it. You can take that trunk to the carriage."

She strolled to the door, opened it to a smiling Lord Thortonberry and waved him in as Mr. Barrett made his way out the door. Lord Thortonberry frowned as he stepped inside. "I wish you would allow my servants to come over and assist you."

"No. I don't want any charity."

Something kindled in Lord Thortonberry's eyes, but exactly what she was seeing, she wasn't sure. He held out a small purse to her. "My solicitor sold your jewels."

She took the purse and struggled to resist the urge to look inside to see if the jewels had brought enough money to survive the next couple of months.

A gentle smile pulled at his lips. "I hope you don't mind, but I took the liberty of requiring my solicitor check with me before accepting an offer for your gems."

Audrey's brows pulled together. "Why did you do that?"

"I wanted to make sure he secured the best possible price. I think you'll be pleased. Why don't you look?"

Her fingers tightened involuntarily around the silk purse. "I'll wait." She was dying to peek, but her situation was already far too embarrassing without displaying her desperation.

He plucked the purse out of her fingers and opened it before she could protest. Withdrawing the money with a flourish, he handed it to her palm-up with a stern expression on his face. "There is no shame in wanting to make sure you have enough money to live on. Please don't ever feel embarrassed over such a thing with me."

His words tugged at her heart, but in a warm, fuzzy way, much like how she felt when Sally, Whitney and Gillian had shown up here. She glanced down to hide the confusion stirring within her. She cared for him as a friend, but if he asked to court her, could she think of him as more?

As she counted the money in her hands, her heart raced and an unstoppable grin spread across her face. There was enough money to live on for the next four months if they were very careful. Looking up, she caught him gazing intently at her. Her breath caught in her throat. She'd seen that look before in Trent's eyes and thought it had meant he cared for her. Seeing it now in Lord Thortonberry's eyes did not rouse the same breathless joy within her as when she'd believed Trent loved her, but she did feel something for Lord Thortonberry. Maybe she would never feel for a man what she'd felt for Trent. Maybe what Trent had inspired in her only came along once in a lifetime, or maybe she just needed to truly forget the devil in order to really open her heart to another man. Not that Lord Thortonberry was asking for her heart.

"Lady Audrey."

His deep voice startled her out of her musings. Heat singed her cheeks. What must he think of her standing here staring into the air and not talking? "I'm sorry. I was woolgathering."

"Over Davenport?"

The heat burning her cheeks made its way rapidly down her neck and chest. She didn't need to glance down to know her chest was splotchy. Clearing her throat, she prayed she sounded convincing. "Certainly not. I never think of that scoundrel."

Lord Thortonberry's eyebrows shot up and an amused smile pulled at his lips.

Perhaps the use of the word *scoundrel* had given her away. Drat it all. She longed to be able to say truthfully she'd forgotten the glittering green-eyed thief of hearts.

Lord Thortonberry's gaze raked over her twice before he spoke. "He's not worth you, nor the heartache you still nurture for him."

Her heart pounded viciously against her breastbone. Lord Thortonberry may well be right. After all, she'd had the same thoughts, but it didn't change how she felt. Still, maybe if she tried harder, she could really forget Trent. She swallowed, her throat dry with her nerves. "Do you have a suggestion?"

"As a matter of fact, I do. I propose you need to fall in love with another man."

His gold-flecked eyes smoldered. If she'd been uncertain previously, she wasn't anymore. Lord Thortonberry wanted her. Her stomach knotted with anxiety. With a little encouragement, he would probably court her and all her financial problems would be solved. She knew exactly what to say, but the words stuck in her throat.

When the front door swung open and Mr. Barrett strode in with an armful of packages, her relief was so immediate her legs trembled. "Mr. Barrett, what do you have there?"

"These packages were just delivered for you, my lady."

She frowned and waved a hand toward the hall table. "Set them there." She followed Mr. Barrett to the table. There were seven packages in all, each labeled from Madam Marmont's dress shop. Behind her, she could feel Lord Thortonberry gazing over her shoulder.

"Are you going to open your packages?"

His breath wafted over her. She inched a little closer to the table to put a respectable distance between them. "Yes, of course. My friends must have sent me something, though I told them not to." With trembling fingers, she quickly opened the first package. She couldn't stop the delighted gasp that filled her when she saw the sapphire gossamer gown nestled in the tissue. On top of the gown was a small card. As she read it, confusion swarmed her.

Dear Lady Cringlewood,

I do so hope these gowns, unmentionables, etc. meet all the requirements that were set before me by your admirer. The silver gown will be done in time for the upcoming ball, as your admirer specifically requested. If you will come see me when you reach London, I will fit you to make sure it's perfect for him and you.

All the best,
Madam Marmont

Audrey froze, very aware of Lord Thortonberry standing so near she could hear each breath he took and feel the heat of his body. He was the only man who knew she was coming to London, and he understood very well she couldn't afford new gowns. His thoughtfulness and generosity touched her to her core. Slowly, she turned toward him and inhaled sharply at just how close he was. She started to fidget but forced herself to stand still. "You shouldn't have had these gowns made, but I vow it's the nicest thing any man has ever done for me."

He swallowed repeatedly, his throat visibly moving in

his neck as he did so. Did he think himself a fool for what he had done, since she hadn't commented earlier on his proposal that she fall in love with another man? The last thing she ever wanted to do was hurt him. "Lord Thortonberry—"

"Can I speak first, Lady Audrey?"

She pressed her lips together and nodded.

He raked a hand through his hair. "I've cared for you for years."

"What about Lady Caroline?" she squeaked.

"It was a ruse to get close to you. I'd tried everything else I could think of, but you never noticed me."

Her cheeks heated instantly. "I noticed you," she whispered.

"As a friend."

That was true. She couldn't deny it.

He gently grasped her elbow. "I know you think you loved Davenport, even though you deny it, but I'm begging you to give me a chance. He's not here, and I don't want to hurt you, but I don't see him as the type to ever marry you. I want to marry you."

"You do?" Her heart thumped wildly, but more out of fear than excitement.

"I do. I've known forever that you're perfect for me. You're strong, determined and brilliant, and you have my heart in your hands."

"Lord Thortonberry," she chided, trying to tug her elbow away. How she'd longed to hear similar words from Trent. Why must she hear them now and not feel as she should?

"Please." He tightened his grip on her elbow, not painfully but with enough pressure that she stilled and met his beseeching gaze. "I'm right for you and good for you. I would never let you down and I would always treasure you, if you would just give me the chance."

How could she not? She nodded. "All right. I promise when I'm in London for the Season to give you a proper chance."

A smile of relief spread across his face and he hugged her to him just as her aunt entered the room. Without a word, her aunt shook her head and tsked. Audrey disentangled herself while glaring at her disapproving aunt. "We better get going. I think a storm may be coming and we don't want to be caught in it as we make our way to London."

"Yes, all right," Lord Thortonberry agreed.

Audrey nearly sighed with relief. Her aunt took her by the elbow and pulled her toward the door. As they stepped outside, Aunt Hillie pressed close to her and whispered under her breath, "The weather looks perfectly lovely to me."

Audrey tensed. "Do be quiet. If I say the weather looks dreadful can you not simply agree?"

"Do you wish me to agree with every ridiculous thing you do or say?"

"Yes," Audrey snapped and stormed toward the carriage, wishing she felt more like the giddy girl she had when she'd gone to London to see Trent instead of like a beleaguered lady going off to participate in a dreadful task otherwise known as the Season.

Seventeen

London, England

By God, it was wonderful to be back on English soil. Trent whistled as he strolled into White's. According to the invitation from the Duke and Duchess of Primwitty, he had a good half hour before he needed to worry about making his way to their home for their annual ball of the Season. He was in a fine mood, but one's mood could always be made a little finer with a glass of whiskey. The liquor would also serve to settle the tension coiling through him. Leave it to an impending encounter with Audrey to make him feel like a schoolboy about to embark on his first attempt at courting.

He grinned in anticipation. He didn't expect Audrey to welcome him with open arms, but nevertheless he was looking forward to the challenge of softening her. He was also anticipating seeing her in the silver silk gown he'd written to his cousin to have Madam Marmont make. In his dreams, she'd looked stunning in an almost sheer gown of silver. Of course, this gown would not be sheer, but he had no doubt she'd be breathtaking.

He would place his entire fortune on the gamble that the reality of her in the gown was better. The silver should perfectly match the flecks in her eyes and contrast nicely with her rich black hair. He warmed just imagining her in the creation. Better yet, he wanted to imagine taking her out of it. Not tonight, of course, but soon, once she realized they were a perfect match even without declarations of the heart.

Trent scanned the few men standing in the doorway of White's but didn't see Dinnisfree. His friend's note had said to meet him here. When Trent had returned from France yesterday, he had sent word to his family and Dinnisfree, though Dinnisfree had already known when to expect him. Trent had written him after he found out Gwyneth was truly gone, and told Dinnisfree he was coming home. And knowing Dinnisfree, he'd likely been keeping a watchful eye on Trent's house in his absence. He'd have to thank his friend for his concern.

Trent moved past the crowd in the doorway and swept the room for the duke. His friend was nowhere in sight, but there was an interesting crowd gathered around White's infamous betting book. It had been ages since he'd done something as carefree as place a bet. He strolled leisurely toward the book, nodding to various acquaintances as he went. The strange looks he received in return struck him as odd.

Even stranger was the way the crowd of men gathered around the betting book parted for him. More awkward greetings, a scattering of mumblings and a few jovial, forced-sounding hellos came to him as he walked up to the book.

Dinnisfree stood right by the book with wads of blunt clutched in his fists. "Ah, Davenport," Dinnisfree boomed. "Gentlemen, see how finely Davenport is dressed? How he fills out his coat. How his gaze pierces. Mark my words, gentlemen, the lady in question will not be able to resist him. I don't care if she has been laughing and dancing on the arm of the Marquess of Thortonberry for two weeks. I tell you, no man is a match for my friend."

The men erupted into noise as more bills waved in the air before being shoved at Dinnisfree. Calls of *double me down* and *increase my bet* sounded around Trent. Anger started to simmer deep within. Anything having to do with Thortonberry was bound to be nefarious, and deadly for the man if the woman in question was Audrey. Trent cleared his throat, hoping Dinnisfree would take a hint and excuse himself. His friend grinned in return.

Dinnisfree bandied a hand in Trent's direction. "Gentlemen, if you haven't bet, feast your eyes on the only man who could possibly win. His hair may be a bit too long, but his tongue is silver. Speak, Davenport, and let these men hear how you will woo Lady Audrey and therefore win her heart and money for them."

Damn Dinnisfree. What the devil was he up to? Trent snatched up the book and searched the bets for anything that might catch his eye. He moved his finger over a sentence and stopped, his anger going from a simmer to a boil.

Lord Justin Holleman, the Duke of Dinnisfree, wagers twenty pounds against Mr. Drake Sutherland that Lord Rutherford, the Marquess of Davenport, will win the heart and therefore the hand of Lady Audrey Cringlewood away from the current forerunning suitor, Lord Clayworth, the Marquess of Thortonberry.

Black fury swept through him. Thortonberry would never be Audrey's husband. Trent may not be able to give her the love she desired, but Thortonberry would not even give her fidelity. He'd come back just in time. Trent threw the book on the table and swept his gaze over the silent group of men. "I'll stake my entire fortune on me," he snarled before turning on his heel and storming out the front door.

The stifling air that enveloped him as he pounded down the steps and onto the street did nothing to cool his temper. He headed for his carriage that still stood at the curb. His coachman blinked at him in surprise. "My lord, are you already leaving?"

Trent nodded. "Take me to Lady Whitney's house." The little fiend had some explaining to do. He didn't doubt for a minute she was somehow behind some part or possibly all of this. The coachman started to nod, but Trent held up a hand, rethinking his command. "Never mind that. Take me to the Duke and Duchess of Primwitty's home."

He slammed the carriage door shut only to have it yanked open as Dinnisfree scrambled in. "Smart move going to the Primwitty home first. You don't want to give

Thortonberry one more minute to gain ground on you. I've lots of coin riding on you."

Trent glared at his friend. "Didn't I tell you to keep Thortonberry away from her?"

"You did." Dinnisfree tugged his coattails out from under him before settling himself.

"Then why the hell didn't you?"

Dinnisfree withdrew a flask from his coat. Slowly, and Trent suspected to get on his last nerve, Dinnisfree unscrewed the top and tipped the container up. After he took a sip, he swiped a hand across his lips and settled the cap before speaking. "I trailed the man the entire first week they were here. He never once visited a hellfire club."

"You're sure?" Trent's brow furrowed.

Dinnisfree leaned forward in his seat. "As sure as I possibly can be. I could not watch him every waking moment, so technically, he could have gone when I slept, but you know how little I sleep."

"Yet you do," Trent said flatly. "So the possibility exists that the man did indeed go to the hellfire clubs while you were sleeping."

"I suppose," Dinnisfree grumbled. But Lady Whitney assured me when Lady Audrey came out of mourning two weeks ago and traveled to London that she and Sutherland were personally watching over her, and when your cousin seemed pleased that Lord Thortonberry was courting Lady Audrey and I had not seen him at the hellfire clubs, I decided not to interfere. I assumed your cousin new best. There are rumors swirling around the *ton* about Lady Audrey's family."

Trent nodded, having suspected that would happen.

Dinnisfree continued. "In light of the rumors, I thought your cousin best situated to help Lady Audrey. Of course, then I got your letter telling me you were a widower and would be back in a week, but I felt I should leave the matter of Lady Audrey to you."

Trent grunted. He'd been right. His cousin had a hand in this, but why the devil was she pushing Lady Audrey into Thortonberry's arms when Trent had very plainly stated in the missive he had sent that he had every intention of coming back to London posthaste and marrying Audrey? He tried to think back to his exact wording, but he couldn't recall it, but damn it, he was sure he'd made his intent clear that he still believed he and Lady Audrey could have a very mutually beneficial marriage. Of course, he could not know for certain what his cousin had thought since she had no way of getting a letter to him.

Trent sat back in his seat as his frustration mounted. He did not believe Thortonberry was a changed man, but not only that, Trent wanted Audrey for himself. "When Lady Audrey arrives at the ball will you keep Thortonberry busy if he's with her?"

"I take it you'll be trying to win my money I put on the bet?"

"I will."

"Please tell me you've a better strategy than offering the lady a loveless marriage of convenience."

"I will offer her the moon and the stars," Trent said half-jokingly.

Dinnisfree chuckled. "I fear, my friend, the lady will demand more than that to even spare you the time of day again."

"I prefer you better when you're quiet and drinking," Trent growled, not liking the fact that Dinnisfree had touched on the one fear Trent possessed when it came to winning Audrey.

AUDREY STOOD BESIDE WHITNEY AND her husband at the edge of the dance floor while waiting for Lord Thortonberry to return with her punch. There was something very odd going on, but she wasn't sure what it was. Whitney was acting unusually edgy, fidgeting with her dress and moving from foot to foot, while her husband, a normally affable gentleman had barely said a word and kept glancing up toward the top of the staircase where the guests were being announced as they entered the Duke and Duchess of Primwitty's ballroom.

"Are you expecting someone?" Audrey finally asked, tired of standing here watching her friend and her husband act like trapped mice. Both Whitney and her husband whipped their gazes to Audrey.

"No," Mr. Sutherland answered with one last look at the stairs before he focused on her.

Audrey snorted. She'd bet all her pin money he was lying, *if* she had any pin money.

Whitney linked arms with her husband and smiled, though the wobbly effort appeared forced to Audrey. "Actually," Whitney said, "I"—she flicked her gaze to her husband—"that is, we, had one more suitor we were hoping would appear tonight that we wanted you to have a chance to speak with."

"Oh, goodness," Audrey murmured, grateful yet a little concerned who else they'd throw in her path. In the two weeks since she'd arrived in London for the Season, she'd had no less than six gentlemen callers show up at her home, courtesy of Whitney, Sally, Gillian and their husbands. It seemed the wives had gently recruited their spouses to persuade their eligible bachelor friends to come and meet her. Not that any of the conspirators had let on to their secret plan. One very nervous yet sweet scientist, who was a childhood friend of the Duke of Primwitty's, had clumsily confessed, after trying to kiss her, how glad he was he had overlooked the fact she had no money to her name and come to call on her.

It was all so embarrassing and gauche, yet well-intended, so she'd kept her mouth shut and dutifully spent the past two weeks going on various outings with her different suitors and her aunt as her chaperone. Enough was enough. She'd made up her mind last night, after another dreadfully boring theater outing with one of Mr. Sutherland's friends, that the only man courting her so far that didn't make her want to run in the other direction was Lord Thortonberry.

She cleared her throat. "You've all been incredibly kind, but I've made a decision that from here on out, I'm going to concentrate on seeing whether Lord Thortonberry and I would make a good match."

"Oh." Whitney frowned. "Have you decided you have a true tender for him, after all?"

Audrey's cheeks heated with embarrassment at having this conversation in front of Whitney's husband. She eyed Whitney and Whitney in turn gave a quick nod of understanding before facing her husband. "Darling, will you please fetch me some punch?"

"But a moment ago you said you weren't thirsty when Thortonberry asked you."

Whitney smiled gently. "I'm thirsty now."

Grumbling, Mr. Sutherland departed and Whitney leaned close to Audrey. "I thought Lord Thortonberry didn't inspire passion in you."

"Hush," Audrey hissed, wishing she'd not confessed her concern to Whitney.

"No one can hear us," Whitney whispered. "Has something changed?"

Audrey nodded. "Yes, my outlook. After two weeks of being courted by seven men, I know without a doubt Lord Thortonberry is the only one I could stand being married to. And I think I felt a stirring of something that might be akin to passion tonight when he read me a poem he'd written for me."

"Really? A poem inspired passion? It must have been a truly magnificent poem." Whitney smirked before she started giggling.

Audrey smacked her friend on the arm. "Do be serious."

"All right, I'm terribly sorry. So you now feel passion for the man."

"I said possibly a stirring of what might be passion." Rather she'd felt more like she did when she had her snuggly nightrail on—*comfortable*. Being with Lord Thortonberry was easy. He accepted her rather opinionated views, didn't seem to want to change her and had professed on several occasions that his heart belonged to her. That was more than she had a right to hope for at this point.

Whitney stilled and her expression grew serious. "Dearest, I hate to see you marry a man who only might *possibly* stir passion in you. I do so wish for you to have a marriage like mine."

An odd knot twisted in Audrey's stomach. "I wanted that too, but you know perfectly well the only man I ever loved was not only possibly, mysteriously already married, but told me quite plainly he only wanted to offer me a marriage of convenience. He did not love me and clearly never thought he would." Her words choked her. In a desperate attempt to regain her control, she bit her lip until it throbbed like her pulse. It worked, blessedly. Swallowing hard, she continued. "I'll never marry a man who cannot love me. My father was incapable of love, and look what happened to my mother. No. Thank. You."

An intense almost secretive expression crossed Whitney's face before disappearing. "What if Sin comes back from France and announces he no longer has a wife?"

Whitney's question caused gooseflesh to cover Audrey's arms. Summoning her will, she shook her head. "What-ifs will not save me or my aunt from starving. Besides, Trent may come back a widower, but I refuse to marry a man who harbors secrets and cannot love me. Let's do talk about something else. Trent is not here, and Lord Thortonberry is making his way back toward me."

Whitney startled her by gripping her arm. "Dearest, I think you're wrong about what no longer having wife would possibly do to Sin." Whitney's gaze left Audrey's face and moved to where her husband had been looking earlier.

"Don't tell me your latest suitor for me is here," Audrey grumbled, irritated her friend was not squarely on her side when it came to Trent.

Whitney's hold on Audrey's arm increased. "Don't be upset with me. I would have warned you, but I was afraid you'd do something rash like flee."

Foreboding swept across Audrey's skin, leaving gooseflesh all over her body and the hairs on the back of her neck standing on end. "If you tell me Trent has returned and is here and you failed to mention it, I'll scream."

"Do so softly, then. Your Lord Thortonberry approaches from the right, as you said, and Sin is coming up fast behind you."

Audrey whirled around and froze. The dreams of Trent that had haunted her and teased her had not done her memory of him justice. Or was it possible he'd become more beautiful in his time away? She laughed nervously. Beautiful was really an odd word to describe a man, but no other word would do. Trent strode toward her, clad head to toe in black. His thick tawny-gold hair contrasted strikingly with his inky clothes. His hair was longer than he'd ever worn it, touching his shoulders and blowing back with the force of his stride. The closer he came, the more erratic her pulse grew.

Five feet. Four. Three. Two. One. She gulped and gulped again. The emotions she'd worked so hard to suppress, the ones she'd thought she had firm control over, broke through the surface of her mind and threatened to drown her in longing. He stopped in front of her, all vital, raw male power, illustrated by the way his broad shoulders strained against the expensive material of his jacket. The shadow of golden beard on his cheeks gave him an even manlier aura if that was possible. His full sensual lips, curled in the sardonic smile she remembered so well. He took her arm, which hung limply at her side, and drew her hand to his lips.

Her mind screamed at her to pull away but she was slow, made sluggish by the shock of seeing him once again. His warm lips pressed against the thin material of her gloves. No silk could hold back the heat that burned within him. She felt singed. Claimed. And foolish. Damn him. With a quick jerk, she tugged her hand away. "I see being shot in the arm did nothing to dim your presumptuous nature. In the future you should make sure a lady doesn't mind you kissing her hand."

"Ah, but I knew you wouldn't welcome my kisses and I was determined to give you one, one way or the other."

He smiled lazily, his gaze raking over her ever so slowly and giving her the distinct impression he was undressing her with his mind. Blasted fiend. His gaze lingered for a moment on the deep V of her dress that she had argued showed to much of her attributes. His eyes met hers before he turned to Whitney. "What's the meaning of this?" He actually waved a hand at Audrey's décolletage. A searing blush, if you could describe the heat of what she was feeling as simply a blush, covered her face, chest and neck. *Wonderful.* She was splotchy and the entire *ton* would know it thanks to the very insistent Madam Marmont for refusing to bring the neckline of this gown up to a more respectable level.

Whitney gave Trent the most innocent wide-eyed look. If Audrey wasn't so confused, angry and flustered, she would have laughed at her friend's obvious ploy. Whitney let out a long huff, then spoke. "You said have a new wardrobe created for her to ease her transition back into Society, and that's what I did."

Whitney's words rang in Audrey's ears. Trent had been the one to commission the dresses she was wearing? The hats. The gloves. The unmentionables. She blinked at him, her heart racing with the revelation. "You were the one who paid for these gowns."

His gaze pierced her as he nodded. "Yes. I knew you probably wouldn't be able to afford new gowns and I wanted to make things a bit easier for you when you returned to Society from your mourning period. I asked Whitney to order the gowns and let you think they were from her."

She furrowed her brow. "But I thought they were from Lord Thortonberry."

A cold expression settled on Trent's face and turned the warmth in his green gaze to iciness. "Why would you think that?"

Audrey glanced at Whitney, who looked positively sheepish. "Why did you have Madam Marmont lead me to believe the wardrobe came from a man?"

Trent let out a soft expletive beside her but said nothing more. Whitney tilted her chin up. Audrey recognized the gesture. It was the one her friend used when she'd decided she was stubbornly right, no matter what. Whitney drew her shoulders back. "Because I assumed you would conclude they came from Sin and possibly make you a little less angry at him when he returned a widower from France."

She turned to Trent. "Are you a widower?" Dear heaven, she wasn't supposed to care. It didn't change a thing, yet when he nodded, she couldn't deny the bubble of happiness that expanded in her chest. She was a fool when it came to him. She pursed her lips and tried to think of an appropriate, impersonal response. "I'm terribly sorry for your loss."

Trent quirked an eyebrow. "Don't be."

Audrey felt her lower jaw drop open. "You don't sound very sad for a man who just returned from confirming the wife he thought was dead, then learned may well be alive, is truly and actually dead. Or is it that she might resurrect again?" Audrey gasped and covered her mouth. Why on earth had she said such an awful thing? Thankfully, Trent did not look devastated. He appeared amused. Still...she lowered her palm. "I'm terribly sorry. That was uncalled for, no matter our past."

He touched her elbow for a brief moment, and the heat of his touch seeped into her skin and awakened a longing in the pit of her belly. Her muscles cramped and her heart thumped slow and hard. She couldn't breathe properly until the moment his fingers fell away. He stepped a bit closer, so the heat radiating from his body surrounded her. "She is truly gone. I'm not as heartless as you must think."

"I think any man who doesn't seem to mourn the loss of his wife is indeed heartless. Then again, knowing you as I now do, it shouldn't surprise me."

Trent's jaw tensed. Audrey counted the rapid beats of his pulse. He raked a hand through his hair before speaking. "You're just going to have to trust me and let me prove to you I have a heart."

"Trust you!" Audrey laughed and was about to blast him with her anger when Lord Thortonberry arrived by her side, looking as irritated as she felt.

He held the glass of punch he'd gone to get some twenty minutes prior out to her. "I'm sorry I took so long. He"—Lord Thortonberry shot a scathing look to his side where the Duke of Dinnisfree had saddled up to him— "detained me with ridiculous inquiries and refused to let me take my leave."

"Say, that's rather rude," the Duke of Dinnisfree exclaimed with obvious mock indignation before exchanging a glance with Trent.

Audrey's anger heated more. She didn't know what Trent was up to, but whatever it was she suspected it somehow involved the duke keeping Lord Thortonberry occupied. Audrey gritted her teeth. She was upset with Lord Thortonberry for lying to her, or rather omitting the truth. The man had never really said he'd bought her the gowns. He just hadn't denied it when she'd assumed it. But she'd hear what he had to say for himself later. *In private.*

She owed him that after everything else he'd done for her. As for Trent, if he thought he could simply appear back into her life and smile that dazzling, rakish smile at her and she'd swoon at his feet and do whatever he wanted, he was even more pompous than she'd previously known.

Glaring at Trent, she spoke. "I will never trust you again."

The pain that stole across his features and hardened them further almost took the wind out of the set-down she had in her mind. She had to press on. If she allowed him close to her, she was afraid of what would happen. "Do not seek me out in Society. Do not buy me things. In fact, forget you know me."

His eyes glittered dangerously as if he might explode at any moment. Her heart skipped a beat and her breath caught in her throat. Perhaps she should have told him those things in private? It was eerily quiet around them, despite the fact that she saw people dancing so knew music had to be playing. No one spoke as Trent stepped so close to her one would have thought he was about to embrace her. Her stomach knotted and her head swam. He leaned down and pressed his lips close to her ear. "I could never, for even a second, forget I knew you. Your image dances in my dreams, toys with my thoughts and makes me contemplate doing things I swore I never would."

She inhaled sharply at his silken words but somehow managed to force herself to step away. Trembling, she slipped her arm into Lord Thortonberry's. He glanced at her with hooded eyes yet pressed her elbow close to his waist. "Do you care to dance?"

Surely he jested. Of course, he had no idea she now knew he'd lied to her about buying the gowns. She shook her head. "Would you mind helping me find my aunt? I wish to leave. I feel a megrim coming on." That was the absolute truth.

He nodded and with a farewell to Whitney, Audrey turned with him away from a glowering Trent. Her head hurt. But her heart... *Blast her heart.* Despite having told Trent to forget he ever knew her, she couldn't forget that he'd worried enough about her he'd commissioned a wardrobe be made to ease her way back onto Society. If she were a foolish woman *that* might be enough to inspire her to hope the man actually did love her and simply didn't realize it yet.

Of course, she was not so foolish. His not telling her he had once been married could be explained away by the fact that he'd thought his wife dead, and from his reaction it seemed the marriage had been painful. But the marriage had also been secret, according to Whitney, and Audrey couldn't fathom how the man could ever explain that. Not that she cared. She didn't. She was curious, of course, but that was different than caring.

By the time she and Lord Thortonberry found her aunt and settled in their carriage, Audrey's head was truly pounding, so there was no acting involved when she closed her eyes and rubbed her temples. She could feel Lord Thortonberry staring at her from across the carriage, so it wasn't a huge surprise when he spoke.

"Do you think you'll be well enough tomorrow to still attend the unveiling of Lord Lionhurst's newest piece of art?"

Audrey tensed and slowly opened her eyes to find her aunt staring at her inquisitively. She wasn't about to confront Lord Thortonberry about why he'd lied to her, with her aunt watching on. "I promised Gillian I would be attending, so, yes, *I'll* be going. Why don't you call on me at ten? I'd like to speak with you on a matter."

He raised his eyebrows questioningly, but she refused to be pulled into the discussion. Once again, she firmly closed her eyes, delighted to realize if she wasn't looking at Lord Thortonberry she was truly hardly thinking of him. It was too bad she couldn't say the same of Trent. His ruggedly handsome face and laughing, secretive eyes danced in her head. It was all she could do to hold in her moan of annoyance.

AFTER AUDREY STORMED AWAY FROM Trent, he excused himself and departed from the ball as quickly as possible. He headed straight for the Sainted Order. Once there, he made a few discreet inquiries about Thortonberry with some of the demireps who were willing to talk for blunt, got the information he needed that proved the man had paid for their services in the past week, and then Trent went straight to the next hellfire club to see if Thortonberry had been there as well.

Six hellfire clubs, three pleasure halls and four long hours later Trent fell onto his bed, exhausted yet more alive than since the night he realized Gwyneth was not at all who she seemed. Thortonberry had been a busy lord these past two weeks. He had stuck to the same pattern all week of not visiting the hellfire clubs until after one in the morning. Apparently, that was well past Dinnisfree's bedtime. If Trent's calculations were correct the man had paid for the services of twenty demireps. That was more than one a night. Trent closed his eyes and grinned. Tomorrow he would make Audrey his and ensure she knew just what sort of man Thortonberry really was.

Eighteen

The next morning at precisely ten, Mr. Barrett, graciously serving as footman so no one who happened to call would know they were desperately poor by the lack of even a simple footman, appeared in her study door and announced Lord Thortonberry's arrival. Her stomach clenched as Lord Thortonberry entered the room and smiled broadly. She nodded to Mr. Barrett to take his leave—and the coachman or rather footman—at the moment, quickly did.

Lord Thortonberry strolled toward her, and taking her gloved hand, kissed it as had become customary for him. She'd spent all morning fretting about how to confront him and had decided she simply had to brave it and ask him the truth.

He seated himself on the settee and motioned for her to sit by him. She hesitated before doing so. Lately she'd grown more and more comfortable with such intimacies with him, but now that she knew he'd purposely let her believe something that wasn't true, she felt awkward. Still, she would give him the benefit of hearing why he'd lied, before she threw him out of her house. Once seated, she turned and faced him.

He reached for her hand, and she pulled away. A frown creased his brow before he spoke. "You look beautiful this morning."

She'd purposely chosen one of the gowns that had

been made by Madam Marmont. "Thank you. This is one
of the gowns you purchased for me. I can't tell you again
how much I appreciate what you did."

Lord Thortonberry squirmed on the couch and
appeared vastly uncomfortable. Audrey smiled grimly. At
least lying bothered him. "Tell me," she continued
ruthlessly, "what made you decide this particular shade
of green would look good on me? I'm assuming you chose
all the colors for the gowns. Or did you give Madam
Marmont the freedom to decide?"

Lord Thortonberry tugged on his collar as perspiration
dampened his brow. "I've never actually met Madam
Marmont."

"Really? How odd. Did you correspond with her by
letters, then, to decide on my wardrobe?" The blasted
fiend could squirm and sweat all he liked. If he intended
to sit here and continue to lie to her, she would take
vindictive glee out of making him regret it.

"I—" Lord Thortonberry stopped talking, threw up his
hands and sighed. "I didn't purchase the gowns for you."

Some of the tension reverberating through her drained
away at his regretful look. "I already know," she
admitted. Her face heated a little as his eyes narrowed.

"Then what's this about?"

"I wanted to see if you would finally tell the truth and I
wanted to watch you squirm."

A bark of laughter escaped him. "You're full of
surprises, Lady Audrey."

She pursed her lips. He wasn't off the hook, by any
means. "As are you." Her tone was purposely chiding. "I
trusted you totally and you lied to me. Why?"

Smiling sadly, he caressed her cheek. "Because I'm
human. Because I saw how happy the gowns made you
when they arrived, and when you assumed I'd purchased
them, I wholeheartedly wished I'd thought to do so. And
because I detected you were on the verge of telling me we
could never be more than friends. Am I right?"

He was right, but what to say? The purchasing of the
gowns had helped her make up her mind to consider
him, though he didn't inspire the passion she wished for.
"Perhaps, but I didn't agree to let you court me simply

because I thought you'd bought me a new wardrobe. You'd been there for me and shown me loyalty, kindness and caring. I greatly admire those things."

"And now?" he asked. "Do you wish to send me away?"

She didn't know. She still needed to marry soon, and despite his having lied to her, he was the best candidate, if he cared for her the way she thought he truly might. "I'm not sure. I want to believe I can trust you."

"You can." He clutched her hand with both of his.

With a firm tug, she pulled away. "We shall see. I'll still see you, but I may need a little time to sort out how I feel."

"You can take all the time you need. I'll wait, but there's something I must say to you."

"Go ahead," she said cautiously.

"I saw the way you looked at Davenport last night. I know you still care for him."

"I don't." Her response rang hollow in her own ears.

"Come now," Lord Thortonberry chided. "Who isn't telling the truth now?"

Embarrassment heated her from her scalp all the way to her slippered feet. "I don't wish to talk about him."

"Neither do I, but permit me to say one more thing to you."

She nodded, though it was reluctant.

"I don't think you'll ever forget him."

Audrey bristled and started to interrupt, but he gently pressed a finger to her lips. "Don't get upset." His voice was pleading. "Not being able to forget him is one of the things that makes you so special. You gave him a piece of your heart. You loved him. You shouldn't forget him. But I want you for myself. If you'll give me the chance, a real chance, I think you'll find there's a piece of your heart you could give to me."

Was he right, or was she willing to believe anything, grasp at what he was saying, because she had to marry very soon? Conflicting emotions battered her, and she wasn't certain how to respond. Before she could decide, Mr. Barrett entered the room. She was relieved and agitated. She'd have to speak with him about knocking before he presumed to enter a room. "Did you need something, Mr. Barrett?

"You've another caller, my lady."

Audrey furrowed her brow. She wasn't expecting anyone. Who would come this early in the morning? No one had the audacity to do such a thing but— She gasped and scrambled to her feet, hoping to rush Mr. Barrett out the door before he said—

"The Marquess of Davenport is—"

"Do be quiet," she snapped, turning toward Lord Thortonberry in time to see his face darken. He stood, anger twisting his mouth.

"Do you wish for me to ask Davenport to leave?"

Her heart thudded in her ears. That would be wise. The exact right path for a woman determined to put a man out of her heart and head. She shook her head, mentally cursing herself. "I don't wish him to think he can cow me." *Liar.* Deep down, the truth was she would never be able to quit wondering why he'd come here this morning if she sent him away without talking to him. And she knew she could never live with that. "Why don't you come back to collect me for the art unveiling at one?"

He shook his head. "I'll wait here to make sure you don't need me to throw him out."

She shoved her hands on her hips. "Careful, my lord. I'm not a woman who has ever enjoyed being told what to do."

"I know," he said. "I'm sorry. Davenport brings out the worst in me."

"Likewise," Trent's voice drawled from behind her.

Audrey gasped and whirled toward the door. Trent leaned lazily against the door frame. His cold eyes belied his easy smile. Dressed in tan leather riding breeches that hugged every bulging muscle of his legs and a dark bottle-green waistcoat cut to fit close to his chest, Trent looked fearsomely handsome and easily capable of stripping off his coat and pummeling any man who irked him into the ground. Audrey gulped, then forced herself to gain control.

"What are you doing here?"

A genuine smile spread across his face as he raked his gaze slowly over her body and lingered at her chest, exactly as he'd done last night. Oh, the devil! She really wished he'd quit doing that. As if he could sense how discomfited he made her, he chuckled. "I'm here to see you, of course. And might I add it pleases me immensely to see you're wearing the chartreuse gown that I chose for you."

She groaned, dearly wishing he hadn't said that. She'd never intended to tell Lord Thortonberry that Trent had actually been the one to purchase the wardrobe for her. By the satisfied gleam in Trent's eye, she could tell he was all too pleased to have revealed it was him. "I intend to help sweep the house later," she snapped. "That's why I chose this gown. I don't care about it, so it's perfect to wear for housework."

"Brava, my lady. I'm glad to see you've not lost your tart tongue while I've been gone," Trent murmured in a way that managed to sound both seductive and genuine and made a blush sear her cheeks.

Lord Thortonberry stepped beside her and pressed a hand against her back. "Lady Audrey has no need for anything from you. She'll be sending the dresses back to you to give to whatever mistress you're currently keeping."

Jealousy twisted her insides as anger made her bite hard on the inside of her cheek to keep herself from being rude to Lord Thortonberry. How dare he suppose he could tell her what to do, even if his pride was prodding him to act so boorish. Still...perhaps he had a point. She'd not planned to send the dresses back, but perhaps it was the wisest thing.

Trent pushed slowly away from the doorframe and came to stand directly in front of them. He didn't presume to touch her, the way Lord Thortonberry had, yet Trent didn't have to. So near to her, he was all she could smell, see and feel. Leather and pine filled her nose with every breath. He'd gone again without shaving, and his whiskers glittered like brushed gold over his skin. His heat wafted to her and made her insides clench.

He looked at her and it was as if it was just the two of them in the room. "I don't have a mistress. And just so there's no confusion, I've not touched another woman since the day I met you." His eyes smoldered as they held hers.

The shock of his words hit her full force. Her legs trembled so that she had to lock her knees to keep the shaking from being obvious. "I see," was all she could manage to say, and that came out as a throaty whisper.

Trent regarded Lord Thortonberry with a coldness that made her skin prickle. "You cannot claim the same loyalty to Lady Audrey, can you?"

Audrey stiffened. Had Lord Thortonberry been pursuing her while sleeping with other women? The rational side of her brain knew it wasn't uncommon, yet she didn't want a man who was common as her husband.

His hand clenched on her back before dropping away. "I don't owe you any explanations," he snapped.

"No, you don't," Trent agreed so readily she gaped. Then he smiled sardonically. "You owe *her* an explanation as to why after you have seen her home every night for the last two weeks you've eventually made your way to every known and unknown hellfire club in the city, where you've not left until the sun rose again on London."

"Have you been following me?" Lord Thortonberry snarled.

Audrey's pulse skittered erratically. Had he? Because of her? That blasted bubble of hope that she was trying to burst in regard to Trent popped up inside her.

"I'm sorry to disappoint you," Trent drawled, "but I don't find you that interesting. Men talk. Simple as that."

That bubble inside her deflated with a pop. Trent hadn't followed Lord Thortonberry because he was concerned for her, and Lord Thortonberry was a beast. Slowly, she turned toward him. "I think perhaps you ought to leave and not bother returning."

"You don't understand," he said, his jaw setting in a determined line.

Trent grabbed the man's elbow. "She doesn't want to understand," he growled. "The lady has asked you to go."

"Stop it," Audrey commanded, fearing a fight would occur if she didn't intervene. "Please just go. That is twice you've lied to me. I'll not allow a third time."

"I've not lied. Allow me to explain. In private. Then I'll leave without argument."

"All right," she huffed. She wasn't such a fool not to

see if the man refused to go Trent might very well forcibly remove him no matter what she said. She eyed Trent. "Wait here. I'll deal with you momentarily." When he opened his mouth as if to protest she glared. "You can always leave too, if you cannot acquiesce to my wishes."

He grinned and rolled back on his heels. "Here will do nicely. I prefer you speak with him without closing the door to whatever room you're in, for safety's sake."

"You may go to the devil," she snapped, then waved an impatient hand at Lord Thortonberry. "Come along." She marched out the door and down the hall.

Once standing in the library, she turned and faced Lord Thortonberry as he strode in after her. He motioned to the door. "May I shut it?"

"No." Her anger made her words short.

"Shall we sit?"

"You've five minutes. What is it you wish to say?"

"I was not with other women in those clubs. I swear it. Or rather I was with women, but not in the way I am sure you're thinking."

She raised her eyebrows. Did he think her so easily manipulated? Surely not. He'd known her all her life, for heaven's sake.

"No? Well, then what you were doing? I know enough to understand that men go to hellfire clubs to either gamble or find pleasure in paid companion's arms, and if you haven't guessed, neither of those lofty pursuits are hobbies I wish in a future husband."

"I've guessed, and I agree with your views. I was there to find my brother, plain and simple."

"But you don't have a brother."

He nodded. "I know. Or at least I did. After my father died, when his will was read, it came to light that I may well indeed have a half brother. My father's dying wish was that I find him and bring him into the fold. I've been searching for the last two years and my search has led me to believe the mother of my half brother once worked in one of London's hellfire clubs."

"I can't believe it," she whispered.

"Neither could I, but then I recall my father and it's not so hard to believe."

"No," Audrey said slowly. "I don't suppose it is." They stared at each other for a moment, leaving his family's history unspoken. His father had not been very good at keeping his affairs secret, though it was customary in the *ton* to do so.

Audrey shifted from foot to foot, trying to order her thoughts. She understood why he would want to fulfill his father's dying wish, and she also understood why he never mentioned what he was doing to her. It wasn't any of her business, after all.

"Lady Audrey, will you consider giving me the chance I asked you for?"

She opened her mouth to answer just as Mr. Barrett stepped into the room.

"You've another caller," her coachman turned footman said in a gruff tone.

She repressed a smile at the way he tugged on the collar of the livery. "Tell whoever it is, I've the plague," she said jokingly, though she was a trifle annoyed.

When Mr. Barrett turned as if to leave, she gasped. "Mr. Barrett, I'm joking. Show them to the salon, and tell them I'll be along in a minute. Is it a gentleman or a lady?"

"A lady."

"Thank goodness for that." She didn't think she could handle anymore gentlemen callers today. As he departed the room, she eyed Lord Thortonberry. She needed time to figure out how to proceed with him. "May I give you my answer this afternoon? I've a lot to think about."

He nodded, but his jaw tightened. "May I still take you to the art showing?"

"Why don't you meet me there?" she suggested, wanting to buy as much time as possible to decide what to do. Her head told her to give him a chance, but her heart—*ah, her problematic heart.* Her heart would not allow her head to rule until she learned exactly why Trent had come here this morning.

"As you wish," he said with a casualness that sounded forced to her ears.

After seeing Lord Thortonberry to the door she made her way to the salon, half expecting to find Whitney there, or possibly Gillian or Sally, though when she'd said goodbye to Sally last night the duchess had been preoccupied with worry over the duke not feeling well. Entering the salon, Audrey frowned.

A petite, fair-haired young lady she didn't recognize sat with her back straight as a board and her hands locked on her knees. Her perch on the edge of the settee made her look as if one wrong word and she would dash out the door. Audrey cleared her throat to get the woman's attention. The woman jerked her gaze to Audrey and quickly rose. "Lady Audrey?"

Audrey nodded. "Yes. How may I help you?" Though she had absolutely no idea who the woman was, something about her was familiar in a way she couldn't name.

The woman fidgeted with the silk reticule in her hands as she stared at Audrey for such an unaccountably long time that Audrey found herself fidgeting as well. She forced herself to still. "Have we met before?"

The woman shook her head. "I'm from Shropshire."

Audrey smiled. "It's a lovely place. I've visited it before. My father's brother lived there."

"Yes, I know," the woman mumbled.

"Did you know my uncle? He passed away some years ago."

The woman nodded. "I knew him. Every time Father came to visit us he would take Mother and me to see Uncle Johnathan."

"Uncle Johnathan?" Audrey repeated, her thoughts spinning dizzily in her head. Did this woman mean Audrey's Uncle John? Was this stranger calling Audrey's Uncle John her uncle? "I think I better sit down." Audrey walked across the carpets and plopped onto the settee. The woman quickly sat and faced her. Trying to calm the quaking inside her, Audrey inhaled deeply. "Perhaps you ought to tell me straight out who you are."

"All right. I'm your half sister, Victoria. Father, *our father*, met my mother a year before he met yours. They were very much in love, but his father, *our grandfather*, threatened to disinherit him if he married her. Grandfather had already promised Father would marry your mother and would lose a great deal of land he was receiving from the union if the marriage contract fell through."

Audrey clenched at the material of her dress. Her mother had never told her any of this. Had she even known? Her tongue felt thick in her mouth, but she swallowed and asked, "I take it he never quit seeing your mother."

Victoria's cheeks reddened, but she nodded. "Shortly after his wedding to your mother, he visited Mama unexpectedly. After he left, she was very ashamed she allowed him to come, so she says, but she loved him desperately and nine months later I was born. Out of love and necessity the visits continued."

Audrey nodded. She was afraid if she tried to speak she would scream. This information certainly explained why her father was always so cold to her mother. He'd never loved her and had been forced to marry her. Forcing herself to meet Victoria's curious gaze straight on, she said, "I assume you knew all about us?"

"Yes. Father kept no secrets from Mama."

Audrey laughed bitterly. She wished she could say the same. "What are you here for? Money?"

Victoria gave her a strange look. "No, Father left us plenty. The solicitor showed up right after his death and gave us enough money to keep us well off for a lifetime."

Audrey's lips were numb but she forced herself to speak again. "A lifetime."

"Yes. And well, the money was such an astonishing sum Mama worried Father hadn't provided for all of you as he should have. She fretted for six months. Afraid to contact you and anger you and your brother by being so bold, but equally fearful that you may need our aid. She always begged him to be kinder to you and your brother, because she worried he took out his unhappiness in the marriage on you both. I told her he'd never do that. He was such a wonderful father, so loving and kind, but she wanted to be sure. So, here I am. I'm embarrassed to inquire, but I assume you're well provided for?"

Dumbfounded, Audrey could do nothing but stare. Hurt heated her and rushed through her body, gaining fire as her shame grew until she was sure her humiliation would kill her. Victoria stared at her, but Audrey couldn't speak. She'd die before ever admitting Father had left her and Richard destitute, without any of his money, love or even the memory of his caring about them. Tears burned the backs of her eyes. By God, she might sit here all day like a statue, but she refused to cry. She willed the tears away.

"Lady Audrey, did he provide for you?"

The ticking hand of the clock clicked five times in Audrey's ear before the soft tapping of shoes startled her and a warm hand pressed down on her shoulder. She whipped her gaze up to find Trent standing over her, a strange faintly familiar look in his eyes. He swept his gaze toward her for a moment, and she caught her breath. The pain she felt seemed to be mirrored in his eyes. *Impossible.* He squeezed her shoulder and spoke. "You must forgive Lady Audrey's silence. She's still mourning the loss of her beloved father, and I'm sure all you've told her has come as a great shock."

"Oh. Oh, yes, of course." Victoria looked at her. "I'm sorry. How unthinking of me."

Audrey didn't need to worry about answering. Trent bowed over the woman's hand, introduced himself and had the lady smiling dreamily at him within seconds and seemingly forgetting all about her question to Audrey. Audrey stared at them both. She knew they were talking, because their lips alternately moved, but she couldn't seem to make out the conversation.

She was horribly hot and her head buzzed with memories of all the times she'd cried over Father not loving her and wondering what she could do to make him give her some affection. He never would have loved her. All his love had already been given somewhere else. To someone else. Another woman. Another child. His preferred family.

She laughed hysterically and Victoria's lips stopped moving. The woman gave her a quizzical look.

"As I was saying," came Trent's voice, crashing through the silence. "Lord Bridgeport provided very well for Audrey and her brother. You may tell your mother not to fret. He loved them dearly and treated them like they were his most prized possessions."

Audrey frowned. Surely the woman wouldn't believe that drivel. Victoria nodded. "I knew it, and I must say, hearing you say it, Lord Davenport, makes me rest easy."

As Trent held out his hand to assist the woman to her feet, Audrey stared at the man before her. He was still a puzzle after all this time. Selfless protector or selfish rake? In this moment, she didn't know whether to throw her arms around him and kiss him or demand he take his leave right along with her half sister.

Nineteen

Trent wanted to take Audrey in his arms and wipe away all the hurt swimming in her eyes. She looked as if she were barely keeping herself together. The sooner her half sister left, the better. "Miss, um, er..." Damnation. He didn't know what surname she went by considering her parents had never been legally married.

Her cheeks turned brilliant red before she spoke. "Cringlewood," she murmured, darting a glance at Audrey. Trent couldn't help but looking as well to see how the news affected her.

Audrey's glassy eyes and flushed cheeks concerned him, but more than that was her silence. She was never one to hold her opinion to herself, but she said nothing. She simply stared at the woman as if the right words would not come. Trent pressed a hand to the new Miss Cringlewood's back and motioned toward the door. "I think perhaps Lady Audrey needs time to come to terms with all you've told her."

"Yes. Quite understandable."

Trent guided Audrey's half sister to the door while sparing a parting glance for Audrey. Silently, she watched them leave. Trying not to appear as if he was rushing the woman out of the house he forced himself to a congenial pace. When the footman shut the door behind her, after a quick goodbye and a promise from Trent that he'd tell Audrey to call on her sister if the desire ever arose, Trent let out an impatient sigh and strode toward the salon, not sure what he might find.

Audrey's crying floated to him before he reached the door. He increased his speed and barreled into the room, stopping short at Audrey slumped over with her head buried in the crook of her arm with her now slipperless feet tucked under her. She looked small and helpless. His heart squeezed mercilessly as he rushed to her side and gathered her in his arms.

He half expected her to fight him, but she flopped against him like a rag doll and sobbed. Instinctually, he ran his hands through her unbound hair while whispering soothing words in her ears. Slowly, she slid her hands up his coat and clung to his arms, tightening her fingers around him. He wanted so badly to take away her pain. If he could have, he would have made it his own. In fact, he'd do anything for her. The thought scared him. It was too close to the hopeless devotion he wanted to avoid. Something inside him was changing, and he didn't like it. Yet, did he have the power to stop it?

After a time, her sobs grew quieter. Of course, that could have been because she'd buried her face in his chest, not that he minded. It had been far too long since he'd touched her and held her so close. When her sobs subsided to nothing but hiccups, he stroked her hair for a few more minutes before asking, "Would you care to talk about it?"

She shook her head against his chest and sniffed loudly. "No. How much did you hear?"

The question made him tense. He didn't want to embarrass her, but he refused to lie to her. "Almost all of it."

Audrey clenched and unclenched the material of his coat but still didn't look at him. "Then you know he had another family and they were the ones he gave all his love to." Her wounded laughter came out in a muffled burst.

Trent cupped her chin and forced her face upward. She swiped her hands under her eyes, blinked and looked at him. "What is it?" she demanded, showing a bit of the bravado he was used to from her. That was a relief. He'd hate to think her spirit had been broken.

"Your father was a fool to deny your love."

With a glare, she shoved away from him. "No more of a fool than you, Lord Rutherford."

"Audrey—"

With a dark warning look, she held up a forestalling hand. "Don't waste your breath. I'll tell you what I told Lord Thortonberry. You've precisely five minutes to say what is on your mind and then I want you out, though I must add, I thank you for helping me keep a scrap of pride in front of my new sister by not telling her the truth of my past and current situation." Audrey paused, took a deep breath, looked at the grandfather clock on the wall and then back at him. By God, righteous anger made her more stunning than ever.

"The clock is ticking, Lord Davenport."

"Don't call me that."

"You are wasting your time and mine," she snapped.

Was she serious? Or merely testing him? "Did you throw Thortonberry out after his five minutes was over?"

"No," she said icily. "You are quite wrong in your views about him. He was not at the hellfire clubs for any untoward purpose."

"You cannot seriously believe him."

"I most certainly can and do. It's you who keeps secrets, not him. He was very quick to tell me exactly what he had been doing there, unlike you, who never could quite explain the secrecy of your former marriage. You've three minutes left, Lord Davenport."

"Damnation, woman!"

"That curse just cost you six seconds, which you could have used to say whatever it is you came to say."

Trent gritted his teeth on another curse. The daft woman truly meant to throw him out. "I came to ask you to marry me." Damn it to hell. That had not at all been the way he'd planned on asking her.

She narrowed her eyes. "Why do you wish to marry me? You don't love me."

"I told you, I believe we will make a good match. I care for you. Admire you. And I want to protect you and give you everything you desire."

He didn't like the way her shoulders sagged at his

words. She shook her head. "I don't need your protection. Lord Thortonberry has asked to court me, and has vowed he wants to marry me, because he loves me. I want to marry a man who loves me. Admiration is nice, but not love. So, you see, your offer pales in comparison to his. My father didn't love my mother and look how that turned out for my mother, my brother and me. I have no desire for that sort of marriage. I tried to give you my love and you threw it back in my face, just like my father."

She loved him. Or she had. His chest tightened as if a vise gripped it. Hearing her say it, he realized he had suspected. Had he hoped she loved him? He rejected the question immediately. He could not allow him mind to tread down that path, could he? "So you'd marry a man you don't love over one you do?" He hadn't meant for his words to come out sharp like a whip, but his control was slipping—on everything it seemed.

She flinched but did not move her gaze from his face. "I suppose we are more alike than I previously thought. You'd marry me, a woman you don't love, simply to get what you desire. Oh, I did forget your admiration." She cast him a cynical smile that made him flinch. She heaved a sigh. "At least I'll end up married to a man who loves me, and I know I'll be a tender and true wife to him, even if I never love him."

"Audrey, please." His words were a desperate hiss.

"You're time is up, Lord Davenport." She waved a hand at the door. "Do you mind seeing yourself out?"

She was throwing him out, and if he couldn't stop her now, his gut told him it would be too late. She demanded too much—wanted too much, but the thought of losing her to Thortonberry was more than Trent could take. As much as he didn't want to love again, he had to try for her. "I'll try to be more amenable to love." He grimaced at his stiff-sounding words.

Her eyes rounded, showing he'd caught her by surprise. It was about bloody time. She'd done nothing but surprise the hell out of him since he'd walked into her home. Slowly, she licked her lips. "I wish I thought you had it in you, Trent, but I'm afraid I don't believe you, as much as I want to."

He slammed a palm down on the table in front of them, making the tea service jump and rattle. "What do you want from me, woman? Blood?"

She shook her head. "Not blood. The truth would be nice for starters. I want you to tell me the truth about your wife and your marriage, and if you can do that, I'll consider letting you court me and prove your feelings to me, but I warn you, I'm not going to quit seeing Lord Thortonberry during this courtship. I've already given my word."

"The truth," Trent echoed. How could he tell her the truth and keep the fact that he had been a spy secret? Carefully. There was no other choice. If he didn't tell her, she'd forget him and never look back. He could see the truth of that in her eyes and he didn't want to be without her. He sat back and stared at his hands, trying to find the right words.

"Because of my station and my exuberance for traveling, I made connections in France that proved valuable to certain men here in England."

She sat back beside him, her shoulder brushing his before she spoke. "Valuable how?"

"These men wanted me to use my connections to be a go between, if you will, among them and men in France who wanted the same thing they wanted. Someone here wrote orders of things that needed to be done, when they needed to be accomplished and exactly how. It was important to keep it very secret, because there were people there who wanted to sabotage what they were doing and help someone very bad escape confinement."

"That is a good start but I need you to be more specific."

He frowned. He'd hoped she wouldn't be her normally inquisitive self, but he should have known better. "They wanted to ensure Napoleon stayed imprisoned and defeated and that those who would see him brought back to power or help him escape his prison never had the chance to do so."

She gaped at him, her hand coming to her throat. "I don't suppose you trust me enough to tell me who it is that wanted you to do this?"

As he sat and stared at her open, honest face it struck him that he wanted to trust her enough to do exactly that. When the hell had that happened? Somewhere between last night and this morning seeing her openly weeping and so vulnerable, she'd managed to slip inside his heart. Sweat dampened his brow. He'd never thought he'd want to trust a woman again. "I'd like to trust you that much, but there are certain things I'll never be able to reveal, for your safety as well as a vow I've given." Like the prince's name.

"Yes." She nodded slowly. "That makes sense. Can you tell me why you kept your marriage secret?"

The sweat on his brow was joined by his heart thudding heavily. "Because I found out after my wife betrayed me that she wasn't who she'd led me to believe she was. And in fact, she worked for the very enemy I was supposed to be helping control."

"Oh, my," Audrey gasped.

"'Oh, my', is an understatement," Trent replied darkly. "Well, what do you think? Have I told you enough to win a spot as one of your suitors?"

Audrey toyed with the necklace she wore, her eyes focused no longer on him, but out the window. Trent tapped his foot against the carpet, hating the waiting. He'd confessed as much to her as he could. Hell, he'd probably confessed too much, but the blasted woman had left him no choice.

He smiled ironically. When faced with spilling his secrets or death in the prison, he'd chosen death. Yet when faced with losing Audrey or telling her enough to make her trust him again, he'd chosen Audrey. Dinnisfree had been right. The woman was his Achilles' heel, and he didn't like it one bit. Not that he could see where he had a choice. How much of a weakness he'd allow her to become was up to him. He was determined to keep his feelings at the level they were at this moment. That little tidbit of truth, though, he would keep to himself.

"All right," she said, meeting his gaze once again. "I'll see you this afternoon at your cousin Gillian's. Her husband is showing his new art piece. You may meet me there."

"And Thortonberry?"

"He'll be meeting me too," she said, her cheeks turning a rosy shade. "Be nice."

He nodded. He'd be nice to her. To Thortonberry, he'd be ruthless. The man needed to find another lady to become infatuated with. Audrey was his, whether she'd accepted it yet or not.

"THEY'RE HERE," WHITNEY WHISPERED IN Audrey's ear. Audrey tensed and gazed at the archway that led into the salon where Gillian's husband's newest addition to his art collection was on display.

Audrey gripped Whitney's arm as she discreetly glanced at Lord Thortonberry and Trent. They stood in the doorway together, both appearing vastly uncomfortable to be sharing the same space. Trent and Lord Thortonberry could not have been dressed in more contrasting colors if they had planned it. Trent wore a single-breasted navy waistcoat, buckskins of a light gray and top boots. His simple cravat and lack of a hat completed his causal outfit. His clothes, obviously from an expensive tailor by the exquisite way they formed to his body, made him appear effortlessly commanding, which was exactly the truth. Her heart flipped, and then flipped again when he smiled at her.

She smiled back, then, feeling guilty that she had hardly spared a glance for Lord Thortonberry, turned her attention to him. His outfit, a double-breasted coat of vibrant green-and-white stripes, a black top hat and cream pantaloons, reminded her of her Aunt Hillie's outrageous outfits. The bold ensemble was rather unlike what he usually wore. Pulling her gaze away from the gentlemen, she whispered to Whitney, "Of all the rotten luck. I never counted on them arriving at the same time."

"No matter." Whitney squeezed Audrey's hand. "Since Sally couldn't be here, because of Peter's illness, I instructed your aunt to run interference if this very predicament occurred.

"How very devious of you," Audrey murmured.

Whitney grinned. "It's the least I can do. However, you know who I think you should choose."

"Yes, I know." Audrey had no wish to have the same discussion they'd had several hours ago after she'd called on Whitney and told her of her predicament.

"In case you've forgotten, I want you to end up with Sin."

"I haven't forgotten." Audrey shot Whitney an incredulous look while keeping part of her attention focused on the men. They were both occupied with greeting the host and hostess, so Audrey had a few minutes to decide who she would spend time with first today.

Whitney nudged her in the side. "I hate to be a pest, but your aunt is waiting for my signal."

Audrey searched the room for her aunt and found her hiding behind a potted plant, which would have been rather clever, except Aunt Hillie had worn her usual shocking attire. The seven feathers in her aunt's hair stuck up past the plant's bushy leaves and gave her hiding place away. Audrey giggled. "I'm not sure."

"Not sure about which man or no longer sure of your plan?"

"Which gentleman," Audrey immediately responded. "I'm still certain of my plan. My head still tells me to choose Lord Thortonberry, while my heart clings to the hope that Trent will realize he loves me."

"Then it's settled. Spend time with Trent first. And then if he has an epiphany, you can send Lord Thortonberry on his way."

Audrey frowned. "I'll spend time with Lord Thortonberry first. I've always followed my heart and look where it's gotten me."

Whitney held up one finger and Aunt Hillie shot Audrey a fierce frown. Whitney snickered. "I daresay your aunt doesn't approve."

"I know. She made her opinion very clear after Trent left. In her mind, true love always wins. Of course, she chooses to forget that Trent has never said he loves me."

"Sometimes men say it without using the words."

"Well, I need the words." After everything that had happened, she wanted that certainty. "Lord Thortonberry is approaching," she warned.

"Yes, yes," Whitney grumbled. "I'll play dutiful chaperone as promised, and you will pretend to be light-headed."

Audrey nodded as she smiled at Lord Thortonberry.

He took her hand and pressed his lips to her glove. "Ladies, you both look exquisite."

Audrey and Whitney murmured appropriate responses and then Lord Thortonberry asked, "Shall we go view the art?"

Audrey shook her head. "I'm feeling rather light-headed." In a way it did not take much acting on her part, because if she thought too long about having to decide who she might marry, she did feel light-headed. Marriage was a lifelong commitment. Could she marry someone she didn't love with all her heart? Then again, could she marry someone who didn't love her? Why did things have to be so complicated? "I need some fresh air."

Whitney clutched her arm on cue. "Lord Thortonberry, won't you help me take Lady Audrey to the garden to get fresh air?"

"Certainly." He grasped her other elbow and pressed his free hand against her back.

Out of the corner of her eye, she saw Trent try to break away from her aunt. Aunt Hillie grabbed his arm and waved her hands in the air while speaking rapidly. Whitney must have seen it as well, because she pulled Audrey along at a clipped pace toward the hall that led to the courtyard.

"Perhaps we should slow down for Lady Audrey's sake," Lord Thortonberry said behind her.

"Nonsense." Whitney strode toward the garden door and practically dragged Audrey down the steps. Before Audrey's feet could gain firm ground, Whitney was pressing her hands to Audrey's shoulders. Audrey landed with a hard thud on the metal bench.

This had not been the plan. They were to stroll in the garden while Whitney fell behind them and allowed them time to talk. Whitney whipped toward Lord Thortonberry as he descended the steps and clutched his arm. "I better go fetch Audrey's aunt, so she doesn't become overly worried. You stay with Lady Audrey and I'll be back in a moment."

Whitney ascended the steps before Lord Thortonberry could agree. Audrey's protest died silently on her lips. Blast Whitney for her scheming ways. She had no idea what Whitney was up to, but she didn't care for it one bit.

Audrey ran a smoothing hand over her skirts as she thought. She could not very well hop up and claim to be all better, but she'd never planned on being utterly alone with Lord Thortonberry. What if he asked her to marry him today? She was not ready to respond.

He sat beside her, so that their knees bumped. "Sorry," he said and tried to adjust himself, but he was a tall man and the bench was small. "Shall I stand and give you more room?"

"No." She took a deep purposeful breath, so he'd believe her next words. "I think I'm already feeling a bit better.

"Excellent."

The gleam in his eyes made her gulp. Perhaps she should have asked him to stand after all.

"I'm glad to get you all to myself." His voice was low and husky.

"Are you?" she murmured, praying Whitney would truly hurry back.

He scooted closer and slid his arm across the back of the bench. His fingers first brushed her shoulder, then moved swiftly to her neck, where he curled his warm, strong hands around her bare skin. Before she could protest him taking any liberties here in a very public garden, his mouth descended on hers, and her heart exploded in galloping indignation.

A thousand rude words rang in her ears. She pushed at his chest, but he didn't seem to notice. His kiss became more fervent, almost bruising in its intensity. Just as she moved her hands up his chest to shove him away, Whitney's voice cut through the silence. "My goodness, you two lovebirds. I leave you alone for one minute and you're in each other's arms."

Audrey was going to throttle Whitney for the game she was playing. She shoved hard at Lord Thortonberry's chest and whipped to her feet, swaying with how fast she came up and her lack of air from the brute's relentless kiss. "Oh my," she murmured, her gaze focusing belatedly on Trent's.

His green eyes bored into her like bits of razor-sharp stones. Her heart sank to her slippered feet, crashing so loudly in her mind she jerked. She wanted to run to him and explain that she'd not been a willing participant in the kiss, more like a ship taken by force, but she stood stock-still. She would not humiliate Lord Thortonberry by saying such a thing. There was an arrested expression on Trent's face that twisted her heart into a tangled mass, but it was the immediate smile that he forced to his lips, which made her tremble and fear he'd never be able to love her now. There wasn't a trace of warmth to his smile, only cold contempt. "I've forgotten something in the salon," he said before turning on his heel and leaving without another word.

His contemptuous tone echoed in her ears. She wanted to run out of the garden go home and sob for what she was sure she'd just lost forever. Instead, she forced her gaze to Whitney, who was staring, with a puckered brow, at the door Trent had slammed shut. Audrey had a strong desire to jerk her friend inside somewhere private and rail at her, but from the utterly bemused expression on Whitney's face Audrey had a sinking suspicion her dear, meddling friend had thought to induce Trent to jealousy so he would admit his feelings. Instead, Whitney had driven him away. Maybe he'd come back?

Audrey found herself staring at the door until Lord Thortonberry spoke beside her. "Shall we go inside and view the art?" His voice was tight with an underlying note of irritation.

Audrey tried to school her features before answering. She nodded, and as he offered his arm to her, the garden door banged open, and Audrey's heart leaped with hope, then fell with such intensity it likely shattered forever. One beleaguered-looking nanny came out with two giggling toddlers. The children darted down the steps, almost knocking the nanny over. As she teetered on the top step, Audrey scrambled toward her to steady her.

The nanny screamed out the children's names with such ear-splitting intensity, Audrey winced.

"Mary and Martin, come back here," the nanny wailed. Audrey caught a glimpse of the little girl's pink skirt just before she disappeared around the corner of the garden maze.

"I'll never find those children before their mother finds me. I'll be fired," the woman wailed. She looked at Audrey with mournful eyes. "I try. I really do. Those children are too spoiled for their own good."

Audrey glanced beseechingly at Lord Thortonberry. "Do you mind?"

"Not at all," he automatically replied, yet had his jaw clenched. Did he not like children? She definitely needed to ask him that. Marrying a man who might be unloving to his children was out of the question. Lord Thortonberry strode toward the garden at a clipped, purposeful pace.

Audrey frowned, a memory of those children nagging her. "Are those the Duchess of Primwitty's niece and nephew?"

"Yes, my lady. The duchess's sister, Lady Brighton, is inside." The woman glanced behind her then turned back. "She insists on bringing them everywhere," the nanny said in a low voice. "His lordship claims it's because their last child died in the care of the nanny while they were out, but I suspect it isn't just that. She's American, you know. She's the daughter from the first marriage and the duchess's half sister. I can tell you she is nothing like the duchess, a true English lady, who I adore."

Audrey shot a beseeching gaze to Whitney to leave rest the reference that the woman being American somehow made her less of a true lady, but it was too late. Whitney gripped the woman's arm and tugged her toward the door. "My husband is American," she said in a torturing tone. "We shall see what their customs are in raising children."

"But my lady," the nanny protested as the garden door once again opened and then banged shut.

Audrey suppressed a hysterical giggle. Whitney had

likely been too livid at the indirect insult to her husband to consider that she was taking the woman away from her charges and leaving the little devils in Audrey and Lord Thortonberry's care. With a sigh, she started toward the garden but stopped when Lord Thortonberry yelped. Not a second later, his voice carried on the wind. "You insufferable beast. Do not kick me again."

Audrey frowned fiercely and crossed her arms over her chest. If Lord Thortonberry was going to speak that way to the child, the man deserved to be kicked. She strolled to the bench and sat down. After the liberties he'd taken with her, he deserved his comeuppance, and perhaps it was best served by a precocious toddler.

Twenty

Trent was five steps away from leaving his cousin's home when Dinnisfree appeared out of the shadows and stepped in front of him to block his path. His friend folded his hands across his chest. "Where are you going?"

"Home," Trent snapped, dodging around the duke and then letting out a warning growl when Dinnisfree grabbed his arm.

"What has happened? I thought I was to keep Thortonberry occupied for you while you made Lady Audrey yours."

Trent ignored Dinnisfree's bantering tone and jerked out of the man's grip. "What has happened is that you bloody failed at preoccupying the competition, and I was waylaid by Lady Audrey's nonsensical, chattering aunt, who I suspect must have been preoccupying me either by her own design or Audrey's. While I was busy answering a thousand mind-numbing questions, all asked with a curious proverb thrown in, the woman I thought to take as my wife was happily ensconced in a lurid embrace." Fierce anger and something else, something raw and throbbing much like—no far greater than—any wound he'd ever received, sliced at him. His chest felt constricted, his throat tight and his nerves on edge.

Dinnisfree cocked his eyebrows. "Lurid, you say?"

Trent nodded.

"Someone was naked, then?"

"Naked? Good God, you reprobate, what sort of woman do you take Lady Audrey for? No one was unclothed. She was locked in Thortonberry's arms, kissing the man."

"And you're certain she wanted to be kissing him?"

"I did not think to ask her," Trent retorted, allowing all the annoyance inside him to pour out with each word.

Dinnisfree shook his head. "Let me ensure I have the right of this. You're leaving with your tail tucked between your legs because you think the woman you claim to desire, *only desire*, mind you, was willingly kissing another man?"

Trent's entire body tensed as Dinnisfree's words broke through his anger and hurt. Yes. Damn it. Hurt. Pain. The very thing he was striving to avoid ever feeling again. "What am I doing?"

"You're losing her." The duke's face became thoughtful for a moment. "I cannot believe I'm about to give you this advice, considering my own repulsion toward the state of matrimony, or any soft emotions, but you're already lost, so I suppose I can do no greater harm than you've already done to yourself by your continual pursuit of a woman who demands your heart. You must find a way to give it to her."

"Give it to her?" Thoughts were crashing around in Trent's head nosily.

"Yes." Dinnisfree flashed an exasperated look. "Allow yourself to fall."

Trent would be damned if he'd discuss the particulars of love with Dinnisfree or anyone else. He cleared his throat. "I'm not prepared to fall, but you're right, I should be fighting for her."

"At least you're taking half my advice," Dinnisfree said with a shrug. "I predict in the end you'll take it all. I'm wiser than I look."

Trent ignored his friend's bantering tone and considered how to outwit Thortonberry. "Come with me." Striding back toward the hall that led to the garden, he motioned Dinnisfree to follow him. He paused in front of the window and watched Audrey. What the devil was she looking at? He glanced at the garden and narrowed his gaze on Thortonberry carrying a wiggling child with another child, a boy, dragging his heels behind Thortonberry. Trent glanced back toward Audrey. She now stood and a huge smile lit her face as Thortonberry approached her. Trent growled, thinking the smile was for the marquess, until he realized when Audrey took the child, then served Thortonberry a dark frown, that the joy on her face was directed at the children. Trent clapped Dinnisfree on the back. "I need you to run interference, but listen carefully to the new plan."

AUDREY SCRAMBLED TO HER FEET as Lord Thortonberry picked his way toward her with the children. The young girl squirmed wildly on his hip, and the boy dragged his heels as Lord Thortonberry tugged him along. When they stopped in front of her, Audrey held her hands out for the girl, who looked as if she might, at any second, take a nice fat bite out of Lord Thortonberry's clutching arm. Without hesitation, he thrust the wiggly child toward Audrey. "Here," he said, his words clipped as he nodded down toward the boy. "Take this one too."

"This one?" Distaste filled Audrey's mouth as she took the young boy's soft hand in hers. His tiny fingers immediately wrapped around hers and she gave him a gentle squeeze. "His name is Master Martin. Isn't it, dear?" She looked at the little boy, who vigorously nodded his head, making his blond curls bounce around. The little girl pressed a sticky palm to Audrey's cheek and tugged, until Audrey turned to look at the child's face.

"I'm Mary," she announced proudly in an angelic voice. Audrey's heart tugged and she grinned at the children. She couldn't wait to have her own children to pour all her love into. She would dote on them the way she'd always longed for her father to dote on her.

Lord Thortonberry cleared his throat. "Why don't we take these two dev—"

Audrey glared him into silence, then blew out an exasperated breath to let him know she was not at all happy with him.

"Darlings," he muttered hastily, but his lips pressed together as the word left his mouth.

Unease crawled up Audrey's spine as she tried and failed to imagine Lord Thortonberry on his knees in the nursery playing with their children. The way the man was acting at the moment, it would be more likely that he never visited the nursery. Perhaps she was being too hard?

"Let us take them to their nanny and continue on with our day," he finished in a strained, awkward tone.

Audrey shook her head. "I'm going to stay outside with them and play. They clearly want to. Don't you?" The children both nodded their heads at once and erupted into chattering over what they wanted to do first.

"Who do we have here?" a deep masculine voice she heard every night in her dreams said behind her. Her heart hitched as she slowly turned toward the garden door. Trent stood on the steps, devilishly handsome, with one hand causally on the railing and the other propped on his hip. The sun shone behind him, making his hair gleam like dark gold.

Her pulsed beat rapidly at her neck, temple, heart, well...everywhere. She wanted to shout *you came back.* Instead she said much calmer than she felt, "this is Master Martin and Lady Mary. These are the Brighton's children."

As Trent descended the steps, Audrey noticed his friend, the Duke of Dinnisfree, was loitering behind him. She inclined her head with a smile. "It's nice to see you, Lord Dinnisfree."

He grinned at her, displaying the bewitching smile she'd heard many a lady giggle over. "Call me Justin," he said casually, as if they were intimately acquainted.

Her response was cut off by Lord Thortonberry. "She won't," Lord Thortonberry said with an attitude of such superiority that Audrey gaped at him. A hot retort scalded her tongue, but Lord Justin's wink eased away her anger.

"I'd be happy to call you Justin," she said sweetly.

Beside her, Trent chuckled before he leaned down to peer at Martin, who was now silent and clinging to

Audrey's skirts. "Well, my lad," Trent said in a pleasant tone that made Audrey smile, "it doesn't seem fair that your sister is being coddled and not you. Shall I hold you?"

"On your back?" the boy shyly asked.

"There's no better way, is there?" Trent bent down and placed his hands on the ground.

"No," the lad replied as he clambered on. When Trent came up with a grin on his face, his eyes shining, and his large hands wrapped protectively around the smiling child, Audrey's heart felt as if it would burst. Trent clearly loved children and she clearly loved Trent. Bother, oh, bother. If only he would love her back, things would be perfect.

Trent started galloping around the grass and pretending to be a horse with the little boy laughing merrily on his back. Audrey hugged the child on her hip who was watching her brother's ride with obvious longing. "Shall I give you a ride?"

"Lady Audrey, why don't you give the child to Dinnisfree, and the two of us can go inside," Lord Thortonberry suggested.

Audrey frowned as Justin held up his palms and shook his head. "Sorry, my lady, I don't give rides." Dinnisfree grinned wickedly. "To children, that is."

A furious blush heated Audrey's cheeks. "Justin, really. Please try and mind your tongue." She could see by the devilish twinkle in his eye it had been the absolute wrong thing to say. She expected another lurid, albeit witty rejoinder, but he surprised her by turning to Lord Thortonberry. "Actually, Thortonberry, I came out here in search of you. Lady Gillian says you must come see the art. She knows you've recently been to Ireland and the piece is from there. She and her husband are having a debate and she insists you settle it."

"I can't leave Lady Audrey."

"Oh, but you must," Audrey rushed out, still irritated with his high-handedness with her and the children, and she had a desperate desire to have a few minutes alone with Trent to try to explain what he'd seen earlier.

"Yes, you really must," Justin added. "It's rude to deny our hostess her request."

"Yes, all right." Lord Thortonberry agreed with obvious reluctance. "I'll be back shortly."

She nodded, then proceeded to help Mary climb on her back and join Trent galloping around the yard. Twenty minutes later, they were all in an unceremonious heap on the grass. Well, all but Audrey. She sat in the grass with her legs tucked under her and watched Trent. He lay back casually as if he could care less about his expensive coat getting dirty, and she believed he truly didn't care. Blast the man. He made her love him more just by being him. He had one child balanced on his knee and the other, Mary, sat by his head playing with his hair. When he finally sat up, his hair stuck up in disarray all over.

Audrey giggled and the children joined in pointing at his hair. "What is it?" he asked, patting the air around his head.

Audrey was quite sure he knew, but it was marvelous of him to entertain the children in such a way. She snickered again before answering finally. "Your hair is a mess."

He stopped patting the air and grinned at her, making butterflies dance in her stomach. Suddenly, he sat Martin beside him on the grass and then reached over and ran a thumb over her cheek. "Your face is a mess."

"I beg your pardon?" she murmured, wanting to press her hand to her cheek that tingled from his touch.

He brushed her face again, making her pulse skitter. "You've something smeared on your face that looks very much like jam, but never fear, you're still the most beautiful woman I've ever seen."

A warm glow of happiness flowed through her. Egads, she was probably smiling like a silly nitwit. She tried to school her features, but the rakish grin pulling at his lips told her she'd failed miserably. She pursed her lips together in an effort to quit smiling like a fool. "Thank you." Heaven above, her voice was husky. Her heart pounded as his eyes devoured her. If they'd been alone she was positive he would have kissed her and that kiss, his lips to hers, would have been heaven. Her toes curled in her slippers at the thought.

"Children, there you are!" a concerned female voice called.

Audrey craned her neck back toward the house entrance. A beaming Lady Brighton came toward them with her arms held wide. The nanny was fast on her heels. As the children rushed to their mother, were properly chastised and then kissed, Audrey exchanged a long, heated look with Trent. He helped her to her feet, his hand lingering on hers longer than was proper but shorter than she wished for.

They traded pleasant greetings with Lady Brighton, then were left in the garden utterly and perfectly alone. She turned to Trent at the same time he turned to her. He took her hand and silently led her behind a large tree and away from anyone who might chance by the windows and see them in the garden. Her heart thundered as she followed him, her pulse becoming even more erratic when he pressed her back to the tree trunk and slid his hands to either side of her shoulders. Trapped in his embrace was the only place she'd ever wanted to be. If only he would open up his heart and love her. If only he would say the words.

"I didn't willingly kiss Lord Thortonberry," she blurted.

"No?" He quirked an eyebrow before leaning so close to her that every breath she took filled her lungs with his masculine scent.

"No," she whispered, barely able to form the one word.

"Shall I challenge him to a duel for liberties taken?" Unblinking, Trent's gaze bored into hers.

She shook her head. "Quit teasing. I just wanted you to know I'm not participating in *that* kind of courtship."

A frown greeted her. "Do you mean the sort of courtship where those participating get to kiss you?"

She nodded.

"It seems only fair since he got to." A faint trace of humor underlay his deep voice and made her shiver with delight.

Her whole body filled with longing for his kiss. "You're right. It's only fair." She closed her eyes and within seconds, his lips descended on hers softly, reverently and perfectly. She would have melted into a puddle, if it were possible. A tingle began in the pit of her stomach as his kiss deepened, and his arms moved from the tree trunk to encircle her waist. She twined her arms around his neck at the same moment her chest crushed against the hard plane of his stomach and chest.

Pressed so close, the rapid beat of his heart pounded against her skin. As their tongues touched, intertwined, receded and mingled once again, she moaned. He wanted her with the same intensity she wanted him, but that had never been in question. The problem was whether he could love her. Not wanting to, but knowing she needed to, she pulled back and flattened her palms against his chest and heart. "Trent—" She looked at his chest as she spoke. "Do you adore children as much as you seem to?"

He nudged her chin up until their eyes met. Something intense flared in his gaze. "I didn't think I wanted children anymore, or cared about having them any longer until you." His hand left her chin, and both palms cupped her face. "You make me want things I never thought I would again, like a home filled with your tinkling feminine laughter and the sound of our children's bare feet pattering wildly through our halls as they chase each other or we chase them."

Audrey stilled, unbelievable hope filling her. His words were so tender. So full of the promise of his loving her. Did she really need him to say it? How foolish would she be to marry Lord Thortonberry when her heart, her soul belonged to Trent. Surely he would come around. The need to tell him exactly how much she loved him exploded inside her. "Trent—"

"There you are." Whitney's voice rang out, making Audrey jump.

Audrey swiveled around to find her Aunt Hillie clutching Whitney's arm. Irritation at being interrupted when she had just gathered the courage to once again confess her heart to Trent flared, but then her aunt swayed a bit and Audrey focused on her with a frown. "Aunt Hillie, what's wrong?"

"I'm sorry, my dear, but I'm not feeling well. I think I've a cold or some such nonsense. I came to see if it would be all right with you if I have Mr. Barrett take me home."

Audrey shot a regretful glance at Trent, which he acknowledge by quickly squeezing her hand before letting her go to her aunt. "Nonsense, Aunt. I'll accompany you and take care of you."

Her aunt, usually so independent, practically wilted into Audrey's arms. "Thank you, dearest. I did hate to ask, but I do feel awful."

Audrey patted her aunt's hand. "Come, then. We better get you home and to bed."

Trent came immediately to her aunt's other side, and Whitney discreetly stepped away before saying, "I'll go tell Gillian you're departing."

Audrey nodded and locked gazes with Trent, glad for a few more minutes with him, even if she couldn't say what she wanted to. Trent asked her aunt, "Might I see you safely to your carriage?"

Aunt Hillie gave him a sardonic smile. "It's about time you thought of someone besides yourself, Lord Davenport."

"Auntie, do hush," Audrey hissed.

Trent chuckled. "Your aunt is undoubtedly correct." After helping Audrey get her aunt settled into the carriage while Audrey exchanged goodbyes with Gillian and her husband, Trent leaned into the enclosed carriage compartment. "Might I take you on a picnic tomorrow, if your aunt is feeling well enough that she doesn't need your care?"

"I'm sure I'll feel perfectly fine," Aunt Hillie said before Audrey could respond. "But where are' you planning on taking my niece on a picnic? I must insist it be somewhere very public, unless I'm coming along as a chaperone."

Audrey gawked at her aunt. It was rather unlike her to demand such a thing.

"Do you approve of Hyde park?" Trent asked.

Aunt Hillie nodded. "Certainly. You'll be surrounded there. Make sure to bring an open carriage."

"Indeed I will." Trent stepped away and tapped on the carriage.

As it pulled away, Audrey turned to her aunt. "Whatever was that about?"

Her aunt smiled gently at her. "Dear, whatever you did to that man today is working. I see a softening in his eyes when he looks at you."

Audrey's heart squeezed a bit. "Really?"

"Absolutely. I cannot in good conscience allow you to be alone with him until you've decided whether or not you wish to accept his proposal."

"Why ever not? You allowed me to be alone with him today."

"Well, yes." Her aunt closed her eyes and leaned back against the seat. "That was before he had that look in his eyes."

Audrey leaned forward, eager to hear what her aunt thought she saw in Trent's eyes. "What look?"

"The look that says it's only a matter of time before he realizes he loves you."

"But that's wonderful," Audrey exclaimed, happy to hear her aunt's thoughts echoed her own.

"To be sure," Aunt Hillie murmured. "But before when he looked as if he merely desired you, I had no qualms the man would keep himself in check. His honor is quite obvious."

"And now?" Audrey clutched at the seat.

Aunt Hillie slit one eye open. "To everything there is a season."

Audrey sighed. "What do you mean?"

Aunt Hillie sat up, her gaze spearing Audrey. "When that man accepts he loves you, I promise you he'll be willing to dance with the devil himself to keep you as his. Honor be damned. Rules of Society won't stop him from claiming you, so I must, until you make up your mind. Tell me, dear, have you any progress with that?"

"I love him." Audrey could not stop the grin from spreading across her face. "And I now have reason to hope he loves me to. The things he said today..." She let her words trail off with a happy sigh. "Perhaps I will have a marriage of love as I always dreamed." She grinned at her aunt. "I feel so happy."

Her aunt patted her hand. "That's wonderful, dear."

Audrey frowned. "It is, and if everything works out it will be almost perfect."

"Almost?" Her aunt quirked an eyebrow at her.

"I wish Richard would return home. Perhaps I can ask Trent if he knows anyone who can help me locate Richard."

"An excellent idea, dear," Aunt Hillie said before succumbing to a coughing fit that took Audrey's concern away from Richard and to her rather flushed-appearing aunt.

Twenty-One

Later that night, Trent ascended the steps to his home with a frown on his face. Things were going perfectly with Audrey, and he should have felt nothing but happiness, but something bothered him and left his gut tight. He'd gone to White's and had a drink by himself to brew over what it could be, but he was no closer to uncovering what was dispelling what should have been an excellent mood, given he was fairly certain today in the garden Audrey had been on the verge of accepting his marriage proposal.

As he opened the door and thought of her laughing in the garden, with the sun beaming down on her hair and the child on her back giggling, Trent's chest tightened almost painfully and it struck him suddenly what he was out of sorts about. It was her. No, it was him and what he was offering to her.

The door swung open before his thoughts got any further and Pickering rushed out of the house, breaking his customary routine of greeting Trent when he stepped through the door. Pickering appeared disheveled and nervous. Instantly, Trent's senses tingled. "What's wrong?"

Pickering waved Trent inside. Once the door was shut behind them, Pickering moved close. "You've a visitor, my lord."

"A visitor? At this hour?"

"Yes, sir," Pickering replied in a whisper.

Trent frowned. "Why are you whispering?"

"The lad is asleep."

"What lad?"

"I do believe she called him Julian."

A knot formed in Trent's stomach. "Julian." A French name. It couldn't be, yet instantly he swept his gaze around the room, looking for Gwyneth, though he knew she was dead. He stopped on the stairs. This was ridiculous. Wasn't it? Could the priest have lied? If Gwyneth wasn't dead after all, but here, and brought a child, did that mean the child was his? He tried to shake the ridiculous scenario his mind had conjured, but it would not shake. It took, it seemed, long moments for his brain to start again. "How old is the child?" he asked woodenly, calculating exactly how old any child he could have had with Gwyneth would be.

"I cannot say for certain, my lord, but he looks to be the age of my nephew and he's half a year shy of his second birthday."

"Bloody hell. I thought you might say that." Any child he and Gwyneth would have conceived would have been just about that age. "Where's the woman?"

"Upstairs in the guest room tending to the child. He is sick. I'm sorry to have taken such liberties, my lord. I did not think you would mind, knowing you as I do, but if you wish to dismiss me..."

Trent waved his butler's offer away and tried to take a deep breath but his lungs did not want to function properly. There was only one way to find out exactly who was upstairs. He took the stairs two at a time, his blood pumping furiously in his veins. Whatever hatred he felt for Gwyneth would never include a child of his. If he had a son, he would love him. An intense ache coursed through his body as he flung open the guest chamber door and stormed in.

For a moment, his gaze focused on the woman's form with her backside to him hovered over the bed. Red hair trailed down her back and he grimaced, recalling Gwyneth's red hair. She stood and turned to him, and relief flowed through him. He walked toward Gwyneth's sister, Bridgette, and paused directly beside her as he glanced down at the sleeping child. Unsure what to think, he silently motioned to the hallway. She nodded and followed him out.

Once they were outside the bedchamber, she closed the door almost all the way and turned to face him. "Monsieur, is there somewhere private we can speak?"

"Yes, my study. Follow me." He had a hundred questions racing through his mind, but they would have to wait. As they descended the steps, his thoughts turned to Audrey. Even if her aunt was better tomorrow, he couldn't take Audrey to the park with Bridgette here. No matter what Bridgette might tell him in a few minutes, it wouldn't make him trust her enough to leave her alone in his house. He doubted he'd feel relaxed until she was no longer in England.

At his study, he waved her in. "Make yourself comfortable. I'll be back momentarily."

A few minutes later he'd located Harris, scribbled a quick note to Audrey telling her an emergency had arisen and he couldn't make tomorrow's picnic. He added a line at the end that he would contact her as soon as he was able. By the time he returned to the study, Bridgette looked agitated in the extreme.

"Please, sit." He motioned to the settee and took the chair opposite of her. What the hell should he ask first? Only one thing really mattered at the moment. "Is the child mine?"

Bridgette quickly nodded, her gaze not wavering from his. "Yes. Why else would I have brought him here?"

He saw her point, still...Trent studied her. Her gaze didn't dart, her hands and feet were still, her breathing normal, if the pulse at her neck was any indication. In every aspect, it appeared as if she was telling the truth. Then again, he'd been utterly duped by her sister. "Can you prove it?"

She smiled gently. "When you look at him, you will know he is yours. He has your exact eyes, color and shape of mouth, full with a slight upturn, and your golden hair with the same wave in the front."

Absently, Trent touched the front of his hair that had

always parted to the right. His gut tightened. Did he really have a son? His mind simply couldn't go there until he saw the child awake for himself. "We shall see." That was all the commitment Bridgette would get from him.

"Completely understandable, monsieur, after what my sister did to you. If I were you, I would want to judge for myself as well and not take anyone's word."

"Tell me of your sister." He braced his hands on his knees.

"She's still dead," Bridgette said bluntly.

Trent exhaled a sharp breath he hadn't realized he'd been holding. "I'm sorry," he quickly said, seeing Bridgette's eyebrows dip inward. "I'm not sure where to ask you to begin, so why don't you decide?"

"The day after I left you at the bar, I received a note from my brother's friend that Pierre was not going to make it through the night and he begged me to come and see him. When I arrived Pierre brought the child out." Bridgette paused and twisted her hands together. "Julian was dressed in rags and filthy."

Fierce protective anger flared inside Trent, surprising him. "Continue," he demanded, wishing the child were awake right now, so he could go and see him and judge for himself if he was his.

Bridgette cleared her throat. "After Gwyneth died Pierre tried to raise Julian, but then Pierre, of course, became ill. When I contacted him, he came to see me to beg me to take Julian, but Pierre decided I would be better persuaded if I saw the child. During the night, however, Pierre took a turn for the worse and feared he wouldn't live another day. That's why he called me to him the next day. On his deathbed, he told me of Gwyneth's British spy husband, whom she'd wed and then left for dead. He told me of the man's escape and how Pierre had seen the man tumble off a bridge and float facedown with the river current. Pierre believed you dead."

Trent stilled, his body tensing. "But you knew different."

Bridgette stared at him, the silence in the room growing until his nerves seemed to crackle within his body. Finally, she spoke. "I asked Pierre to describe Gwyneth's husband. His description didn't fit you, except for your eyes. You have unusually green eyes. Pierre said the same thing. Besides that, I had just met you and you had claimed to have loved Gwyneth. I put the pieces together, and it made sense that you would have lied to me and disguised yourself so Pierre wouldn't recognize you."

Trent clenched his jaw to stop the ticking on the right side. Once sufficiently under control he asked, "What did your brother want you to do with the boy?"

"He thought I might be able to bring Julian to London and find you, or rather since he believed you were dead, he supposed I might be able to find your family. He knew you were wealthy and I believe he had hopes your family would take one look at Julian and see the resemblance and take the child, because he was yours. Despite everything bad about Pierre, I believe he loved Julian."

"Do you want me to take the child?" When he saw Julian, if he believed the child was his, he would not let her leave with his son. He had to know what he was going to be up against.

She cast her gaze down. "I love my nephew, but I cannot raise a child on my own. I deserve a life, and he's *your* son. Will you not take him, because of Gwyneth?"

"Gwyneth be damned," Trent snapped. He gentled his tone when Bridgette flinched. "If I see the resemblance you say is there, the child will never be apart from me again."

Bridgette grabbed his hand, surprising him. "You are a good man. You will see it."

Trent pulled his hand away and stood to pour himself a drink but halfway to the liquor cabinet, he remembered Pickering saying the child was sick. "Is Julian sick?"

"A small cold. Nothing serious."

Trent strode to the door and flung it open. "Pickering," Trent bellowed down the hall.

Pickering appeared before him within minutes. "My lord?"

"The minute Harris returns send him to fetch my physician to the house with all due haste."

"Yes, my lord. Shall I prepare the lady a guest room?"

Trent caught Bridgette's wary gaze. Damnation. He couldn't turn the lady out in the middle of the night, whether the boy was his or not, and he certainly couldn't put her up in an inn. Too many prying eyes would see them and he couldn't chance questions that may lead anyone to delve into his past. The best course of action would be to keep her here, until he could see her safely on a ship headed back to France. Yes, that was a good plan and would ensure Audrey didn't hear anything questionable.

He nodded at Pickering. "Prepare the lady a room."

After Pickering departed, Bridgette walked out of the study and stood by Trent. "I'd like to check on Julian if you don't mind."

"Yes, of course," Trent replied, eager to see the child himself.

A few minutes later they stood at the child's bedside. Julian's breathing rattled in his tiny chest. Trent reached out and placed his hand over the boy's heart. Underneath his palm, he counted a steady beat. Trent's heart constricted in response as he evaluated the boy's face. Julian's hair was the same golden color as Trent's and it did seem the child had the same full lips, but it was hard to tell while he slept.

Moving quietly away from the bed, he waited as Bridgette bent down and pressed a kiss to Julian's forehead. After they departed the room, Trent walked her down the hall to the guest chamber Pickering had prepared for her. "Why don't you wash up and try to get some rest." When she started to protest, he held up a forestalling hand. "I'll check on Julian while you're sleeping, and the minute the physician arrives, I'll wake you. You have to be exhausted."

Bridgette nibbled on her lip, but the dark circles under her eyes revealed what she would not say with words. Finally, she sighed. "You promise to check on him and wake me when the physician arrives."

"I promise."

"All right, then." She stepped into her bedchamber as Pickering came out and closed the door, leaving Trent standing in the hallway with his butler. The silence stretched for a few awkward moments before Trent turned to Pickering. "Bring me a glass of whiskey to the boy's room."

"Right away, my lord."

Trent made his way back toward Julian's room as the sound of the butler descending the steps echoed in the quiet house. Once Trent pulled up a chair to the child's bed, he yanked off his cravat and loosened his shirt. His throat tightened as he stared at Julian. Was this his son? The funny feeling he always felt in his chest when he was around Audrey tugged inside him.

A few minutes later, Pickering returned and Trent accepted the glass of whiskey his butler silently handed him. Without drinking it, Trent sat in the dark contemplating what it might mean if this boy was his. He squeezed his eyes shut, losing track of how long he remained that way, his mind locked with disbelief. Then a memory of earlier today skittered across his thoughts. His belly had ached when he'd given the boy Martin a pony ride. He loved children, and no matter what havoc Julian being his son might cause his life, he would accept him.

Trent slowly opened his eyes and stretched his hand out to lightly touch his fingertips to Julian's brow. By God, the boy was hot.

Fear lodged inside Trent's gut. He shoved the chair back and was out the door, down the hall at Bridgette's room and rapping on the door within a few breaths. She opened the door right away. "What is it?" Fear made her voice tremble.

"Julian is burning up."

"Mon dieu!" Bridgette pushed past Trent and his anxiety escalated as they raced down the hall. When he entered the room, she was already shaking the child. "Julian!" She babbled some words in French while patting the boy's cheek. He moaned and slowly opened his eyes. First just a bit, and then he brought his tiny fists to his eyes, rubbed them and opened them all the way.

Trent met the child's frightened green gaze and all the

air in his lungs expelled in a rush of astonishment. The hairs on his neck stood on end as Julian blinked. It was like peering into a looking glass at a younger version of himself.

The boy cocked his head, causing a lock of golden hair to fall over his right eye. Immediately, he shoved the hair back. That gesture. That flick of his hand, all wrist and arrogance. Trent's heart seized in his chest, then exploded into a vicious beat. He scrambled onto his knees by Julian's bedside. On his son's level, staring into his eyes, the anger that had festered since the day he realized who and what Gwyneth was dissolved. He reached a hand out and Julian glanced at it, then looked to Bridgette for guidance of what he should do. Bridgette gave his son an almost imperceptible nod.

Trent held his breath until the moment the soft, small hand came to his and he wrapped his long fingers around the tiny, chubby ones. He brought his face close to his son, his vision blurring with tears. "Julian," he croaked. "Do you know who I am?"

"Qui," Julian answered in a tiny, unsure voice. "Papa."

"Yes," Trent agreed, warm tears trickling down his cheeks. "I'm your papa and you've come home." He gently pulled the child to him and hugged him to his chest. Julian wiggled in his arms until Trent reluctantly released him.

Bridgette set her hand on Trent's shoulder. "He'll accept you quickly. Children are like that."

Trent nodded, and smiled as Julian picked up his hand and played with the crest ring on his finger.

"Mine," the child said petulantly.

Trent ruffled his son's hair. "Someday," he answered as footsteps sounded behind him and the physician followed Pickering into the room.

Trent stood and turned to greet the physician. "Otts. This is my son. I trust you'll take excellent care of him."

The physician gaped at Trent for a moment before recovering his composure. "Of course, Lord Davenport."

Stepping aside, Trent motioned him toward Julian, but Julian held his chubby hand out to Trent. "Papa. Stay."

Trent's heart constricted as he took his son's hand

and locked gazes with Bridgette. She beamed at him. As the physician examined Julian, the child played with Trent's ring some more, twisting it on his finger. Trent suspected Julian had wanted him to stay by his side more to fiddle with his ring than for his sake, but it didn't matter. He was reluctant to part from the boy. It was astonishing to think he had a son. More shocking than that was the instantaneous intensity of his feelings for Julian. He wanted to protect him from any harm anyone would ever intend him. The first order of business before Julian was introduced to Society would be to make up a story he could tell about Gwyneth. People would talk, of that Trent was certain.

As the physician examined Julian, Trent couldn't help but worry about Audrey. He was certain she'd been on the verge of accepting his proposal, but what would she do now that he had a son? Julian was his rightful heir, no matter whether he and Audrey had a son or not. Could she accept that? Fear twisted his gut. He didn't want to lose her, but he wasn't sure there was going to be a way to entice her to stay.

Unless... He squeezed his eyes shut for a moment, then slowly opened them. Could he offer Audrey his love and trust? Tiny fingers twisted his crest ring as the question rang in his mind. Trusting and loving a child was simple. But a woman?

"My exam is complete," the physician announced.

Trent nodded and motioned toward the hall. "Let's speak out of the room. Bridgette, I'll inform you of what Dr. Otts says."

Bridgette nodded and moved to sit by Julian.

Once in the hall, Trent's concern exploded. "Well?"

"You boy's lungs sound excellent."

"I heard a rattle," Trent countered.

"It's nothing serious."

"What of his fever?"

"Children run warmer than adults, which often worries parents." Otts clapped Trent on the shoulder. "I wasn't aware you were married."

"I was. My wife died," Trent said evenly, not wishing to discuss the situation before he knew exactly what he wanted to say. "I trust you can keep my personal life to yourself."

Otts nodded his head. "Of course, my lord."

"Excellent. Is there anything you recommend I do for Julian to help speed his recovery?"

"Cool cloths to help with the fever and then fresh air once it breaks."

"I'll do it personally," Trent replied. He'd been absent for too much of Julian's young life already. He wasn't about to miss any more.

Much later in the evening Trent held his sleeping, less feverish, son in his arms. He hadn't felt this relaxed and happy in a very long time. The moment was almost perfect. He wanted to share his happiness with Audrey, and for once, the idea of opening up to her didn't set him on edge.

Twenty-Two

After five days of catering to her sick aunt and four days since she had last seen Trent at the Lionhursts' home, the moment the physician's carriage pulled into the drive of her home she scrambled to her feet and flew out of her study, anxious for Dr. Otts to pronounce her aunt in good health. If Aunt Hillie was truly better as she seemed to be, maybe Audrey could somehow see Trent today. She raced down the hall, ignoring the look of astonishment Mr. Barrett gave her when she soared past him and to the door. Flinging open the door, she rushed down the steps and halted as the carriage door slowly opened and doctor Otts descended followed by a young gentleman who resembled the physician. The man had to be Dr. Otts's son. He was in training to practice with his father, so it made sense.

"My goodness, Lady Audrey, has your aunt taken a turn for the worse?" doctor Otts asked.

"No." Audrey blushed.

The physician chuckled. "Tired of being cooped up in your home and playing nursemaid, are you?"

Audrey nodded. "I should be ashamed to admit it, but I daresay I'm not. She's a rather demanding sick person."

Otts patted her arm, as he used to do every time he came to attend to her mother on the many frequent occasions she took to her sick bed. "All persons who are used to being physically active are terrible sick patients."

"Especially children," the man behind Dr. Otts said, stepping forward.

Otts inclined his head to the gentleman. "This is my eldest son, Charles. I've told you about him. You met him years ago when he accompanied me once to care for your mother, though I would not think you would remember that. Do you mind if he is here today?"

"Not at all." Audrey met Charles's friendly gaze. "Your father tells me you want to be a physician."

"I did."

"Did?"

Charles grinned. "After treating Lord Davenport's active son this morning, I'm not so sure."

"Charles!" Doctor Otts snapped before looking warily at her.

"I was only making a joke," Charles sputtered.

"It's not that," Doctor Otts said, glaring at his son. "Lady Audrey, I must beg a personal favor of you."

She forced herself to nod, though she suddenly felt violently ill.

Doctor Otts's shoulders slumped with relief. "Please forget what you just heard. Lord Davenport would be highly agitated with me for my son's slip regarding Davenport's personal affairs, and I fear he would terminate my services with him as well as his entirely family if news of his son gets out before he wishes it to."

Audrey's heart pounded dreadfully. It took all her inner reserves to resist pressing her hand to it. "I understand." Her words shook with the raw emotion coursing through her. *A son?* Her mind reeled and a flush swept across her skin as she recalled the note on her desk she'd received from Trent this morning. How foolish she was. She bit hard on her lip to stop any trembling. He'd asked to call on her today. The note was the first he had sent since canceling their picnic four days ago, and though the note had seemed oddly stilted for him, she'd secretly hoped it was because he was struggling to accept that he loved her.

He didn't love her. He was still harboring secrets from her. Enormous secrets—*like a son*. Was this his child from his first wife or a child from a mistress? Either way, it didn't matter. The man would never trust her enough to love her. She wanted to curl into a ball and weep all her sorrows. Instead, she drew herself to her full height. There was not time to break down and weep. Her aunt waited upstairs to be pronounced well, and Lord Thortonberry also planned to call today.

"Follow me." She couldn't seem to speak above a strangled whisper. Motioning to the stairs, she turned without bothering to ensure they did as she asked. As she ascended, the men's footsteps tapped on each step behind her, the noise almost drowned out by the roar in her ears. Lord Thortonberry would be here soon, and she suspected it was to formally ask for her hand in marriage. Her gut clenched at the thought of saying yes, but what choice did she have? Could she be so selfish as to turn Lord Thortonberry away and cast her and her aunt's future into shadowy doubt?

Within moments, she stood at her aunt's bedside as Dr. Otts examined her. The physician and his son spoke in quiet whispers as her aunt chattered cheerfully about all the things she was going to do when she was able to leave her sickbed. Audrey forced a smile to her lips and kept it there, though her mouth trembled with the effort. Hopefully no one noticed. After a time, Dr. Otts put his instruments away and closed his case.

"My lady," he said as he looked down at Aunt Hillie, "you seem recovered quite nicely. You may get out of bed today, but take things slowly."

Aunt Hillie beamed. "I will. But being in bed like this has made me realize I've allowed myself to get far too soft in my ageing years. I think I'll start walking for exercise every day."

A crease appeared between Dr. Otts's eyebrows. "Exercise is advisable, but nothing strenuous. Remember what I told you yesterday."

"Hush," her aunt snapped.

Suspicious, Audrey carefully observed her aunt. Her lips were pressed hard together. Audrey didn't bother asking her aunt what the doctor had told her yesterday. She could tell by the stubborn set of her aunt's chin the woman clearly didn't want Audrey to know. Audrey reached down and straightened her aunt's covers. "Auntie, I'm so glad you're all better. I'll just see the doctor out and return shortly to help you get up and moving."

"Thank you, dear," her aunt responded without meeting Audrey's gaze.

Audrey frowned. Something was definitely amiss. Once she was downstairs with the doctor, she determined to try to get an answer from him. "Tell me what's wrong with my aunt."

The physician furrowed his brow. "I'm afraid I cannot do that without your aunt's permission."

"She'll never give it, and you know it. But if she dies because of some condition that she has that I should know about, it will be on your conscience." She gave him a stern look.

Doctor Otts glanced at his son. "This is the sort of dilemma you'll face, my boy. The confidentiality you've promised your patient weighs against their life being at risk if you don't tell anyone. What would you do?"

"I'd tell her," Charles said immediately.

Audrey smiled gratefully.

"We're in agreement," the physician said. "Lady Audrey, it's her heart. It's beating irregularly."

Audrey gulped in a breath. "Is she going to die?"

"Not today, my dear. But the irregular beat is a concern. I simply told her to try not to put herself under any undue stress. I imagine your aunt should be around for years if she will simply endeavor to live a peaceful life."

A peaceful life. Audrey's stomach rolled with nauseating despair. Her future had just been decided for her. Her aunt needed peace, not turmoil and uncertainly. A marriage to Lord Thortonberry would afford her the ability to give Aunt Hillie the stability she required.

After seeing the physician and his son out, Audrey didn't go up to her aunt. Instead, she made her way to her study and sat staring out the window, the thoughts in her head so loud she wanted to scream. She was helpless to stop them. A son of Trent's she could accept. That was not it at all. It was the lack of trust. The lies. Or withholding of the truth, which was the same as lying. Pressing her hands to her ears, she squeezed her eyes shut but her thoughts bombarded her like sharp drops of rain. Fast. Cold. Stinging. Was the child from a mistress? Or his former wife?

She swiveled back toward the desk and pressed her cheek to the cool wood. She'd had such hopes and dreams of a marriage filled with love and that was gone. She had to accept and face the harsh reality of life. Her throat tightened and tears stung the backs of her eyes, but she swallowed the sob that rose in her throat. She could fight back the tears, but she couldn't stop the gnawing pain in her belly or the loss making her heart feel as if someone squeezed it.

"Trent," she whispered before allowing her body to slump with despair. She sat there, listening to the groans of the house and watching the sun grow brighter as the hours slipped by.

Above her, the hardwood floors creaked. Was her aunt out of bed? Did she need something? Audrey shoved herself up. How utterly selfish she was being. She had not even spared a thought for her sick aunt's needs.

As she stood to see to her aunt, a rap sounded on her door. Trying to quickly tidy herself she called, "Enter."

Mr. Barrett entered the room with a grin on his face that faltered when he looked at her. "My lady, are you unwell?"

"No, simply tired." She smiled, sure he'd been grinning because he'd finally remembered to knock before entering a room. If Lord Thortonberry would allow it, she wanted to take Mr. Barrett with her when she was married. "Did you need me?"

"Lord Thortonberry has arrived."

"Show him to the library. I'll be there in a moment." To her dismay, her voice broke slightly. Egads, this would not do. She was not a woman without strength. She squared her shoulders and stood before Mr. Barrett had time to respond. "Never mind." She glided past her him. "I'll retrieve Lord Thortonberry myself."

She trod down the hall, determined to quit acting as if a marriage to Lord Thortonberry was a death sentence. It would be a good match, and she had to accept it. Entering the foyer, she held out her hands.

His eyebrows rose in surprise, but he took one of her hands. In the other, she noted he held a black velvet bag. Her stomach tightened as she considered whether a betrothal ring was in the bag.

He gently squeezed her hand. "Lady Audrey, you look exquisite."

"Thank you," she replied. "Why don't we speak in the parlor where we can be private?"

He started to nod, then stilled as his brow furrowed and his gaze settled somewhere behind her. "My lady. It's wonderful to see you out of bed and better."

Audrey's jaw dropped open as she swirled around and faced her aunt. "Aunt Hillie!" she admonished as she rushed to her aunt's side and grabbed her elbow. "However did you manage to get out of your bed and dress yourself?" Audrey eyed the seven feathers in her aunt's hair. "You even did you hair," she said, a bit bemused.

"I'm not so old and feeble that I can't take care of myself, no matter what that traitor physician told you." Her aunt's voice had dropped low.

Audrey gazed into her aunt's narrowed eyes. "Were you eavesdropping?" Audrey whispered.

Her aunt tugged her arm out of Audrey's grasp. "Most certainly." She brushed past Audrey and strode toward Lord Thortonberry. "Shall we all move to the parlor?"

"No, Auntie." Audrey answered for Lord Thortonberry, whose irritated face told her the last thing he desired was her aunt in there with them. She marched up to her aunt. "This is a private affair between Lord Thortonberry and me."

"I'm still your chaperone, my girl."

"Indeed," Audrey snapped, irritated that her aunt was trying to interfere when she had to understand there was no choice. "You may chaperone from outside the door." She grabbed Lord Thortonberry by the arm, tugged him toward the parlor and firmly shut the door on her aunt's protest.

Even with the door closed, her aunt's murmuring

infiltrated the silence. "Don't be foolish," Aunt Hillie whispered from the other side of the door. "Don't throw your life away for me, child."

Turning away from the door and toward Lord Thortonberry, she pressed her trembling hands to her forehead. "I'm sorry."

He took her gently by the elbow and led her to the settee. "It quite amused me to see you stand up to your aunt that way. I take it she doesn't think we will make a good match."

"No she doesn't," Audrey blurted, not wishing to lie to him. If she was going to do this, he needed to understand everything.

"What do you think?"

"I think," she said in a strangled whisper, "that you're getting a terrible bargain if you're here for what I think you are."

"I'm here to ask you to marry me, and if you say yes, I'll be the luckiest man in the world."

Heaven help her, all she could think was that she only wanted to hear these words from Trent. As wonderfully kind and attentive as Lord Thortonberry had been and as much as she understood that she should say yes, she wasn't sure she could make herself form the words. "Lord Thortonberry—"

"Call me Liam," he interrupted. "I have loved you since you were fifteen."

"What?" she gasped.

He nodded. "It's true. I was going to confess all to you years ago at my father's annual summer picnic, but when I went to find you at the stables with my brother. You were locked in Oscar's embrace and kissing him." Liam's face twisted savagely. "I'd dreamed of hearing my name on your lips, but then you were saying Oscar's name. I hated my older brother after that."

Audrey's mind reeled at his confession. She'd utterly forgotten the kiss his deceased older brother had stolen from her so many years ago. Perhaps she'd pushed it out of her head. Oscar had been her childhood crush, until she'd realized his true distasteful nature. Yet after he died that very summer he stole that kiss she'd felt terribly guilty for her cruel words to him that day in the stables after he'd cornered her. A terrible, sinking thought struck her. Liam had worshipped his older brother. "Have you been pursuing me because of that long-ago kiss? Because you wanted to somehow have what you thought your brother wanted and never had the chance to have?"

"No." His reply was vehement. "You've got it all twisted. Oscar was the one..." Liam's words trailed off and he jerked a hand through his hair. "Never mind. The past isn't important now, as long as we're together for the future."

Audrey tensed. "I don't love you."

"You will. You'll grow to love me."

"Yes." She nodded. "Perhaps. But not ever like I love him." She didn't bother to name Trent. The angry flare of Liam's eyes revealed he knew exactly who she was talking about.

"You'll forget him in time. And I love you enough for both of us." He grabbed her and crushed her to his chest.

She stilled, not wanting to be cruel and pull away. Her head spun with her thoughts. "If this is about a competition with your dead brother—"

Liam released her. "I've told you it isn't. I admit I was insanely jealous that day I saw my brother kissing you, but I was jealous because I already knew you were the girl for me."

She stared at his earnest face, unsure what to believe. Liam and his brother had always competed with each other for everything, as far as she could remember. Her gut told her she was the ultimate competition Liam had no intention of losing, even if his brother was long gone. "I'm not sure what to do," she admitted.

He shoved the black velvet bag at her. "Maybe this will make up your mind."

She shook her head and tried to push the bag back to him. "A betrothal ring will not clear my thoughts."

"It's not a ring. I have one for you, but this is something entirely different." He opened the bag and withdrew the jewelry she'd given him to sell.

Dumbfounded, she took the jewels from him. "You never sold them?"

He shook his head. "I couldn't. They're yours."

"But the money?"

He shrugged. "Mine. I knew you wouldn't take charity, so..."

"So you made me think you'd sold them for me."

"Yes. I'm sorry I lied."

"No." She briefly placed her hand over his, touched by what he'd done for her. "I understand why you did it."

"So, Audrey, will you marry me?"

Panic seized her voice, so when the door to the library banged open and Mr. Barrett charged in all she could do was gape.

"My lady, your aunt has fainted!"

Audrey jumped up and raced out the door, almost tripping over her aunt's crumpled body. Sinking to her knees, she turned her aunt's head to the side and caught the faintest flickering of her aunt's eyelids as Hillie squeezed them firmly shut. Audrey was alternately relived and irritated. Irritation won out. Oh, she'd singe her aunt's ears good when they were alone for pulling such a ploy.

Behind her, Liam hovered. "Shall I fetch the doctor for you?"

Audrey welcomed the reprieve, though her aunt was foolish indeed. Relinquishing her dreams was harder than she'd anticipated. "No, the doctor won't be necessary." Audrey squeezed her aunt's arm encouragingly. "Aunt Hillie." She spoke to her aunt. "Did you break your fast this morning?"

On cue, her aunt fluttered her eyelashes for a second before opening them. "Dear me," Aunt Hillie exclaimed. "I didn't. That must be why I fainted."

Audrey suppressed the hysterical laughter rising in her throat. "Liam, if you'll just help her up, I'm certain she simply needs nourishment."

Together, they got her aunt to her feet, and by the time she was righted Mr. Barrett stepped in to help. Audrey bit her lip to fight off the smile caused by her aunt's dramatics. "If you don't mind, I'll see to my aunt and meet you in the park later this afternoon?" she asked Liam. "I'll have your answer then."

He looked as if he wanted to argue, but when he nodded his head in assent, Audrey nearly expelled a relieved breath. Letting it out slowly and subtly, she saw him out. When the door was firmly shut, she turned to her aunt, who stood a few paces away with Mr. Barrett gripping her elbow.

Audrey glared at her, and Hillie smirked back. "No need to thank me," Hillie chirped as she removed her elbow from Mr. Barrett's grasp.

"My lady, can you stand on your own?"

"Certainly," Hillie replied, reaching up to adjust the crooked feathers in her hair. But I am starving. Why don't you run along and see that breakfast is set out?"

Once Mr. Barrett departed, Audrey wilted into a wingback chair and pressed her fingertips to her temples. "Whatever am I going to do?"

Twenty-Three

Trent knew he was driving his carriage recklessly toward Audrey's home, but he couldn't seem to restrain himself. Julian was settled with the new nanny, Bridgette was on her way back to France and all he could think about was telling Audrey about Julian and seeing her reaction. For some reason, his instincts told him her face would solve a good deal for him. What that was, he had no idea, but he wanted to trust his instincts as he used to before Gwyneth had made him trust no one, least of all himself.

After arriving at Audrey's he tethered the horses and rapped on the door. He blinked in surprise when Audrey's aunt answered. Her eyebrows arched and her mouth momentarily formed an O before settling into a hard line. "What do you want?"

Her tone was less than friendly. He forced a casual smile, though tension vibrated through him. "I assume you are feeling all better?"

"I feel perfectly fine. But try telling that to my stubborn niece. She's determined to ruin her life and sacrifice herself for me. I tell you, I'm fit as a fiddle no matter if my heart beats strangely or not. I've never felt better. I'm going to give Dr. Otts a scalding he'll never—"

Trent held up a hand, his mind grasping her words as coldness seeped into his bones. "Otts is your physician?"

She gave him a narrow-eyed look. "Yes. So you might as well turn around and head back the way you came,

Lord Davenport. My niece is not here, and I highly doubt even if she were that she would see you."

Fear pummeled his gut like a well-trained fighter. Digging deep, he forced a lethal calmness. "Do you mind telling me why Lady Audrey would refuse to see me?"

Audrey's aunt observed him with a look of utter distaste. "I don't mind telling you at all. My niece is a lady. As such, it would be highly improper to allow you to call on her when she's to be betrothed to another man."

Through the roaring dim of blood rushing in his ears he asked, "Lady Audrey is going to marry Thortonberry?"

"Seems so," Audrey's aunt snapped. "Between you with your secrets and her worry over my health, the foolish woman seems to feel she has no choice."

He clenched his teeth against his flaring temper. "My secrets? Such as?"

"It's incredibly hard to keep a child secret, Lord Davenport, no matter how much you wish to."

He was going to throttle Otts, but first he needed to find Audrey. He refused to believe she no longer loved him because of Julian. It went against everything he knew of her character. "I want to be certain I understand you. You're telling me Audrey would rather marry a man she doesn't love than me, simply because I have a child."

"I daresay she would have rather married you, but you never could quite come to snuff, could you? And to keep such a secret as a child..." Audrey's aunt clucked her tongue.

Damnation. He had to have the chance to explain about Julian. "Please." He touched Lady Hillary's elbow. "I need to see her."

The woman's face remained cold. Hell and damn. Now he knew where Audrey got a bit of her inner strength from. He was going to be forced to grovel. So be it. "I came here today to tell her about my son."

"And?" The one word was frosty.

He refused to lose Audrey to his fear. "I love her. I love her and it's useless to fight it." Saying the words released him. By God, he felt like a new man. Now, if only he could convince Audrey he was a changed man and worth her love.

A slow smile pulled at the older woman's lips. "Now, then." Her tone had become sweet and motherly. She grasped him to her and gave him a hug. "Was that so hard?"

"You've no idea," he admitted, returning her embrace before extracting himself.

"Yes, well..." She chuckled. "The course of true love never did run smooth."

"Shakespeare," Trent supplied, wanting to hurry Audrey's aunt along.

"Indeed. I knew I liked you. She's at Hyde Park. She planned to take a stroll and clear her mind before meeting with Lord Thortonberry."

Hope filled Trent's chest. "So she's not betrothed yet?"

"Not yet, though I doubt that will make it much easier for you. Her mind seemed set when she left here, though I tried to make her see reason. You know how stubborn she is, though."

"I do. It's one of the things I love best about her."

After saying a quick goodbye, he rushed to untether the horses and depart. Once on the road to the park, he pushed the horses harder than he normally would, driven by the fear he would be too late to stop Audrey from accepting Thortonberry's offer. Once she gave her promise, Audrey was not the kind of woman would ever break it. His breaths came in short gasps as his blood surged in his veins. He had to make it to her on time.

A short time later, he entered the park and spotted Audrey strolling alone down the narrow footpath along the southern end of the Serpentine. Sunlight flittered through the bright green and yellow leaves of the tall oak trees that lined either side of the path. She moved under a particularly shady spot where the overhead tree was especially dense, strolled out of the shadows and meandered behind a row of full green trees whose branches started at the ground and swept up to completely canopy her.

Jesus, he prayed he wasn't too late to stop her from accepting Thortonberry. After everything, he was at her mercy, a state of existence he'd tried to avoid repeating. Yet it was unavoidable. He slowed the horses, his movements made jerky by nerves. Once he dismounted, he quickly saw to the horse, and then abandoning all pride, he raced to her. She turned as he rounded the corner, her delicate brow crinkling. His heart jerked in response to the lovely picture she presented in a yellow walking dress with the thick green canopy of leaves as her background.

"Your aunt told me you were here."

"I wish she wouldn't have done that."

Audrey's frosty tone was expected, but her anticipated reaction didn't make the clenching of his gut less painful. "I'm glad she did," he replied, determined to push through and do what he'd come to do. "She tells me you know of my son already, but I'd like the chance to explain."

The guarded green gaze that stared at him ripped at his heart. Her distrust and pain was obvious. But she hadn't refused to hear about his son. He hesitated, measuring her for a moment. He'd pushed her away—hell, everyone away—for so long. It seemed impossible for him to form the bluntly honest words that might put him back in a position of weakness he'd done all in his power to avoid. It had been easier to tell her aunt how he felt, which was ridiculous.

Audrey sighed loudly and crossed her arms. "If you've nothing to say, I wish you would leave. Lord Thortonberry is meeting me here and he expects an answer to his proposal. Three would make a crowd, don't you think?"

Coward, his mind taunted. He couldn't let her go without ever having tried. "I cannot believe you no longer want to marry me because I have a son."

Her lower jaw fell open. "Don't be ridiculous. I'd never be so shallow. If anything, it would be because you hid the boy from me. But more so it's that you don't love me." Her voice shook and her eyes glistened. He struggled against himself not to yank her into his arms. Every part of him warned to let her finish even as relief flowed through him at her words.

"Go on," he encouraged gently.

"Go on?" She sounded incredulous. "All right, I might as well. I think I fell in love with you the first day I met you, and I've done nothing but offer my love to you ever since. You returned my offer with lies, secrets, more lies and a cold heart. I would never marry a man who doesn't have the capacity to trust and love me and you've shown that time and again. How could you hide the fact that you had a son from me?"

"I didn't know I had a son."

"You didn't know?" She grunted. "Do you expect me to believe that?"

He scrubbed his hand over his face. "Yes, because it's true. I had no idea until several days ago I had a son. Gwyneth's sister, Bridgette, showed up at my home with Julian and that is the first I knew of his existence. I wanted to tell you in person, which is the reason I came to see you today. A note will not do for that sort of thing. Do you not agree?"

Her mouth turned down further, but at least she nodded her agreement. He relaxed his ridged stance. "I had to get Julian settled and see Bridgette safely back to France."

"I can understand that," she said slowly. "What I don't understand is what you said a moment ago. Why ever would I not accept your child? He is your flesh and blood, and therefore I would love him. Do you really think I could be that cold?"

"No, darling, I don't. You misunderstood me a moment ago. What I meant was I refused to accept you are anything but the honest, kind-hearted woman that I love."

"That you what?" Her words were a shaky whisper.

"I love you," he said simply.

Her breath hitched, but she didn't respond. The three words hung in the air between them, the moment stretching until his taut nerves strummed in his ears. Desperation curled in his belly and knifed a path to his heart. "Am I too late? Is your mind set against me and for Thortonberry?" His heart pounded against his breastbone.

AUDREY COULD SCARCELY BELIEVE WHAT she'd heard. "Too late," she mumbled, too shocked to make her incoherent thoughts come out correct.

Audrey blinked as a pleading look swept across Trent's proud face. Heaven above, now he was misunderstanding her! Before she could say a word to clarify, he dropped to his knees and wrapped his arms around her waist. "Audrey." His hoarse whisper filled with entreaty shook her so badly she placed her hands on his shoulders to steady herself.

He glanced up at her, his green eyes glowing with pain. "I've been a fool. Desperate not to be hurt again. Until the moment I held my son and felt immediate love for him shove its way into my heart, I thought I could live without ever loving anyone with a completeness that left me vulnerable again."

She swayed toward Trent, his confession filling her heart, body and soul. Gently, she stroked a hand through his hair and sighed when he curled his fingers around her hips tighter, possessively—like he would never let her go. She grazed her fingers lovingly across his cheek. "What do you think now?"

"That if I'd been smarter, I would have realized months ago my fight against loving you was hopeless from the moment I met you. You smile, and my heart tugs. You flay me with a rejoinder and my chest tightens. You sway your hips and my body burns. But most importantly, you've shown me what it is to truly be loved by someone. You never gave up on me. On us. Please, I beg you—"

She pressed a finger to his warm lips, a ripple of awareness flowing through her as their skin made lingering contact. "Don't beg." She tugged on his arm to make him rise.

Slowly, he moved to stand, but instead of letting her go he slid his arms up her back and locked his hands around her waist. He pulled her against his hard chest while his eyes implored her. "I will gladly beg, if it will make you reconsider marrying Thortonberry and marrying me instead."

A happy chuckle burst from her. "I have no intention of marrying Lord Thortonberry."

"You don't?" Astonishment crossed Trent's face, followed swiftly by a look of stark relief. "Did your aunt know that?"

"Of course. Why?"

"She tricked me, but I'm damn glad she did."

She twined her hands around his neck. "I'd convinced myself it was my duty to marry and provide my aunt with the comfort she deserved, but in the end, I just couldn't do it. And after I talked to Whitney I felt secure in my decision and not as if I was abandoning my aunt."

Trent grinned. "What did my cousin say?"

"She delicately pointed out I would be acting just as my father had if I married Lord Thortonberry. I don't know why I didn't see it before. Maybe my father thought he would be a good husband to my mother." Audrey shivered at the possibility that she'd been thinking exactly as her father might have so many years ago. "Between Whitney and myself we came up with an alternative solution to my financial dilemma other than marriage."

"And what was that?" Trent asked, grinning at her.

"Sally needs a new nanny, so she agreed to let me take the position, and your mother, it seems, wants a companion to live with her, so I was going to send my aunt there. My mother always said a million tears won't change a lady's life but a well-thought out plan can alter her future."

"Your mother was clearly a brilliant woman," Trent said huskily before cupping Audrey's face and bringing his lips mere inches from hers. "Will you marry me and let me love you forever?

The tenderness in his gaze made her heart flutter. "Forever?"

He nodded as he pressed his lips gently to hers and then drew back. He took her hand and laid it against his pounding heart. "What I feel for you will never die, even when I do. Marry me."

She curled her hand over his. "Gladly."

His tender gaze turned possessive and bright. A tingling burst in the pit of her stomach as he claimed her mouth in a hard, hungry kiss. She met his hunger with her own need to possess him and make him hers. His heart thudded against her breasts as he deepened their kiss and bid her silently to open her mouth for him. She did so willingly wanting to taste him once again, as only dreams had allowed for so long.

The sweetness of his kiss made her head spin, but he gathered her more firmly in his embrace so all her worries fell away. Her mouth burned with his branding, but it was a sweet fire. He kissed her lips, then trailed a blazing path of kisses across her neck before lavishing his attention to her jawbone, her nose, her eyelids, and finally when she thought she would die of wanting his lips on hers once again, he settled there with a ragged moan.

Blood pounded in her head, swirled in her veins and made her body tremble. As his lips gentled, her pulse dipped, but he traced his tongue seductively across her lower lip before delving into her mouth and making her pulse leap while her body tensed with longing.

She plunged her hands into his hair to tug him closer, but as she did, a sound behind her stilled her. Trent pulled back at once, a cold, hard look crossing his face. She knew before turning that Liam had arrived. Nervousness and regret twisted her stomach into knots. "Please," she mouthed at Trent in way of asking for his cooperation.

He gave a terse nod and turned toward Liam. "Keep your hands off her, Thortonberry." Trent's voice held a menacing note, but at least he had been kind enough not to blurt the news of her decision. It confirmed what she'd believed all along. Trent was a man who cared deeply for others' feelings, which was why the wound his deceased wife had inflicted on him had taken so long to heal. She watched as he moved a far enough away to give her privacy yet still, she assumed, be where he could see her.

Audrey took a deep breath and focused on Liam. "I'm sorry," she said simply. "I love him, and I cannot change that. I am going to marry him."

"Sorry," Liam snarled. "Sorry is not good enough."

She blanched at the bitterness in his voice. "It wouldn't be fair to you if I married you. You deserve a woman who will love you with all her heart."

He yanked a hand through his hair. "I lost you to my brother and now Davenport. At least my brother loved you."

"Loved me?" Audrey wrinkled her brow. "That kiss you saw in the stables was the first I ever exchanged with your brother, and he stole that kiss. He didn't love me. I was on his long list of the debutantes he fancied he could seduce. Surely you knew that. My brother warned me away from Oscar, because he'd heard through mutual acquaintances about his list. You had to know."

Liam shook his head as he stalked back and forth in front of her. "I confessed my feelings for you to Oscar and the next thing I knew I stumbled in on the two of you kissing in the stables."

"Oh, Liam." Pity swelled in Audrey's throat. If he'd only told her this sooner, she would have understood they were both wanting the other for the wrong reasons. He thought he loved her, but he didn't. Not really. "I suspect your brother pursued me because he knew how you felt about me." She touched his cheek, biting her lip when Trent growled intensely. She prayed he wouldn't interrupt. "What did your brother tell you after you saw us that day?"

Liam stopped pacing and gave her a narrow-eyed look. "He said you told him you loved him."

"No." She shook her head and dropped her hand, impressed and glad Trent had kept his temper this long. No need to push him further. "I never said that. The only man I've ever told I loved is Trent."

Liam reached for her as if to grab her by the arms and she scuttled backward but behind her Trent bellowed. She whirled toward Trent to beg him to stay put and as she turned Liam raced by her and charged into Trent. The two men flew back and hit the ground hard. Audrey's breath seized in her throat as Trent somehow came up on top, flipped Liam onto his back, and straddling him in a blur, shoved his forearm against Liam's neck to pin him to the ground. She raced toward Trent, fearful he might hurt Liam without truly meaning to.

"Trent!" she gasped.

He flicked his cold gaze to her and it immediately softened before he returned his attention to Liam, who gasped and bucked under Trent's hold. "Cease moving and I will lessen my hold so you may breathe a little easier."

Liam immediately quit bucking and Trent whipped his

arm off the marquess's neck and shoved his palms against Liam's shoulders. Audrey bit her lip, unsure whether to interfere or not.

"Get off me," Liam snarled.

Trent shook his head. "Not until you hear me carefully. I understand the pain you must be going through to lose her. The agony. The anger. I would want to pound my face if I were you, but it's no use Thortonberry. You will never get a punch in and you will lose her respect for trying. Say goodbye to her and walk away, man. Save your dignity."

Audrey held her breath as Liam's wild gaze swung between Trent and her. Finally he nodded. "I'll go peacefully, so get off me."

Trent surged to his feet in a blur and stood beside her before she could even release her breath.

Liam staggered to his feet, his cravat undone and his hair in wild disarray. He fixed her with a hostile stare. "I pity you," he said tonelessly. "I would have given you my heart. All he will do"—Liam glanced at Trent then back to her—"is break yours."

"Liam—"

"No. Do not even bother. There is nothing you can say to me anyway that I want to hear."

She nodded and held her silence as he strode around the majestically sweeping branches of the tree that hid them and disappeared out of her sight.

Trent gathered her into his arms and a bit of the tension coiling in her shoulders and neck released. "I feel dreadful for having hurt him so."

Trent nuzzled her neck. "I know you do, darling, which is one of the many reasons I love you."

She melted easily into his arms, relenting to the happiness and pushing the sadness for Liam away.

"I am"—he gave her a quick kiss on the lips—"irrationally jealous over you. When it seemed he would touch you—"

Trent quit speaking and raked his gaze over her body before continuing. "I wanted to smash him in the face when I had him pinned simply because he had tried to touch you."

"But you did not," she murmured, glad he had controlled himself.

"No. I did not. I'm not a ruffian, but I cannot say I will always hold my temper if another man dares to put his hands on you."

Audrey smiled up at him. "Well, I'll just make sure to never give you reason to be jealous."

"Excellent. Then you promise to never speak alone with another man."

She started to laugh but stopped at the intense look on his face. "You're serious?"

"Quite."

She slid her hands up his chest. "Darling, if we're going to be married, then you must trust me completely."

"I trust you." His intense tone told her he believed it to be true.

"It's the men I don't trust. I saw the look in Thortonberry's eyes. He would have done anything to win you, if he thought there was anything that could be done."

She cocked her head to the side while playing with a particular enticing golden lock of hair that curled against Trent's neck. "How do you know that's what his look meant?"

"I saw that same look on my face this morning as I was shaving before coming to tell you of my son. I contemplated every possible scenario of what might occur and what I might do. I concluded in the end, I would do anything to make you mine."

Her breath hitched in her throat and her pulse beat a rapid tattoo in her neck. "Such as?"

"If I couldn't convince you to marry me now that I have a son, I planned to kidnap you and ruin you so you'd be forced to marry me."

She pulled back, scarcely able to take a proper breath at the unrestrained possessiveness gleaming in his eyes. "Scandalous," she whispered throatily.

He pressed a kiss to the vein on her neck where the blood pumped through savagely. "I'm sorry you're angry with me."

She smiled wickedly, enjoying the widening of his eyes

and the dawning smile of realization that tugged at his lips.

"You want me to ruin you?"

She batted her lashes playfully before coyly looking down. "Only if you think you must in order to ensure I'm yours."

Grinning, he swept his arms under her legs and picking her up held her against his chest.

Laughing, she pressed a hand against his shoulder. "Someone might see us." She didn't personally give a fig what the *ton* said. After all, she would be Trent's wife, and if she knew him it would be sooner rather than later. But she would hate for her actions to cause her aunt heartache or Trent's mother concern.

"No. I brought my carriage, so you can hover inside. If it makes you feel better, stay down until we reach my house."

A thrill shot through her, dampened only by one dark shadow still hovering over her life. "Trent, will you help me find Richard? Do you know someone we can hire to locate him?"

A twinkle filled Trent's eyes. He kissed her on the tip of her nose and then said, "Leave it to me. I know the perfect man, and if it is at all possible, I vow he will find your brother and bring him home to you."

Audrey hugged Trent as he set her on her feet, grabbed her hand and tugged her around the low-hung tree toward his carriage in the distance.

She pulled to a stop as they neared it. "Will you tell me all the details of your meeting? I want to help."

He winked at her. "As soon as I know more details, I'll tell you. Come." He let down the carriage stairs and helped her inside. "Let us think on only the two of us for tonight."

She nodded and closed the curtain to the carriage window. With a smile, Trent shut the door and the carriage dipped as he took the driver's seat. Nerves made her stomach turn as the carriage moved out of the park, yet excitement filled her as well. She loved Trent with all her heart, and she wanted nothing more than to spend the first night he'd declared his love for her in his arms.

Twenty-Four

"You're certain of this?" Trent asked as he took Audrey's hand and led her down the garden path that meandered beside his London townhome and to the garden house that set at the back of his property well hid from anyone's view.

Audrey nodded. "I've never been more certain of anything in my life."

Her words still confirmed what she'd been saying since he led them out of Hyde Park, but her voice quivered. He paused on the darkened trail and turned to her, brushing a branch out of his face as he did so. With the sun waning, shadows loomed over her forehead and eyes and made seeing her expression difficult. He tugged her gently to his chest, then encircled her small frame. When she sighed, slipped her arms around his waist and pressed her cheek to his heart, a knot lodged in his throat.

He leaned his face into the top of her hair and inhaled the scent of honeysuckle that always lingered on her. His chest tightened almost painfully. The love he felt for her robbed him of the ability to speak for a moment. More than anything, he wanted to spend the rest of his life making her happy, and despite the fact that he'd dreamed nightly of holding her naked in his arms since the day he met her, he'd wait until they were married, if she had any doubts. But how to get her to be truthful with him?

"Audrey." He kissed the top of her head and hugged her. "I don't want you to ever lie to me, even if you're worried you'll displease me. I'd rather be momentarily annoyed than either of us breach the trust our marriage must have."

Her shoulders sagged and he inwardly cursed. So be it. They would wait until their wedding day. His hardened body tensed at the thought. What he needed was a tub of cold water to cool his lust.

She leaned back, so he could just see her somber expression. His heart twisted at the worry on her face. "Darling." He cupped her cheeks and kissed her fully on the mouth. "Do not fret yourself. Many women are scared of what happens between a man and a woman. Once we're married, I'm sure a bit of your tension will ease." A disgruntled smile stretched across her mouth, but he forced himself to continue. She had never been with a man, after all, and it pleased him to think he would be the only one to ever know her intimately. "I'll be very gentle on our wedding night."

When Audrey erupted into laughter, he frowned. She leaned into him, her soft chest pressing against his hard one, which did nothing to dampen his lust. The woman would be the death of him.

"I'm not nervous about what occurs between a man and a woman. Whitney and Sally are married and have told me a few things. So rest assured, I know exactly what to expect."

Imagining the sort of education she might have gotten from Whitney and Sally made him bark with laughter. He plunged his hands into her hair and drew her face near his. He nibbled first on her upper lip and then her lower, reveling in the soft mewling noises that came from her and the way she squirmed under his administration.

He'd been a fool to think she would be afraid to be with him. She was a passionate woman. Leaving one hand braced around the slender nape of her neck, he moved the other to her exposed collarbone and traced a slow path across her chest. A hiss of air escaped her, and his already hard body strummed with the desire touching her inflamed in him. He swallowed and searched his mind for what he had meant to ask her. Oh, yes, the concern on her face. "Something is worrying you. If it's not what we will be doing when we join, then what had you looking upset?"

She gazed down, but he cupped her chin and forced her to look at him. "Tell me. Let me soothe your fears." With his hands. His tongue. His—he groaned at the direction of his thoughts.

She blew out a long breath. "I'm afraid I'll fail to compare to *her*."

Damn Gwyneth. Even dead, she caused problems. It was time to bury her once and for all. He placed his hands gently on Audrey's cheeks and stared into her eyes. "There are many different levels of love, Audrey. I'll not deny I loved Gwyneth at one time, but it was the most simplistic layer of love—the one where someone intrigues you and captures your attention and then your passion. There was never time for more to develop and then when I really came to know who she was there was only room for pain. But with you—" His emotions rose up and choked him. He cleared his throat. "Ah, my love, with you, our love is complex, rich, multilayered. You have my respect, loyalty, passion, admiration, heart and soul. You have everything within my power to give to you and when I hold you in my arms there's not a speck of room for another woman in my heart or my head."

She flung herself at him as if his words had released her fears. Thank God.

AUDREY'S HEART FILLED WITH ACHING happiness as she grasped clumsily at Trent and kissed his lips. His confession set her free. She was no longer afraid he might think of Gwyneth. Her only fear now was wasting a single moment of this night. "I love you." She crushed her lips to his, desire curling in her belly, tightening her loins and making her breasts grow heavy with need.

His mouth moved over hers, hard and possessively. She needed more. Wanted more. When his hands roamed up her back in an exploring motion and slid back down in a seductively slow slither, she whimpered into his mouth. He answered her with a throaty chuckle as he curled his fingers into her burning flesh and squeezed her bottom repeatedly.

For a few moments, she stood locked in his embrace, a prisoner to his feverish kisses that matched the intense need burning within her. She had no desire to back out of his arms or stop the building passion, so when he pulled away and buried his head against her neck she protested with a cry. His panting breath tickled her ear as his hands came to her hips and tugged her against his hard erection. "If we don't go inside the garden house I'll take you on these hard steps and you deserve better than that."

She giggled at his thick, unsteady voice. It amazed her that she had the power to elicit such unbridled need in him. "I wouldn't mind being taken here one bit, except for the fact that I worry someone might chance by."

Trent groaned. "No danger in that. The servants know not to come out here, unless I specifically instruct them to, and Julian is no doubt being tucked in bed by his new nanny. Besides that, too many trees surround the garden house for anyone to see us. Still it might be uncomfortable."

The cautious expression on his face made her smile. "I rather like hard spots," she said, plucking her hands on her hips and allowing her gaze to travel down between his thighs.

"Then let me oblige you, my love," he growled.

Her gaze flew to his as he cupped her breasts and slipped his fingers over the top edge of her bodice, giving the material a hard jerk down. Her breasts spilled forward into his hands and hot desire exploded within her.

He lowered his mouth to her left breast and flicked his tongue over the hardened bud. She squealed with delight and pleasure. "More," she whispered, burying her hands in his thick hair and tugging his mouth more firmly over her breast. His tongue circled the bud slowly, each delicious swirl around her sensitive skin making sensations spark through her from her breast all the way to her toes. She arched her back toward his mouth and almost screamed with delight when he took her farther

into his mouth and began to suck greedily. Her breast
tightened almost unbearably and her body throbbed from
the inside out.

He moved his mouth away from her breast only to
claim her other one and lavish it with the same wicked
attention. Within seconds, she clung to him, her legs too
weak to hold her upright. Somehow, miraculously, he
seemed to sense her state and held her with one muscled
arm gripped around her waist.

The need within her built. She wanted to touch him.
See him naked. Explore his body as he was exploring
hers and bring to him the same place he was taking her.
She tugged his head up. "I want to touch you. And see
you everywhere."

A sensuous smile pulled at his mouth. He stepped
back and stripped off his clothes, layer by heart-
pounding layer. When he got to his shirt and pulled it
over his head, she thanked God for the now full moon as
the corded muscles of his abdomen rippled with the
movement of his powerful arms. He tossed the shirt
away, bent to tug off his boots and then stood for a
second, perhaps to let her drink him in.

She did, ravaging his gleaming flesh with her eyes,
and when she couldn't resist a second longer, she flew
against him, running her hands over the hard ridges and
secretive planes of his sculpted body. His muscles
jumped under her exploring fingers and her heart
jumped right along with his body. She lowered her
trembling, eager hands to his breeches and fumbled
trying to get them undone. His large hands covered hers
at once, calming, stilling, reassuring. Together they
undid the ties and she pulled his remaining clothing
down until he was able to kick the layers away.

She didn't have time to right herself. Strong hands
came under her arms and pulled her gently up the length
of his overwhelming body. The heat of his desire singed
her through the thin material of her gown.

He raked his eyes up and down her length and
motioned her to turn around. When she did, his hands
circled around her body just below her chest and hauled
her up against his body so that the length of his need

prodded her lower back. She threw her head back with longing as a moan escaped between her pulsing lips. He slid his hands slowly over her exposed, sensitive flesh, gently pinching one bud and then the other. She gritted her teeth against the scream of pleasure that wanted to erupt.

A hoarse growl came from behind her, as his hands cupped between her legs and started massaging her until she wiggled and whimpered. She was coming undone from the inside out. Soon, she'd splinter if he didn't take her. She was sure of it. "Please," she demanded.

His hands stopped their motion abruptly and then flew to her back, and before she knew it, she was standing perfectly naked, her back pressed to his throbbing length. The springy hairs of his powerful thighs tickled her skin as he nudged his leg between hers until she spread them apart for him. Inside her body, a great tug and pull commenced, starting in her belly and spiraling downward to her core, where an ache blossomed.

As he kissed a fiery trail over the backs of her shoulders and up and down each side of her neck, gooseflesh rose over her entire body. She shivered with unrestrained need. "Now?"

"Soon," he promised in a throaty voice.

His hard, hot, slick length came between her legs and she tensed in expectation and a bit of fear. He slid his hand over her hips and between her thighs to the valley of her most private area. His fingers gently parted her throbbing parts and playfully caressed her.

She couldn't stand the painful need building from within. She grabbed his thighs and dug her nails in and tugged in a desperate attempt to make him come inside her. His fingers touched on the spot between her legs that pulsed with its own life and when he started gently to massage her there, her entire body strummed to the beat of his movements. He played her like an intimate instrument, bringing her body to a deafening crescendo that culminated in spasms, stripping her of all her strength. She arched out like a bow about to break, quiver after quiver racking her, and pure, sweet heat flooding her veins.

She sagged into his hands even as his member nudged farther between her legs to tease the heated opening of her body. She spread further for him, his hotness and hardness consuming her. She wanted him. Expected him. Hoped for him. Withdrawing with a growl, he whipped her around and gave her a hard kiss on the mouth.

She blinked at him, dazed. "Is something wrong?"

He raked a hand through his hair. "You strip me of my control. I want to take you hard and fast, and I will, but not today. Not when you've never had a man inside of you. There's a time for romance and a time for rough play. Today is the time for more gentleness."

She opened her mouth to disagree, but he placed a finger over her lips. "Trust me."

She nodded numbly as he strode up the steps of the garden cottage. His firm buttocks flexed as he walked. He belonged to her, body and soul. He'd said so. Joy took her breath once more. Before she knew it, he came back out holding several blankets. He laid them in the entranceway and then took her by the hand and gently guided her to her back.

Before she could settle fully, he loomed over her, his hands coming to either side of her shoulders. He bent down until his mouth found her neck and he alternated between kissing and sucking his way down her neck to her breasts. He lavished one breast with attention and then the other. And as he started to move down her stomach with feathery kisses, she grabbed his shoulders and stopped him.

He glanced up, his eyebrows arched. "What is it, my love?"

Silently she tugged him again, until he was above her once more. She reached down between them and stroked him between his thighs. The groan of pleasure that came from him made her smile. He'd undone her moments ago. Now it was her turn. She may not know exactly what to do, but his responses would guide her.

Releasing him so she could push up toward him on her palms, she said, "I want to touch you as I've dreamed of so many nights."

"You've dreamed of touching me?"

The husky incredulity in his voice helped chase away the heat of the blush staining her cheeks. "Yes. For quite some time now. Will you let me?"

"Will I let you?" He grinned wickedly and in a flash was beside her on his back. "Do with me what you will, my little wench."

A thrill coursed through her and filled her with boldness unlike anything she'd ever known. She scrambled to her knees and knelt over him, touching him tentatively at first. The smooth hard length of his desire both fascinated and amazed her. Every time she stroked him, he growled in a way that told her she was bringing him painful pleasure. Embolden with her newfound power, she stroked him faster, her heartbeat increasing with each sweep of her hand.

Suddenly, he grasped her shoulders and pushed her onto her back before coming over her as her lips parted in surprise. His eyes burned as sweat dampened his brow. "If you keep that up, I'll succumb before I want to."

She pouted playfully. "But I want to bring you pleasure."

He reached down, grasped her hips and lifted her bottom toward him. She opened her thighs to get closer and as she did so, the hard length she'd stroked only moments before came to the juncture between her legs that throbbed with need. A momentary spasm of fright took her. She curled her fingers into his muscular thighs. "No hesitation."

"You're sure?"

His voice was no more than a raw rumble. She nodded and his hands pressed tighter, lifted her higher, and in one quick thrust he filled her. The pain was sharp and made her cringe. Trent held very still, which she was utterly grateful for. The sensation of having him inside her was very foreign. She felt stretched, full and at first uncomfortable, but then something happened. She locked gazes with him and offered a wobbly smile at the tenderness filling his eyes. The pain was dulling quickly and as it did, she noticed the other sensations curling in her abdomen. The pulsating ache was back and she desperately wanted him to help her make the ache stop.

"Trent." His name was a plea for understanding from her lips.

He didn't say a word but gripped her hips tighter and withdrew himself almost to the tip, leaving her feeling empty until he slowly slid all the way back in to the hilt. He repeated the motion with such exquisite preciseness that she caught his rhythm, learned it, met it and matched it to her own.

Soon nothing but dizzying tingling sensations filled her as her body clenched tightly around his. His movements became faster and harder. Whether he was matching her pace or leading her, she wasn't certain anymore. She had to reach some peak, she knew it instinctually. Only he could take her there.

Heat built within her with each slick stroke he offered. She wanted to scream out but feared being heard. "Trent, please," she managed between her clenched teeth.

"Shh, darling. I know." His strokes didn't lessen as he leaned his body toward her, and his hips rested on hers, causing his body to rub at her most sensitive parts. A scream of delight ripped from her mouth, but the noise was lost to Trent's lips coming over hers.

He plunged his tongue inside her mouth and moved his hips in slow, torturous circles. Inside, she burst as spasms took her. Above her, Trent grunted, lifted her to his chest and thrust deeply. His hands circled her back as hot liquid poured into her. They stayed locked in each other's embrace and panting heavily. She rested her chin on his shoulder, glancing up at the starry night sky and bright moon while marveling at the perfectness of the moment.

"You're mine," she whispered and then kissed his neck.

He pulled back and stared into her eyes. "I was yours from the moment I met you. It just took me a while to admit I'd been captured."

Twenty-Five

Later the next day Trent strolled into Wolverton's club, which was empty due it being midafternoon. Business hours at a hellfire club like Wolverton's did not begin until late at night. Trent kept his bag of coin out he had used to convince the young lad at the door to let him in. No doubt it might take more blunt before Wolverton's notoriously protective employees would let Trent see the man. Trent was prepared to pay, cajole or threaten, whichever the situation may call for, to get the conformation and information he had come here for.

The scent of smoke and whiskey lingered in the air and the main gaming room, which was the first room one entered after winding down the hall from the front door, was dark, except for a table in the far corner where several candles glowed. A man sat at the table, his face not discernible due to the darkness and because his head was bent as he counted money. The soft tap of coins being placed on the wooden table and the man's low murmuring voice as he counted to himself filled the air. The clap of Trent's shoes joined the sounds as he moved off the carpet and onto the marble floor.

The man counting the money immediately raised his head, his voice and the click of coin against wood ceasing abruptly. "We're closed. Come back at ten."

Trent kept walking but spoke. "I'm not here for leisure or gaming." As he neared the table he blinked at the sight of Wolverton, unshaven with his sleeves rolled to his elbows and the typical black coat and white cravat he wore gone. "I'm surprised to find you in here, but glad I did."

Wolverton stood. "What can I do for you, Davenport?"

"Are we alone?" Trent asked, pulling out a chair and motioning Wolverton to sit once more.

The owner eyed him warily but obliged by sitting. Leaning back in his chair, he said, "We are. No one comes in before three. Even us working cits need time off, Davenport."

Trent let the biting comment go. Wolverton could not know that Trent heartily agreed with him, and he did not have the time to discuss the plight of the working class right now. "Tell me what you have done with Lord Bridgeport."

"What makes you think I've done anything with the man?" Wolverton asked, reaching forward and scooping a shiny pile of coins toward him. The money scraped against the table and then a soft chink filled the momentary silence as Wolverton dropped the coins one by one into a black bag.

"I know you took him. There is no doubt in my mind and I'll tell you why." Satisfied he had Wolverton's attention by the man's flared nostrils Trent continued. "I spent my morning making inquiries to the more nefarious men I know and they all say the same thing. Bridgeport owed a great many people, but he owed you the most."

"That proves nothing."

Trent smiled. "No, of course not. Not alone. My fiancée, Bridgeport's sister, Lady Audrey, saw your carriage at her home the day her brother disappeared and she heard your voices raised in argument."

Wolverton shrugged. "I went to collect my money. Simple. That does not mean I collected the man."

"True." Trent splayed his hands against the table. "I've, of course, heard stories of men disappearing who fail to pay you what they owe you, but again, that would prove nothing."

"Exactly," Wolverton agreed with a hard voice. "Are we finished?"

"Not quite. You see, I am a curious man. A thorough one too. And I am driven by the desire to make my future wife happy. This ambition sent me to the docks before I came here." Trent was pleased to see Wolverton's fingers flex and then curl tightly around the bag he held. He gazed intently at the man. "I spoke with several dock workers who saw a man fitting Bridgeport's description unconscious and being dragged onto the ship the South Star, but conveniently there's no record of Bridgeport on the ship."

Wolverton smiled. "I'm afraid I cannot help you."

"You don't need to yet." Trent allowed his tone to grow cold and menacing. "I took it upon myself to slip into the ship's office and check the records of where the ship was bound for. It was headed for the Indies that day, which I must say did not come as a great surprise, considering that is exactly where I would send a man I wanted to get rid of but not kill."

"Yes, well, I'm not a murderer. You still can prove nothing."

Trent drummed his fingers on the table. "No, but I don't have to have definitive proof. I'm normally not a vindictive person, but if you refuse to tell me what you have done with him, I will ruin you. I will make sure every gentlemen of the *ton* quits frequenting your establishment and we both know I have the power to do it."

"I like you," Wolverton said unexpectedly. "You dress like a gentleman but you are not soft, unlike most men in the *ton*. And I do believe you will carry out your threat. I did not set out to send Bridgeport anywhere. I went to see him to get my money. When he said he could not pay me and he kicked me of his property, I left a man of mine to watch the house. I suspected he would try to flee town and his obligations, and I was proven correct when I followed him to the docks and ascertained him trying to board a ship bound for America.

"I decided then and there to teach him a lesson about repaying his obligations that he would never forget. Bridgeport will be back once he pays the debt he owes me. I am keeping tabs on him and calculating how much money I think he earns each day for the labor he is doing. When I think he has learned his lesson about the dangers of gambling and not paying I'll return him only mildly scathed."

"I applaud your strategy, but I would like to see him home by my wedding as a gift to my bride. I'll pay his debt to you and I vow he will understand the dangers you spoke of when I am done talking to him."

"You have a bargain, Davenport. I never turn down a chance to obtain more money, and I am not one to intentionally cause a lady pain, even if I suspect your betrothed is better off without her brother." Wolverton picked up the quill on the table, wrote something down and slid the paper toward Trent. "This is the amount of the debt."

"Excellent." Trent glanced at the paper and folded it without a word. The money meant nothing compared to making Audrey happy. "I'll send the money around this afternoon once you have sent me written notes on where he is and how to go about getting him."

"I can do that, but I would be happy to have my men return him and spare you the trouble."

Trent shook his head. "I prefer to have the control." An old habit left from spying.

"Very good, then. You have not only paid his debt, you have saved me the expense of bringing him home. Next time you are in here, you will have a credit."

"That is not necessary. I will not be visiting hellfire clubs anymore." He had no desire to and he knew Audrey would not like it. With a wave, he departed the building and headed across to town to see his future wife. She wanted him to help decide the menu for their wedding breakfast and he wanted nothing more than to spend every second with her.

Two months later

TRENT STOOD AMONG THE BUSTLE of the guests at his wedding brunch and grinned. He had been smiling like a fool all morning, but he could not seem to stop himself. Across Whitney's dining room, Audrey knelt, her hair falling over one side of her face, with Julian on her hip, and gestured animatedly to a group of children surrounding them.

Trent's heart constricted with joy. Julian and Audrey had taken to each other as if they were meant to be mother and son. He could have stood staring at them all day and counting his blessings, but Dinnisfree entered the room and giving Trent a slight nod strode toward him and clapped him on the shoulder.

The duke leaned close to Trent. "I have Bridgeport in Sutherland's study, as you instructed.

"Thank you for collecting him at the shipyard. I would have done it myself—"

"And miss your wedding breakfast? I think not. I was happy to do it for you. In fact, I have to admit I was eager to. I much preferred watching Bridgeport's face drain of all color as he read the letter you wrote to him outlining the conditions of his staying in England to sitting in church and watching you marry. Sorry."

Trent laughed. "No apologies necessary. Did the marquess readily agree?"

"Surprisingly, he did. I suppose being kidnapped and made to work under slave conditions has made him willing to do anything to have a fresh start."

"Excellent. My relationship with him will be far more pleasant if I am not constantly having to threaten him to keep out of trouble and become a respectable man worthy of his sister's love."

"Marriage has softened you," Dinnisfree accused.

Trent chuckled. "Audrey softened me. Marriage has made me happy, my friend. You should try it."

Dinnisfree shook his head. "I've nothing to offer a woman but heartache."

"I don't think I've ever heard you admit a flaw, Dinnisfree."

"And you won't again." Dinnisfree darted his gaze around the guests close to them, and Trent could not help but notice, let it linger on the widow Lady Claremont. She smiled invitingly at Dinnisfree.

"If you do not need any further assistance..."

"No." Trent smiled. "Go and have fun with Lady

Claremont. I'm going to fetch Audrey and present my surprise to her."

With a nod, Dinnisfree walked away and Trent strode across the room to the cake table where Audrey now stood talking to her aunt. Every time his gaze landed on her in her delicate dress of lace and silk with the ring of white flowers in her flowing hair, he wanted to take her away from the celebration and strip off her wedding finery and show her with his body how much he loved and desired her. That would have to wait for tonight. As he approached Audrey and her aunt they both smiled at him. "Pardon me for interrupting, ladies, but I would like to speak with my bride for a moment. I have a surprise for you." When she looked as if she might protest being taken away from her wedding breakfast he added, "Well, not a complete surprise. We have been discussing it. Remember, I told you I was unsure when it would arrive but I hoped very much by today."

AUDREY GASPED, UNDERSTANDING IMMEDIATELY THAT Richard was home. Trent had confided in her over a month ago that he was bringing Richard home to her, but he could not say for certain the exact day of his arrival because of the uncertainty of travel times when one traveled by sea.

Immediately, she took Trent's hand and said to her aunt, "We will not be long."

"Come." Trent tugged on her hand. "We can slip out quickly and be back before anyone notices we are both gone.

Audrey nodded and they darted around the edge of the foyer toward the hall. She giggled as they slipped behind a plant and ducked out. Once well into the hall Trent slid his arm around her waist and hauled her close as they walked. Her heart thumped with happiness and a touch of nervousness. "Have you seen him?"

Trent shook his head. "Not yet. I imagine since he came straight from the ship that he is not fit to come into the breakfast, though."

"Yes." She bit her lip. "I already thought of that. It does not matter. I'm so happy he is back. That is all that matters." She stopped in the dark hall before the door to the parlor and faced her husband.

Her heart flipped as she stared into his loving eyes. Standing on her tiptoes she pressed her lips to his and drew away to look at him. "Thank you for all you have done. For unraveling the mystery of what happened to my brother, for going to see Mr. Wolverton, for paying Richard's debt and for bringing Richard home to me. Most of all, though, thank you for trusting me enough to tell me the entire truth about Richard rather than keeping me in the dark as my father did."

"Darling." Trent traced a finger over her lips and his touch set her body to flames. He leaned down and kissed her neck, then withdrew. "I trust you completely. Implicitly. With all my heart and with all my soul."

Audrey's heart swelled with love. She slipped her hand into the crook of Trent's arm and nodded for him to open the door. It had taken a bit longer than she hoped, but in the end she had captured her prince and married for love.

World of Johnstone Teaser
Keep reading for a peek into the first
Lords of Deception novel!

What a Rogue Wants

**London, England
1804**

LORD GREY ADLARD ENTERED WHITE'S gentlemen's club, intent on one purpose—to find and wring the neck of Gravenhurst, his former best friend as of roughly twenty minutes ago. Before Grey got two steps into the entranceway, Henry, White's stuffiest and Grey's favorite footman, appeared.

"Milord, may I take your hat and coat?" As usual, Henry's droopy eyelids made it hard to gauge his reaction, but Grey bet his soggy state shocked the proper footman. Hell, it shocked *him*, and he was far from proper.

He held out his dripping coat and hat, trying to ignore the water pattering against the floor from his garments. He looked like a damn fool. At Henry's annoyed inhalation, Grey narrowed his eyes, daring Henry to say a word. After being forced to traverse down a thorny rose trellis and take an unplanned midnight swim in a freezing lake to escape the sudden appearance of Lady Julia's irate father, Grey was in no mood for Henry's reproach. "Is Gravenhurst here?"

"Of course." Henry took Grey's coat with the tips of his fingers and eyed it distastefully. "Lord Grey, you are dripping on my floor."

Grey glanced at the puddle at his feet, his neck warming in irritation. His favorite shoes were ruined, not to mention his trousers. Tiny rips covered the front of the fine, black material. Gravenhurst would pay to replace these, *if* he decided to let the man live. "Sorry, Henry. Might I have a towel?"

"You might. But first, you must promise no fisticuffs. I'd hate to have you and Lord Gravenhurst thrown out again."

Grey scanned White's for Gravenhurst. He found the man positioned diagonally from the entranceway, one blond eyebrow raised, left foot propped leisurely on his right knee, coat off, cravat loose, drink in hand, and perfectly dry. The man deserved to be dumped in the lake. "Might I have that towel before I catch my death?"

"Milord, your promise?"

Henry's brazenness made Grey smile. He preferred audacity over timidity any day. "You're impertinent." He said it to goad Henry. The man's sharp-witted responses never disappointed.

"Yes, milord."

"That's it?"

Henry's mouth twitched upward in a faint smile. "I'm afraid so, milord. We're very busy, and short-staffed."

Bollocks. There was no fun to be found anywhere tonight. "Fine. I promise no fisticuffs." He dried himself with the towel Henry handed him. When he was as dry as he could manage, he handed the towel to Henry. "I'd like to remind you that my fight with Gravenhurst was years ago."

"All I remember are the broken chairs and tables, milord."

Grey eyed Henry. "Gravenhurst and I are now far too old and wise to engage in fisticuffs inside White's." *Outside* was implied, of course.

"I agree with too old." Henry's eyebrows rose in challenge.

Entertainment at last. "You know—" Grey ran a hand through his disheveled, wet, hair. "—I'm not sure why I put up with your insolence."

"I believe, milord, it's because you know I'm right, and our verbal sparring amuses you."

"I'll never admit such a thing," Grey tossed over his shoulder as he strode away. He nodded to Lords Peter and Perkins, who gaped in return. He could count on those two dimwits to gossip all over Town about his appearance, which if nothing else, would cause his father a moment of discomfort. Grey smiled. The night wasn't a total loss after all.

He pulled out a chair and sat, his trousers smacking wetly against the wood. The candlelight from the center of the table glowed on Gravenhurst's tan skin and light hair and made him look wicked. Fitting. No telling what the man was up to now. "Do not," he said as Gravenhurst started to snicker, "laugh or say a word to me until I've had a drink or I'll rearrange your nose for you, which might be an improvement to the crooked thing."

Grey grabbed the full glass Gravenhurst put in front of him and downed the liquor. A slow warmth started in his mouth and spread to his chest, pushing away a little of the iciness clinging to his damp skin. He would need a least two more drinks to warm himself and cool his irritation, but now he could talk civilly. Setting his glass down, he leaned back and allowed himself to relax for the first time in over an hour. "Your information was incorrect."

"You don't say?" Gravenhurst replied, a smile pulling at his lips. "I thought as much when I saw you enter. So her father's back in Town?"

"He is indeed."

"Bollocks. I'm sorry, Grey."

"Think nothing of it. I almost broke my neck climbing down a rickety trellis and nearly froze to death swimming in their lake escaping, but don't hold yourself accountable for giving me incorrect information."

"Seems to me being caught by Lord Blackborn in his daughter's bedroom would've been the perfect opportunity to finally get your father's notice."

"I stopped wanting my father's notice ten years ago. I'm perfectly happy being the invisible second son of the mighty Duke of Ashdon." He ignored the inner twitch that always occurred when he lied. Someday, he'd master that reaction.

"So your constant exploits are for—?"

"Irritating him." He wasn't about to begin exploring

why he acted as he did. He had an agreement with himself to never examine his actions toward his father. So far, the agreement had worked out perfectly. He raised his hand and signaled the server for another glass of whiskey. "It's a perverse but enjoyable pastime. One I'll not see ended by being snagged in marriage with a lady like Julia who beds all who take her fancy. That would irritate me, not my father."

Gravenhurst regarded Grey over the rim of his glass. "If you really want to shock and irritate your father, I have a way."

Grey leaned his elbows on the table. The sympathetic look on Gravenhurst's face bothered Grey more than his wet state. Pity, even from his best friend, made him uncomfortable. "I want nothing more than to be the exact opposite sort of man than my stick-up-the-arse father. What's this way you speak of?"

"Marie Vallendri is now living in Golden Square. I propose we go there tomorrow, you meet her and invite her to your parent's country party."

"That's brilliant." Grey slid his chair back and stood. "Father hates anyone French, and he'll despise a former rumored courtesan of Napoleon's, famous opera singer or not, dining across from him at dinner."

"You'll really do it?" Gravenhurst's face had gone pale.

Grey chuckled. He hadn't been sure, but now he was. Passing up a chance to shock Gravenhurst was out of the question. "Were you trying to call my bluff? Really Grave, you should know better. Pick me up at ten and we'll make our way to Golden Square. By dinner tomorrow night, I expect Miss Vallendri to be my newest mistress and sitting at my parents' table eating turtle soup." Never mind he didn't particularly want a new mistress. That wasn't what this was really about. "If this doesn't make my father want to secure me a commission and send me far from him, I don't know what will."

"You're sure this is wise?"

"I'm sure it's not, and that's what makes it perfect," Grey said and strode toward the door with as much dignity as he could muster over the squishing of his shoes.

LADY MADELAINE ALDRIGE SCRAMBLED OUT of the hired hackney and tugged on her dearest friend Abigail Langley's hand. "Do hurry."

Madelaine nearly careened down the steps when Abigail jerked her hand away. She whirled around to face her friend. "Why'd you do that?"

The bright morning sun in her eyes made it hard to see Abigail's expression, but her frown was apparent in her tone. "Look at these people." Abby cast her voice low, though only God above knew why she bothered.

"No one can hear you, Abby." Madelaine raised her voice above the merry music drifting from Golden Square and scanned the perimeter of London's art district. Vendors lined the streets with their wares and mulled about in small clusters while laughing and joking. The sight was glorious. Ladies strolled along the paths without chaperones or companions, couples sprawled in the grassy banks on blankets with picnics and art canvases clustered around them, jugglers performed by the spouting fountains and in the distance Madelaine could swear she saw a woman shooting an arrow at a target. Her heart nearly exploded with excitement. There *was* more to life than following societal dictates! It felt grand to be right about something for once.

She rummaged in her reticule, fumbling in her impatience to find the coins she needed for the hackney driver. Once secured, she paid the man and sent him on his way before Abby changed her mind and forced them both to leave. Abby was a worrier that way. Her friend chewed on her nail, a sure sign she was having serious doubts.

Madelaine linked her arm through Abby's and led them toward the sound of a trumpet, or was that a saxophone? Who really cared? It was beautiful music filling the air. "Abby, do quit looking as if someone's going to point at us and shout 'frauds!' Artists don't give a whit about two women from Lancashire coming to explore a little." At least she didn't think they did. "We're safe here. Free to roam around and do exactly as we wish. Artists live as they want without the restrictions of Society."

"How do you know?"

"I read it in the gossip sheets, so it's at least half true."

"I suppose." Abby did not look convinced with her creased brow. "We cannot stay long. An hour at most."

Madelaine sighed. "I know." Why couldn't her one voyage into freedom and the glorious unknown be longer? "Now stop worrying. We'll be back at the townhouse long before my father. He'll never know we were anywhere but Bond Street shopping for ribbon and all the other ridiculous things girls are supposed to love."

"I do love ribbon." Abby twirled a strand of her brown, curly hair around her finger.

Madelaine patted her friend. "I know, darling. I can't for the life of me figure out why. You're so sensible in every other way. But because I love you so, I left you all my best ribbons in your room." The fact that it had been an utter relief to leave the ribbon behind didn't matter. Abby had a gift for twining ribbon in her hair while Madelaine had a knack for somehow getting it knotted in her hair. "You won't forget me, will you?" Madelaine's throat suddenly ached with emotion.

Abby clutched Madelaine's arm tighter as they strolled toward the first row of vendors. "I would never forget you, Maddie, with or without the ribbons. But next time I see you, I daresay you'll be a proper lady, likely betrothed to a handsome man you meet at Court, and you'll probably not wish to talk to the housekeeper's daughter any longer."

Since she'd never been very good at being a proper lady, Abby's prediction wasn't likely to come true. She held in a sigh. She wanted a husband, but she didn't want to pretend to be someone she wasn't to get one. Yet, she knew she was odd, and her father wanted her married, no matter the pretense she employed.

"I'd never forget you," Madelaine swore as she stopped under a pretty tree blooming with pink flowers. Perching on the ledge of the stone wall that surrounded Golden Square, she inhaled the unfamiliar sweet scent. "Let's sit for a moment and take it all in, shall we?"

Abby nodded and sat beside Madelaine. The sadness that had pressed against Madelaine's chest since her mother's death felt lighter here in the square. The lightness was short lived. Tomorrow Father would deposit her at Court where he demanded she find a proper husband to marry. Not even her usual stalling tactics had talked him out of it. "No dallying," he said. No pressure there. It was only her mother's dying wish that Father had zealously embraced. She pressed her fingertips to her throbbing temples.

Tomorrow she would be a lady-in-waiting to the queen, manipulated like a puppet by the queen's dictates. Even if by some miracle Madelaine found a man who suited her, that wanted her in return, the queen's opinion could sway any match to be denied or accepted. She prayed the queen liked her. If not, life could be intolerable. She couldn't botch it this time. She'd failed her mother in life, but she would not fail her in her death, nor would she cause her father any more pain and sorrow than she already had. Failing to find a husband, after he'd used his friendship with the king to secure her a position with the queen would mortify her father.

Somehow, she would become a proper lady, though the idea of spending the rest of her life only concerned with sketching, embroidering, and the pianoforte made her clench her teeth. Thank God she had today to do as she pleased. It might be her last ever.

"Come on." She stood and brushed her skirts off. "I want to eat sticky treats, look at scandalous art, and wander over to that group shooting arrows."

"The gypsies?" Abby's voice hitched.

"They're not going to rob us. It's broad daylight for goodness sake."

Abby stood and shielded her eyes. "We can do as you wish for *one hour*. I won't have us coming in after your father. There'd be the devil to pay if he found out we disobeyed him." That was an understatement. "You might be leaving for Court tomorrow," Abby continued. "But I have to go back to your father's house and live as his servant. I can't afford his wrath."

"Neither can I," Madelaine muttered. The last fight she'd had with her mother was ever present in her mind. Fresh regret pierced her heart and made her rub at her chest as they walked toward the smell of gooey rolls.

"THIS TRIP HAS BEEN A bloody waste," Grey growled as they made their way out of Marie Vallendri's townhome and into the bright sunshine of Golden Square. "Who am I going to shock my father with at dinner tonight since Miss Vallendri already has a lover?"

"How about that chit right there." Gravenhurst pointed toward a band of gypsies who'd set up a shooting booth.

"I said I wanted to shock my father, not give him a death fit."

Gravenhurst chuckled at Grey's side. "Look closer. See the tall, pretty brunette? From my experience women with curly hair have rousing personalities to match, and the chit may be dressed as a proper lady, but she wouldn't be in the art district if she was. She's ripe for adventure. I say go pluck her."

"I like your thinking." Grey studied the woman. "She's pretty enough but see how her mouth is puckered in disapproval. She's not here of her choosing. Likely she'd faint if I propositioned her."

"You may be right. Perhaps you should select a new mistress from Madam Landry's women."

"I think not," Grey said, distracted by the sudden shouting from the group of gypsies. As he moved across the square and closer to the group he could hear wagers being bantered back and forth between the men and women alike. The excited buzz of the crowd was like a drug. He stopped by a sleek-haired gypsy with keen black eyes who struggled to take the money shoved at him while scribbling wagers in a little book.

"What's the wager?"

The gypsy acknowledged Grey with an upward flick of his eyebrows and a sardonic smile. Grey instantly liked him. "The lady claims she can split the arrow lodged in the target over there." The man pointed to a target so far away Grey had to squint to see it.

"Impossible. Unless the lady is built like a man. Which lady?" He glanced at the women gathered around the group. A few of them were thick in arm and might be able to do it if they'd been shooting all their lives.

"There. That fair *ghel* with the sun on her head."

"The fair what with what on her head?" Grey reached into his coat and brought out a bag of coin.

"Come, I'll show you." The gypsy eyed Grey's coin and then wound through the throng of people. "You going to wager?"

Was he ever. No need to go showing his excitement and get taken advantage of. "Yes, but I'll see the lady before I decide for or against."

"And your friend?"

Gravenhurst shook his head. "I'll keep my funds in my pocket where they belong."

Leave it to Gravenhurst to try to spoil the fun. Nothing could spoil this novelty though. Grey shrugged. "Sorry—?"

"Romany." The gypsy stuck out his hand. Grey shook the man's hand with enthusiasm. His wasted trip was just about to become profitable and entertaining. Toward the inner circle the man stopped behind a woman whose waves of flaxen hair tumbled invitingly down her back and marked her as the woman with the sun on her head. He chortled at the description. What a preposterous idea to imagine the petite creature standing in front of him had the strength to wield the bow and shoot the arrow true enough to split the one already lodged in the target.

She had a right lovely round backside, he'd give her that, but he'd not give her his confidence. He jingled the bag of money with a grin and held it toward Romany who'd begun taking bets again from the people around him. "I'll put the whole lot on the lady's failure."

With a gasp, the woman whirled around and speared him with a dark look as well as nearly stabbing him with her arrow. "You're mistaken to wager against me, sir."

There was something invitingly erotic about the pale-skinned, bronze-eyed beauty wrapped in delicate, lilac silk. She looked dainty and helpless yet she wielded a weapon that could kill and boasted of skills no proper lady would dream of admitting. His lust awoke in a heartbeat. This was the woman he needed to prickle his father and push him toward agreeing to secure a commission. "I'll be happy if you prove me wrong, yet your stature does make me question your abilities, Lady...?"

"Miss Prattle," she responded with a conspiratorial look at the curly-headed brunette.

"What an unusual name." He winked to prod her and was rewarded when her eyes rounded.

"Yes, well, Lord...?"

"Drivel." He could barely contain his amusement.

She burst out laughing, the merry sound making him smile. "Your laugh is lovely," he said. Instantly, she sobered, eyed him warily and turned her attention downward on her arrow. She was right to be guarded. His blood hummed in his ears with his desire. Forget his parent's boring dinner. By tonight he'd have this chit in his bed. The contradiction she presented was irresistible. "I'll put my money on you *and* give you all my winnings to make up for offending you, but if you lose, you must accompany me to my townhouse."

"She'll not!" her friend exclaimed before the lady herself could reply. When the lady gave her friend a cool look, Grey had to work not to show his satisfaction. She was just as interested in him as he was in her. Today was turning out to be splendid, indeed.

"I'll take your offer."

"Excellent." He ignored her friend's outraged huff and Gravenhurst's indiscreet snickering into his hands. "There's much I want to show you." Grey imagined her excited expression when she saw his collection of archery sets. Her mouth dropped open. By God, the chit thought he was referring to something sexual. Her expression of barely contained outrage was priceless and intrigued him all the more.

"What precisely do you think to show me? Are you a collector of art?"

Her tone was brittle as glass. The challenge of making her pliable in his hands was going to be quite enjoyable. For now, it might do her good to wonder what he was about. "I only have one piece of art that's worth your seeing."

At that, Gravenhurst started guffawing but stopped promptly when the brunette lady glared him into ashes. The woman's obvious protective instinct over her friend was admirable, even if he didn't like her interference.

"I won't be seeing your art, but I will take your money," the blond-haired chit replied before turning away, raising her arrow and saying in a loud, confident voice, "I'm ready."

Romany and his cronies immediately called for last wagers, collected the money, and then a hush fell over the crowd.

Grey moved so he could see the woman's face. He was rewarded for his effort. An adorable crease appeared on her forehead as she pulled the bow back with a creak. Her teeth bit down on her lower lip in concentration, and he could see her doing all the same small calculations he did every time he practiced his archery. She tested the tautness of her bow, the weight of her arrow, and the direction of the wind. Her knowledge impressed him. Her weight subtly shifted, but her skirt swished around her ankles and alerted him to her change in stance.

Fascination stilled him. He might lose, but the loss of his money didn't worry him. Her fingers lifted off the bow and the arrow buzzed through the air true and straight. He'd underestimated her. Her arrow sliced down the middle of the other arrow and a collective gasp, followed by cheers and groans filled the air. He wanted to cheer too, but jaded lords didn't cheer.

She whooped, her arms flying above her head in victory and her feet leaving the ground with her enthusiasm. He grinned as he watched her. She had real spirit. He no longer gave a damn about needling his father. He wanted to get to know this chit for her sake alone.

She faced him with a grin that lit her whole face. The sight was breathtaking. "I thank you kindly for your money," she said. He grabbed her arm before she disappeared into the swell of people wanting to congratulate her and those who wanted a chance to earn their money back.

"I'd still love for you to come to my town home."

"To see your one piece of art?" She tilted her head challengingly to the side.

"No. To see my archery collection."

"Oh!" The smile on her face filled her eyes and made them shine like polished bronze.

"By God, you're lovely." He'd not been so taken with a woman's beauty since he'd been old enough to understand women used their appearance to scheme and manipulate.

Her light eyebrows tilted into two twin arches as she gently pulled her arm from his grasp. "Thank you."

"Miss Prattle," her friend said through clenched teeth. "Our hour is over.

"Tell me your name," Grey insisted as his intriguing, blonde beauty started backing away from him. He didn't want her to go. Not yet.

"You already know it."

"Your real name," he amended, advancing toward her so she couldn't simply vanish into the thickening crowd. "I could call on you. Take you to the theatre. Show you things you've probably only imagined."

A lovely pink blush stained her cheeks. "I've a great imagination."

"Then let's explore it together." He didn't give a damn how forward he sounded.

"Enough!" her annoying companion said. "We must go now. It's been two hours."

"Two hours!" his beauty gasped. "Dear me. I really must go, but thank you for the offer."

He sidestepped in front of her and looked down into her upturned face. "Meet me here tomorrow," he said, desperate to ensure he would see her again. Her indecisiveness showed as she bit on her lip. "I won't let you leave unless you agree."

"That's coercion."

"Whatever it takes." He loved the word "whatever". It left so many intriguing possibilities open to explore.

"Please remember that tomorrow." She sidestepped around him.

A sense of satisfaction filled him. "I'll see you at the fountain at ten."

Already a few steps away, she looked over her shoulder. A frown marred her beautiful face. "Goodbye, Lord Drivel."

He loved that she was willing to play the game. "Fair well, Miss Prattle."

He watched her depart, her hips rocking enticingly with each step, until he could see her no more. If he was any other sort of man, he would have followed her all the way to her carriage just for a few more minutes in her company. Gravenhurst nudged him in the side. "Do you really think that piece will meet you here?"

"Of course I do. I'd not have let her leave, otherwise."

About the Author

Julie Johnstone is the bestselling author of Regency romance and paranormal romance. She has been a voracious reader of books since she was a young girl. Her mother would tell you that as a child Julie had a rich fantasy life made up of many different make believe friends. As an adult, Julie is one of the lucky few who can say she is living the dream by working with her passion of creating worlds from her imagination.

When Julie is not writing she is chasing her two precocious children around, cooking, reading or exercising. Julie loves to hear from her readers. You can send her an email or visit her at her website below.

juliejohnstoneauthor@gmail.com

www.juliejohnstoneauthor.com

Made in the USA
San Bernardino, CA
22 March 2014